COURT OF ASSASSINS

THE RANGER ARCHIVES: VOLUME ONE

PHILIP C. QUAINTRELL

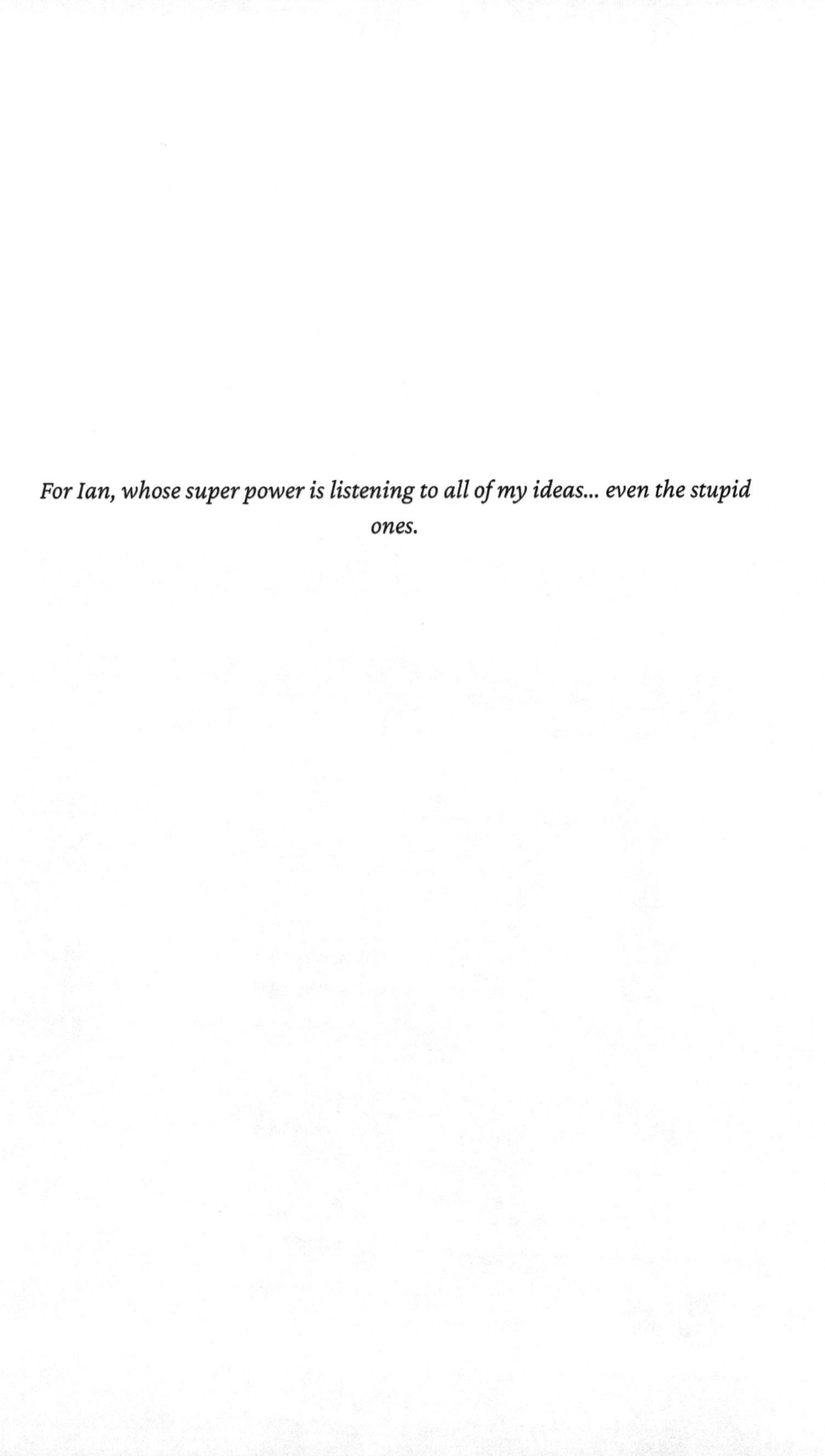

For Ian, whose super power is listening to all of my ideas... even the stupid ones.

ALSO BY PHILIP C. QUAINTRELL

THE ECHOES SAGA: (9 Book Series)

1. Rise of the Ranger

2. Empire of Dirt

3. Relic of the Gods

4. The Fall of Neverdark

5. Kingdom of Bones

6. Age of the King

7. The Knights of Erador

8. Last of the Dragorn

9. A Clash of Fates

THE RANGER ARCHIVES: (3 Book Series)

1. Court of Assassins

2. Blood and Coin

3. A Dance of Fang and Claw

THE TERRAN CYCLE: (4 Book Series)

1. Intrinsic

2. Tempest

3. Heretic

4. Legacy

GRIMWHAL
BHAN DORAL
KHALDARIM
THE WHISPERING MOUNTAINS
DHENAHEIM
THE VENGORAN MOUNTAINS
SILVYR HALL
THE KING'S LAKE
NAMDHOR
HYNDAERN
SKYSTEAD
THE WHITE VALE
ILLIA
NIMDUHN
WOOD VALE
KELP TOWN
THE KING'S INN
IKIRITH
GREY STONE
THE EVERMO
SNOWFELL
CARSTANE
BLEAK
THE NORD
LIRIAN
VANGARTH
THE WILD MOORES
ELETHIAH
WEST FELLION
THE NARROWS
THE MOONLIT PL
QAMNARAN
ILYTHYRA
LAKE NUBIA
TREGARAN
HALL
AMEERASKA
THE ARID LA
THE HOX
THE OLD GARDEN
KARAT
SYLA'S GATE
SYLAS PASS
THE UNDYING MOUNTAINS
ITHILI
LAKE RAND
THE BLACK LAKE

VERDA
THE LONELY WASTES
THE BLACK WOOD
LONGDALE
HOGSTEAD
DUNWICH
KWELL
THE UNMAR
OS
STOWHOLD
KORKANATH
VELIA
SSH
TOWER OF DRAGORN
DRAGORN
THE WILLOWS
THE LIFELESS ISLES
RDRA
THE ADEAN
DROWNERS' RUN
THE HOOK OF THE WORLD
ATILAN'S LANDING
THE LIVING SEA
THE SPEAR
SHALARIA
THE AMARA
THE DARVIN MOUNTAINS
ELANDRIL
THE ELMEER FOREST
MOUNT GARGANAFAN
THE ESSIANT LAKE
LAKE KAHEARE
THE CRYSTAL SEA
AYDA
THE Q'OL
THE RED MOUNTAINS
THE FLAT WASTES
DRAGONS REACH
THE TRIDENT
MALAYSAI
THE GREAT MAW
DAVOSAI
GRAVOSAI

DRAMATIS PERSONAE

Alidyr Yalathanil
Elf/Master of Nightfall

Artem Gorinson
Ranger

Asher
Assassin of Nightfall/Ranger

Bail
Blacksmith

Borvyn Murell
Lord of Dunwich

Dunkan
Ranger

DRAMATIS PERSONAE

Davin Mendal
Ranger

Demry
Assassin of Nightfall

Eckard
Master of Inquisition in Nightfall

Everic
Assassin of Nightfall

Geron Thorbear
Ranger

Hanaghan
Alchemist

Jorgan
Assassin of Nightfall

Kalantha
Ranger

Kalben Tarn
Lord of Skystead/Leader of the Ironsworn

Krain
Master of Nightfall

Melekish
Assassin of Nightfall

Nasta Nal-Aket
Father of Nightfall

Rendal
Assassin of Nightfall

Ro Dosarn
Assassin of Nightfall

Rolan Vask
Ranger

Royce Mendal
Ranger

Uthork
Assassin of Nightfall

CHAPTER 1

KILLING STRANGERS

It is easy to kill a man. Men have been killing each other since the dawning of the First Age. It is said, however, that living with it can be difficult, a weight upon one's conscience.

So say the weak.

Your conditioning begins here, in the embrace of Nightfall. This conditioning will allow you to shed the weaknesses that plague the ordinary.

You will fight this training, 'tis only natural. But know this: you will either be broken down and built back up into something worthy of the name Arakesh, or you will be broken down and the pieces discarded.

The Night Codex, Introduction, Page 1.

Master Ingrit, 332 of the Third Age.

The quiet of winter's early dark was cut by the ringing of a single church bell. It carried across Wood Vale, signalling the end of the service in which many had given thanks to Atilan, the king of the gods. Under a cold moon, hundreds filed out of the imposing church and dispersed into the street as they met the biting chill.

They did so under the watchful gaze of a predator, a creature bred to stalk the world of man and kill with both efficiency and discretion. Though this creature looked like them, walked among them, and even talked their many languages, this creature could not be described as a man. For how could a lion ever be described as a lamb?

Perched on a roof across the street, his hardened leathers blending in to the dark stone of Wood Vale's architecture, Asher scanned the flock, his blue eyes focused on the church's main doors.

Most were wrapped in cloaks, furs draped over their shoulders, and with heads bowed against the howling wind. But one, bound by the traditions of his ancient order, walked out of the church in flowing robes of dark maroon. He was a high priest of Atilan, a position that gave him religious power over the entire town; even the governing lord would bend to his suggestions and requests.

Despite the hubbub below and the blasting winds that swept over Wood Vale's rooftops, the world drew in on itself, becoming so quiet that only two things existed for Asher - his heart, a steady drum beat that murmured in his chest, and his target.

That's all the priest was: a target.

"This should be easy."

The voice came from the shadows beside him, its timbre and words reminding Asher that he was in the company of a younger and less-experienced assassin. Foolishly, he edged forward to join Asher by the lip, his movement unnecessary given their vantage.

"Stop moving," Asher instructed, his voice gruff from disuse.

Everic heeded his superior's words and froze, mimicking the gothic statues either side of them.

"Welcome to the shadows," Asher said, the phrase raising an eyebrow on Everic's angular face. "Those are the first words every recruit hears upon entering the halls of Nightfall," Asher reminded him. "They are said to you for a reason."

Everic failed to conceal his irritation before adjusting his position in the darkness. Asher gave the young assassin a fleeting glance - all that was required to take the measure of him. They hadn't travelled to Wood Vale together, nor would they be leaving together, offering Asher a limited time to assess the man. But assess him he would.

He guessed Everic - a northman by his accent - to be ten years his junior, perhaps more, with only twenty or so winters behind him. He had killed for Nightfall already, and several times at that, but always accompanied by the critical eye of a more experienced assassin like Asher.

Upon their first meeting, Asher had been struck by the beauty of the man. His sandy blond hair curled in waves to his shoulders and his blue eyes, a shade lighter than Asher's, were piercing. They were also memorable, which Asher disapproved of. An assassin of Night-fall needed to blend in to every crowd at a moment's notice: something one with princely attributes could never do. Asher knew, though, that there would be times when his appearance opened doors while others would be forced to use more extreme measures.

It was what lay beneath his looks that truly irked Asher. Everic carried with him an arrogant undertone he had yet to earn. The pitiful lives he had taken up to now had emboldened him. Asher remembered that feeling: invincibility. It only lasted until everything went sideways.

"Never underestimate your target," he said, continuing Everic's dark education.

"What is there to overestimate?" the younger man countered, feeling a length of red string between his finger and thumb. "High

Priest Valyn…" Everic was shaking his head. "He's just a man of the cloth. His skin will break as easily as everyone else's."

Asher whipped his head around to lay eyes on the string. He had seen hundreds just like it during his career, every one dotted with knots in the secret tactile code of Nightfall. There were always two names, the target and the patron, and their last known locations.

"Eat it." Asher spoke those two words with a clarity and an edge that informed Everic that he wasn't being hyperbolic.

The young assassin hesitated, his state of mind caught somewhere between righteous anger and embarrassment. Still, he used a small knife to cut the string into pieces and swallowed every bit without protest.

"That should never have left Nightfall," Asher scorned. "Commit it to memory next time."

"As you say," Everic muttered. "But I'm not wrong," he continued, his arrogance showing through again. "He's just a priest."

"He's a well-guarded priest," Asher corrected, watching Valyn shake various hands of his congregation.

Everic frowned. "I only see two guards of the faith," he observed, gesturing to the pair of lightly armoured men standing off to the side, each carrying a small club.

"Look again," Asher instructed.

Everic narrowed his gaze at the church doors, his frustration showing. "Why are we using our eyes?" he questioned, reaching for the red strip of cloth on his belt.

Asher pulled back from the edge, sinking deeper into the shadows, and gripped Everic's wrist in the same movement. "If you *need* that you aren't fit to call yourself an Arakesh," he stated, using the elven word for assassin, the name by which the legend of Nightfall had grown. He released Everic's wrist, satisfied that he was going to leave the blindfold where it was for now. "Look again," he repeated. "There is more to our target than you believe."

Creeping back to the lip of the roof, the assassins located their target once more and renewed their assessment. They had been observing Valyn for three days, from dawn till dusk, and then into the night until he was in a deep slumber. Everic's eyes darted from face to face, desperately trying to see what was all too obvious to Asher.

Everic's face dropped. "There are five men who do not belong to this congregation," he finally declared.

"Explain."

Everic tilted his head. "They are alone."

"So are others," Asher pointed out, teasing the details out of the young assassin.

"They carry themselves differently," Everic went on. "Like soldiers. Their cloaks are concealing weapons."

"And what else?" Asher enquired.

Everic paused. "They're assessing the crowd, just like us."

"Correct. But there are *six* of them." Asher jutted his chin in the priest's direction. "The cleric standing behind the target."

Everic took a moment to observe the diminutive figure hooded and robed in navy blue. "We have been watching the high priest since we arrived - that's his *assistant*. He's older than the target."

Asher was shaking his head, disappointed. "The real assistant was left at the lodge house. That *cleric* is part of Valyn's personal protection."

Everic scowled at the bold assessment. "How could you know that?"

Asher turned on him. "The better question is, how could you not?" After noting his barbed words had sunk in, he continued. "The cleric you see before us is shorter than the one we've seen serving the high priest. Observe their height relative to those around them."

Everic squinted, but when the revelation hit him he quickly moved past it. "Since when did high priests surround themselves with sellswords?"

"They don't," Asher replied. "And the church won't be paying for them either. Their pockets are being lined with Valyn's own coin."

Everic turned to Asher in light of another revelation. "He knows we're coming," he concluded.

"You saw the other name," Asher remarked.

Everic ran his tongue along his gums, no doubt clearing what was left of the string. "It was another high priest, from Grey Stone."

"They're clearly vying for a higher position within their order," Asher reasoned. "Valyn is expecting an attempt on his life. The sellswords must have arrived this evening."

Everic shrugged at the mounting odds, his body lacking the scars that would have made him think twice. "It makes no difference. Six sellswords, two guards of the faith, and four more back at the lodge house - they are no match for two Arakesh."

"They do not face *two* Arakesh," Asher pointed out, his gaze never straying from the target. "This is *your* trial, northman. Should I be required to assist you, the Father will never grant you the title of Arakesh. It would be better to die here today than face the alternative," he opined.

A flash of uncertainty crossed Everic's expression before he quashed it. "That priest is already dead. He just doesn't know it yet."

Asher reached for the red blindfold looped around his belt. "We shall see." He proceeded to cover his eyes with the strip of cloth and tie it into a knot at the back of his head. Without a single spark of light pressing against his eyelids, his vision was cast into true darkness and, with it, a luminous world was born around him.

He sat back, away from the edge, as he no longer required his eyes to see. His every sense was enhanced magnitudes beyond even that of the fabled elves. By touch and pressure alone, he could feel the density of the icy stone beneath his fingertips. Its every imperfection stood out to Asher like words on a page. He could also feel the blood cooling under his skin where he brushed the snow.

After running the edge of his tongue over his bottom lip, Asher was able to taste the very air, sampling the acrid sweat of both Everic and the crowd below. There was a note of sweet spice from the incense that had been burning inside the church, something he wouldn't normally have been capable of tasting even if he was standing next to it.

His intensified sense of smell increased the clarity of it all, adding individual scents from the numerous people departing the church. Through their sweat and breath he knew what they had eaten over the last day, who among them had recently bathed, and even discern those who lay with each other.

Aiding his mind to build a three-dimensional image of the surroundings, Asher's hearing intensified to such heights that he could hear Everic's heart beating in his chest. Having long learned to hone his focus under such conditions, Asher moved past the distracting sounds of his companion and turned his attention to the crowd below.

Hundreds of voices bombarded him, some coming from inside the adjacent buildings. Again, he blocked out everything he didn't need. The multitude of voices slowly died away, taking with them the sounds of shuffling feet, the crunching of snow, and the billowing fabric caught in the wind.

Steel. He could hear it lightly knocking against belt buckles. He could taste the mineral in the air. He could smell the sweat-soaked hilts and the debris that marred the blades. Every sellsword was armed with a well-used blade among other weapons. That informed Asher of their experience and thus informed him of the best approach to the target. He doubted, however, that Everic would come to that same conclusion.

Asher didn't need his eyes to know that the younger man had similarly donned his red blindfold. "Learn what you can," he remarked. "But you will not be permitted to hunt in this manner. The trial demands it."

Everic made no comment on that fact, though Asher heard his jaw clench and his teeth come firmly together. He obviously didn't agree, but tradition was tradition and Asher was there for the sole purpose of upholding it.

"Tell me more about the *cleric*," Asher demanded, his senses having already revealed all the secrets of the so-called assistant.

Everic was quick to respond, a display of disciplined command where his heightened senses were concerned. "He is a *she*," he said, with just the slightest hint of surprise in his voice. "Early forties. She's hungry - hasn't eaten since this morning. Surprisingly few weapons," he added softly, his mind unravelling the sellsword. "A small dagger at the base of her back." Everic paused, double-checking his tastebuds. "There's rabbit hair on the blade - she only uses the dagger for preparing food," he reasoned.

"What else?" Asher pressed.

Everic raised a hand and rubbed his fingers and thumb together, his senses so attuned to the world that he could actually feel objects as if they were within his reach. "There's something up her sleeve," he assessed quietly. "The bark of an oak tree. No... A willow. It's slender, no wider than her finger. And..." The northman's expression soured.

"Dirt," Asher finished. "It's the Demetrium in the core of her wand - it tastes like mud. The exterior wood can mask it if you don't know what you're looking for."

Despite his calm appearance, Everic's increased heart rate betrayed his concern. "A mage," he uttered.

Though the intricacies of the magic world were never taught in the halls of Nightfall, every assassin was well versed in its devastating capabilities. In a situation such as this, the mage was to be considered a real threat, an obstacle that could interfere with the kill. To Asher there were two paths that now led to the success of their mission: kill the mage first or kill the target without being detected. The latter was the obvious and easier choice in his mind, but Everic didn't see all as he did.

"How does a mage end up among sellswords?" the younger man enquired absently.

"Not every student of Korkanath winds up as a court mage to

some king," Asher explained. "The smart ones put their magic to better use."

Everic briefly pursed his lips. "I'd say this mage should have chosen a different line of work."

"Don't get on the other end of her wand," Asher advised dryly. "Magic is loud and bright, and neither is good for you."

"I thought you weren't supposed to interfere in the trial," Everic remarked with a clipped tone.

Asher suppressed his exasperated sigh. "The target is yours to kill however you see fit. But a true Arakesh is never seen and never heard. We do not fail and we leave nothing but shadows in our wake. If you die out there, I will be expected to dispose of your body before it can be found. So-don't-involve-the-mage," he added as a matter of fact.

Before either could say any more, their senses were flooded with the arrival of something new: heavy footsteps from the east, flattening the fresh powder on the road. Experience on his side, Asher was able to make sense of the information in a second and knew that eight people were approaching the church, their formation tight enough to suggest they were together.

A few more seconds of listening to his senses and Asher knew so much more about this new group, enough to make him swear under his breath.

"What's wrong?" Everic asked.

"*Graycoats*," Asher said gruffly.

Everic's heart rate quickened all the more. "You're sure?" There was an edge of excitement in his voice now - the promise of a real fight.

A low growl rumbled from Asher's throat, speaking of his growing impatience. "Your life expectancy is short if you can't tell a Graycoat from a sellsword."

The northman's expression pinched in a moment of anger. "They each carry a sword of identical weight and length," he began, in an attempt to prove himself. "The steel is clean, their blades regularly cared for. The same applies to the bows and quivers on their backs - identical and even made from the same wood. Their coats are a strong leather and *long*; I can hear them flapping about their ankles, though they're fastened tight around their chests. They walk with a warrior's confidence. They smell like horses," he added with disdain.

"They've ridden far to get here," Asher concluded, having already picked up the individual scents of their mounts.

"There are two females and six males," Everic continued. "Their ages vary. The youngest is barely a man, sixteen perhaps; the oldest fifty. Judging by the bones crunching in his left knee and the depth of his impression in the snow, I'd say he favours the right."

"Their ages are irrelevant," Asher told him. "Their training is rigorous and West Fellion takes them in as young as Nightfall does. As far as you're concerned, Graycoats are your equal in the field."

Though he didn't need to, Everic turned to face Asher. "The Father would have you whipped for that opinion."

No he wouldn't, Asher thought, words he knew well to keep to himself. "The Father hasn't left Nightfall in a very long time," he said instead. "The Graycoats have changed. To the rest of Illian, the Arakesh are more myth than real. The Graycoats know better. They consider us their sworn enemies."

Everic chewed over Asher's words. "Well what are they doing in Wood Vale?"

"Why are there eight of them?" Asher questioned, offering up a more interesting query. "Graycoats patrol the realm in pairs, not groups. Something's brought them together."

The assassins waited and observed from their high perch.

The last of the congregation moved aside for the Graycoats while, in the face of a potential threat, the sellswords finally gave themselves away and reached for their concealed weapons. The hooded mage subtly flexed her fingers, however, and the mercenaries refrained from drawing their swords.

"High Priest Valyn, I am Marik Sal-Nareen," one of the male Graycoats began, his distant voice crystal clear in Asher's ears. He also recognised the man's accent, placing his origins to that of either Karath or Ameeraska, in the southern Arid Lands.

Valyn looked the group of warriors over. No explanation was required as to who they were or where they had come from, their signature coats more than enough for anyone to identify them. "I always have time for any who carry the honour of West Fellion," he replied. "Might I ask what business you have in Wood Vale?"

"And how you came to know the high priest's name," the mage cut in, standing directly beside her client now.

Marik looked at the mage before casting a cursory glance over the sellswords. "I don't answer to the likes of mercenaries," he simply announced, the derision audible in his voice. "We have been sent at the behest of the Lord Marshal of West Fellion," he continued, talking directly to Valyn. "We have received word from our sector house in Grey Stone. We believe an attempt is going to be made on your life." Again, the Graycoat surveyed the six mercenaries. "Clearly you are in possession of the same knowledge."

"I am," the high priest said. "And, as you can see, I have taken precautions."

"They won't be enough," Marik told him flatly. "I know what hunts you."

As a sense of dread began to rise up in Valyn, the all too familiar scent of fear reached Asher. It was intoxicating to one trained in the art of death. Asher felt the pull of it, pressing him to advance and display his superiority. Instead, he clenched his fists and took a long steadying breath, calling on his years of discipline.

"To the hells with this lot," one of the sellswords snapped.

The mage flexed her fingers again and the loudmouth was immediately silenced. "What is it you believe we should so fear?"

Marik paused. "Our source in Grey Stone indicates the Arakesh are involved."

The high priest raised a greying eyebrow. "You have travelled a long way to warn me of naught but myth and legend."

"Nightfall is no myth," one of the female Graycoats interjected, her tone grave.

"And we aren't here to warn you, High Priest," Marik added. "We're here to protect you."

"No," the mage disagreed. "That's what we're here for." She turned to Valyn. "The Graycoats are here to use you. You're nothing but bait to them."

The high priest looked Marik in the eyes, perhaps expecting the man to rebuke the mage's accusation, but the Graycoat remained a sentinel in the snow. "Be that as it may," Valyn accepted, "I will not shun the extra swords on my side. What do you need?"

"Access to the lodge house," Marik answered.

Valyn responded with a short bow of the head. "Granted. I was about to retire anyway. You can follow us."

As the now larger group departed the church, Asher removed his blindfold and blinked hard to rid himself of the disorientation that accompanied the transition. He looked on the sellswords and Graycoats with his own eyes, an uneasy feeling settling over him.

"Well this just became interesting," Everic commented, a hungry smirk pulling at one side of his face. The young assassin then made to stalk the group, moving towards the adjacent rooftop.

"Where are you going?" Asher demanded.

Still blindfolded, Everic half turned around. "To eliminate my target," he said.

Asher frowned. "The target is surrounded by eight Graycoats and six sellswords, one of whom is a mage."

"You're saying I should abandon the kill?" the northman argued.

"Nightfall never abandons a kill," Asher replied firmly, the words practically etched into his bones. "I'm saying you should *wait*. A few more days and the priest won't be able to afford the continued protection of the sellswords and the Graycoats will grow bored and leave."

"That might be how you would do it, *old man*, but I am done waiting. I will get in and out without notice and with the priest's blood on my blade." With that vow, Everic continued towards the western edge of the building.

Asher raised his arm and opened his hand in the northman's direction. He need not speak while Everic was blindfolded, his senses more than aware of Asher's actions. The young assassin sighed and quietly returned to his superior's side before removing his red blindfold and dropping it into his waiting hand.

"I was like you once," Asher offered, halting Everic on his way back to the edge. "And I have the scars to prove it."

The northman met Asher's gaze, though he was clearly too young and foolhardy to understand wisdom when he heard it. Instead, he leapt from the roof and disappeared into the night. Asher rested his head back against the stone and exhaled a cloud of hot air. This was going to be a long night, he knew.

Replacing his own blindfold over his eyes, the Nightseye elixir, that had been coursing through his veins since he was nine years old, came to life once more. From his seated position, he detected Everic two buildings over, his fingers and toes finding every groove in the sheer wall. Deciding that it would be prudent if he was closer, Asher found his feet and hurried after the northman, his own path taking him along a different set of rooftops.

His advanced senses allowed him to hone his centre of gravity and navigate every nook and cranny of Wood Vale. All the while, his mind pieced together the movements of both Everic and the target, each closing in on the church's lodge house.

Arriving in the western district, Asher jumped the gaps between the buildings in a bid to put some distance between himself and the raucous tavern that sat on the corner. With the lodge house between them, he could focus all the better on Everic's attempt.

The high priest's dwelling was, in fact, home to several members of the faith, though Valyn occupied the largest chamber at the top of the four-storey building.

The breeze swept over Asher, bringing with it the odour of unwashed sellswords. Besides their old sweat and general filth, he could smell the curdling breath of two as they patrolled the outer walkway on the third floor. Above and below them were identical wooden walkways that wrapped around the entire lodge house, the highest of which granted a regular view of the sunset over Wood Vale's western district.

Tonight, however, the light was gone and the dark left to reign.

Everic's timing was perfect. He sprang from the closest rooftop and fell through the air without a sound. As a Graycoat entered the lodge house on the ground floor, the northman came down and found a hold on the railing of the second-tier walkway. To Asher, it was a deafening infiltration but, to those patrolling nearby, all they heard was the creaking door before it shut.

The young assassin continued to hang by his fingers, waiting. He was right to do so as both a Graycoat and a sellsword passed each other. The two men were so occupied in flashing the other a disparaging grimace that they missed Everic's gripping fingers down by their feet.

The subtlest shift in his muscles led Asher to believe that the northman was about to propel himself onto the walkway and challenge them. He was relieved to find that Everic was simply bracing himself to climb up onto the railing and jump up to the next tier.

Asher flinched as he detected the creases that formed in the Graycoat's leather coat - he was turning around. If he saw Everic ascending the walkways all hell would break loose. Asher tensed, ready to intervene but, thankfully, the northman cleared the next railing up before the Graycoat could see his feet disappear onto the third-tier walkway.

Moving along the southern side of the lodge house, Everic kept his body close to the wall, his sight fixed on the corner up ahead.

"Check your surroundings," Asher muttered to himself.

The young assassin was so used to relying on the Nightseye elixir that he was forgetting to check the path behind him. Had he spared a moment to look back, he might have noticed one of the doors opening. Asher already knew there was a sellsword on the other side, an unlit pipe gripped between his lips. As the wood creaked, Everic realised he wasn't alone. Almost at the next corner, he had only to rush ahead and he would avoid detection.

But he didn't.

Soaking in the instincts of a killer, the northman freed one of the slender daggers from his belt and hurled it at the mercenary. His aim true, the steel sank deep into the man's head and dropped him dead. Asher tasted the blood spoiling the air and sighed with disappointment. Though Everic was permitted to kill anyone who put themselves between him and the target, he should never be so loud about it. And the large body hitting the walkway was, indeed, *loud*.

Above and below, Asher noted two Graycoats and a sellsword had stopped moving, alerted to the sound. One of the Graycoats climbed the interior staircase and began making her way towards the fallen body. She entered the room and discovered the open door that led onto the walkway. She would have seen the sellsword's corpse had Everic not backtracked and dragged it out of sight. What he couldn't hide, however, was the dark blood staining the wood.

The Graycoat moved closer to investigate. A seasoned warrior, she approached the curious stain with a steady heart rate and measured breaths. Her sword was slowly drawn from its scabbard and the tip pointed at the doorway. Though she made cautious steps, Asher heard the bones clicking in her feet and the floorboards taking her weight.

As the Graycoat stepped onto the threshold, her suspicion was realised. The sight of the blood set her heart racing with anticipation. That was, inevitably, until Everic stopped it forever. The northman had remained concealed beside the door, waiting for his moment to strike. His dagger pierced her chest and the force of his attack sent them both into the darkened room beyond. Adhering to his training this time, Everic caught her body before it fell and lowered her without a sound. He then quickly recovered the dead sellsword and concealed them in the empty room.

The other Graycoat who had been alerted to Everic's first kill appeared on the highest walkway and looked over the northern edge. A short sharp whistle caught the attention of his remaining comrades on the ground, bringing them inside. Within seconds, seven Graycoats and five sellswords were inside the lodge house with Everic.

It was all going wrong.

Instinctively, Asher retrieved the folded bow from his back and thumbed the small lever to unfurl it. The intricate mechanics rotated and the weapon snapped to life, pulling the bow string taut and ready to receive an arrow. His fingers hesitated as they felt for the projectile resting in the quiver. He wasn't supposed to intervene - this was Everic's trial. He stayed his hand, for now.

Instead, Asher shifted his focus from Everic's infiltration to the top floor, where the mage was quietly arguing with Marik Sal-Nareen. "You aren't needed here," the mage disputed with some posturing. "Whoever this assassin is, we can handle them."

Marik turned to gesture at the other Graycoat standing at the end of the hallway. "You see that boy? Galfrey! How old are you?"

The young Graycoat didn't hesitate to answer his superior. "Seventeen, Brother Marik."

Marik returned his attention to the mage. "That seventeen year old boy has more skill than all of your sellswords put together, and he is the least-skilled of us all. So you see, mercenary, it is *you* who is not needed here."

As the mage abandoned her post, leaving Marik outside the target's door, Asher turned away from their petty argument and listened for Everic. The northman had the perfect opportunity to sneak past a pair of sellswords who were checking every room, but he wasn't moving. The assassin was positioned in the shadows above them, his limbs braced against the wooden beams. He was going to kill again.

"Fool," Asher whispered to himself.

Only when the two sellswords were beneath him did Everic reveal himself. Before his feet were forced to take his full weight, the northman's twin short-swords were freed from the scabbards on his back. The hour-glass blades, identical to the pair on Asher's back, were the finest steel coming out of Karath - home to the world's greatest sword makers. In the right hands they were instruments fit for Death itself. Everic, however, was only an emissary of that dark entity.

He pivoted one way then the next, his short-swords flashing steel in a rotating pattern. Those exquisite edges sliced through mail, leather, and finally flesh. The blood of both sellswords was splattered up the walls, three of their major arteries exposed to air. Their deaths went unheard by all but Asher, who perceived their last ragged breaths from across the street. That still left three sellswords and seven Graycoats to deal with, and two of the latter were quickly making their way up to Everic.

"Get a move on," Asher urged frustratedly.

But without complete darkness, the Nightseye elixir in Everic's veins remained dormant, leaving him with all the senses of an ordinary man. He moved slowly and cautiously down the hall, unaware that he was about to be flanked by a pair of Graycoats.

Asher had to wonder at what point the mission was utterly compromised beyond repair. Did he step in now? Or did he give the northman the benefit of the doubt and wait to see if he recovered? Everic was certainly less-experienced than Asher, but he had already proven himself more than competent in the art of delivering death.

A door slammed open somewhere on the street below and a group of men staggered into the snow, singing at the top of their voices. It broke Asher's concentration, drawing his senses to the ale on their breath and the vibrations inside their throats, their every sound affecting the world around them in ways they couldn't possibly know. They continued their merriment down the street, away from the lodge house, and towards the tavern that promised more drink.

Asher tilted his head back to the lodge house and discovered an impending calamity he could do nothing about. Everic had succeeded in evading multiple foes on his way to Valyn's chamber, but he now found himself in the one place Asher had warned him to stay away from.

The young assassin, who had apparently chosen the wrong moment to enter the top floor, was looking down the delicate shaft of a wand. A devastating blast of light and sound exploded forth from the wand tip. Everic was taken from his feet in a whirlwind of debris stripped from the floor and walls. The magic launched him at an awkward angle, shoving him through the wall to his left and into a small supply room.

The mage lowered her wand and a new spell took effect, releasing three long strands of glowing gold. The whips dragged along the floor, sizzling and sparking, as she slowly approached the jagged hole in the supply room wall. One swing of her arm curled the golden whips in a ruinous arc, each strand capable of cutting through the walls like a hot knife slicing through butter. Within seconds of meeting the mage, Everic was on his back and surrounded by utter destruction.

Across the street, Asher was gritting his teeth. Every Graycoat and sellsword was now rushing up to meet the injured northman, who was soon to meet his end at the hands of the mage anyway. Besides the fact that they would then be in possession of an Arakesh's body, the target would be whisked away, and likely granted refuge in the high walls of West Fellion itself.

Time to go to work.

With muscle memory alone, Asher nocked an arrow and let it loose on the world. To any archer's eyes there was no shot to be had, but nothing escaped a blindfolded Arakesh. The breeze on his skin informed him of the intensity and direction of its currents. He could hear that same breeze funnelling through the narrow slit of a window that illuminated the supply room. The pressure on his bow string had been just right, allowing the arrow to sail rather than fight the wind. And so it soared up into the night air before curving to angle down at the lodge house.

The mage couldn't have predicted such an attack, as evidenced by the pained surprise that shot through the fine muscles in her face. As Everic groaned and crawled through the debris, the mage collapsed to her knees in the hallway. With her remaining seconds of life, her eyes flickered down to inspect the arrow protruding from her chest. Death was ineluctable, however, and claimed the mage as its own, her wand slipping from her dead fingers.

Asher flicked the switch on his bow and punched the air with it, folding it neatly in one swift movement. As he clipped it to his quiver, he was already moving along the roof top, away from the lodge house - he needed speed.

Dashing back, he leapt from the roof as Everic had done, his arms outstretched and waiting for the railing. He slammed into it with his feet coming up to brace against the railing, there to absorb the impact. With no delay, the assassin propelled himself over the side and entered via the same room where Everic had stashed his two kills.

The stench of their blood filled the room now like a thick soup. Asher had long been accustomed to the smell of death and simply stepped over the bodies. Approaching the door to the interior, he felt the vibrations of two sellswords hurtling down the hallway. They were slower than the Graycoats, their conditioning having slipped over the years. They were still trained to fight though, a fact only the foolish would soon discover.

Asher planted his feet like the roots of a great tree, waiting for the opportune moment to make himself known. The sellsword in the lead was the heavier of the two, his broader shoulders having a greater impact on the dusty atmosphere around him. Trailing close behind him, the second and last of the mercenaries was a slimmer build, but his lungs crackled with every breath, likely due to the pipe he had been sucking on for most of his life.

Braced, his left leg slightly behind his right, Asher kicked out, thrusting his boot into the closed door. The force of it swung the door open at significant speed and provided a wall of wood for the slim sellsword. He crashed into it mid-run and was sent flying in the opposite direction.

Asher didn't wait for the fight to come to him. He drew both of the hour-glass short-swords from his back and entered the hallway, there to face the larger sellsword.

Fear. It swelled within the man and poured out in waves, easily interpreted by almost all of Asher's acute senses. Credit to him, it didn't stop the larger man from lunging with his sword.

There was a split second, from the moment he raised his weapon to Asher's response, when something switched in the assassin's mind, a lever that had been created after twenty-six years of brutal conditioning. It redirected Asher's consciousness, making him oblivious to his own actions. When next his conscious mind caught up with him, both sellswords lay dead at his feet, their blood dripping off the tips of his blades. Only an echo of the fight remained, if it could have been called a fight at all.

Having killed this way all his life, Asher paid it no heed and sprinted down the hall, making his way to the winding staircase. A couple of lowly priests dared to open their doors a crack and spy the violence. The sight of Asher saw them retreat without a word, their doors quickly barred by furniture.

By the time he reached the fourth floor, the remaining seven Graycoats surrounded Everic, his weakened body having been dragged into the hallway and dumped at their feet. They were examining him like a wild animal, deciding whether to kill him immediately or imprison him in West Fellion for questioning. Neither could be permitted.

Asher presented himself at the end of the passage, his short-swords held casually by his side. He waited for them to notice him, the man standing as still as the shadows themselves. He knew the effect his appearance had on others, and how it was made all the more menacing with fresh blood staining his weapons. It was the red blindfold, however, that had always brought out a person's fear the most. The ordinary man found it disturbing, he supposed.

The same could still be said of the Graycoats. Unlike the ordinary man, however, the knights had been trained to quash their fear with righteous anger. Buried though it might be, even a sliver of fear could not escape an Arakesh.

They left Everic to his wounds and strode towards the assassin, emboldened by their greater numbers. That was their mistake. The hallway forced close-quarters upon them all, reducing the significance of their advantage.

As the gap closed between them, Asher steadied his breathing and tightened the grip around his weapons. How many times had he faced similar odds or worse while training in the depths of Nightfall? He knew how to mentally and physically prepare for a fight. Reaching within ten feet of him, the Graycoats weren't people anymore. They weren't men and women. They were just obstacles in his way.

Switch.

The assassin took control once more, always ready to take a life. It was as simple as blowing out a candle to those who knew what they were doing. Since Nightfall had been instructing Asher in the art of killing a man from the age of nine, he knew exactly what he was doing. At least his body did. The clash of steel and dying cries were so distant as to hardly be perceived at all. Yet men *were* dying. One particular cry was higher in pitch than the rest, suggesting that a woman had now been added to the dead, but Asher couldn't rightly say.

His mind had been cast back to his earlier years in Nightfall. The lesson that day had concerned Graycoats, an order as ancient as the Arakesh, though they walked a very different path. Most called them noble knights, their services collectively paid for by the six kingdoms of Illian. Nasta Nal-Aket, Asher's closest mentor, had not referred to them as noble knights. Nasta had called them *hammers*.

He was right.

Asher's mind was hurled back into the present as a Graycoat heaved him off his feet and into a closed door. The assassin's back took the brunt of it, shattering the door into its individual planks. Adding to the assault, the Graycoat's weight then came down on top of him. By his scent alone, Asher knew he was fighting the one called Marik.

Despite maintaining his grip on both short-swords, Marik knocked each aside, leaving him free to beat one fist after the other into Asher's face. The assassin took the punishment and waited for his moment to strike. Raising his hips and lifting his right leg, he twisted it with swift speed and wrapped the limb around the Graycoat's midriff. Ensnared, he forced Marik to one side and through the bottom half of a bookshelf.

The reprieve was momentary, but it was enough for Asher to detect the five dead Graycoats he had left in the hallway. He also felt numerous cuts and growing bruises where his enemies had found a way past his defences. There was no time to assess the seriousness of them as Marik was already rising to his feet.

The two men collided in a flurry of martial arts known only to their orders. Though the fighting style of any Graycoat was more than sufficient to best most of the realm's warriors, it could not stand up to the more varied combat skills of an Arakesh. And so Asher quickly assumed command of the fight, repeatedly striking his opponent's nerve clusters to induce maximum pain. The pain made the Graycoat angry, which only served to cloud his judgement all the more. He began swinging wildly, relying more on his strength than any skill.

Asher heard the bones in Marik's left arm grinding as he raised it, his tendons pulling taut as he closed his fist. The Graycoat's every movement, seen or otherwise, gave his intentions away. Asher blocked the obvious attack and locked the arm in place, ensuring the elbow was lined up. With all his strength behind his own palm, the assassin broke Marik's arm. Had he been using his eyes, Asher would have seen the bone that cleared his foe's arm and kissed the air.

Marik's agonised roar was cut short when Asher planted a boot in his chest and kicked him back into the hallway. His victory assured, the assassin walked out of the room to stand over the beaten Graycoat. Not far away, Everic was attempting to stand, his hand reaching blindly up the wall for something to help him rise.

"Asher!" the northman called.

His warning was unnecessary, the assassin well aware of events unfolding down the corridor. He could hear, smell, and taste the youngest Graycoat emerging from the chamber with High Priest Valyn in tow.

Seeing Asher, the Graycoat froze like a deer that had seen the hunter. Still, the brave knight drew his sword and prepared for battle.

His short-swords left behind, Asher retrieved the dagger from his belt - it was sufficient to put the baby Graycoat down. It was overkill where the priest was concerned.

"Nathaniel!" Marik called out. "Get him to the horses!"

Asher took one step towards his target, his mind already slipping into ignorant darkness. But Marik Sal-Nareen wasn't out of the fight it seemed. The Graycoat dug into his reserves and threw himself at Asher, taking them both into the wall, hard. With his only working arm, Marik snatched at Asher's leathers and dragged him across the hall and through another door.

The assassin tripped over debris and went down inside the room, landing awkwardly over Marik. The Graycoat freed one leg and kicked Asher across the jaw, sending him reeling away.

The continuous input from his environment informed the injured assassin that the young Graycoat had already rushed past and escorted Valyn to the staircase, the pair disappearing into the depths of the lodge house.

Everic was on his feet now, staggering from one side of the hall to the other, as he moved to investigate their fight. Asher had harsh words waiting for the foolish whelp, but his breath was taken from him when Marik's body slammed into his back and a cool blade of steel ran up between his ribs.

Everic reached the broken doorway and set wide eyes over

Asher's predicament - it was a mortal blow regardless of his training and experience.

"You're scum," Marik hissed in his ear. "And you'll die like scum."

Asher could feel his lung filling with blood. He had only seconds before he began to drown in a room full of air.

Embracing pain was among an Arakesh's earliest and most regular lessons. In the right circumstances it could gift a level of strength and endurance one needed to survive. And so, on the cusp of death, he welcomed it.

His head snapped back and broke Marik's nose. It also sent the Graycoat scrambling away and his dagger with him. Blood spilled over Asher's dark leathers while Everic stood by and watched. If he died, the northman could spin a tale about how the mission's failure was Asher's fault. Unfortunately for Everic, Asher had no intention of dying in some lodge house at the hands of a Graycoat no less.

With what breath he could still muster, Asher got to his feet as Marik did. The Graycoat sneered at his enemy and spun the dagger around in his grip. Having only one arm, there were only so many ways he could come at Asher, and the Arakesh knew them all. He intercepted the predictable swing and broke Marik's wrist in the process. In the same fluid movement, Asher claimed the dagger as his own.

When next he registered his surroundings, the Graycoat was stumbling back towards the far wall. The dagger was in his throat. Asher had no memory of putting the blade there, his body an extension of Nightfall itself.

Marik slid down the wall, one hand covering his bloody neck. What he had left came out in sputters, though it didn't last long. He grew very still, his gaze distant.

Asher heard Marik's final heartbeat before he himself collapsed to his knees. It was getting harder to breathe and the pain in his chest was clawing at his insides. The assassin ignored whatever mutterings were coming from Everic - he had to focus. His bloody hands pulled at his tough collar while his fingers reached for the necklace concealed against his chest. He tugged it hard, snapping the leather, and retrieved the ring that slipped off the broken end.

It wasn't beautiful. Had it been laid out on a market stall, none would have looked twice at it. The circlet was a dirty silver in colour and cheap iron in make. Its only unique feature was the dull black crystal that rested in the ring's claws, its jagged edges spilling over here and there.

As Death's icy hand reached out for the assassin, he put the ring on and poured his will into it, a will to live. The magic therein rushed through his body, soothing and healing his fresh wounds as if they had never been there. Second by second, his breathing eased and the pain in his chest subsided before vanishing altogether.

His strength returned, Asher rose to his full height.

Everic stared at him, his eyes calculating. "How in all the hells did you do that?" he demanded, a trickle of blood running down from a cut on his hairline. "You should be dead," he insisted. "What is that?"

Asher's hand, unseen by the northman, slipped down to one of the throwing knives on his belt. His fingers felt the edges of the small hilt. In one smooth movement, he could take the blade in hand and lend it flight, right into Everic's skull. That would silence him for good and Asher's secrets would remain his own.

But he didn't. His hand left the throwing knife where it was and he turned to put a hand on the northman's chest, shoving him back to the other side of the hall. Everic had a stream of questions for him but Asher ignored them all and retrieved his fallen short-swords, each fitting neatly over his back.

"What are you doing?" Everic pestered.

Asher rushed the petulant assassin and pinned him to the wall with one arm across his chest. "Finishing the job!" he growled.

He pushed off hard from the northman and strode into the room where Marik's body sat lifeless. A swift kick knocked open the door that led onto the highest walkway, returning the Arakesh to the dark of night and the chill of winter. The breeze brought with it so much about the world, informing Asher of Wood Vale's secrets. He cared little for any of them. There was only the kill now.

Horses were even easier to find than people. Their stench was greater and they knew nothing of stealth, their hooves beating the mud beneath the snow. Cocking his head to one side, Asher heard the high priest panting after their mad dash to reach the stables, across the street.

When the doors burst open, the young Graycoat was the first to ride out, and at speed. His right hand was outstretched, holding tight to the reins of Valyn's horse. "Quickly!" he urged the priest.

Both horses were set to a gallop down the road, a path that would take them into the heart of The Evermoore, a forest easy to get lost in. Asher remained calm, inhaling through his nose and exhaling through his mouth. With one hand, he snapped his bow to life and with the other he nocked an arrow. He welcomed the input from his surroundings, using it to build a picture of the arrow's path in his head.

The bow went high, the string taut. Asher turned his left ear down the shaft of the arrow while his mind steadily grew blank, his consciousness stretching on and on, unfocused. His reflexes told him when the time was just right and he relaxed his fingers. The arrow was given flight. It arced over the roof tops with barely a whistle before the currents of the wind took control.

A satisfying thud reached his senses, rousing the Arakesh from his moment of absence. Asher removed the red blindfold from his eyes and shook his head to move past the brief daze. When, finally, he set his eyes to the distance, the target was falling from his horse with an arrow lodged in his back, the tip having pierced his heart. The young Graycoat brought his horse to a stop and looked over the dead priest before searching the heights of the lodge house. After spotting Asher, he turned his horse back to The Evermoore and bolted.

Asher considered nocking another arrow, but his arm remained dormant by his side. He told himself that leaving one Graycoat to spread the word of Nightfall's ferocity was a good enough reason for letting him live. It had nothing to do with him only being seventeen years old. He told himself that three more times before returning to the blood-splattered hallway.

"It's done," he said gruffly.

Everic winced as he pulled a splinter of wood, the size of his finger, from his thigh. "That was *my* kill," he dared to reply.

"The target should have been the only kill!" Asher spat. "None of these people needed to die!"

Everic frowned. "What does it matter? They were just Graycoats and sellswords. They were the enemy."

Asher didn't have the energy to argue with the man. "Return to Nightfall," he commanded. "You will have to face the Father now."

"I could have—"

Asher whipped his head around. "Return to Nightfall," he repeated. "And I warn you, northman, should you run, the Father will enact our traditions and I will personally volunteer to be the one who hunts you down."

Everic didn't say another word. He glanced at Asher's ring one last time before dropping his gaze and navigating the fallen Graycoats.

Asher was left in the midst of his work. He turned his right hand over and examined the mysterious black crystal. How many times had he used it to save his life? In all his years, none had ever seen him use it.

Until now...

CHAPTER 2

HALF-REMEMBERED DREAM

You are myth. You are legend. You are a whisper on the breeze. In the halls of Nightfall, you are unborn of the world and given to shadow and dust. That which you were is dead, forgotten. You are now a blade in the dark. In this new dark, you will embrace Death, for it is your faithful companion. Your every action is an extension of its will. You have but to listen to your instincts and fate will unravel according to the gods.

The Night Codex, Principles of an Arakesh, Page 13.

Master Arun-Suun, 337 of the Third Age.

After arduous weeks of riding south from The Evermoore, Asher entered the city of Calmardra and left his mount with a trusted stable that had long been financed by Nightfall. He treated himself to a night in a real bed and acquired fresh supplies to see him through the remainder of his journey. Come the morn, he set off on foot from the reprieve of civilisation.

Beyond Calmardra's towering iron gates, The Arid Lands awaited, an unforgiving desert of hard ground that baked during the day and froze overnight.

Asher took to The Selk Road, the only road that connected every kingdom in Illian. Were he to continue on this path, alongside the many caravans and merchants, he would eventually find himself in Karath, the most southern city in all of Illian and capital of The Arid Lands. He had learned numerous lessons in that sprawling city, from pickpocketing to stalking targets through bustling areas.

Of course, he had no intention of making the journey to Karath - he simply wished to make it look as if he was. Making himself look like something else was an essential skill in the tradecraft of an assassin. He had eliminated a dozen targets during his career having simply walked up to them, unnoticed. Now, on the road, his toned physique and plethora of scars were hidden by loose-fitting clothes and a ragged brown cloak marred by holes. A dirty hood concealed his light brown hair, though some spilled over the tops of his shoulders. Asher pulled it low over his face, using the shadow to conceal the black fang tattoo below his left eye. Being identified as an Outlander would carry the same consequences as being identified as an Arakesh, whatever the kingdom.

Adjusting the large bag slung over his shoulder, his weapons and dark leathers wrapped in cloth and stashed within, Asher put one foot in front of the other and continued his trek for three more days. The sun beat down on him during the day and the night tested the strength of his camp fires. On the third night, while the merchants set up their camp, Asher stepped off the road and vanished into the east.

When the sun next rose over Verda, the assassin was standing on the lip of a vast canyon, a scar on the land. Had he travelled directly from Wood Vale, he would have found himself standing there a week earlier, but no self-respecting assassin took a direct route anywhere, especially if it risked revealing Nightfall's location.

Now to finish the last leg of his journey and return to the only home he had ever known.

Following the edge of the canyon north for a mile, he came across a natural gully by the edge. Like every time before, he paused as one of his earliest memories rose to the surface. At nine years old, or so he had always believed, Nasta Nal-Aket had brought him to this same marker and told him he was about to take his last steps as a boy. He was right. Nightfall didn't suffer children. It moulded them into a weapon or discarded them - there was no in-between.

Asher stepped into the smooth cleft and turned immediately to his left, where a single step, roughly carved from the canyon rock, awaited him. It was a short drop that took him below the lip of the canyon and, from there, he had only to follow the jutting stones along the sheer wall. The assassin descended into the shadows until he came across a platform, a slab of stone that extended from the wall. It was there that Nightfall's entrance called to Asher. It had always looked like a jagged arrow head to him, devoid of any mark-ings that might identify it as a dwelling. Such were the ways of the Arakesh.

The darkness soon enveloped him, the light of the world left behind. The Nightseye elixir in his veins took effect and created an intimate connection between Asher and his environment. He felt the rough walls of the triangular passage transition into dressed stone. The distant clamour of training came from various passages, along with the taste of blood on the air - there were no training swords in Nightfall.

In the pitch black, Asher passed many of his fellow assassins, exchanging respectful nods of the head. There were no friends in the ancient order, only allies and those who were not allies. In light of these unspoken rules, Asher was given a wider berth than most due to his closest ally and mentor.

The succulent aromas drifting out of the kitchens called to him, but his need to sleep was more powerful. Turning away from the smell of roasting pork, Asher made for the sleeping quarters located deeper inside the labyrinth. He had enjoyed the basic comforts of his own room since passing his own trials, sixteen years previously.

The dorms were the only sections of Nightfall to be illuminated, the walls adorned with blazing torches and small braziers between every room. The light provided privacy in a place where the dark revealed all.

Possessing the only key to his door, Asher opened it an inch, wary of new traps. Attempts on his life had been a regular occurrence since he was a young teenager. He couldn't blame them. Asher had lost count of the number of traps *he* had set for others, sometimes at the behest of his mentor before he ascended to the grand position of *Father*.

Exhausted from his extensive journey, the assassin was grateful for the lack of traps this time. He locked the door behind him, set his gear down, and welcomed the abyss that accompanied sleep.

In his deepest slumber, Asher dwelled between the past and present. Every day of his life seemed to have been one of violence, blood, and pain, all of which vied for control of his dreams, throwing him into restless turmoil. But the past clawed at him, refusing to let go of the assassin.

Images of a foreign life flashed across his vision. He saw winged beasts spitting fire across an unknown battlefield. He heard the cries of war, despite the fact that he had never fought in one. And there was a woman, always the same. Her jet-black hair flowed over narrow shoulders and an ethereal white dress.

Her face remained hidden, as ever, masked behind too many years of brutality under Nightfall's rule. How long would it be before his earliest memories were lost to him forever?

Asher shifted in his sleep, disturbed by the images that clashed in his mind. The woman reached down and put something in his child-like hands.

The black crystal...

"Run, Asher!" the woman hissed.

And so he did. He ran straight into that hallway in the lodge house, where six Graycoats held their ground to protect the high priest. There was no escaping what he did in his dreams, a place where memory and nightmare collided outside the confines of his conditioning. Asher relived that fight in all its violent detail. His hour-glass blades cut through the air and deflected the Graycoats' attacks before turning to their flesh.

He always found the weak spots.

The oldest of the knights did, indeed, rely more on his right leg, just as Everic had informed him. Asher danced around the man, using his previous injury against the Graycoat, until he was in position to impale him in the back. Skewered on his short-sword, the assassin used him as a human shield and intercepted the next swing of Graycoat steel. There was no life in him after that. Asher let the body drop to the floor, his weapon sliding out of the corpse.

He faced the next of the knights after using the wall to jump into her. The tip of one blade batted her sword aside before the second thrust into her heart, pinning her to the opposing wall.

Without turning to look, he dipped under the incoming swing of another and popped up to drive a sword into their gut. The expression of pain and shock that racked the man's facial muscles haunted Asher's sleep. And he wasn't done yet. His dreams dredged up every second of the fight, leaving nothing to the imagination.

His only reprieve was the moment Marik picked him up and slammed him into a door. The jolt was enough to make the assassin call out in his sleep and wake up to the sound of his own voice. Asher wiped the sheen of sweat from his brow and sat up, adding his shadow to those that danced in the flickering flames.

Like every such room in Nightfall, Asher's personal dwelling was illuminated by a small fireplace, fitted with a winding and complex chimney system that fed the smoke into the tunnels of the canyon. The blaze served to gift privacy and rest for without the light pressing against his eyelids the Nightseye elixir would never let him sleep. The potion would force his senses to interpret every scent, sound, and taste around him, not to mention the feel of every weave in his sheets. The dark was an overwhelming place.

"More nightmares?" a familiar voice announced from the corner.

Asher would know that voice anywhere, especially with its exotic accent from The Arid Lands. It required every ounce of his training though to refrain from instinctively attacking. It was unbecoming of an Arakesh to ever do anything so mundane as to appear startled.

"How long have you been sitting there?" Asher rasped, his throat dry.

"Too long," Nasta Nal-Aket replied with an edge of disappointment. "I taught you better than to fall into such a deep sleep. You must meditate more."

Asher scrutinised his door or, more specifically, the lack of traps he had failed to set in his fatigued state.

"You are lucky it is me sitting here and no other," Nasta continued. "There are plenty of assassins in these halls who would slit your throat in a bid to gain my favour."

With a smile on their face, Asher thought.

"Breaking into my room is only half the fight," he said confidently. His hand slipped under the pillow and his fingers searched in vain for the slender dagger.

"Half the fight indeed…" Nasta held up the previously hidden blade with a coy smile pushing his wrinkles together.

Embarrassed, Asher took the dagger back and swung his legs out of the cot. "Why are you here?" he asked, this time allowing his irritation to be heard.

Nasta tilted his head. "In private, you are granted liberties no other enjoys, but you *will* mind your tone, boy."

Absorbing the sigh itching to be released, Asher nodded apologetically. Were any assassin of Nightfall to address Nasta by anything other than *Father,* they would suffer painful consequences.

"Forgive me - I forget my place." Asher bowed his head in respect to find Nasta's bare feet flat against the floor.

The Father leaned forward, bringing his face out of the flickering shadow. No matter how much he pressed into the light, however, there would always be shadow in the deep pits where his eyes had once been. In the absence of eyes, Nasta lived in permanent darkness, allowing his heightened senses to constantly feed on his surroundings.

"Confidence can quickly become arrogance," the Father declared. "You would have this be a cause for your death? I entered your room without protest and took your weapon. I could also have taken your life."

"Thanks to your teachings," Asher replied, "I don't need a blade to defend myself."

"You miss the point," Nasta was quick to respond. "There are many in these halls who want nothing more than to replace me as Mother or Father. It is known that I have designs for you to be that replacement. That makes you a target. Never forget what I taught you, Asher: in Nightfall, the predator can become the prey in a heartbeat."

"I have not forgotten," Asher assured. Nor was he ignorant to Nasta's plans for him, though assuming the role of Father was not something Asher particularly desired. Besides the fact that he would have to have his eyes gouged out, a tradition no Mother or Father could avoid, he would also have to kill Nasta to take his place. That in itself would be no easy feat, but he simply couldn't picture the murder in his mind.

"It is far easier to die in here," the Father said, "than it is out in the world."

Asher bowed his head in understanding.

Nasta sat back in his chair. "While we're on the subject of lapsing judgement, why am I sitting in your room instead of listening to your report in The Cradle? You should have come to me before all else."

"I could barely stand—" Asher began before the Father held up a finger to silence his defence.

"I brought you here," Nasta continued. "They told me you were too *old* and too *wild* to be trained in our ways. How could an Outlander rise to the standards of an Arakesh they said. I took responsibility for you. Even today, as the Father of Nightfall, that still stands. Everything you do is a reflection on me. You openly disrespect me in the eyes of the masters - you cannot be seen to go unpunished."

Asher wanted to strongly argue his case but knew better than to do anything other than nod in agreement and offer another apology.

"You are to assist Master Yalathanil in his lab. His equipment requires a lot of cleaning."

Asher opened his mouth to condemn the punishment, a task for any initiate rather than a highly regarded Arakesh. His jaw, however, clamped shut. He had, after all, insulted the Father of Nightfall - any other in Nasta's position would have had him whipped.

"What haunts your dreams?" Nasta asked, changing the subject so suddenly that Asher struggled to comprehend the question. "You have trained in these halls and killed in the name of Nightfall for more than two decades - does this trouble you?"

"Of course not," Asher responded instinctively.

Nasta twisted his mouth. "Lying is easy, isn't it?" he mused. "A product of your training. You were just a pup when I found you, soaking wet and freezing in the swamps of Elethiah. You didn't even know what a lie was then. A virtue of youth, I suppose."

Mention of the conditions in which they met brought with it the woman's voice again. *"Run, Asher!"* she had said, though he couldn't recall why. Nor could he recall with any clarity as to why he was soaking wet and freezing in those swamps in the first place. It was only thanks to the small wolf's fang under his eye that he even knew he had once been an Outlander of The Wild Moores - a savage in any other's mind. Asher shook his head to rid himself of the questions that had plagued him for so many years.

"I am an Arakesh," he declared boldly. "That does not trouble me. And my dreams are my own," he added darkly, hoping to keep something to himself.

"Do you still see her?" Nasta enquired, his curiosity delivered with an even tone. "The woman who gave you that."

The Father had no eyes to direct Asher, but he knew exactly what his old mentor was talking about. The assassin reached into his shirt to reveal the new necklace he had stolen from the markets in Calmardra. The silver-coloured ring sat in the centre of his chest, the black crystal absorbing the firelight.

"I thought you had discarded it," the Father remarked.

"Most of it," Asher replied quietly.

"But you kept a piece," Nasta observed.

Asher stumbled over his response. "It's all that I have from... *before.*"

The Father remained quiet for a moment. "I see," he finally said, his words only more than a whisper.

"It's just a worthless gem," Asher told him, pouring all of his belief into the statement.

Nasta, who could hear his heartbeat as easily as his voice, remained silent for a time, his thoughts his own. "It is not worthless to you. The original gem was the size of your finger if I recall, yet you have gone to the trouble of carving a piece off and fixing it to a ring."

Asher shrugged and looked down at the gem. "I can't remember who I was."

"Is it so important that you cling to your old life?" Nasta questioned. "A life you can no longer recall. You were abandoned by your tribe and left for dead. So ends the story of Asher the Outlander. You are a killer of the highest order now, a predator among men."

Asher would have liked to believe that. "I nearly died in Wood Vale," he admitted without the details.

Nasta's expression fell. "And who, may I ask, was so skilled as to nearly deliver a mortal blow?"

"A Graycoat."

The Father ran a hand through his white goatee. "Perhaps I should have been informed of this mission earlier," he suggested sourly.

"The target was—"

"No," Nasta exacted firmly. "All will be revealed in The Cradle, as it should have been." The Father drew in on himself, his senses likely focused on the crystal. "We have been here before, Asher. Possessions are frowned upon," Nasta reminded, his hand reaching out to touch the air around the crystal. "But possessions from our previous lives are *forbidden*. I will counsel you again on the matter: get rid of it. You have no need of trinkets."

Asher had no response that would please his mentor, so he simply tucked the ring beneath his shirt. Nasta rested back in his chair, accepting the only answer that he was going to receive.

"Come," the Father bade, rising from the chair. "Everic was discovered passed out on the canyon steps some time ago - he barely made it home."

"He was injured," Asher began, before Nasta put another hand up to silence his report.

"To The Cradle. Everic's judgement awaits."

CHAPTER 3

JUDGEMENT

The principal weapon of any Arakesh is that which lies between your ears. Your weapons training will be as extensive as it is rigorous, but no steel in all of Verda can best the mind of an Arakesh.

You will never be unarmed so long as you can think. To that end, there are no obstacles, only opportunities.

Assessing your environment will become as instinctual as breathing. In time, you will come to see the weak points, places where civilisation itself is weak. These weak points extend to people. Exploiting their vulnerabilities will grant you access to the impenetrable.

Then, there will be no fortress you cannot breach, no prison that can hold you, and no target you cannot kill.

The Night Codex, You are the Weapon, Page 28.

Master Kentris, 335 of the Third Age.

In a darkness worthy of the ocean's depths, Asher stood before the throne of Nightfall. It was a simple block of carved stone protruding from the rocky wall. Like all things in Nightfall, it was devoid of aesthetic features and, as all things should, it served a purpose. Right now, that purpose was to seat Nasta Nal-Aket, the Father.

He remained perfectly still. Were it not for his slow and steady heartbeat, the old man could easily have been mistaken for dead. His was not the only heartbeat to occupy The Cradle. A handful of masters observed from the surrounding balcony, their curiosity always piqued when the Father's prodigy was involved.

They were all vultures as far as Asher was concerned, waiting for their anticipated meal to present itself so that they might gorge and consume him. Without Asher, Nasta would be left with few allies, leaving him vulnerable to a would-be successor.

Among them was Master Krain, easily detected by Asher's sense of smell. The master was rarely seen without a cup of steaming sweet Ameeraskan tea, its aroma clouding the air around his mouth. Of all the masters in Nightfall, Krain was Nasta's greatest threat and, therefore, Asher's greatest threat. He had several Arakesh in his pocket, all under the belief that they would receive special treatment once Krain was declared Father.

Asher could still clearly recall the time when one of those foolish disciples had been tasked with killing him, paving the way to Nasta. They had both been on assignment in Namdhor, the capital of the north. Krain's man had nearly compromised Asher's kill that day, taking what he believed to be the ideal moment to surprise him. Asher had gutted the assassin and burnt the body, leaving Krain with no illusion as to what had happened to his servant. Upon returning to Nightfall, Nasta had ordered Asher to kill another of Krain's trusted Arakesh as retaliation.

Back and forth their deadly games had continued. Asher knew exactly how many throats he had slit for Nasta, though he didn't care to dwell on the number. He shouldn't even have let his thoughts drift as they had - the next few minutes were vital, especially for Everic.

The northman had returned to Nightfall while Asher had been sleeping and, considering his condition, had been given very little time to rest before being forced to stand in The Cradle. Asher gave him credit for returning at all, but it was near impossible to fight their conditioning.

"Everic," Nasta announced, his voice slicing through the tension. "You entered these ancient halls with a mere five winters behind you. You trained in the ways of the Arakesh for fifteen years and went on to survive the pit. You have since completed four assassinations in the name of Nightfall. This was your fifth and final trial. But is the time upon you to hold the title of Arakesh?" The Father tilted his head towards Asher, who stood beside Everic.

"No, Father," Asher answered formally.

The northman stiffened, the tension in his muscles sending out waves to the sensitive onlookers. His dry lips parted, though he knew better than to speak until spoken to.

"No?" Nasta echoed. "Was the target not eliminated?"

"High Priest Valyn received an arrow to the heart and died moments later," Asher reported succinctly.

The Father's head shifted back to Everic. "Did the arrow belong to the initiate?"

"No, Father. It was mine, fired from my bow."

"You were only there to oversee," Nasta continued. "Your intervention was only permitted should the target escape, something no Arakesh could ever allow to happen." His last words were delivered with a condemning tone and clearly aimed at the northman.

"The target succeeded in reaching a horse," Asher explained, "and was moments away from disappearing into The Evermoore."

"Had I been given the chance," Everic spat, "the priest would never have left the forest!"

Nasta tapped a firm finger against the stone of his throne, a sound as loud as any gavel to an Arakesh in the dark. It stopped

Everic from saying another word, his head lowered in shame and fear.

"Continue," the Father demanded of Asher.

"The target was being escorted by a Graycoat," Asher continued, "who had been instructed to take the priest to West Fellion for protection."

Nasta pursed his lips. "A Graycoat?"

Asher was impressed; his mentor's surprise and intrigue sounded genuine to his ears. "The target suspected there was a price on his head. For three days we gathered information, but on the third night we discovered six sellswords - including a mage - had been paid to protect the priest. They were soon reinforced by eight Graycoats."

"Eight is a large number for their order," Nasta remarked.

"They reported word from Grey Stone, Father, where the patron's request originated. They suspected our involvement."

A wordless tone reverberated from within Nasta's throat. "This mission grows more intriguing by the second. One target, six sell-swords, and eight Graycoats. You were certainly being tested, young Everic," he added, offering the northman an ounce of sympathy. "And what was your assessment of the situation, Asher?"

"Patience," he replied flatly. "The sellswords were being funded directly by the priest, a man of little personal wealth. Another day or two and they would have moved on in search of the next job. The Graycoats would have remained in Wood Vale for longer, but even their interest would have waned with inactivity. I calculated that the target would be vulnerable in less than a week."

"And the initiate's assessment?" the Father enquired.

"He believed he was skilled enough to eliminate the target without being caught."

"And what did you make of the initiate's skills?" Nasta pressed.

Asher took a breath. "During his infiltration of the lodge house, he successfully killed one sellsword and one Graycoat. The initiate displayed efficiency and focus in both kills and even used one to bait the other."

Nasta's brow pinched into a crease. "Go on."

"Without use of the Nightseye elixir, the initiate displayed a lack of awareness for his surroundings. It is my belief that he considered himself vastly superior to his foes and he conducted himself in this reckless manner."

"I see," Nasta drawled. "And at what point did you feel your involvement was necessary?"

"When the mage knocked him through a wall," Asher answered simply. It was subtle, but he detected a ripple of amusement from the masters above.

The Father tapped his finger again and the masters grew still. "Have you not been instructed in the ways of assassinating mages?" he asked the initiate.

Everic lifted his chin in the dark as the lump in his throat slowly fell away. "Yes, Father. Always with surprise, attacking from behind or from a distance so as to avoid their wand or staff."

"Then you do not adhere to your lessons," Nasta reasoned but, since it wasn't a question, Everic kept his mouth shut. "Continue with your assessment, Asher."

"It was at this point I deemed the initiate to have failed and compromised the kill. I intervened and eliminated the remaining sellswords and Graycoats before assassinating the target on the road."

"A modest recounting," Nasta complimented. "You are a testament to Nightfall's training, Asher. And it is a blessing from Ibilis that you were there to lend your blades to the kill."

Asher didn't believe the god of shadows had anything to do with it - he was simply the killer his conditioning had bred him to be.

"What to do with you then?" the Father pondered, his attention returned to the northman. "Not only did you fail to make the kill, you exposed the order to outsiders. Had Asher not been there, you would have been captured by our enemy. I wonder how quickly our secrets would have come spilling from your mouth in the company of Graycoats."

"I would die first!" Everic assured.

Nasta leaned forward on his throne. "Would you now?" he replied ominously. "Approach," he ordered.

Everic knelt before the Father. Nasta held out his hand and turned it palm up, the motion detected by all. The northman hesitated before placing his own hand in the Father's. Asher focused all of his senses on the exchange, unsure what was going to happen next. He heard his old mentor grip Everic's wrist and flip his hand over, granting him access to the initiate's palm.

"I'm going to give you a word," Nasta told him calmly, his finger lightly scribing the word over Everic's skin. "Do you have it?"

"Yes, Father," he said quickly.

As did Asher and the masters, the shape of the letters easily interpreted. It was a word of ridicule and weakness never to be spoken in Nightfall.

"That word is now a secret," Nasta decreed. "You are not to say that word aloud for any but me. Should any in these halls hear you utter it, you will be stripped, bound, and thrown into the pit, a feast for the monsters of the deep."

Everic's confusion was as clear as a ringing bell. "I would never say it, Father."

"We shall see." Nasta sat back against the cool stone. "Master Eckard..."

Asher felt the atmosphere move around the master as he stepped forward on the upper tier. Eckard was always accompanied by the bitter aroma of fresh blood. Even now, Asher could smell the blood in the grooves of the master's hands and under his nails.

"Father," Master Eckard replied obediently, his harsh accent forever tying him to The Ice Vales.

"I believe your latest subject recently expired," Nasta said, his ageing voice easily heard above.

"Indeed, Father."

Asher called on all of his teachings to remain steady on his feet. He deduced the brand of punishment that awaited Everic and, though he was angry with the young northman for causing the needless loss of so many lives, what he was about to receive felt disproportionate, evil almost.

"Then I give to you your new subject," Nasta announced, gesturing to the northman. "Should he survive the month without revealing his secret or dying at the hands of his fellow initiates, he may enter the trials again."

Everic too, it seemed, had come to understand what awaited him. The northman stepped back from the throne without permission, his fear taking hold. Nasta's hand snapped to the hilt of his scimitar resting beside the throne. Everic froze in place, not so bold as to face the Father, especially when he had Reaver in hand. The blade had been handed down through the generations of Nightfall, along with the enchantment engraved into the steel. Were any to suffer its bite, they would be left with its sting for some time, as Asher had personally learned years ago while sparring with Nasta. The wound had taken over a year to heal and left Asher with numerous sleepless nights.

"Two months," Nasta dictated.

Asher sighed inwardly as his senses detected Everic's sharp intake of air - the fool was about to speak.

"I saw Asher use—" he spat, before Nasta rose from his throne like a cobra ready to strike. The northman swallowed his next words.

"Master Eckard," the Father said firmly. "How long do your subjects survive?"

"That depends on the stock, Father. The average criminal of Karath... maybe a week. The criminals we take from the north tend to endure the lessons for longer, sometimes as much as a month."

Asher had loathed those lessons, an instruction in the art of interrogation. Really, it was an instruction in the many ways of inflicting pain on a person without letting them die. There were many ways of learning the truth and, in Asher's experience, pain yielded questionable results. But it was not his place to dictate the lessons of Nightfall - he just had to survive them.

"Everic is of northern stock," Nasta commented. "Perhaps he will prove stronger than his kin."

The initiate opened his mouth again, perhaps to attempt one last plea, but Nasta held up a slender finger. "Speak one more word in my presence, boy, and I will let your peers carve you up for no more than fun."

Everic bowed his head, accepting his fate. Per Nasta's next command, Asher removed the northman's weapons and stripped him of his leathers, so that he stood with naught but cotton to fend off the chill. Taking him by the arm, he then escorted the initiate through the dark halls, to Master Eckard's chamber.

"It didn't have to be like this," Everic growled as Asher thrust him through the doorway.

His next line of argument was taken from him, his senses distracted by the exotic instruments that lined the walls of the training room. So much steel. So much blood. It often proved over-whelming to the youngest initiates, who had yet to master the ways in which the Nightseye elixir affected their body.

"You didn't have to sell me out," the northman fumed, his fear bubbling into anger now.

"And you didn't have to enter that lodge house," Asher countered. "The mission was yours to conduct. You had the option to wait - I even counselled as much and you ignored me. Only *one* needed to die."

Everic snapped and lashed out at the only chair in the room. He kicked it with some force but it was bolted down in the centre of the floor. "Do the deaths of a few Graycoats and mercenaries weigh on your conscience? Perhaps it's you who should be stuck in this chamber; after all, you do have a few *secrets*."

Asher took one meaningful step and placed himself nose to nose with the northman. "Do yourself a favour in here - keep your mouth shut. There are monsters in the pit that prefer to digest their prey slowly, while they're still alive."

Everic's fists balled up, his knuckles cracking. "We're supposed to kill, Asher. And we're supposed to *like* it."

"We're *supposed* to be blades in the dark, not butchers," Asher corrected. "You were sloppy, arrogant even. Our every action has consequence. Welcome to yours." He turned to leave, confident that Everic wouldn't be so bold as to try and escape before Master Eckard and his next class arrived.

"When I get out of this," Everic said, giving Asher pause, "and I *will* get out of this, I'm going to use that ring of yours to heal myself. You will watch me do this. Then I will *kill* you."

Asher wanted to offer a barbed retort of his own and have the last word, but Everic simply wasn't going to survive even the next month. The initiates were clumsy, inevitably going too far and spilling too much blood. The northman was already dead.

CHAPTER 4

THE NATURE OF MONSTERS

The Nightseye Elixir: *Of all the gifts Nightfall will grant to you, the elven elixir known as Nightseye is, perhaps, the greatest. Introduced to the order in its earliest days by Master Alidyr Yalathanil, the potion must be consumed every day for a number of years before its effects become permanent.*

After such time, it will grant you power over the dark for the rest of your days. When cast in total shadow, your senses will be amplified beyond even that of an elf, which Master Yalathanil has proven to be considerable.

Though this advantage will give you complete awareness of your surroundings, it can also make you vulnerable to overstimulation, be it an overwhelmingly loud noise or even, in some cases, a potent odour. In these instances, you will be disorientated and open to attack. You must learn to hone your senses, lest the predator become the prey.

The Night Codex, Nightseye Elixir, Page 101.

Master Fin, 341 of the Third Age.

Asher's feet skipped and danced from post to post, always on the move. His twin short-swords were an extension of his hands, working furiously to keep his opponents at bay. Like him, the two Arakesh vying for first blood were leaping from post to post, wary of the twenty-foot drop and the array of spikes that awaited any who miscalculated their surroundings.

In the heart of the vertical arena, Asher found himself between the two assassins. Though it was every man for himself, it had become clear that his foes had made some silent alliance opposing him. Their attacks against each other were often feigned, bait to lure Asher in to their combined assault.

Jumping to the side, his sense of balance allowing him to find perfect equilibrium in his movements, Asher avoided their blades and rested on one foot atop the adjacent post. "You boys are working awfully hard for a single drop of blood," he provoked.

"As are you," one of the Arakesh replied with venom.

Asher knew the man as Ro Dosarn, an assassin of equal renown. It had come as no surprise to him when Ro quickly volunteered to ascend the fighting posts to challenge him - he had been seeking the Father's favour for years.

"This is just my warm up," Asher said with a shrug.

Ro snarled and came at him with a leaping attack, his short-swords raised over his head. The second Arakesh, an older assassin whom Asher couldn't name, attacked from the side, limiting any possibility of escape. There was, however, an unorthodox angle of evasion, one that required Asher to leap diagonally while twisting his body into a corkscrew.

With no other choice to make in the split-second he had, Asher tossed one of his short-swords into the air and made the calculated dive. As predicted, he narrowly missed the incoming steel of all four of his enemies' blades. His free hand caught the top of a distant post and allowed him to pivot around until his feet found purchase, spread wide across two other posts. He heard the spin of his flying short-sword, his throw having lent it just the right amount of force to reach his current position. Head bowed, he caught the weapon and braced himself into a fighting stance.

Ro and his ally flipped and dashed, closing the gap. Their swords rang out, clashing in a flurry of skill and focus all around them. Bare chested, all three men were sweating, tainting the air with their individual musk. To some, it would have clouded their senses as the sweat left too much of an echo, creating false copies of their opponent. The three currently atop the fighting posts were not *some*. They had been fighting and killing for decades and knew where their enemy was at all times.

To that effect, Asher knew the older Arakesh had once again angled himself to attack from behind. As that thrusting blade came for his back, Asher threw one of his blades up high again and stepped off the post. Before he could plummet onto the spikes, his fingers gripped the edge of the post and his bare feet pressed into the stone. Positioned beneath the advancing Arakesh, he had only to swing up and slice at his leg. It was by no means a killing blow but, then again, Asher hadn't intended to kill him.

His blood spilled, the older Arakesh groaned in both pain and defeat. He also had the good sense to move aside before Asher's airborne sword speared his foot. Instead, the steel tip dug into the top of the post where it briefly stood before Asher retrieved it on his way up.

With only Ro Dosarn opposing him, Asher rolled one of his shoulders and cracked his neck, preparing himself to push through to the end. As Nasta had said, everything he did was a reflection upon him - including losing in front of his fellow assassins, many of whom had crowded around the edge of the fighting posts to observe.

Ro skipped forwards, the balls of his feet projecting him from every post at considerable speed. Asher continued to face him while simultaneously retreating, keeping himself just beyond the reach of Ro's swords. After observing his foe's repeating pattern, Asher knew exactly when to cease his evasion and offer a counterattack.

His sudden halt put Ro off balance, but the slash and thrust of his twin blades sent his opponent hopping awkwardly to the side. His footing compromised, Ro slipped off the edge of the post and lost one of his weapons in a bid to reach out for safety. He deftly used his momentum to swing up and return to the fight. Asher was waiting for him.

With only one sword, however, Ro was at a disadvantage. Asher pressed his attack, pushing his enemy towards the edge of the arena. Forced to think about fighting differently, Ro used his legs more, taking Asher from his feet in one swift kick. At the last moment, Asher was able to support himself with one hand and respond with a kick of his own, catching Ro across the face.

Asher tasted blood on the air.

Ro Dosarn roared in the manner of a beast, his arm tensing from his shoulder down to the fingers gripping his short-sword. He was going to launch it. If the blade struck home, it would do a lot more than draw blood. Killing another Arakesh was forbidden and punishable by death - at least being *caught* was forbidden.

The sound of a man clearing his throat brought Ro to a sudden stop and turned everyone's attention to the large archway. Both assassins straightened up atop the fighting posts, their match quickly forgotten. Asher didn't need to interpret his senses for any more than a second to know that the figure observing from the archway was no man.

Everything about Alidyr Yalathanil was different, from the sweet scent of his skin to the fine silk of his midnight hair. He also possessed an aura of authority and confidence, likely lent to him by his superior strength and speed, if not his incalculable age. Were he human, he would be considered arrogant and obnoxiously so. As it was, Alidyr's regal nature was befitting of his immortal race, for he was an *elf*.

His true age was unknown to the inhabitants of Nightfall, including the Father. But from the feel of his skin on the air and the vibrancy of his voice, the heightened senses of every Arakesh informed them that the elf was somewhere between the ages of twenty and thirty. Of course, that wasn't nearly true. Like every assassin who currently called these halls their home, including Nasta Nal-Aket, Asher had been taught by Alidyr since childhood. He was a daunting master to behold, and one who had always taught his lessons in the elven language. You either picked it up or suffered his wrath.

"Blood has been drawn," the elf declared softly. "The contest is over."

Asher and Ro bowed their heads in respect of the master's judgement. Even Ro, whose righteous anger was emanating from him in waves, wasn't about to disagree. After they dropped down from the posts, the crowd quietly dispersed and returned to their training, giving Asher a clear path to Alidyr. He hardly paid Ro a moment's notice, his focus stolen by the pile of clothing and leathers next to the archway. The black gem was hidden inside the folds of his belongings, only ten feet away from the elf.

Though Alidyr had never detected the gem before, Asher was always wary of being around him. Elves were in tune with the magic world and the gem was certainly of that realm. Like every time before, though, Alidyr remained fixed on Asher, oblivious to the powerful artifact beside him.

"You were supposed to meet me in my chamber," Alidyr chastised, as Asher approached.

"My apologies, Master," Asher replied with a deeper bow.

"You might be the Father's pet," Alidyr remarked, "but that does not make you invincible. Should I have to find you again," he added threateningly, "it will be me you face up there."

Asher knew there was no correct response other than to keep his head bowed and await an actual command.

"Dress yourself and meet me in The Cradle," the elf finally ordered.

Asher waited until the master had returned to the passage before reclaiming his belongings. With all haste, he fitted his leathers and various weapons to his person, including the concealment of the ring beneath his shirt.

"Next time, Asher," Ro whispered from across the chamber, "I'll be coming for more than a drop of blood."

Asher gave a wry smile in the darkness before leaving the training hall behind. At somewhere between a stride and a run, he made his way to The Cradle. Nasta was nowhere to be detected, the shrine to Ibilis left untended. Rather than dwell on the whereabouts of his old mentor, Asher walked past the empty throne and down the shallow steps, into the adjacent chamber.

His nose and tastebuds had to search through the debris that wafted up from the pit. Only then could he feel the twelve initiates gathered around it and Alidyr off to the side. All of their heartbeats were slightly elevated and rightly so; there was no ignoring the odour of monsters and death.

Alidyr began to circle the ring of initiates. "*The fact that you twelve are standing here,*" he said in the elven tongue, "*means that, thus far, you have displayed qualities worthy of an Arakesh. But Arakesh you are not,*" he stated flatly. "*Less than half of you will survive the labyrinth of tunnels below. Should you ever see the sky again, you will have the opportunity to prove yourself in the five trials.*"

The elf paused and gestured with one hand. Asher detected the movement and found the clay jug resting in a slender alcove in the wall. Without further instruction, Asher retrieved the jug and held it in both hands, awaiting the master's next command.

"*Stretch your senses into the pit,*" Alidyr continued, "*into that ravenous abyss. The monsters that dwell in the deep of the earth have no name, their ilk never seen by man or elf. I have witnessed thousands of initiates enter the pit,*" he said, a hint of amusement in his voice. "*I can assure you, the monsters know you're coming. You will need more than the sum of your training to survive down there. Only a true Arakesh will find their way through.*"

Asher felt Alidyr's finger beckon, calling him over. "*Turn around,*" the elf commanded the initiates. Facing away from the pit, they each raised a shallow bowl in both hands and waited patiently. "*Nightseye elixir,*" Alidyr continued ceremoniously, "*the lifeblood of every Arakesh. The single element that binds us all and, in the darkness, frees us all.*" Asher made his way around the circle and poured the purple liquid into the waiting bowls. "*You have ingested it every day since you began your training. Survive the pit and you will find another dose awaits you. It will be your last,*" he emphasised. "*Upon taking that final dose, the Nightseye elixir will course through your veins for evermore.*"

Asher knew the *last dose* Alidyr spoke of was ritualistic - they had all been taking the Nightseye elixir for a decade or more, making its effects permanent. The last dose was simply ceremonial.

Making his way around the circle again, Asher collected their bowls and returned to the corner. A final command from Alidyr had the initiates descending the pit one by one, using the ladder that had been carved into the rock. He didn't envy them. The monsters that swarmed beneath Nightfall showed just enough intelligence that they could be described as cruel. He would never forget his own time down there, running for his life. He had only just made it, finding a way out on Illian's eastern shore, before the nightmarish beasts carved him up.

Alidyr didn't even wait for them all to descend before he turned to leave. "Have everything washed and returned to my lab," he ordered Asher on his way out.

The assassin knew better than to audibly sigh. Instead, he diligently stacked the bowls on a tray, collected the empty jug, and made for the kitchens. He hadn't even made it to the door, however, before the sound of screaming reached his ears. Asher quickened his step into the passage before he could taste the blood on the air.

Of course, the initiates in the pit weren't the only ones suffering. There was another scream that soon made itself known, a crying howl that echoed through the halls of Nightfall. Everic had survived just over a week in Master Eckard's chamber, his body a canvas for the uneducated. Asher had welcomed the light of his own room every day since, his only escape from the northman's torment.

"Asher," came a distant whisper.

The assassin stopped and turned down the adjacent passage, his senses easily picking out the initiate walking towards him. She was young, nearing twenty-five years, he guessed. She was likely in the middle of the five trials, as Everic had been. Asher recognised her scent and the distinct way she walked, the heels of her feet rarely touching the cold stone. Her name, on the other hand, entirely escaped him.

"Seriah," she said, placing a hand to her chest.

Asher heard her heart speed up and felt the temperature of her skin rise in his presence. She was attracted to him, if a little fearful. Either way, he didn't suspect a scheme to kill him and so he continued to hold the tray in both hands.

"What do you want?" he asked bluntly, embarrassed by the obvious task he had been set to do.

Seriah straightened up, her own task clearly one of importance. "The Father sent me to find you. You are to meet him on the surface."

Asher prided himself on his adaptability, a survival instinct that always saw him come out on top, but he hesitated in his response, his mind stumbling over Seriah's words. "On the surface?" he questioned incredulously.

"Immediately," the young assassin confirmed. "I will assume your task," she added, holding her hands out to receive the tray.

Catching up with himself, Asher gave the tray to Seriah. "See that it's all returned to Master Yalathanil's chamber when you're done."

Seriah bowed her head and deliberately brushed Asher's arm on her way past, ensuring her personal scent could be found on him. Asher had performed the same manoeuvre himself on numerous suitors. Now Seriah would linger in his senses for days, keeping her ever-present in his mind until his desire forced him to seek her out. It was a welcome development, but Nasta demanded his attention.

As he approached the end of the triangular tunnel, true darkness began to fade and with it his heightened senses. The gradual change, however, was preferable to the sensation he always experienced when he removed his blindfold after an assignment.

Following the steps along the canyon wall, Asher rose up into a twilight sky as the east slowly gave way to the approaching sun. On the surface, the desert stretched out into the west, where the stars still held sway over the world. Looking down the jagged edge of the canyon, to the north, he discovered Nasta Nal-Aket standing on the lip, facing the sunrise.

"The last time you asked me to meet you up here," Asher commented, "you had eyes in your head."

Nasta nodded along. "Before I made my final move against the Mother," he recalled. "You kept her allies well occupied."

Asher couldn't remember the moment he had killed the opposing assassins, but he had relived it several times in his dreams. He had challenged them in their rooms, where he had been able to make the light an unlikely ally.

"Is someone moving against you?" he asked his old mentor.

"Always," Nasta replied cryptically.

"I only need a name," Asher told him.

"If only it was so simple," the Father lamented. "They are coming at me through you," he explained.

"Through me?" Asher echoed. "How so?"

Nasta raised his chin to the east. "I have always enjoyed this part," he said. "I can feel it on my skin, the reaching sun. It bathes the land and wakes the world. Its very touch changes everything. The smell of the grass, the feel of the sand, the sound of the plants and trees. Everything from insects to Giants welcomes the sun. I do miss the colours though."

Asher frowned at the Father - he hadn't heard him speak this way for a long time. "Nasta, what's happening?"

"You are bound for Orith," he declared, calling the north by its regional name.

"A new target?" the assassin enquired.

"*Targets*," Nasta corrected, emphasising the plural. "Esabelle and Thomas of house Murell."

Asher's brow pinched in thought, the name familiar to him. "Murell... As in Borvyn Murell, the lord of Dunwich?"

"As in his *children*," Nasta specified.

Asher's control slipped and his heart began to pound in his chest, a rapid thunder that betrayed him. The only thing Nasta couldn't interpret was the sinking feeling that opened up in Asher's stomach. The Father made no comment.

"Who has made this request?" Asher demanded, if softly.

"In all your years," Nasta stated, "you have never asked me that question."

Asher had no response and so the Father held out a length of red string, the ends blowing in the morning breeze. The assassin accepted it and ran his finger and thumb over the names and locations knotted in their secret language.

"Lord Kalben of Skystead," he announced.

Nasta looked briefly to his left. "From The Vengoran Mountains to The Shining Coast, the northern realm is a battlefield for the lords of wind and snow. More often than not, they fight for King Merkaris's favour, but Kalben Tarn is more than just a lord; he is also the head of the Ironsworn."

"The crime guild?" Asher pondered aloud. "I heard whispers of them the last time I was in Namdhor," he remarked. "Their influence had little reach at the time."

"Times have changed, especially since their leader rose to the loftiness of Lordship. The last report I read had their influence growing far beyond Skystead. It seems he wishes to destabilise Lord Borvyn's grip on Dunwich."

"By having his children killed?" Asher knew, as soon as the words had left his lips, that he should have done a better job of hiding his disgust.

"You think it monstrous," Nasta observed.

Asher paused. "Isn't it?"

"Of course," the Father agreed. "But isn't it a monster's nature to be monstrous?" he added, tilting his head towards his protege. "This is a world of monsters, Asher. We might set ourselves apart from them but we cannot deny what we are. We just have to be the monsters that *eat* the other monsters."

"Why have I been tasked with this?" Asher asked, working to keep his tone even.

"It's a test," Nasta said simply.

A sense of injustice cut through Asher's calm demeanour. "I survived the pit. I completed the five trials. Since then I have spent years in service to Nightfall. Why am I to be *tested*?" he spat.

"Tone," Nasta reminded him firmly. "And the test is not only for you, boy. The masters are applying pressure. Some know that one day you will be the Father of Nightfall, *their* master. They wish to make certain that you can do all that is required for the order and they know you have never taken a child's life."

"And the others?"

Nasta took a breath. "Those less accepting of your potential ascension wish to reveal your weakness for all to see. Should you fail, I too will fail. Then the wolves will really come for us."

As the sun crested the horizon, Asher let his shoulders sag and cast his eyes to the chasm below. "I will be accompanied then," he assumed.

"Of course. A kill of this nature always requires a second to see it done."

"It *will* be done," Asher assured.

Nasta remained quiet, basking in the morning sunlight. He was, no doubt, dissecting the cadence of Asher's voice, searching for any modulation or inflection that might reveal the truth behind his bold assurance.

"Do *you* believe I need testing?" the assassin asked earnestly.

Nasta didn't immediately reply, his hand dancing through the rays of light. "Yes," he finally answered.

Asher looked away from his old mentor, his jaw clenched. "Why?"

Nasta raised an eyebrow. "That is another question you have never asked of me. Curious…" The old man folded his hands into the opposing sleeves of his robe. "You are to be the Father of Nightfall," he went on. "It is the only path that lies ahead of you. You have spilt all manner of blood in your time, but none so young as this. One day, you might have to command another Arakesh to do the same. How can you do this if you have never done it yourself?"

Asher wanted to argue his own brand of logic, but a new question rose to the surface. "Have you ever killed a child?"

"My story is my own," the Father told him. "I am more concerned now with my legacy. You will be the only echo of my presence in this world. Will you see this through?"

"You're asking if I can kill you?"

"And more besides," Nasta replied casually.

Asher glanced at the enchanted scimitar resting on the Father's hip. "Will you put up a fight?"

Nasta chuckled to himself. "Oh, my boy, it will be the fight of your life."

Asher would have shared in the amusement were he not dwelling on the terrible task that awaited him in Dunwich. "Who will be overseeing my *test*?" he asked irritably.

"I wanted to send Rynona," Nasta said. "She's one of mine," he added, leading Asher to wonder how many allies the Father had beyond him. "Master Krain, however, insisted that Jorgan accompany you - he has accomplished a task such as yours… more than once. He's in Longdale right now. He will meet you in Dunwich."

"Jorgan's in Master Krain's pocket," Asher stated as an obvious fact.

"That he is," Nasta confirmed. "So watch your back."

Asher didn't need the warning to do such a thing. "Why didn't you refuse Master Krain?"

"The masters agreed that Jorgan had more experience and they were right - it would have been clear favouritism had I refused to see logic."

Asher nodded once and turned back to the south. "I will leave at once."

Nasta stopped him with an outstretched hand, his fingers grasping Asher's arm. "Wait," he whispered, turning the assassin towards him. His hand gently ran down Asher's face, taking in the contours of his stubbled jaw. He opened his mouth to speak but words failed to follow. Instead, he squeezed one of Asher's shoulders. "Go," he said, before returning to the sunrise.

CHAPTER 5

A COLD GREETING

*When your training is complete, you may count yourselves among the
most exquisite killers in all of Illian. Your knowledge of weaponry will be
vast, your skill with a number of blades incomparable to the ordinary
soldier.*
*But what good are you to the service of this great order if you cannot kill
with your bare hands?*
*Before you touch steel, you must first learn an extensive array of hand-to-
hand combat and breathing techniques. Once these are mastered, you will
be a living weapon.*

The Night Codex, The Art of Combat, Page 52.

Master Ventrello, 367 of the Third Age.

Making the arduous journey up the east coast of Illian, Asher left The Arid Lands behind, passed through the realm of Alborn, and pushed on into Orith, the north. After numerous weeks on the road, spring was beginning to settle over all of Verda, bringing with it the promise of summer and pleasant days.

There was little promise of it in the north.

Winter's grip hardly lessened over the snowy land. And so Asher kept his horse ploughing on, putting one mile after another behind them until the flat and dreary town of Dunwich came into view. It certainly wasn't a highlight of the north, nor Illian as a whole, but it was undoubtedly a well-situated town. Built around The Selk Road, travellers from either north or south had no choice but to pass through.

Trade was ever-constant and expanding by the look of the sprawling market that had burst out of the town and taken over the plains to the south. Asher climbed down from his horse and directed the animal by the reins, leading it through the crowds. The market was loud, oppressively so after such a long time on the road with only his horse for company. Dozens of vendors attempted to sell him their goods but he kept his hood low over his face and continued through to the town proper, where smoke rose from every chimney.

Bar one decrepit-looking tower to the west, there were no buildings higher than two storeys. Having perused the extensive maps of Dunwich, including the lord's traditional homestead, before leaving Nightfall, Asher knew that his targets were located in the very north of the town.

As it had since departing Nightfall, imagining his intended targets opened that bottomless pit in his stomach. More than once he had struggled to eat his meal or even sleep.

Asher took a breath to clear his mind, relying on that empty space he was able to pour his consciousness into. There was only the Father's will. His life had no meaning beyond that. He had but one fate and it was to rule Nightfall. What else had all his training been for?

Walking past the grand house, he could see that it was set back from the street and walled off. Three soldiers guarded the wooden gate and, though they protected the lord's manor, they were the king's men before all else. As such, they were attired in the golden cloaks of Namdhor, the capital city of the north, where King Merkaris dwelt. Their chest plates were emblazoned with the head of a lion, the sigil of house Tion, Merkaris's bloodline.

The men of the north were a hardy folk and their warriors even more so. Asher had crossed a few in his time and knew well of their stubbornness when it came to backing down, even in *his* shadow. They weren't bad with a sword either. Tackling the three at the front gate would be an immediate mistake in the assassin's mind. He didn't doubt his ability to kill them, and two of them quickly at that, but the third would inevitably make some noise before he died. And, even if he did drop the third man without a sound, there would still be three dead bodies to move, the effort of which could expose him.

The rooftop would have been an obvious and unseen way of infiltration, but it was too far back from the surrounding buildings. There were plenty of windows and even a balcony he could see on the first floor. The western wall had a naked trellis that almost reached to the lip of the roof and there was a window to the side of it. In the north, of course, it was more than likely that every window was either locked or frozen shut.

From the street, that was all he could see, and with a mere glance at that. Keeping his mount between him and the manor, Asher never stopped moving, making his way through the streets in search of one of the town's undertaker's office. He knew there were two in Dunwich, but the undertaker in the north-east district was his intended destination.

Bellman and Sons was an unassuming family business that offered a small variety of burial options for the people of Dunwich. It was, in fact, underperforming in comparison to its counterpart in the town's southern district, yet the lack of customers never seemed to put Bellman and Sons out of business. The truth of the matter was known only to Asher and those of his order who, long ago, had reached out to a multitude of undertakers across every town and city in Illian, setting up surreptitious services for Nightfall. They had deliberately targeted the businesses with the lowest profits and, therefore, the lowest foot traffic.

Gripping the door handle on his way inside, Asher noted the red string tied around the neck of the handle. Few, if any, would have noticed the bound string, but to an Arakesh it was as good as an invitation. Inside was a man, with a couple of decades on Asher, poring over parchments on a tall reception desk. It was doubtful he was one of the sons in Bellman and Sons, though he had, likely, been so some years earlier.

"Can I help you?" the older man enquired, with hardly a glance at Asher.

The assassin walked right up to the desk. "A dark dawn this morning," he uttered, drawing a slow gaze from the undertaker.

Without a word, the man retrieved a key that had been threaded on his concealed necklace. He proceeded to unlock a drawer in the desk and then another compartment inside of that. Appearing somewhat paler than when Asher had first entered, the man presented the assassin with a red piece of string. Asher never took his eyes from the undertaker as his finger and thumb ran over the sequence of knots in the string. He read Jorgan's message only once before handing it back to the undertaker, who knew to burn it at his earliest convenience.

Since Nightfall compensated the undertaker, Asher wasn't required to give him anything in return, freeing him to simply turn around and leave Bellman and Sons behind. Following Jorgan's instructions, he was brought to a crossroads dominated by a large tavern, The Gilded Crown. Directly opposite, enjoying a pipe on an old bench, was Jorgan and his wicked grin. Upon sighting Asher, he thumbed at the small stables across the street before nodding his chin at the tavern.

A simple exchange of coin ensured his horse was given shelter, though Asher's attention had been preoccupied watching Jorgan disappear inside the tavern. He had met the man a handful of times in Nightfall and knew him to be an excellent assassin, his skills worthy of Master Krain's attention. He also came across as someone whose personality was just as wicked as his smirk.

Making his way back to The Gilded Crown, Asher scanned the building's surroundings, including its structure. In the few seconds it took him to cross the street, he knew there were eight windows and a side door that led into the alley. The thick wooden beams on the outside were easily climbable, granting him quick access to the roof should he require it.

Inside, he naturally sought out the barkeep. He was a heavyset man with forearms like most people's upper arms. The man had a look about him that told Asher he had been dealing with trouble most of his career and he settled for no nonsense in his establishment. It also told the assassin that there was, in all likelihood, a weapon concealed behind the bar. A hammer perhaps, something small but powerful that could be used without deadly consequences.

Asher knew there would be very few incidents that gave him need of the barkeep's weapon, but it was just another piece of information that informed the assassin of his environment.

With his sack of weapons and gear slung over his shoulder, Asher approached the gloomy booth Jorgan had chosen to occupy. There was already a tankard of honey mead waiting for him, another resting in Jorgan's hand.

"It's a little early," Asher remarked as he took the bench opposite his fellow Arakesh.

"Not round here it's not," Jorgan replied cheerily, his harsh accent that of Grey Stone, to the far west. "Got to blend in with these northerners now," he added, taking a swig. "You took your time getting here," the man went on, his bald head catching a beam of dusty light through the window. "Stop at a Velian spa did we?"

Asher pushed the mead aside, his gaze unwavering.

Jorgan gave a short sharp sniff. "I've been here for over a week. I can assure you, Dunwich has nothing to offer men like us."

Asher took umbrage with Jorgan's last three words but he kept his feelings to himself. "Where are you staying?" he asked gruffly.

Jorgan's eyes flitted to the ceiling. "Upstairs. There's another room available—"

"I'll find lodging elsewhere," Asher interjected. "Tell me what you know - you've been here long enough to have assessed the manor."

Jorgan sat back and smiled through Asher's rude interruption and subsequent demand. "The message that found me in Longdale carried quite the specific mandate. This is *your* test, not mine. You find a way in and I will follow."

Asher frowned, his blue eyes narrowing on the man. "I work better alone."

"Don't we all," Jorgan agreed, lifting his tankard. "Nevertheless, I *will* accompany you inside and observe the task myself."

Asher looked away with a tight sigh escaping his gritted teeth. He thought, for just a moment, about leaving Jorgan half dead in a gutter somewhere while he saw to the task on his own, as planned.

"Though I would do you a favour," Jorgan continued, his long face leaning forward across the table, "if you would permit."

"I require no favours," Asher stated.

"Of course not. Perhaps you would do *me* a favour then?"

Asher tilted his head a degree. "Speak plainly."

"You have two targets," he uttered, his voice carrying no further than Asher's ears. "I would ask that you let me see to one of them. The girl perhaps? Officially, I am happy to report that you killed them both."

Asher swallowed once, his hand clenching under the table. There were any number of responses one assassin could give the other in this position, but reaching over the table and cracking his neck should not be one of them. Yet, that was all Asher could visualise in the moment. Why didn't he agree? Or simply refuse the offer in favour of eliminating both targets himself?

Everic's words came back to him. *"We're supposed to kill, Asher. And we're supposed to like it."*

It was a simple truth applied to the Arakesh as a whole... almost.

Again, Asher found himself in need of a clear mind to move on. He pushed his knuckles up into the table until the pain banished his wild thoughts. The pain reminded him of who he was: an Arakesh.

"We move tonight," he announced, shifting his weight back towards the end of the bench. "Meet me outside the town, north of the manor's outer wall."

"You want to move tonight?" Jorgan questioned as Asher rose to his feet. "You think you can learn all that you need to know in a day?"

Asher heaved his gear. "I learned everything I need to know on the walk here. Tonight: north of the wall. If you're not there, I'll move in without you."

"Oh don't worry," Jorgan called after him, "I'll be there, Asher. Every step of the way."

Asher's growl was drowned out by the creek of the tavern door on his way out.

CHAPTER 6
SWITCH

You will wear many faces as an Arakesh. It will not always be enough to spill the blood of those in your way until the target is at your mercy. There will be times when deception is required. In order to convince others that you are someone else, you will need to practise being someone else.

You must master the various accents and languages of Illian and understand the nuances of high borns and plebs alike. Prior planning and adaptability will be key to your success in this.

Always have another language on the tip of your tongue. Know the variations in culture between the six kingdoms, including the bloodlines and houses of the ruling class.

Succeed in this, and you will be able to walk up to your target, kill them, and even walk away - a master of death.

The Night Codex, The Many Faces of Death, Page 249.

Master Oblandra, 351 of the Third Age.

Braced between the branches of a tree, all four of his limbs gripped against bark, Asher looked on, observing the manor house from the rear. Under the canopy of night, his dark leathers and motionless form allowed him to blend into the tree, an imperceptible watcher from beyond the wall.

His approach was entirely wrong and he knew it. He had only arrived in Dunwich that morning - he should have spent days scouting the area before infiltrating. He didn't even know if this was the best place to eliminate his targets. They had passed some of the windows throughout the day, playing as children did, but they weren't confined to the house. Had he taken time to observe them, a potentially superior alternative might have become clear.

And he certainly needed more than one day of scouting to make sense of the guard pattern when it came to patrolling and switching shifts. Yet here he was, ready to enter and kill without real preparation - he was no better than Everic.

A gust of cold wind blew through the trees and brought with it the smell of honey mead. Asher focused his senses to the east and heard a faint heartbeat, the sound almost masked by the crunching snow. Jorgan was moving slowly through the undisturbed powder, his footsteps indiscernible to the ears of an ordinary man, thanks to the wind. But not to Asher.

He now knew everything about the assassin making his cautious approach around the edge of the town. Jorgan had the scent of another resting in the pores of his skin, a young male who, in turn, had the scent of numerous others about him. Had he wished, Asher could have tracked the stink of that other man back to his dwelling. The assassin had no doubt as to what that dwelling truly was - nor did he care for how Jorgan spent his time. It was just more information that informed him of his environment and those around him.

"Eventful day?" Asher whispered from his perch.

Jorgan paused in his tracks. "Better than yours, I expect." The bald Arakesh ascended the tree beside Asher's, his acute senses taking in all that the manor house and its grounds had to offer. "Three beyond the gate," he said.

"And three more patrolling the grounds," Asher relayed. "Only one of them has been replaced - the one relieving himself in the south-west corner. The others have been on duty for most of the day."

"They will be tired and slow," Jorgan reasoned happily.

Asher tilted his head, feeling for the vibrations in the manor's north wall. "There are two more inside. One is sleeping by the front door—"

"I could hear him snoring *without* the elixir," Jorgan cut in, his comment amusing only himself.

"The other is on the first floor," Asher continued, hearing the boards squeak beneath his regulation boots. "Two of the servants are live-in; they're already sleeping. Three more are in the kitchen," he added, hearing the light clatter of plates amidst their hushed gossiping.

"What of the Murells?" Jorgan enquired lazily.

Asher could still hear the incessant scratching of a quill on smooth parchment. "Lord Borvyn is still in his study. He's only left to relieve himself."

"I suppose a lordship isn't without its work," Jorgan commented unhelpfully.

"His wife is absent," Asher informed, having pieced snippets from several people inside the manor. "She left for Darkwell over a week ago to visit her sister."

"And the *children*?" There was a disturbing eagerness in Jorgan's tone.

"The *targets* are sleeping - they share a room in the east wing."

"Very good. And your approach?"

Asher didn't feel he needed to justify his chosen point of entry. "When I open the door," he said dryly, "feel free to walk through it."

With that, Asher released the tension in his muscles and dropped down with barely a sound. What sound he did make, however, found the stone wall that surrounded the manor and informed the assassin of how far away it was. Given that knowledge, he calculated the speed and force he would require to reach the top. When the moment was right, he broke into a sprint and leapt at the wall. Two steps up the jagged stone was enough for him to reach with both hands and curl his fingers over the lip.

There he remained, fixed in place, while he waited for the opportune moment. It was coming. Two of the three guards patrolling the grounds were rounding the back of the manor. Seven out of ten times, one of the soldiers, whose sweat stank of roasted chicken, had stopped to look through the kitchen window and spy one of the servants he liked the look of. Every time he did this, the other soldier would chuckle to himself and carry on his patrol.

Asher had a plan to deal with both men, regardless of the brief pause outside the kitchen window, though his swiftest plan favoured the growing gap between them. Had he been a religious man, like so many in Nightfall, he would have thanked the god Ibilis when the soldier stopped to look at the servant.

The assassin sprang.

His feet cleared the top of the wall, his body angled to come down beside the bewitched man. Asher's arms crashed onto the soldier, crumpling him just enough for the Arakesh to slip his hands under the victim's jaw and behind his head. As Asher rose to his full height, the weight of the soldier's head sat firmly in his grip. As always, his conditioning took hold of his mind and ran his limbs through the motion of killing a man.

Though sensitive ears heard the soldier's vertebrae in his neck snap out of alignment, Asher was too removed from the moment to fully grasp its meaning. When next he returned to his right sense of self, the man was dead at his feet and the second guard, who had walked a little further ahead, was dropping to the ground with one of Asher's throwing knives protruding from the back of his neck.

The assassin pressed his back to the manor wall and touched the palm of his hand to the stone. Had any inside been alerted to his attack, their sudden movements would send vibrations through the floors and walls. Nothing. Even the servants in the kitchen had missed his first kill.

There was, however, one heart beating much faster than those around him. Asher cocked his head and tracked the source through to the third guard inside the grounds. His steps quickened as he crossed the courtyard but slowed as he neared the east corner of the manor, where the second guard had fallen. He must have heard the body.

The path along the side of the manor was covered in slushy ice and snow where their constant patrolling had flattened the powder, but Asher could still hear the man's boots crunching small chunks of ice. The assassin braced himself low and set into a dash towards the corner of the manor. Again, his timing was easily managed by his senses and he jumped into a flying push kick as the man cleared the edge of the wall. The side of his face took the full force behind Asher's boot, throwing his head and then his body into the outer wall that ringed the grounds. Asher heard the *click* as a hairline fracture cut across the soldier's skull, but it was his slow and steady breathing that informed him the man was unconscious.

Moving to the back door, the assassin crouched down and removed the lock pick from the back of his belt. Opening a locked door was child's play when he could hear and feel the individual pins slotting into place. In less than a minute, he had access to the manor and no one to stop him.

Jorgan dropped down behind him with his signature smirk pulling at his cheeks. "Not bad," he complimented.

Asher ignored the comment and crept inside the Murell's home. Only the grand foyer was illuminated by torchlight and it was easily navigated thanks to the sleeping guard. Asher and Jorgan avoided the creaky steps by climbing up the beams that rose to the first floor. From there, they had only to wait until the patrolling guard passed the staircase and entered the west wing, leaving the targets' chamber to the east.

Moving down the hallway, Asher could feel sweat on his palms and fingertips. If he could feel it, so too could Jorgan. Asher gritted his teeth and focused on placing one foot in front of the other. He had two targets to eliminate - nothing more.

By the time he was reaching for the door handle to their room, the Arakesh had repeated that statement a dozen times like a mantra. Opening the door, the sweat on his hand was all the more obvious to him. When was the last time he had sweated with anxiety before a kill? It was most likely his first, though he could scarcely recall it.

Asher took a deep breath as he entered the room trying, as he might, to clear the doubt raking at his insides. He was a killer. There was no denying that, nor that he was a very good killer. If anything, the children were lucky that an Arakesh had been tasked with their death and not some Ironsworn brute. At least he would grant them a swift and painless death in their sleep.

Inside the room, his senses built a picture of his environment, informing him of the wooden toys scattered around a large chest at the far end and the quaint den made out of bed sheets in the corner. There were two single beds, side by side, with a cabinet between. To the assassin's left, Lord Borvyn's daughter, Esabelle, was sleeping soundly, her face hidden by dark ringlets. To the right of her, Thomas was lightly snoring, his arms stretched around his head.

Targets... They were just targets. Names on a length of knotted string.

Approaching the boy's bed, Asher carefully removed the dagger resting on his hip. The steel was an inch longer than his hand and recently stoned, its tip and clean edge as sharp as could be. As his grip intensified around the hilt, the assassin's mind withdrew from the task until he was floating in a dark ocean, far removed from the grit of reality.

This was the moment. Moving past this, his test would be over and Nasta's judgment could never be called into question where his chosen successor was concerned. Asher held on to this as he drifted through blissful ignorance.

A sudden, if faint, gasp reached through the ether, however, and took Asher's heart with a vice-like grip, dragging him back to the present. For a second, every muscle in the boy's small body tensed and his eyes opened wide. That gasp was his last breath before his body went limp in the arms of death.

Asher's breath went ragged, his heart thundering in his chest. His hands felt weak and the pit in his stomach dropped to new depths, pushing him down to his knees beside the bed. The red blindfold began to absorb fresh tears while his mind split open into warring sides.

What had he done?

In all his years, the switch in his mind had never failed him, protecting his consciousness from the darkest part of his vocation. Now it had abandoned him, leaving him vulnerable, his nerves exposed and raw to the reality of what he did. He wasn't just a killer, for it was too simple a word to describe what he was. He didn't kill; he snatched innocent lives from the world because another had paid for the privilege of keeping their hands clean.

He was a monster.

One hand slid up his face and pushed the blindfold off. In the cool light of the moon, he saw the boy's last expression. It was haunting. The image burned into his mind like a forest fire, purging so much of who he was and replacing it with crushing guilt.

"Wakey, wakey," Jorgan whispered over the girl, his words dredging Asher from his new burden.

The sadistic assassin was trying to wake Esabelle up before he killed her, relishing the moment of fear this would elicit. This was what made Jorgan feel powerful, and he loved every second of it.

The girl's eyes fluttered open before snapping wide at the sight of Jorgan leaning over her, his blade pointed down at her throat. Her reaction was to scream but the sound was muffled by the assassin's hand covering her mouth, his weight now pressing down on her. He was dragging it out, soaking up the moment as she squirmed beneath him.

Asher's guilt was instantly transported into a forge and reborn a searing fury.

Without thinking through the consequences of his actions, as he had always been taught to do, his hand whipped out and clamped around Jorgan's wrist, halting the mortal blow. The murderous assassin turned questioningly, but there was no time for words before Asher threw himself into the man, taking them both over the other side of the bed and onto the floor.

Esabelle was screaming by the time Asher had rolled to one knee and blocked Jorgan's first swipe with the blade. Coming together, the two Arakesh rose to their feet and slammed into the wardrobe, caving one of the doors in. Steel flashed up and down as Jorgan slashed and thrust at his foe's midriff. Asher felt the blade slice through his leathers and even cut through the skin below his left ribs, but Jorgan failed again and again to deliver that final strike.

Through the girl's hysterics, they continued to hurl each other around the room, exchanging attacks in the shadows. Asher wanted to reach for one of the weapons he possessed, but his hands needed to be in constant motion if he was to keep Jorgan's blade at bay. Batting his next swipe aside, Asher darted forward and landed three successive punches to his enemy's gut and chest before clasping a hand around the back of his head. With great satisfaction, he rammed the wretch's face into a book shelf before forcing him down through the next.

Jorgan roared with pain and came back at Asher with a wild upwards slash of his dagger, drawing a red line across his chin. It stung, but not nearly enough to slow Asher down. He blocked high and stopped the dagger from coming back down on him, but Jorgan took advantage of Asher's exposed ribs and launched a balled fist. The second punch cut up and caught him under the jaw, staggering Asher back two steps. In his daze, he missed the boot coming up into his chest. There was no missing the floor that rose up to greet him.

The landing was made all the more painful by the wooden toy that came between his hip and the floor. As much as he wanted to massage the area, his hands were again required to keep steel from sinking into his flesh. Jorgan had come down on him, his arms and full weight behind the hilt of the dagger. Asher had enough strength from his prone position to keep the blade from plunging through his throat, but not enough to stop the tip from piercing his skin.

As blood trickled down the side of his neck, the chamber door burst open, a northern soldier filling the frame. His cry of shock turned into one of rage, his sword swiftly drawn from its scabbard. Jorgan had little choice but to cease his assault on Asher and turn his attention to the incoming attack. Asher could only watch as Jorgan rolled aside, launched a single throwing knife to stagger the northman, and popped up by his side, the assassin's dagger sliding nicely up between the soldier's ribs and into his heart.

Esabelle screamed all the louder and pushed herself towards the headboard, her blanket concealing her face. Jorgan made the mistake of giving the girl a thought, his focus drawn to her and fantasies of the kill to come. In that moment, Asher dived through the air and caught him in the back. They flew over the guard's body and tumbled to the floor in a heap of punching limbs. Asher felt more than a few stabs from Jorgan's blade and knew his blood was spilling across the boards.

As the pair brought their skills and experience together, each vying to come out on top of the other, Asher looked to his environment for the advantage. In the chaos of their fight, the stand next to Esabelle's bed had been knocked over and debris scattered over the floor. Among this was a quill, no match when compared to Jorgan's fine dagger but, with enough force behind it, Asher was able to jam it into the assassin's hand and damage the tendons that secured his grip.

The dagger fell amidst his pain-filled cry and landed neatly in Asher's waiting hand. Their roles reversed now, Asher pressed himself down on top of Jorgan, flattening him to the floor with his own dagger angled towards his right eye. They pushed against each other, the tip of the blade inching closer and closer until it was touching Jorgan's blindfold.

Asher didn't let up.

A primal rage had been awoken in him, his various disciplines forgotten in the heat of the kill. He waited for his consciousness to retract and seek comfort in the dark folds of his mind, as it had always done, but he remained present for Jorgan's final moment, the levers of control finally broken.

He felt the dagger push through the material of the assassin's blindfold before Jorgan's resistance increased, his fear lending him new strength. Asher, however, wanted to experience every facet of the wretch's death, and nothing was going to stop him: nothing ever had.

With one hand, Asher slammed the pommel of the dagger. The first strike hammered the blade through Jorgan's eyeball, dragging a howl of pain from the man. The second strike shoved the dagger down into his head, killing him instantly. The third strike drove the steel into the boards beneath his skull.

His breathing ragged, Asher rolled aside and lay flat to the floor beside the corpse. He could hear rushing footsteps beyond the room. He didn't care. All he could see was Thomas Murell's face, his last expression etched into his mind.

Esabelle's muffled whimper broke his plummet into misery. Asher groaned through the fresh wounds Jorgan had inflicted on him and rose to his feet. He rounded the girl's bed, pausing only to retrieve his fallen blindfold. He wanted to sit on the edge of her mattress and tell her everything was going to be alright now, that she was safe. But he didn't want to peel back her blanket, lest she see her brother.

Asher had never considered himself a coward, the word incon-gruous with the life of an Arakesh, but he knew that's exactly what he was. Only cowards killed from the shadows. Only cowards killed innocent and defenceless people. But, in truth, there was no word to name those who took the life of a child - even monster seemed too fair a word.

Instead of approaching the girl, he gave in to his instincts and began backing away towards the window. Halfway there, the second guard - previously asleep - rushed into the room, his sword already drawn. His face said it all upon seeing the ruin and death that awaited him. It took the man an extra second to spot Asher, his body naturally finding the shadows in which to linger.

Rightly so, the man charged at him with his sword raised. Again, the assassin's instincts took control, urging him to replace his blindfold and flee the scene. In total darkness, his senses returned to their heightened state. He could taste the boy's blood and feel his cooling skin as he lay utterly still. It was almost enough to keep him rooted to the spot, there to wait until the guard ran him through.

But the instincts of an Arakesh were hard to ignore.

He turned and bolted for the window, a single leap taking him through it. As he flew and then fell through the open air, he was aware of every splinter of glass around him, as well as his distance from the ground. He landed in the courtyard amidst the raining shards, his knees bent to absorb the drop, before rolling towards the main gates.

"Murderer!" came the cry from the shattered window.

The three guards on the other side of the gate had already heard Asher's dramatic departure and were entering the grounds. Asher could hear leather gloves squeaking as fingers grasped hilts and freed cold steel. His own hand lifted - a reflex - and nearly drew one of the short-swords on his back. But that would, inevitably, lead to more blood and bodies in his wake. Hadn't there been enough of that?

The three warriors had no trouble finding Asher in the middle of the snow-covered courtyard - nor did they slow down, ignorant, perhaps, of his origins. Remaining on one knee, his head bowed, Asher waited until all three were upon him. Then he moved like a Wraith. He pivoted to the side, avoiding one incoming sword that rang out against the stone, and sprang up in front of another. His limbs extended into one unorthodox display after another, allowing him to evade, block, and dance between his three opponents.

One by one, he delivered an incapacitating strike that knocked the men to the ground. While they rolled around in pain and disorientation, Asher sprinted towards the street and the freedom beyond. He was brought to a skidding stop, as he crossed the threshold, by the uncontrollable sobs of a man reaching his ears. Tilting his head, he quickly tracked it back to the children's room and knew it to be the sobs of Lord Borvyn.

For the first time in his life, the cold and impenetrable wall that had surrounded Asher's heart cracked. There was no source to the pain that racked him, but it felt crippling. Again, it was only his instincts that set his body into motion. This time, the sound of bells ringing out in the night turned him away from the manor and into the nearest alley. It wasn't long before more bells were ringing, all across Dunwich. Candle and torch light began to illuminate the dark parts of the town.

Rushing feet and clattering steel filled the nearby streets, forcing Asher to seek safety on the rooftops. Across the street from the manor, crouched beside a brick chimney, the assassin removed his blindfold and watched as dozens of town watchmen and hardened soldiers converged on the courtyard. The three men he had put in the snow were only just beginning to rise. They would continue to suffer for days, if not weeks, from their injuries but, at least, they were alive.

Asher slumped against the chimney, his head resting on the snowy bricks. Everything hurt. Jorgan's dagger had apparently found every vulnerable spot in his leathers and sliced through his skin in multiple places. His knuckles were swollen and cut, the blood a mixture of his and Jorgan's. An acute pain stabbed at his left shoulder and he heard something metallic knock against the chimney.

There was a throwing knife in his back.

The assassin sighed, unsure when exactly his opponent had caught him in the fight. He welcomed the momentary reprieve the pain brought him, muddying his focus. After pulling the blade out and discarding it across the roof, Asher naturally reached into his shirt for the black gem, its mysterious properties capable of healing him.

Thomas Murell's face flashed across his vision, his guilt pushing through the fading pain.

Asher released the ring, letting it fall back to his chest. He decided to keep the pain. He deserved it. What he actually deserved was something more final.

"FIND HIM!" The command was roared from the manor's front door, where Lord Borvyn stood with a sword in hand. "I want his head!" With that final order, he stormed back inside his house.

The soldiers began to divide themselves up and assign streets and districts. It was clear that no one would be sleeping in Dunwich that night. Asher knew that to be especially true of one young girl who had borne witness to murder and bloodshed. He couldn't imagine how Esabelle Murell would ever recover from it all. At least she now had her whole life to find a way, he thought, for what little comfort it was.

An alarm suddenly rang in the assassin's mind, so clear and so loud it could have been one of the many bells currently waking up the town. Esabelle didn't have her whole life ahead of her. She only had until the next Arakesh was sent to finish the job. Asher himself had been that very Arakesh on one occasion, sent across the realm to see Nightfall's oath fulfilled.

Asher knew there and then that he would stay in Dunwich and wait for that next killer. He wouldn't let them touch her. His iron resolve faltered. Nasta would only send another and another. Though Asher was confident he could protect the girl - for years if he must - he also knew that, eventually, more than one Arakesh would be dispatched to investigate the multiple deaths. How many could he really fend off? It would only take one assassin to distract him while the other killed Esabelle.

As the girl's inevitable death loomed over him, Asher was awash in deep depression. There was no stopping Nightfall. The ancient order was akin to the ever-reaching hand of Death - it could never be stopped, only delayed. And so, in the coming weeks, a new murderer would walk into Dunwich with two names and two locations on a length of knotted red string. Then, Esabelle would face...

Asher's mind stopped in its tracks having stumbled over a detail that gave him pause. Two names. Two locations. The target and the patron.

Lord Kalben of Skystead...

Asher could still feel the touch of the knotted string as if it was between his fingers. Kalben Tarn was the only man in the world who could save Esabelle now. Or, more specifically, the death of Kalben Tarn could save Esabelle. The lord could, of course, request that Nightfall not kill the girl, but there was no guarantee that he wouldn't look to an Arakesh in the future to see the deed done. Only his death granted her life.

That seemed a fair exchange to Asher. He knew time was against him. Word would reach Nightfall and Nasta would waste no time assigning another. Only the Father knew where every Arakesh was currently located in the realm, so Asher could only hope there were none close by.

There was no time to sit around and debate the idea, no time to plan and assess his options. He simply had to act, and fast. Scrambling over the roof, his movements put to haste, the assassin set himself the task of liberating his horse and riding hard to the west, to Skystead.

CHAPTER 7

OLD WELL

Fingers, toes, knees, and elbows. Every man, woman, and child in Illian possesses some or all of these anatomical elements. They are all joints that work in the same manner as a door hinge - they can only bend one way. Break your opponent's toe and they will struggle to walk. Snap their knee and they will fail to stand. Snapping fingers will hinder their grip on any weapon. Snap their elbow and you face a foe with limited range. These are but a few of the weaknesses that can leave even the strongest of enemies at your mercy (see No Mercy, Page 10). Severely injuring these joints is also a useful technique when dealing with multiple opponents at once.

The Night Codex, Disabling and Maiming, Page 127.

Master Bok, 377 of the Third Age.

Reaching his horse had been the easy part. The stables were quiet and dark with only two horses left for the night. Asher stroked the neck of his mount, calming it after creeping in. He had only just concealed himself inside the stall before a group of soldiers with torches passed by, one of whom paused to scan the stables from the entrance.

Asher had remained still, his back pressed flat to the stall door. All the while, he had kept one hand on the hilt of a short-sword, over his shoulder. It was only when he considered what he would actually do with it that he lowered his arm and considered the non-lethal techniques he could employ. After all, the northern soldier was just doing his job... searching for a murderer.

Alone again, the assassin moved about the stable with practised caution, his steps as light as falling leaves. He went about fixing his saddle to the horse's back, noting with irritation that the bags were empty. He had taken the contents to his room, a room that was situated on the first floor of The Gauntlet Inn, two blocks over. They were all lost to him now, including his clothes.

This wasn't how he had intended to leave Dunwich. Everything about his person told of his identity, be it the nature of his dark leathers, the plethora of knives concealed across his body, or the twin short-swords on his back. And then there was that other thing, the part of him that lived in his eyes and revealed his predatory nature. He had seen men look at him the way they might look a Sandstalker in the eyes. They just knew.

The horse exhaled a cloud of hot vapour as he led it out of the stall, pulling it along by the reins. "I hope you've had your rest," he whispered to the animal. "We won't be walking out of here."

As he raised one foot into a stirrup, heavy boots approached the stable doors. Asher paused in his ascent only as long as it took him to realise the person was, indeed, going to enter. He groaned to himself - this wasn't how assassins were supposed to leave anywhere. He should be better than this. Perhaps, he considered, his days of being a *better* assassin were gone. There would certainly be no going back after tonight. Then again, he thought, there might not be any going forward either.

The stable door scraped across the stone as it was dragged fully open. The owner, a man who smelled like the inside of a smoking pipe, looked on in shock and then terror as Asher's steed bolted from the stable, almost knocking him over.

Out on the street, Asher kept the horse's speed up and began searching for the nearest path that would lead to the north road. The stable owner, however, was shouting for guards before the horse had even turned the first corner. The night soon rang out with new cries of warning as the soldiers and town's watchmen tried to narrow down his whereabouts.

Every new street he galloped past, soldiers and watchmen would begin their chase on foot, hounding him with curses and hollers. Inevitably it drew more down on the assassin. Soldiers and watchmen were diverting to get ahead of him, but they were no match for a horse in full flight. Asher was forced, only once, to kick out and catch one of the guards in the helmet before he could swing his sword.

Upon reaching The Selk Road - which ran from north to south through the heart of Dunwich - Asher escaped the cramped streets and turned right, where the road continued into the furthest reaches of Orith. The open road, of course, came with problems all of its own for the Arakesh. Six riders, clad in northern iron and draped in golden cloaks, blocked the way.

Asher brought his horse to a skidding stop with fifty feet to go and turned it in a tight circle. He scanned his surroundings, his mind trained to find every way in and out of an environment. More soldiers were spilling out from the side streets while the towns-people looked on through their windows.

With only seconds in his favour, Asher laid out Illian's terrain in his mind. Skystead was his destination, to the west of Dunwich as the crow flies. Between here and there lay the sprawling White Vale, a barren landscape of snow and nothing else. Only fools would go out into that white, a featureless desert that could turn a man around for days. It was the only reason Asher was trying to reach the north-bound road, a path that would take any traveller along the edge of The Vengoran Mountains. After coming across Namdhor, the capital in these lands, he would only have to follow the shore of The King's Lake south until he came to Skystead. It was a journey measured by time not miles, but at least he knew the road would take him there.

Turning his horse back around to face the riders in his way, the assassin contemplated the fight he faced. On horseback, the advantage was theirs, the reach of their swords greater than the two on his back. They had but to injure his mount and that would complicate matters all the more. He needed to evade, though a part of his mind now wondered if he would have made that same decision prior to the night's horrific events.

The sound of galloping hooves turned the assassin's head over his shoulder. There were three more riders approaching from the south, their blades already drawn. It emboldened the six blocking his way, setting them all at a charge. Though he felt like fighting his instincts, Asher let them bleed through as he adopted a survival mindset. He knew instantly what he was going to do and had to consciously ignore how reckless it was. After all, Esabelle Murell's life was in his hands, bloodied as they were.

Yanking the reins, he directed the horse to the west, where an alley cut through two blocks of shops and led to further streets. "Ya!" he called, spurring the mount into a new gallop.

The riders gave chase with fire in their veins. Asher couldn't blame them. Were Esabelle's life not in danger, he would have surrendered already and faced the death he so deserved.

Navigating the western district, Asher made one turn after another until the darkness beyond the town was finally in sight. His horse made for the narrow gap between two houses, shortly followed by the pursuing riders. After breaking away from the town, the northmen spread out, their mounts thundering through the untouched snow. One of the soldiers attempted to bring Asher down with an arrow, but firing at a moving target while riding a horse wasn't an easy skill to acquire. The arrow whistled through the air, missing the assassin by a clear foot.

Asher's left hand naturally made to retrieve the folded bow on his back - firing an arrow under these conditions was not a problem for him. It would have been even easier were he wearing his blindfold. Resisting the urge, the assassin squeezed the leather of his horse's reins all the tighter and hunkered down in his saddle.

On he rode, his only company the howling wind that brought with it the threatening cries of his hunters. And they were gaining on him. A glance over his shoulder told him as much, the northmen almost upon him. Asher cursed the fatigue of his horse, for it was not only to be the end of him but Esabelle too.

But his escape plan was only moments away from taking effect.

Riding hard through the darkness, there was only one thing that dominated the land to the town's immediate west. Asher heard it before he was aware of it, the lake known to the people of Dunwich as Old Well. The sound of hooves galloping across the ice was deafening. Another glance over his shoulder proved his plan had worked to some extent for, of the nine riders who had given chase, four had seen enough sense to keep their horses on the shore and abandon the pursuit.

That still left five capable killers on his tail. Asher swore under his breath. While the bite of the wind proved winter had yet to release its full grip on the north, it was likely that the lake, even now, would be thawing, weakening the ice. It was a good gamble, however, that the frozen lake could cope with a single horse galloping across its hardened face. Asher didn't like the odds though when there was five times the weight in the equation.

Looking down, there was no way to see if the ice was cracking and there would be no hearing it over the sound of the horses. Fortunate that he had left the knot in his blindfold, Asher was able to pull it from his belt and fix it over his eyes with one hand. Now he knew true darkness, and the world came alive in a way that even the sun could never bring.

Every hammering step his horse made was an impact that connected the ice to Asher's senses. He could feel it cracking all around them, completely shattering in places. The smell of his mount's foamy sweat was impossible to ignore, the animal's run almost at an end. Yet the lake was vast and the land beyond even more so.

In the lead, the assassin could hear the fissure that was about to race out to his left. By the time the northmen were aware of it, one of them plunged into Old Well. The soldier's horse dropped through, its front half disappearing beneath the black water, while its rider slammed into the edge of the ice, the wind knocked out of him.

One of the remaining four pulled hard on his reins and moved swiftly to assist his fallen companion before the weight of his armour dragged him down to the depths. Another rider simply peeled away, his fears getting the better of him. That left two on the hunt, each coming up on Asher's side.

As the three rode over a particularly strong patch of ice, the assassin took the moment to rid himself of another foe without sealing the man's fate. Freeing one foot from its stirrup, he lashed out with a kick and shoved the soldier hard in the ribs. It was enough to dislodge him and launch the man free of his mount, where the hard ice was able to take his impact. Without a rider, the horse slowed down and veered away from the seeming race.

Now there was only one who could potentially stop him from saving Esabelle. Before he could formulate a plan, however, his heightened senses detected the devastating shockwaves that had gone on ahead of them and severely weakened the ice. Asher immediately redirected his horse to the north, but the damage to the ice spread even faster than his senses could keep up with.

Crack.

It sounded like thunder to Asher's ears. His horse was instantly swallowed up by the lake, its cry of surprise short-lived. The assassin became a slave to his momentum and was thrown ahead. A slight adjustment in the angle of his shoulders allowed him to roll before skidding across the ice on his back. All the while, his senses built a picture of his surroundings, informing him that the last rider, while slightly slowing, had avoided the breaking ice and was still coming for him.

Twisting his hip, Asher swung his legs around and continued to slide on his arms and knees, desperate to create some kind of meaningful friction. Seeing his end approaching, the assassin pulled free the dagger from his belt and plunged it into the ice. He stopped dead and wasted no time rolling to the side, missing the horse's relentless hooves by inches.

The rider slowed his mount down and turned it back to face Asher. The assassin could tell a lot about a person from the beat of their heart and, credit to the northern soldier, he had no fear about him. He was all determined rage as he dismounted and drew his sword.

"You would murder a child, coward!" he spat. "I will take your head back to my lord," he panted, "and leave your body for the fish!"

Asher rose carefully, able to *see* every crack in the ice like a flame in the dark. On his feet, his centre of gravity purposefully positioned to apply pressure to the weakest parts of the ice, he waited, without a word, for the soldier to close the gap. As the northerner came in with a high swing, an attack that required a firm footing, Asher stamped his foot once and dived aside.

The man gave a sharp yelp before his legs disappeared into the water. He abandoned his sword to the depths in favour of reaching out for solid ice. His gauntlets scraped repeatedly against the ice's edge, his fingers clawing for purchase. Before long, he was almost submerged to his chest. It wouldn't be long, Asher knew, until the water's numbing temperature stopped his legs from kicking. Then he would be at the mercy of Old Well, his end assured.

Asher crossed the ice and gripped the soldier by both wrists. Sure now that the northman had no capacity to chase him any further, the assassin dragged him up and out of the water.

With laboured breaths, Asher pointed directly north and said, "Go straight from here. Don't deviate or you'll fall through again."

"Wait," the northerner stammered. "You're... under... arrest."

Asher ignored him and made his way to the only horse left standing on the ice. The soldier's mount was restless, aware of the dangers it had already witnessed. The assassin held out one hand and approached cautiously, soothing the animal with a quiet voice. After taking it by the reins, he patted its neck and ran his fingers down its long face.

"Good boy," he uttered, moving to investigate the large saddle bags either side of its rump. He was pleased to see that the soldier had recently stocked them with supplies and even strapped a blanket to the back of the saddle.

With that, he mounted the horse and turned it westward. He estimated three weeks before Skystead was in his sights - if he made it traversing the wilds.

CHAPTER 8
TRADITIONS

There is but one ruler of Nightfall - you will have met them by now. For me, in the year 391 of the Third Age, it is Maelstra, the Mother. Like her predecessors, Maelstra honed her skills over many years before challenging the sitting ruler - in her case it was a Father. The only rule of such a challenge is to defeat your opponent in combat and kill them.

Upon attaining her new position, the Mother had her eyes removed, a ceremony traditionally performed in silence as a sign of strength and endurance. Mothers and Fathers live out the rest of their days in a heightened sense, lending to the belief that one must have been an Arakesh for decades before being capable of enduring this aspect of the title.

A historical reminder of this occurred in the year 219 of the Third Age, when an initiate succeeded in killing the sitting Mother of the time. It is noted in the records that the initiate went mad before their 20th year of life.

The Night Codex, Know Whom You Serve, Page 2.

Master Obadiah, 391 of the Third Age.

. . .

To Nasta Nal-Aket, the world and its inhabitants were an open book. To the Father, body language was just that, a *language*. The human body was always broadcasting the thoughts and feelings of the mind, be it in the twitch of fine muscles around the eyes or the dilation of the pores of the skin.

And there was so much more beneath the surface that betrayed secrets. It was all there for Nasta to interpret, including the functions of his own body. He could hear his heart beating and even feel the hairs in his nose and ears growing day by day. His heightened senses knew no rest.

While every Arakesh in Nightfall slept in the light, the Father lived in permanent darkness, his mind an abyss. Like every Mother and Father before him, he was only able to find rest in meditation, a state in which he could pull back from the constant input. Still, he heard the hurried steps beyond The Cradle's walls.

The owner of those feet was young, fourteen perhaps. His body felt abound with energy, his muscles coiled in tight cords, ready to be honed for the service of Nightfall. The boy was stopped mid run, a wall of experienced assassins standing in his way. Had Nasta any eyes to open they certainly would have done so with a snap. The eldest assassin took a length of string from the younger hands and ran a sensitive finger over the knots, reading the coded message as he did. He then dismissed the boy with a flick of two fingers, a common gesture of Master Krain's.

Nasta, fully roused from his meditation, pivoted away from the altar to Ibilis and rose to his feet without need of his hands. He was standing in front of the main doors by the time Master Krain entered The Cradle, his proximity putting the other assassin instantly on edge.

"Father," he greeted more loudly than was necessary.

"Master Krain," Nasta replied evenly.

Master Krain held the string up. "Word from Dunwich," he said, an unfortunate smirk creeping up one side of his face.

"Yet it remains in your hands instead of mine," Nasta pointed out.

Krain bowed his head by way of a stiff apology and offered the knotted string. Nasta accepted it and turned his back on the master while his finger and thumb interpreted the knots. The message had come a long way and been held by two men prior to the boy Krain had taken it from. Nasta could smell both the northman who had journeyed south with it and the man who had accepted the report in Calmardra and brought it out into the desert.

It was the message itself, however, that brought the Father to a halt. *Well done, boy,* Nasta thought. *You made your choice. Now I only hope you have the will to fight for it.*

As he read it a second and even a third time, The Cradle began to steadily fill with the other masters who had heard Krain's words. Of course they had gathered, Nasta thought. Had it been any other put to the test the masters would have left it to the Father to handle, but Asher was another matter altogether. Even Alidyr entered behind them, his interest piqued.

"Ill news?" Master Bantara enquired, her voice sounding nearly as ancient as the stone around them.

Nasta half turned and lazily gestured at the gathered masters. "You are already aware of the facts, Master Krain..."

With no lack of satisfaction, Krain addressed his peers. "We have word from trusted contacts in Dunwich," he began, enjoying his tale. "Two weeks ago, the son of Lord Borvyn was assassinated in his bed. His sister, Esabelle, yet lives."

"Asher and Jorgan have failed?" Master Bantara questioned incredulously.

"The task was Asher's alone," Master Eckard reminded.

"Jorgan is dead," Krain announced, silencing the chamber. "His body is in the custody of the town's watchmen."

"One of the targets lives *and* Jorgan is dead?" Master Vor-Kana echoed, the vertebrae in his long spine lining up quite neatly as he straightened his back. "How could this have come to be?"

"The northmen are good fighters all," Master Eckard remarked, "but none compare to Jorgan."

True as it was, Nasta would have expected nothing else from the inquisitor, for he had imparted much of himself to Jorgan over the course of his training.

Krain held up a finger. "Jorgan did not suffer the blade of a northman. The report is quite specific. The girl claims to have witnessed his death... at the hands of *Asher*." The master paused for dramatic effect, allowing his words to sink in. "There are a great number of eyewitness reports that state Asher then fled the scene and the town itself."

"He spared the girl?" Master Vor-Kana questioned, cupping his trimmed goatee.

"This is most disturbing, Father," Master Bantara voiced. "We are talking about a rogue Arakesh - an accomplished one at that. Asher poses a great threat to Nightfall."

Nasta detected no animosity towards Asher or himself, her tone and reasoning born of good sense.

"A threat that could easily have been averted," Master Krain stirred, "by one who knew Asher so well."

Nasta maintained complete control of his mind and body, presenting the masters with an unnervingly calm figure. There was blood in the water. Now, more than ever, it was important to appear the predator. In truth, he would have been disappointed if Krain missed the opportunity to strike. And he wasn't saying anything the other masters weren't already thinking.

"Why would Asher betray us?" Master Bantara questioned rightly, steering away from any accusations. "He has served the order well since his trials."

Krain waved her logic away. "What he possessed in skill he lacked in the mind. Asher was riddled with weakness from his first day. He should never have been brought here."

The second strike was twice the blow of the first, his words a direct attack on the Father. Still, Nasta continued to slowly run his finger and thumb over the knots in the string, his mind cast adrift. Krain had made no mention of it, but there was a curious detail in the report that stood out to Nasta. It seemed Asher had fled the manor and then the town under the duress of a manhunt that ended on the frozen lake. Besides the fact that Asher had been so clumsy as to be seen leaving anywhere, there were no further casualties after slaying Jorgan. Of all the soldiers who confronted him, Asher had killed none of them.

Curious...

"Our traditions are quite clear on the matter," Krain continued, eager to get a rise out of the Father. "Asher has betrayed the order. He has killed one of our own. He has allowed a target to live. He has brought Nightfall into the light. He must be placed in—"

"You do not exact our traditions, Master Krain." Nasta's tone was even, if firm. Now he had the masters' full attention. If his reaction to Asher's betrayal was anything but swift and decisive, they would all turn on him.

"How are we to deal with the matter, Father?" Master Eckard asked, eager to have one of his most accomplished students avenged.

Nasta took in all that there was to glean from those before him. All were poised, ready to receive his word and cast their judgement on his decision. All except for Alidyr, who appeared wholly exasperated with the affair. How many times, Nasta wondered, had the ancient one borne witness to an event identical to this one? History must surely be seen to repeat itself in the eyes of an immortal.

"As of this moment," Nasta declared, "Asher is placed in the court of assassins." He instantly detected an array of changes in Krain's manner that spoke of his deep irritation. Had Krain suggested it first, the Father would have been made to appear all the weaker, his judgement seen to be impaired.

"The court hasn't been enacted since I was a boy in these halls," Nasta continued, "but I know our *traditions* well," he added pointedly. "Asher has killed a brother of the order, allowed a target to live, exposed Nightfall, and he has not returned to face the consequences of his rash actions. He shall be set upon by an Arakesh for every sin."

"Four?" Krain concluded in disbelief. "Besides his skill, Asher poses too high a threat to leave it to four. We should send ten at least. Asher knows too much of our ways," he continued to argue. "He cannot be allowed to live."

"Our traditions are quite clear on the matter," Nasta said, echoing Krain's own words. "They bend for no one. Asher shall face an assassin for every tenet broken. Now, we the masters of these hallowed halls, must choose our Arakesh."

Master Vor-Kana clasped his fingers behind his back. "Uthork. He is of The Ice Vales; the hunt was in his blood long before his time in Nightfall."

Master Bantara tapped the bulbous top of her cane. "Melekish. He is well versed in the art of deception. I believe he could walk right up to Asher and he wouldn't suspect a thing." Master Eckard was nodding approvingly, agreeing with his fellow master's choice.

Nasta disagreed with both, but he didn't protest.

"Ro Dosarn," came the whisper of an elf, his tone as bored as his demeanour.

"I sent Ro to Ameeraska three days past," Nasta informed. "Choose another."

Alidyr took a breath, though it did nothing to invigorate him. "Demry," he said, choosing the only woman who had been in Asher's training cohort.

Nasta accepted the elf's choice of Arakesh, and it was a good one at that. Of all the assassins available to them, those from Asher's cohort knew him best and often enacted similar, if not identical tactics. There were also only three still alive from that particular cohort.

Master Krain had been rubbing his finger and thumb together since the Father had enacted the court, clearly indecisive about who among his allies was best equipped to kill Asher.

"Borman," Krain put forth as the final assassin. "He will rectify this mistake."

The Father knew of Borman, a brute of an Arakesh who had been in Krain's pocket since his early teens. Nasta had never liked him, his frame larger than average - not a quality best served in an assassin that needed to blend in where required.

"No," Nasta said evenly, confident issuing commands without the need of a firm tone.

Krain's facial muscles creased into a scowl. "No? Borman is the only one among the court who will actually see the task done."

"Must I repeat myself?" There was an edge to Nasta's voice now, speaking of his irritation.

"You have someone else in mind, Father?" Master Vor-Kana queried.

"I do," was all Nasta offered.

"What of the target?" Master Bantara questioned, content to leave the Father's private thoughts to himself. "Two lives were paid for. Two lives must be taken."

Nasta regarded Master Bantara. "I leave it to your judgement on who to assign."

Master Bantara bowed her head. "I have someone already in mind, Father. I believe Rendal has executed a mission such as this twice already."

"Very good," Nasta replied with hardly any interest.

"*Who* is your choice, Father?" Krain pressed, his intractable demeanour growing all the more tiresome.

Nasta answered to none of them, but he was presented with an opportunity to detach himself from Asher and, at the same time, reduce Krain's remarks to hot air. "Have you ever played a game of Gallant, Master Krain?"

It was not the response Krain was expecting, slowing his time to answer. "Not in many years, Father, I must admit."

"Every deck contains one wild card," Nasta explained. "The inexperienced player will keep this close, believing it can elevate their hand. Of course, in the long game, it rarely counts for much. No, the wild card is to be played against your opponent, putting them off balance and thus forcing them to change their tactics part way through the game. This need to change can be a mistake, one that often leads to miscalculation and ultimate failure."

Master Bantara pursed her lips. "Do you have a wild card to add to our deck, Father?"

"I do," he replied, before informing them of his decision. Their responses were mixed, though none - not even Krain - offered protest.

Nasta returned the coded string to Krain and strode past them all, making for the doors. Initiates and Arakesh alike pressed themselves flat to the walls as the Father weaved his way through the labyrinth. He didn't stop until he was inside Master Eckard's chamber, a place even a witless fool could have found had they followed their nose.

It had the smell of a person's insides, a raw and individual odour that assaulted the senses. Fiery braziers illuminated the chamber from all four corners, though the Father was only aware of their heat. Ignoring the dirty implements that lined the walls, Nasta's bare feet crossed the floor slick with blood and stood before the room's only other occupant.

Everic's head tilted just enough for the northman to spy Nasta between two matted strands of blood-soaked hair. Listening intently to his breathing, the Father was sure the young man had suffered no broken bones. Good, he thought. His skin, however, was another matter altogether. The damage done to him was irreparable, the flesh fated to scar in horrible ways. The question was, how much of the assassin remained inside such a broken shell?

"We are alone," Nasta told him. "You may utter the word I gave you."

Everic twitched and the leather straps around his wrists squeaked. He opened his mouth, tearing open a wound that had yet to properly seal, and fresh blood spilled over his lips. The northman winced at the pain before licking the blood and swallowing.

His voice was a rasp after so much screaming. "Help..."

There it was, the secret he had been given. He was only allowed to speak it in Nasta's presence and Nasta's presence alone. To the Father's knowledge, Everic had suffered the worst Master Eckard had at his disposal and never did he utter the secret word.

"Your two months are up," Nasta said, though Everic was in too much pain to smile. "You have the iron will of an Arakesh," he complimented. "I would even go so far as to say you have the makings of a Father in you."

Everic pushed through his pain. "I live... to serve... Nightfall."

"You have proven yourself worthy of a second chance," Nasta went on. "A rare thing in this world and even rarer in these halls. The five trials should be all that awaits you beyond this chamber. But I would have you attain the title of Arakesh with only one."

Everic's brow furrowed and a new line of blood ran down the ragged edges of his mutilated nose. "One... trial?"

"One trial," the Father echoed. "One target."

"Who?" Everic rasped.

Nasta raised his chin. "Asher," he announced.

At last, Everic smiled.

CHAPTER 9
FOLLOW THE MONEY

Ensuring the death of your target or opponent is essential and, in some cases, you will have little time to do so. A quick death is attainable if you know where to strike (see below for anatomical diagram).
You need only target one of the major arteries - these are large passages in the body that carry a critical volume of blood. Severing one of these arteries can result in unconsciousness in as little as 30 seconds and death in minutes. Just try not to slip afterwards.

The Night Codex, Knowledge is Power, Page 60.

Master Gaelish, 334 of the Third Age.

After weeks of defying the north's freezing hospitality and feeling quite dead on his feet, Asher finally looked upon the city of Skystead. Once home to the elves, before their exodus nearly a thousand years ago, the ancient city curved around the southern shore of The King's Lake. Namdhor, the capital city in this part of the world, rose from the ground and shared the shore in the north-east, a glimmering speck on Skystead's horizon.

In the passing millennium, humanity had moved in and claimed Skystead as their own. Now, the crescent city was an overlapping mixture of elven and human architecture, boasting the elegant spires and arching halls of the immortals, and the squat and bulky dwellings of the northmen. Most of these enjoyed the lakeside view, its flat surface gleaming in the midday sun.

To Asher, it was a warren of opportunities, as were most bustling cities in the eyes of an assassin. Though, right now, he was finding it hard to think of anything but food. The paltry supplies he had rationed from the saddlebags had run out two days past; even the horse he had stolen was flagging. To that end, he relieved the animal of its saddlebags and slapped its rump, sending it towards the city alone. Someone would adopt the mount and make coin in the process no doubt.

The only thing Asher kept was the travelling cloak the previous rider had stuffed into one of the bags. While on the outskirts of the farmland, shielded within a copse of trees, the assassin inverted the scabbards on his back so that the hilts crossed over his hips rather than jutted over his shoulders. The travelling cloak, a voluminous piece of grey fabric, concealed much of his tough leathers and weapons. He tucked most of his folded bow into one of the saddle-bags and slung the whole thing over the shoulder that hadn't recently received the cold edge of Jorgan's blade. The quiver of arrows he clipped to his belt, from where the black fletchings poked out of the cloak. At a passing glance, people would likely believe he was a hunter of some description and leave him to his business.

Crossing what remained of the land, Asher stepped off The Selk Road and passed between the two enormous statues that marked the entrance to Skystead, each a hooded elf in need of repair. The city quickly rose up around him, blocking the view of both the lake and the mountains that surrounded the western landscape.

It was ten times the size of Dunwich and the population was a testament to that. The assassin fell into the embrace of his training and weaved through the teeming streets, hectic with activity. All, it seemed, were preparing for the festival of Ymir which was quickly approaching before the summer.

These were perfect conditions for an experienced pickpocket, one of the earliest skills an initiate of Nightfall was expected to learn. Asher scanned every person walking towards him and brushed past the ones who only *thought* their coin purse was securely tied to their belts. Some were even easier and he was able to deftly snatch them from behind before disappearing down another avenue.

Asher didn't need to read the signs posted on the street corners to find his way to The White Citadel, Lord Kalben's home on the lake front. It made Lord Borvyn's manor house in Dunwich look like an Outlander's hut. The assassin had never been assigned a target inside the fort but, like every ancient major fort or keep that the high borns of the world had called home, Asher knew the internal layout as well as its location.

The citadel rose up in tiers, granting its inhabitants a view of both the city and the lake. It was heavily guarded by soldiers of the north, who patrolled the ramparts of the outer wall and stood sentinel before the gates. Asher didn't need to look inside to know that the grounds and the fort itself were populated by more of their ilk. And he didn't miss the raggedy Ironsworn who passed freely between the soldiers.

The waterfront was his best point of access - a conclusion he had come to before arriving at the fort. He could either steal a small rowing boat and set off in the dark of night, or even brave the daunting temperature of the water. Whatever his attempt was to be, the assassin had to be certain that it would end in his target's death, for Lord Kalben needed to die as soon as possible.

As always, his rigorous training was there to catch him, determining his path and offering him solutions in the art of death. If he couldn't get to his target, then he would make the target come to him. The only question was what bait to use?

The smell of hot food got in the way of his thinking and brought his feet to a sudden stop. More than one person barged past him, knocking his shoulder, unaware of the killer who had walked into their midst.

Following his nose, Asher turned down the street to his right, away from The White Citadel, and found himself entering a cosy tavern by the name of The Gobber's Revenge. He cared little for the name or the few patrons that occupied a handful of stools at the bar. He claimed the only booth in the tavern and signalled the barmaid, a plump woman who looked like she would rather be anywhere else, especially if it meant taking the weight off her feet. Good, the assassin thought. She was less likely to remember him if her mind was so obviously elsewhere.

"A pitcher of water," he ordered before she could ask, "and a cup of Velian mint tea," he added, the specific tea only available in the larger cities in Illian.

"Any food?" she asked, inspecting one of her finger nails.

"Whatever's hot," he replied gruffly, eager to consume it. "What's that sweet smell?" he enquired of the aroma that had drawn him to the tavern in the first place.

"The pie."

"I'll take two."

The barmaid finally gave him more than a glance. "You got coin?" Her tone suggested Asher was no more than a vagrant in her eyes, though his rough and ragged appearance didn't help him.

Beneath the grey cloak, his hand retrieved one of the small coin purses he had pilfered. He dropped it on the table top by way of an answer. The barmaid scooped up the purse and disappeared without a word. Asher waited, his fingers drumming impatiently against the wood, until his food and drink arrived, at which point he consumed everything without thought as to what any of it was.

When, at last, he looked up from his empty plates, the afternoon drinkers had departed, leaving Asher as the only patron inside The Gobber's Revenge. He contemplated ordering the same again - and would have - but now his mind and body demanded sleep, preferably in a bed beside a fire. He could see, though, that the tavern didn't offer accommodation. As he gathered his things, the door opened and a cold draft swept through the small interior.

Everything about the man that walked in to The Gobber's Revenge set alarm bells ringing in the assassin's mind.

His walk was a display of arrogance, his shoulders dipping with every step, broadcasting the man's cocky nature immediately. The smile he flashed the old man behind the bar was meant to intimidate, reminding him who was on top in the food chain. His physique of toned muscle was mostly hidden beneath pricey furs and a thick blue cloak. Tattoos ran up his neck, worming out of his collar and up into his cropped blond hair. Asher noticed a few scars here and there, mostly on his hands - he was a fighter then. And, of course, there was the one-handed falchion sword on his hip.

"Can I help you?" the tavern owner asked innocently enough.

The stranger raised his left arm and pulled back his sleeve. Asher was unable to see what he was showing the old man, though it was likely another tattoo and, judging by the barkeep's expression, it was a very meaningful tattoo.

"Collection," the stranger said with a broad smile.

The old man hesitated. "You're not Kovar," he remarked.

"Good eye," the stranger complimented mockingly. "Kovar was found to be skimming. You won't be seeing him again. I'm Yarisk. Collection," he repeated, holding his hand out.

The tavern owner produced a single coin purse from a box hidden under the bar. The stranger accepted it and hefted the coins between his fingers, feeling for the weight. His smile vanished.

"You're light," he stated, his tone laced with a threatening edge.

The old man swallowed. "Tell Lord—"

"We don't say his name." Those five words saw the old man retreat into himself. Yarisk dropped his hand and the sack of coins onto the bar. "I will inform the boss of your contributions. Be seeing you."

The thug turned around and spotted Asher for the first time, the sight of him enough to give the man pause. Asher didn't shy away from his scrutiny. In fact, he let Yarisk see his eyes. One killer always knew another when they saw one.

"Greetings, friend," the young thug offered as he approached the assassin's booth. "Do yourself a favour," he said, tossing a couple of coins onto Asher's empty plate. "Forget ever seeing me. You might sleep better," he added with a wink.

Asher said nothing, unsettling Yarisk. As the moment crossed the line into awkwardness, the thug pivoted on his heel and marched out of the tavern.

"Damned Ironsworn!" the barmaid seethed. "Gods curse the lot of them!"

The old man's hand whipped up to stop her tirade, his head looking towards Asher.

The barmaid waved Asher's presence away. "I'm just saying it was better when the Faceless Ones ruled the streets. At least they had some decency about them!"

"Ironsworn," Asher muttered under his breath, examining one of the coins between finger and thumb.

There was every chance Yarisk was too low down in the Ironsworn's pecking order to actually exchange words with the *boss*, as he had boasted, but he did have money bound for the Lord's coffers. Money, Asher knew well, was any rich man's weakness.

The perfect bait.

Asher took the coins Yarisk had tossed on his plate and left The Gobber's Revenge to its own troubles. Returned to the swarming streets, the assassin took to the nearest corner - where he could lean against the stone, out of everyone's way - and surveyed his options. He needed to wait until darkness before making his move and, undeniably, he needed to sleep before exerting himself.

If he failed, a little girl in Dunwich would die.

It went against his better judgement, but he accepted directions to the nearest inn and had every intention of staying there. Nightfall's training demanded that he appear to sleep in one place while actually seeking rest elsewhere, so as to remain a ghost in the world of man. But he was exhausted, increasingly so, and he didn't have time to seek out two locations.

Acquiring a small room at Gal's Inn, Asher took only the time required to remove his cloak and twin short-swords before his head hit the pillow and sleep dragged him down into the depths of his mind.

It was there that he relived the events of Dunwich, including the two soldiers he murdered at the back of the manor. He tossed and turned on the bed, his hands grasping at the sheets as he felt the first northman's neck break, his death exaggerated by the Nightseye elixir. And he didn't miss any of the moment he twisted the throwing knife in his hand and launched it into the second's head. Both were likely someone's husband, father, or son, never to return to their families for doing no more than their lawful job.

"Run, Asher," that familiar female voice called out from the depths of his memories.

With the black gem in hand, he did, indeed, run away from the murders he had committed. But there was no outrunning Thomas Murell, nor the last gasp he ever made. Only after killing the boy a dozen more times in his head did Asher wake up in a cold sweat, his whole body bolting out of the bed. Scrambling on all fours in the light of the moon, he worked hard to get his breathing under control again. He almost succeeded when the pain in his wounded shoulder got the better of him and his left arm failed to hold him up.

A pained groan found its way through his gritted teeth. He told himself that he deserved it, easily believed after the nightmares that had haunted him across the north's vast wilderness. The assassin pushed himself up and resisted the urge to reach for the black gem under his shirt.

Turning to the window, he was satisfied to see that the night had finally blanketed the realm. Time to go to work.

His short-swords strapped upside down on his back again, Asher climbed out of his window and ascended to the roof, quietly passing by the rooms of his fellow patrons. Crouched in the darkness, he wrapped the red blindfold around his eyes and submerged into the gritty details of the world.

Cities were hard places to focus senses as heightened as those of a blindfolded Arakesh. Thousands of people crammed into tight spaces, their constant noise and odour polluting the air. Animals, domesticated and wild, roamed the streets night and day, always adding to the input. He welcomed the icy wind that blew in off the mountains and overwhelmed his sense of touch, the power of it blocking out all else.

Rising into those cold currents, Asher broke into a run and left Gal's Inn behind. It was only a short journey across the roof tops to The Gobber's Revenge, the beginning of his hunt. Balanced on the very lip of the roof, the assassin brought Yarisk's two coins to his nose, inhaling his scent. They had been in the thug's pocket for a handful of days before he deigned to drop them on Asher's plate. The assassin could smell the oils secreted by his skin where his fingers had mindlessly rubbed the coins together in his pocket. Combined with the odour of his clothes, Asher was confident he could track Yarisk to the ends of Verda.

But not from up on the roof tops.

Had he been in a town or a village, he could have hunted his prey from the high vantage, but Skystead had so much more to bombard his senses with. He needed to track from street level. And he needed to remain blindfolded. Asher's mind worked furiously to solve the problem when he was reminded of a trick Nasta Nal-Aket had shown him while tracking a target through the winding streets of Velia. With this in mind, he focused his senses while searching for a particular person.

It was only seconds before he located what he was looking for, the stench unmissable. He skipped and leapt across three rooftops before descending into an alley betsween a tailor's shop and a tanner's workstation. Each place of business had its own distinct note on Asher's tongue, but it was the homeless beggar huddled against the alley wall that had caught the assassin's attention.

Before emerging from the shadows and revealing himself, Asher removed his blindfold and blinked hard as he readjusted to the gloom. Approaching the beggar, he was pleased to see that the man possessed exactly what he required.

"This is for your cloak," Asher said by way of a greeting, his hand tossing a small purse of coins at the beggar's feet.

The man appeared too weary and haggard to be surprised by Asher's sudden arrival. "Ye want... me cloak?"

"There's a tavern two streets over from here who will accept your coin," Asher went on. "Why barter words in the cold when you could be eating a hot meal?"

The beggar swallowed and licked his lips as he savoured his great turn in luck. "No funny business!" he blurted, finally wary of the forbidding figure now standing over him, his hot breath misting his features.

"Just the cloak," Asher repeated.

It was only after the man had removed his cloak and walked away with the coins that Asher reflected on the exchange. He couldn't decide whether he would have paid for the stinking cloak or simply taken it by force prior to recent events. He was sure he knew the truth but he didn't dwell on it - there was a hunt to be had.

Putting on the cloak, hood and all, was a task that required little thought, lest he consider the bodily fluids that lent the cloak its particular reek. That was almost impossible to do, however, after returning his blindfold to his eyes. Resisting the urge to bring up his pies from earlier, Asher leaned against the wall and steadied himself with slow breaths.

Completing his new look, Asher picked up the shaft of wood left behind by the beggar in his haste. It came up to his neck until the assassin deliberately lowered his head so that the quiver hidden under the cloak was presented as a hunch on his back. Adopting the walk of a blind man, his stick tapping the ground from left to right, Asher departed the alley and made his way back to The Gobber's Revenge, where he had last seen Yarisk.

To those who wandered the streets, searching for a good time, the assassin might as well have been invisible to the eye. Only his stench garnered attention and criticism from passers-by, a fact that granted him a wide berth.

Outside the tavern, Asher once again brought the thug's coins to his nose, so that even his tongue caught the taste of the man. He moved away, further into the street, as Yarisk would have done, and soon found his trail amidst the hundreds of others who had walked through the district. Continuing his ruse as a blind beggar, the assassin moved from block to block, occasionally pretending to bump into people or stationary carriages.

After an hour of walking the streets of Skystead, Asher concluded that Yarisk had visited multiple places of business, collecting for the *boss*. He had also been accompanied by two of his fellow Ironsworn, their scent always mixed with his own. They were obviously the muscle, there to ensure that anyone who refused was severely dealt with.

Following the trail left by all three of them, Asher was brought to the north of the city, where it began to curve around the edge of The King's Lake. It was a livelier district, a place where the taverns could be found on both sides of the street and on every corner. Drunkards were staggering and falling over in every direction, while others grouped together and belted songs out into the night with sloshing tankards and bottles in hand. With so many clogging up the streets with their noise and odours, the assassin began to lose Yarisk and his thugs.

He paused by the side of the street, hunched over his staff. He let his heightened senses build a more accurate picture of his surroundings. It didn't take him long to find the only two people who weren't moving. They were standing side by side, a door behind them. They were guards. With no armour or tough leather about them, Asher quickly concluded that they weren't members of the city watch, though they were each armed with a sword on their hip.

Ironsworn, he deduced.

The assassin pushed his senses beyond the pair and investigated the building they were protecting. He could feel the wind impacting the east wall and instantly knew that it was the largest building on the street. The way the breeze flowed around the curves informed Asher that it was elven in design. It was a church most likely - after all, it had been the elves who, centuries ago, had passed on their religion to the humans. But why would the Ironsworn be guarding a church?

Tapping his stick as he clumsily made his way across the street, he detected Yarisk on the air. He had gone inside the church. The closer he got to the building the more he discovered about the day-to-day activities that took place in the area. More specifically, he could smell coins. Lots of coins. Horses too, dragging heavy carriages if the grooves in the road were anything to go by. The answer struck Asher in that moment. It wasn't a church. It was a bank.

There was only one bank in all of Illian that dealt with coins in the volume Asher was sensing. This had to be the Skystead branch of the Stowhold banking guild. Only they could afford such a grand elven building, notoriously expensive property. But Stowhold were a respectable establishment, offering financial aid to kings and queens even. They wouldn't be in business with the likes of the Ironsworn. Unless, of course, the authorities of the bank didn't know this branch had been adopted by the criminals. They were obviously using it as a place to store their illegally gained fortune, a part of which they were using to buy off the staff and the local watch.

Asher didn't much care for the details of how the Ironsworn had come to claim the building as their own. He only cared that his target had gone inside. Deciding that his current disguise was still his best way in, the assassin wandered back into the street, perfectly timing his interception of a rowdy group. The man on the wing had one arm over the shoulder of his friends while the other swung lazily with a bottle of brandy clutched loosely in his fingers. As they reached the crescendo of their incoherent song, Asher reached out and deftly snatched the bottle from his hand on the backwards swing.

Veering away, he began to move closer to the guards, all the while blindly monitoring raucous activity around them. As the Ironsworn thugs noted his approach, Asher let loose a few lines of song he had picked up before swigging the brandy. To onlookers, he was just a blind beggar who had spent his day's coin on too much drink. Coming to this conclusion themselves, the men notably lowered their guard. Asher could hear their heartbeats returning to a steady drum as their hands released the hilts of their swords.

One was even grinning at the inebriated beggar that stumbled towards them. His muscles were tensing, preparing to shove Asher back as a bit of fun. But Asher knew that a group of patrons were about to burst out of the tavern across the street after an argument had arisen between them. It was all so perfectly timed, just as he had been taught.

"He stinks," one remarked, his expression souring.

"Get lost!" the other thug barked, his hands coming up.

Asher spat his mouthful of brandy in the Ironsworn's face as the brawl spilled into the street across the way. Their clamour drowned out the guard's cry, though Asher soon ended it himself when he drove the base of the bottle into his throat. The second man, taken by surprise, was too slow to realise what had happened, his attention having been diverted by the brawl. He received a back-hand from the assassin, his face used to shatter the brandy bottle. He didn't get back up.

The choking Ironsworn crumpled back against the bank's outer wall and slid to the ground. Asher could feel the blood bubbling under the surface of the man's face, changing the colour of his skin through his need for air. A swift strike with the end of the staff put him out of his misery. Within a few seconds, both guards had been rendered useless, each appearing as drunkards who had passed out in the street.

Leaving the brawl to fizzle out, Asher opened the outer gate just enough to slip through. He wasted no time in ridding himself of the filthy cloak and wooden staff, throwing both into the well-groomed grounds that lay between the gate and the bank. Before taking another step, Asher raised his hand into the air and rubbed his fingers and thumb together. Moisture was gathering in the air, heralding the rain to come.

Under the arching alcove of the bank's entrance, the assassin pressed the flat of his hand to the door. He could feel the vibrations from two men talking, but they were inside a room towards the back of the main chamber. It surprised him that they were the only two he could detect, making him doubt, for a brief moment, that the Nightseye elixir in his veins was working. As the first rain drops began to touch down, Asher knew that had never been the case and proceeded to pick the lock and enter the bank.

It was cathedral in size, his senses taking in the open space that loomed high above him. He could smell the ancient crevices in the elven stonework, where damp had taken root out of sight. Walking through the foyer, Asher ran one hand along the wall, his fingers dragging along the runes carved into the stone long before man had emerged from The Wild Moores.

The assassin retracted his hand and clenched it into a fist. He needed to focus on the matter at hand. Esabelle's life was still in the balance. Word of his treachery had to have reached Nightfall by now, which meant Nasta had already dispatched another Arakesh to finish Lord Kalben's despicable request.

Moving through the bank, across the vast floor that provided numerous tellers workspace during the day, Asher skipped over the counter that separated staff and clients. He could already feel the great quantity of steel that lay beyond the double doors at the back of the room - the vault. The presence of the vault was made all the clearer by the two Ironsworn guarding it, their voices impacting the sturdy metal.

"I hate this job," one was complaining in a dreary tone.

"Why?" the other questioned. "It's the easiest coin we make."

"It's boring," the first answered. "There's not a thief in all of Illian that can crack a Stowhold vault."

"We're not guarding the vault," the second replied, somewhat exasperated by the sound of it. "Why would we be guarding *this* vault? It ain't Stowhold that put coins in our pockets. Yarisk told us to wait here, so we wait."

"We've been waiting all day!" the first went on. "I just want to stretch my legs."

Asher put his nose to the divide in the double doors and inhaled what he could of their scent. He knew immediately that these were the two men who had accompanied Yarisk from business to business.

"Yarisk has to triple check the count," the second reminded. "If he gets the number wrong, Menvin will drag his guts out of his mouth."

Asher withdrew from the door. Yarisk was close by, checking over the money. But where? Asher couldn't hear, taste, smell or feel another person inside the bank. He considered the vault, but there was limited air inside. Even if Yarisk was inside, Asher knew he didn't possess the skills to open the vault.

Moving away from the doors altogether, the assassin tilted his head left and right, shifting his focus from room to room. Perhaps there was a hidden chamber or a concealed door. He began to search for unusual drafts, places where there shouldn't be a cool breeze.

Nothing.

Hopping over the counter again, he moved into the middle of the open floor, his frustration growing. He raised his chin towards the high ceiling, where arch upon arch came together in a single point. There was nothing up there but a family of bats that had found a large enough crack in the stone to get in and out of the building.

It was then, he realised, he had been right from the start. It was a church. Or, at least, it had been a thousand years ago. Thinking of his surroundings like a church instead of a bank, Asher knew there was one direction he had failed to check. Resting on one knee, the assassin put a hand to the cold smooth floor. It took a moment to decipher the layers of rock and various insects before Asher discovered the hollow space beneath the old church.

"Catacombs," he uttered, a little impressed with the gang.

At that same moment, the doors to the vault room opened and Yarisk's men emerged. "Why don't you nip across the street and get us a couple of ciders?" one of the thugs was suggesting to the other. "We're wasting the night away here."

The second man stopped in his tracks and hit the other in the arm. They had finally discovered the stranger in their midst.

"What in all the hells..." The larger of the two began to make strides towards Asher.

"Who are you?" the other demanded, reaching for the hammer on his belt.

The assassin held up a single finger to the men, requesting a moment's reprieve from their questions. They looked to each other, baffled by Asher's blatant lack of distress and unsure how to proceed. The assassin took the extra seconds to verify his findings below. It was faint, but he could hear the metallic sound of coins knocking together and, fainter still, the sound of footsteps echoing through the rocky catacombs. Lord Kalben was definitely running his illegal profits through the bank's ancient foundations.

One of the Ironsworn laughed to himself, a hint of nervous energy about him. "You're in for a world of hurt, my friend."

The other squeezed the haft of his axe, his knuckles cracking. "How did you even get in here?"

Asher heard the last question but his senses were still following the sound of cracking bones from the man's hand up to his shoulder. The grinding therein informed the assassin that this particular thug had dislocated his right arm numerous times. That kind of injury could be the cause of chronic pain, pain Asher could use.

The larger of the two reached down with a meaty hand, oblivious in the gloom to the twin short-swords resting upside down on the assassin's back. A flash of steel arced high from Asher's hip. So swift was his blade that the Ironsworn barely winced as he was relieved of his fingers. Shock, however, was quick to set in. His mouth fell ajar, a scream mounting in his throat. Asher was already moving, his leg sweeping to take out his foe's legs. The moment his head impacted the floor, the thug was robbed of all sense.

Laden with shock of his own, the remaining Ironsworn was slow to raise his hammer. Too slow. Asher replaced the sword on his back with one hand and took the guard's wrist in the other, clenching the limb within a vice-like grip. He had only to yank it high to yield the required *pop*, tearing through muscle, ligament, and tendon. The pain caused him to drop his hammer and then drop to one knee, where Asher caught him by the throat in another constricting grip.

"Shh," Asher hushed, placing a finger to his own lips. The Ironsworn gurgled and squirmed, his eyes bulging. "Where is the entrance to the catacombs?" he demanded in his gruff voice.

The Ironsworn's facial muscles twitched in an expression of defiance. "You're... a dead... man."

Asher's free hand fell upon the man's injured shoulder, eliciting a wave of pain and nausea over his victim. "I'm not in the habit of asking twice," he warned.

Still, the thug turned his pain into anger and clamped his teeth together. "You're... already dead," he seethed.

Asher dug his thumb into the shoulder joint and irritated the nerve that had been partially damaged in the dislocation. As the Ironsworn thug howled in new heights of agony, the assassin increased the grip around his throat, limiting the volume.

"If the next words out of your mouth aren't directions," Asher threatened, "I'll dislocate your other arm. After that, I'll move on to fingers and toes. Next it's the knees. After that—"

"Through there," the guard hissed, his head gesturing to the doors they had come through.

"The vault?" Asher queried, wondering if he needed to press his thumb a little harder.

"The passage," he managed, his airway restricted. "Behind the... tapestry."

Asher dropped low and pivoted to one side, putting considerable force behind his rising elbow. After being slammed in the temple, the Ironsworn joined his companion in the painless realm of sweet oblivion.

Ignoring the rectangular door that secured the vault, the assassin ran his hand along the hewn wall as he made his way down the adjacent passage. Where most would have continued to follow the passage around the corner, Asher was drawn to the alcove, where the sound of his scraping fingers was being absorbed by material instead of stone. He could taste the earthy tones of the tapestry draped over the wall, its intricate details illuminated by the single torch fixed to the wall.

The assassin gave no thought to the art - he was more concerned by the cold draft that filtered between the tapestry and the wall. He clicked his fingers inside the alcove and heard the noise reverberate into a hidden chamber beyond the arras. A rough tug reduced the artwork to a crumpled pile on the floor, revealing a jagged opening in the wall.

Clicking his fingers again, Asher was taken on a journey with the sound as it expanded and descended through a spiralling staircase, cut into the stone before any inhabitants of Skystead were born. Taking to those steps, the assassin put the bank of Stowhold behind him and entered the catacombs of the once elven church. The sound of burning torches filled the immediate passage. Beyond that, he could hear voices and clinking coins. One of the voices was certainly that of Yarisk.

Asher moved down the passage without a sound, his senses drinking in the environment. The closer he got the more detailed the picture in his mind became. There were three women round the next corner, the majority of the coins passing through their fingers from one pile to another before being stored in a chest. Yarisk was close to them, and sitting by the rate of his heart. He was likely watching them count the coins, ensuring none were to go astray.

There was only one other in the rocky hollow and his size was big enough to absorb a decent portion of the sound being generated. His heart was larger than the average person, further suggesting that this was the Ironsworn's living vault, the defence against foolish robbers. Indeed, leaning against the wall, beside the big man, was an equally big axe, the combination of wood and iron mixing on Asher's tongue.

His head cocked at an angle, the assassin knew this big man was facing the others, oblivious to the killer who had silently approached. All in all, Asher felt the Ironsworn had done a terrible job of protecting their illegal activity. This lapse, however, informed him that Lord Kalben's gang had well and truly subdued Skystead, for they feared little in the way of reprisals or attacks on their business.

Perhaps it was time to remind them of the things that dwelled in the shadows.

"Menvin's expecting a final count, ladies," Yarisk was saying as he bit into an apple. "Let's get a move on."

Asher broke into a sprint, making no effort to hide his rapid footsteps. The big man's heart rate increased immediately, his hand snapping out to grab his axe. Before passing their hollow and revealing himself, the assassin leapt into the left wall, propelling himself into the right wall, until he was high enough in the passage that his legs could split and brace him in place. The big man naturally moved into the passage to investigate the sound, unaware that a predator lurked above.

They quickly lined up and Asher dropped down. The dagger in his hand would have easily plunged through the big man's skull, sinking to the hilt, but Asher over-extended his arm mid-fall, causing the wound Jorgan had inflicted on his shoulder to flare up in that final and crucial moment. He grunted in pain, giving his foe just enough time to react and reach up. The assassin's attack was foiled and, worse still, the wind was knocked out of him as his midriff slammed into the big man's shoulder.

Before he could do anything to correct his error, the Ironsworn thug was flipping him over and throwing him onto the floor. Painful as the whole thing was, his senses didn't miss the blade of an axe cutting through the air. Asher rolled to the side and avoided the mortal blow by inches. Though he continued to struggle in his effort to breathe, the assassin managed to lash out with his foot, launching a kick into the big man's leg. His intention had been to drop the thug down to one knee and introduce him to the dagger. Unfortunately, the leg in question didn't budge and the big man maintained his towering stature.

Asher swore, though the word could barely be heard.

The Ironsworn heaved him off the floor with one hand and pinned him to the wall as Yarisk dashed into the passage. Asher ignored the smaller thug and threw a couple of punches into the big man's gut before stabbing him with the dagger his fingers had refused to let go of. The big man hissed, baring his teeth and unleashing his terrible breath upon the assassin. But his hand never relented, keeping Asher firmly in place. So he stabbed him again and again, spilling blood over their feet.

"What are they feeding you?" he questioned in disbelief.

A feral growl rumbled out of the Ironsworn's throat. He dropped his axe and grabbed Asher's wrist, manipulating it until the dagger was pulled free and he was able to bend the limb. The pain proved too much and the assassin had no choice but to drop the dagger. As it clattered to the floor, the big man head-butted him twice, the second one almost robbing Asher of his grip on reality.

Rough hands took the assassin by his leathers and tossed him from wall to wall like a rag doll. With every new injury, Asher saw Esabelle's life slipping through his fingers. What a fool he had been. Never in his career had he attempted an assassination while so injured. He should have healed himself, he knew, though the thought of restoring himself to full health while Thomas Murell's body grew ever colder sickened him.

But he couldn't let another child die, not when he had the power to save them.

The man mountain employed to guard the Ironsworn's loot finally grew tired of hurling Asher around. One hammer-like fist to the face put the assassin on his back again.

"Who in the hells is this?" Yarisk was asking, spectating from afar.

Asher crawled across the floor, feigning the extent of his wounds, though they had become considerable since entering the catacombs. All the while, his hand fumbled inside his leathers and under his shirt as he tugged at the ring on his necklace. Curling up into a ball as the big man retrieved his axe, Asher slipped the ring over his bloody finger and clenched his fist. He willed the innate magic to flood his body and make him whole again. It was like taking a hot bath, the water cleansing the dirt and grime from his skin.

His strength restored, the pain resigned to memory, Asher rose from the floor with renewed determination. He decided there and then that every Ironsworn was culpable in the death of Thomas Murell and the attempted murder of Esabelle Murell. Every one of them was a child-killing wretch and he would treat them as such.

Yarisk frowned at the sight of him. "What the..."

The big man wasn't one for questioning anything. He simply hefted his axe and lunged at Asher. The assassin, however, had already determined his enemy's fate - the artery pulsing under his opponent's arm like a geyser in Asher's ears, the sound homing him in. As the Ironsworn's swing went high, Asher darted forward and slipped through the gap with one of his hourglass blades in hand. The tip of the short-sword sliced neatly through the underside of the big man's arm but, more importantly, it sliced through a vital artery. For the first time, it felt satisfying to take a life and be present for the moment.

Asher continued his momentum and strode towards a terrified Yarisk. Behind him, the big Ironsworn turned to pursue him as blood gushed from his arm. After three steps he wobbled from side to side and staggered to one knee, his hand reaching out for Asher. More blood spurted up the walls, the colour draining from his skin. As

Asher took Yarisk by the throat, the big man dropped senseless, soon to be dead, his face pressed into a pool of his own blood.

Yarisk squirmed as the assassin forced him into the hollow, the violence of it all eliciting gasps from the three women. They huddled together against the rocky wall and watched Asher lift Yarisk to his toes with a wrenching gut punch. The Ironsworn collapsed at his feet and vomited.

Asher removed the blindfold and looked upon the pile of coins with his own eyes. Chest upon chest filled the hollow, stacked to the ceiling. More still were spilled across the only table, where the women had been in the process of counting.

This was Lord Kalben's weak spot. Without any of this, his power would be severely depleted, for who would work for him without the promise of coin? Now he just had to get his attention.

Yarisk turned on his side, his face flushed. "Who... are you?"

Asher looked down at him with his predatory eyes. "I'm the monster that eats the other monsters."

CHAPTER 10

INTO THE LIGHT

It has become clear over the centuries that we have but one thorn in our side: the Graycoats. They have become aware of our existence and have taken it upon themselves to eradicate our order.

Their own order of so-called noble knights was formed after The Dragon War, a time when King Gal Tion ruled over Illian from north to south. His general, and proclaimed hero of the era, Tyberius Gray, founded the Graycoats and was even gifted West Fellion, their fortress home on The Moonlit Plains.

In the centuries since his passing, they have continued to show great skill in the art of combat, mastering numerous techniques unknown to the warriors of the six kingdoms. Reports of violent encounters with their ilk are becoming regular occurrences with deaths on both sides. More on their side... obviously.

The Night Codex, The Graycoats, Page 211.
Master Baris, 601 of the Third Age.

Returned to the familiar and comfortable heights of Skystead's rooftops, Asher watched his trap take shape. Using the horse and wagon waiting in the bank's yard, Yarisk and the women had been forced by the assassin to load it up with all the Ironsworn's ill-gained coin. All but one, which Asher had instructed they leave on the floor of the bank, a token to enrage Lord Kalben.

After the wagon had been loaded beyond its capacity, Asher tied Yarisk's hands to the reins and set the horse off at speed. Now, he observed from an adjacent roof as thousands of coins spilled into the street, leaving a golden trail behind the departing wagon. It was made all the more beautiful when the light of the rising sun caught them all, glistening a blinding gold.

Word would spread quickly, Asher knew. Hundreds of people were already rushing to scoop up the coins in whatever they could. The entire street would be cleaned of Ironsworn coin in minutes.

Asher just had to wait.

The city watch were the first to arrive at the bank, there to discover the four Ironsworn that had been left unconscious and in various states of injury, some more long-term than others. None of them were placed in chains, their presence at the bank expected by every member of the armed watch. Asher noted one return to his horse and ride hard towards The White Citadel, while the others went about dispersing the people before they could take all the coin. Only when their weapons were drawn did they succeed in moving them on.

The next group to ride up were from the local barracks, situated north of the city. They were soldiers of King Merkaris, but they all took orders from a lord of the north. Whether they knew about Lord Kalben's command of the Ironsworn remained to be seen.

Finally, after much debating had taken place, both inside and outside the bank, a carriage bearing the sigil of house Tarn arrived. This was closely followed by a dozen men on horseback, Ironsworn all by the look of them. The driver stepped down to open his master's door but Lord Kalben Tarn burst forth, slamming the door open with his boot. He was a barrel of a man, his bulk making it hard to decide whether he had spent many years in the illegal fighting pits or a lifetime of constant eating. It was likely a bit of both, Asher concluded.

His cloak of expensive red cloth billowed out behind him as he stormed towards the bank entrance, his large hands shoving anyone too slow to get out of his way. A wild mane of chestnut hair suggested he had recently been woken up and all since had been done in haste. Of all his entourage, only one accompanied him inside; a slender man in tight-fitting robes of deep purple and blue.

In order to follow them beyond sight, Asher tied his blindfold around his head and let the Nightseye elixir connect him to the world. There was a lot to push through, his focus tempted by the distraction of restless horses and soldiers pocketing stray coins. By the time he found the voice of Lord Kalben it was distant, the words growing incoherent beyond the ancient stone. It helped, however, that he was mostly shouting.

"I want every coin returned by sundown!" he fumed. "Go from door to door if you have to! If there's coin in these houses you can bet it's mine!"

"It will be done," the slender man promised.

Lord Kalben was standing over the blood stain on the bank floor, where Asher had relieved one Ironsworn of his fingers. He crouched down and picked up the single coin left standing on its edge. "I'm going to personally gut the fools who did this," he seethed. "Speaking of fools - where's..." The lord clicked his fingers repeatedly.

"Yarisk," the other man finished.

"Yarisk." Lord Kalben enunciated his name as if it was venom in his mouth. "Where is the pathetic excuse of a turd?"

"He's being brought back here as we speak," the slim Ironsworn answered. "The horse he was tied to made it beyond the city before tiring," he added, a hint of amusement in his voice.

"No," Tarn commanded sharply. "Have him waiting for me in the fort. I would like to express my displeasure in private." The lord turned swiftly back to his subject. "And Menvin," he said as an afterthought, "bring anyone Yarisk considers a friend or family."

Menvin, a name Asher had heard several times now, bowed his head. "As you wish, my Lord."

He lost the pair soon after, their distant voices overwhelmed by the competing hubbub below. Asher moved along the rooftop and sought a better position that allowed him to utilise his bow. The elaborate puzzle of cogs responded to his touch and the weapon snapped to life in his hand. There were fourteen arrows in his quiver, but he only needed the one to eliminate his target. His fingers brushed through the fletching before he pulled the arrow free and casually nocked it onto the string.

While he waited for his target to emerge, the assassin listened to his senses and got a feel for the shifting breeze. He sat in it for a while, his breathing falling into a steady rhythm. He could taste the iron plating beneath the painted boards of Lord Kalben's carriage. It was reinforced to protect against arrows and, likely, magic too. That meant he only had a small window of opportunity when his target walked from the bank door to the street. An old oak tree, however, shielded most of the grounds, shrinking that window all the more.

"Do you know how hard it is to find a beast like that?" Tarn growled as he returned from the catacombs, his voice echoing through the vast bank chamber and out of the open doors. "Men his size don't fall off trees! Hells, they usually fell the bloody things with their bare hands!"

"They must have swarmed the bank, using their numbers to their advantage," Menvin suggested calmly.

"This is *my* city!" the lord barked as they stepped into the sun. "The advantage should always be mine! Triple the guard on this place."

"I fear, my Lord, that this particular branch of Stowhold has lost its usefulness. Word will inevitably reach the executive barons and they will send their own people to investigate the matter. They will not take kindly to their property being used by any other."

Lord Kalben ground his teeth, mulling it over. "Hmm. It would be folly to aggravate the barons of Stowhold now, when we're on the verge of real expansion. As you say, Menvin, it has lost its usefulness. As have the cretins that were supposed to be guarding it last night. Dispose of them all."

"Very good, my Lord."

The pair had passed under the oak tree now and were about to cross the threshold of the outer wall. Between them and the carriage were twenty-feet and over a dozen men milling about nervously. This was the moment he had spent all night working towards. He wasn't going to miss it.

Had the breeze been more significant, the assassin could have fired his arrow from the safety of cover and let the wind guide it to his target's heart. Since the breeze between the buildings was insufficient, Asher was forced to stand up and aim over the lip of the roof, his weapon pointed in the direction of his victim. Doing such a thing in broad daylight went against his instincts, those tenets engraved in his mind, but time was ever against him.

The Nightseye elixir in his veins, however, shaved off those precious seconds an ordinary man would have required to make the shot. The arrow set sail across the street, the angle and force just right to intercept Tarn's confident stride and deliver a blow that would pierce his broad chest.

Asher's mouth fell open. In his haste, he had forsaken so much of his training, lessons he had even pressed upon Everic only weeks earlier. So focused was he on killing Tarn to save Esabelle that he hadn't stopped to assess those in his target's company. Now, as the arrow closed the gap, he tasted dirt on the tip of his tongue. Demetrium.

Menvin was a mage.

The arrow speared the invisible surface of a protective shield and flared with every colour of the spectrum. The projectile was immediately splintered and all eyes turned skyward. Menvin was the quickest to react, brandishing the wand that had been concealed in his hand inside his voluminous sleeve.

Asher's escape plan was instantly nullified, his reliance on the rooftops well within the reach of a mage's spells. Instead of scaling the wall behind him and taking to the building's highest roof - a feat no man on the ground could have prevented - he dashed to the right and simply fled.

Menvin's magic was on his heels. The first spell he unleashed was cast with a flick of the wrist. The staccato of lightning burned brighter than the rising sun and impacted the building just behind Asher. The pale stone exploded and the concussive wave caught the assassin from behind, throwing him forward. The second spell followed a moment later and sent more rubble high into the air, some of which landed atop the assassin and cut into his skin where the leathers failed to protect him.

Dazed and sluggish, Asher picked himself up and removed the blindfold that had been scraped up one side of his forehead. He stuffed it into his belt and reached for his bow, half aware of the shouting voices that began to fill the street.

"Get up there!" one was yelling above the rest.

Asher blinked hard and pushed his pains aside, his mind desperately trying to grasp at the immediate priority. Evade and escape. It was the only thing left to him in the wake of his error. The assassin hesitated. Kalben Tarn needed to die and he needed to die right now.

In the not too distant past, Asher knew he would never have ignored his instincts, especially those worked into him by Nasta Nal-Aket. But, with a set jaw and a low growl in his throat, Asher was about to make a stand and break every rule he had ever assimilated.

Through the cloud of white dust, the assassin popped up with an arrow already in his bow. He assumed Lord Kalben would have been rushed to his carriage so he aimed for the driver instead, hoping to keep his target grounded until he could get up close and finish the job. The arrow was let loose and it did, indeed, strike the Ironsworn driver, a gut blow that saw him fall from his seat. But Menvin let loose another spell.

Asher had the good sense to dive out of the way, but magic was fast, faster than an arrow. The spell was one of ice, and it burned the assassin's left arm before covering the rear wall in a glistening sheen. The pain was almost overwhelming, but he still managed to collapse his bow and returned it to his back. Time against him, he proceeded to crawl one-handed along the lower roof, his movement hidden by the tall lip.

Menvin, it seemed, wasn't taking any chances. He spat the ancient language and hurled spell after spell at the area around Asher.

Amidst the falling debris, the assassin strived to find that quiet place in his mind where his focus was forged into an iron will. Nasta had always referred to it as an island, a place known only to Asher where he could retreat from the chaos and pain around him and bind himself to a singular purpose.

Lord Kalben Tarn had to die.

To that end, that singular purpose, Asher pushed himself up and broke into a flat run. Flashes of magic impacted the building in front and behind but none succeeded in striking the assassin. He leapt to the adjacent roof, catching the edge with his fingers before climbing over the lip. Menvin's fire spell charred the patch of wall where Asher had been hanging, missing him by naught but a second.

"Get him out of here!" the mage cried, gesturing at the carriage.

Another member of the Ironsworn accepted the order and moved to ascend the carriage's driving seat. Asher wasn't accustomed to letting his targets escape. The thought of it spurred him on to make bolder choices that he knew Nasta would have called rash. But he had been a man against time since he put a dagger through Jorgan's eye.

Reaching the other side of the building, the assassin flipped over the edge, upturning his body to grip the roof, and swung his legs down and through the top window, taking him inside the building.

He skidded across the floor in a rain of glass and yet more broken masonry as Menvin hounded him with another spell. A variety of screams came from unseen rooms as the mage's magic threatened to bring down the entire northern wall, exposing the building's innards.

Asher shoulder-barged his way through a door and bounced from wall to wall until he regained his balance enough to run straight. Menvin's spells were tearing through the stone as if it was soft cheese now, eliciting more screams and cries of help from the top floor. The assassin hopped over the banister at the end of the corridor and took the stairs down to the next floor.

Now to be bold.

Lining himself up in the corridor, Asher faced a room that would offer a view of the street below. With one determined breath, he stormed through the door and continued through the far window. His knees tucked up, one arm shielding his face against the glass, the assassin crossed the street by air and landed atop the carriage as it made its escape. Whether he liked it or not, Asher had to accept the fact that he had now left the shadowy confines of an Arakesh and entered a whole new realm in the light.

A tuck and roll saved him from the bone-breaking fall but sent him skidding over the side of the carriage. At the last moment, his arm outstretched, he was able to find purchase with one hand and press himself into the door. This left the remaining Ironsworn and city watch in a frenzy to coordinate a pursuit. Only Menvin maintained his cool and calm demeanour while mounting a horse and giving chase.

Meanwhile, Asher continued to brace himself against every bump along the road. He reached down and strained his fingers to grip the door handle, but every time he touched the cold metal another jarring bump would slam him into the carriage. The driver forced the horses to take a tight turn, briefly rocking the carriage up on two wheels. The citizens of Skystead did everything they could to jump out of the way and lift playing children to safety.

Looking through a narrow slit that cut horizontally along the carriage, Asher narrowed his eyes to see his target, hoping the man was a picture of fear. He was dismayed to find that the carriage was devoid of occupants and, making matters worse, the driver had used the moment to leap from his bench and was now rolling across the street.

Setting a hard gaze to the road ahead, Asher berated himself for his foolishness. He had allowed his determination to blind him. Now, like the horses and the carriage they pulled, the assassin faced the end of the road and a thirty-foot drop into The King's Lake. The horses saw their fate all too late and failed to stop before their momentum - and that of the carriage behind them - took all three over the edge. Asher jumped away as the front wheels found naught but air, his impact turning into an uncontrollable roll. Coming to a stop by the lip, he looked down to see the violent crash as the horses met their end between the water and the falling carriage.

With a plethora of new injuries, the assassin slowly rose to his feet. His back cracked upon straightening up and he felt more than one shard of glass protruding from his skin.

Turning away from the glistening lake, Asher glimpsed Menvin and his pointed wand before a flash of light tore through the street. The spell struck the stack of crates beside the assassin, the heat washing over him before the explosion took him off his feet and launched him through a large sliding door.

Shock prevented him from feeling the wooden door he blew through, but nothing could stop him from feeling the hard floor that awaited his limp body. Tumbling limb over limb, Asher finally came to a stop after hitting a thick wooden pillar. New levels of pain racked the assassin, urging him to release his grip on reality and succumb to the sweet bliss of oblivion. But half of his training had been about pushing through pain, so that's what he did.

Welcoming the pain as a reminder of what he had already overcome in his violent life, Asher found his feet and used the pillar to support himself, his shoulders shrugging off the splinters of wood. A foul smell had him scanning his environment. He was in a fishery warehouse, surrounded by hooks, nets, and a couple of old rowing boats. There was only one way in and out and he had just been thrown through it. That same door was slid fully open by a flick of Menvin's wand, the slender figure standing in the light.

"I must applaud your efforts," Menvin said, stepping inside the warehouse. "You're certainly hard to kill. If you hadn't caused us so much trouble I would have happily offered you a job in our organisation."

Asher let him talk while he considered his options. Facing a mage head-on was suicide, especially given how close they were, though the assassin did wonder whether he could hurl a knife quicker than his foe could raise his wand. Unfortunately, his mind struggled to work through anything more complex than that. It was then that he discovered the blood trickling from the back of his head, the cause of his increasing disorientation.

"Obviously," Menvin continued, "I have a number of questions for you but..." The mage gestured to their stinking surroundings. "Perhaps we should retire to a more appropriate venue."

As his wand came up Asher reached around his belt for one of the throwing knives, but his reactions were wholly too slow. Menvin uttered a single word and his spell was manifest. The green flash illuminated every dark corner of the fishery and crossed the gap in a heartbeat. An unmissable target, Asher barely had time to wince before the magic hit him square in the chest.

Though the world was beginning to lose its harder edges and the shadows were steadily creeping upon Asher's vision, the assassin didn't miss the fact that Menvin's spell had done nothing but wash over him, no more harmful than a cloud of green smoke. Mirroring some of the mage's confusion, Asher rubbed his chest where the spell had struck him. Nothing. Not even a tear in his leathers.

Menvin's confusion turned swiftly into frustration and then anger. The mage whipped his wand through the air again and again, every flick a new spell that moved over Asher like water on rock.

"Impossible," Menvin muttered, examining the tip of his wand.

With what remained of his strength, Asher offered the Ironsworn a wicked grin. "My turn."

"I think not," Menvin replied confidently, his wand thrusting through the air before Asher could grip one of the hilts on his back.

The mage's next and last spell went high and obliterated half of the tethering that kept the row boat strapped to the rafters. His mind almost set adrift, Asher failed to even conjure surprise as the boat swung down and rammed him into the pillar.

At last, sweet oblivion was achieved.

CHAPTER II
MAN ON VALA

A cold awakening brought Asher's slumber to an end. So horribly biting was the water thrown over him that his gasp was delayed by a moment of shock. A heavy hand pressed into his face and pushed the matted hair back from his eyes. As he blinked the water from his vision, a number of figures began to take shape before him.

Lord Kalben and Menvin were the most prominent in his blurry vision, their shapes most recognisable and even more so when standing next to each other. Another hard blink and the two Ironsworn guards at their back became clear. A third stood sentinel in front of the door, his frame almost as wide if certainly shorter.

Asher took a breath and flexed his muscles, coming swiftly to the realisation that his wrists were bound together with manacles and suspended by a chain from the ceiling. His toes were able to touch the damp floor, though only just. Besides the torches providing illumination to the bleak chamber of black brick, there was a single shaft of cool moonlight that cut through from a high and narrow window. This informed the assassin that he had lost the day to his injuries.

"Welcome to The White Citadel," Kalben Tarn said in his booming voice. "I would enquire of your name but what import is the name of a dead man? Since you came to my city and went out of your way to make a fool of me, I'm assuming you know who I am."

Asher deliberately avoided giving the man any more than a glance, his attention drawn up to the pulley system that kept him stretched. "I came here to kill you," the assassin replied evenly. "Making a fool of you was just to pass the time," he lied with some amusement.

Lord Kalben nodded along as if they were enjoying a pleasant conversation. Then he buried his meaty fist in Asher's gut. The force of the blow should have doubled him over, but the chain kept him upright. Kalben lightly patted his cheek before throwing a second punch, catching him in the jaw this time.

"Who sent you?" Menvin demanded, his hands clasped behind his back. "The Faceless Ones? The Death Mongers?"

The lord of The White Citadel didn't look to be paying much attention to his lieutenant's interrogation. Instead, he had cupped Asher's jaw in one hand and was in the process of inspecting his face. His thumb ran over the black fang tattoo under the assassin's left eye.

"There aren't many in this world who mark their face as such," Kalben remarked. "You're not a savage are you?" He gave Asher's attire a cursory inspection before dismissing the notion. "No, the Outlanders don't have fancy leathers like yours. And they definitely don't have your training." The Ironsworn's dark eyes moved past Asher. "I think you're something much worse."

The assassin followed his target, twisting as much as he could to see under his arm. Lord Kalben approached a table behind Asher, where all of his gear and weapons had been laid out. Kalben fingered a couple of daggers and ran his hand over the collapsed bow before he picked up one of the twin short-swords. He drew the blade a few inches and admired its hourglass shape but, apparently, it hadn't been the weapons that had garnered the Ironsworn's attention.

He soon returned to Asher with a strip of dirty red cloth in his hand. "Every witness we have questioned states that you were wearing this as a *blindfold*," the lord told him, his voice ominously low now. "Yet you are not blind," he continued. "In fact, you are quite the shot with a bow." Kalben rubbed the material between his fingers. "There are a lot of myths and legends surrounding the Arakesh of Nightfall, but the one you hear more than the rest speaks of blind warriors, men and women who can kill without sight." Tarn grabbed Asher by the throat. "Is that what you are? Have we caught ourselves a real, living, breathing Arakesh? You're supposed to be a nightmare you know, a shadow given form. That's why I paid damn good coin for you," he whispered in Asher's ear.

"You paid for the lives of children," the assassin spat, his rage getting the better of him.

Lord Kalben was taken aback and his grip relented. His eyes narrowed as his thoughts were brought to a point. "Is that why you're here?" he asked. "I have heard of what transpired in Dunwich. Two assassins. One murdered the other before fleeing. Are you the Arakesh who failed to do the one thing you were created to do? And now you come for me," he said, holding his hands out. "Are you trying to save that little girl?"

"Your blood for her life," Asher replied with something close to a shrug. "It seems like a fair trade to me."

"What a strange thing for one of your ilk to say," Kalben remarked, genuinely baffled by Asher's incongruous nature. "Speaking of your mysterious ilk, I have already received word from Nightfall. An apology," he explained. "And reassurances that the matter will be resolved," he added with a tight smirk. "Hmm. I wonder how much Nightfall will pay for a defective assassin?" Kalben pondered. "You must hold many secrets they wish to keep in the dark. Perhaps I will alert the Graycoats to your existence. We could have a bidding war! Who knows, I might even make a profit on this whole venture."

Asher's muscles had a physical reaction to Tarn's hearty laugh. The chains rattled above as he tensed and pushed himself forward. The lord of Skystead had only to tighten his grip around the assassin's throat and he was easily held at bay.

"An assassin with a conscience," Kalben mused. "What an abhorrent thing you are." He let go of Asher's throat and made for the door, pausing to throw the blindfold at Menvin. "Break him, good mage. Break him until all of his secrets come tumbling out."

"My pleasure," Menvin replied with a bow of the head.

Asher used their brief exchange to again assess the pulley system and bolts that kept him suspended. As subtly as he could, he raised his knees a few inches and pulled his weight down through his arms, testing the strength of it all. The chain could take a heavier man than Asher, but how much heavier was the question on his mind.

Menvin waited in silence after his master's departure, his immaculate robes perfectly still, just like his short dark hair and well-trimmed goatee. Satisfied that Lord Kalben was truly gone, he dismissed the three Ironsworn guards, commanding them to wait outside. They didn't hesitate, clearly confident that the mage could handle one detained prisoner.

"How did you do it?" he finally asked, looking the assassin up and down. "You possessed no wand, no staff, and I have yet to find one measly scrap of Demetrium among your things." The mage pursed his lips. "Some Arakesh secret perhaps. I once knew a man who had the ancient language carved into his bones," he began, stripping Asher of his leathers until he was wearing only his trousers and shirt. "He barely survived the procedure but, afterwards, he boasted many defences against magic." Menvin went on to tear open his shirt. "I see many scars of your trade but none that suggest you have undergone a similar procedure. So, I will ask you again - how did you do it?"

"I can do a lot of things you can't," Asher quipped. "You're going to have to be more specific."

Menvin brandished his wand and uttered, "*Vala.*" The Demetrium core inside focused the mage's magic, honing it perfectly to his will until the tip burned like a hot iron. "How," he began again, pressing the searing wand into Asher's stomach muscles, "did you resist my spells?" With every word he drew the wand up the assassin's torso. Though hot enough to melt through to bone, the spell didn't so much as singe a hair.

"What *are* you?" Menvin's question died on his lips as he arrived at the ring hanging around Asher's neck. His eyes were lost to the rough cut of black crystal fixed into the iron ring.

While the mage's curiosity grew, Asher's own curiosity was mounting to new heights. Having adhered to his training and dealt with mages the safest way, he had never been struck by magic before. Now, in a single day, he had been exposed to more spells than he could count. The logical conclusion to his survival lay in the black gem, though it only provided more questions where the mysterious artifact was concerned.

"What do we have here?" Menvin questioned. His wand tip sizzled out and quickly returned to its normal temperature, allowing him to hook it under the necklace and raise the ring for better scrutiny. "Do all Arakesh carry such trinkets?" he asked without really wanting the answer. "I feel nothing from it, yet it is an unusual gem. Where did you get it?"

"I couldn't say," Asher told him, sure that the mage was too light to aid in his plan to escape. "I don't mean to rush the torture we're heading towards," he continued with an exasperated tone, "but I really need to be getting on with killing your boss. Could we move this along?"

Menvin found the humour in his comment. "I would hate to rush such an experience. You are an *Arakesh* after all. And," he added with an air of superiority, "I have a feeling *this* is the key to your protection."

Asher concealed his discomfort as Menvin's bony fingers reached up to take the ring as his own. To make the theft worse, the ring's absence would leave him vulnerable to the most despicable of Menvin's magic.

With a sly smile, Menvin clasped his fingers around the ring and the gem. The mage's smile was wiped away in an instant, his every muscle gripped in spasming agony. His knuckles whitened around the wand and his teeth clamped together, chomping through the end of his tongue. Soon, his eyes were rolling into the back of a head that was riddled with pulsing veins.

Entirely surprised by the reaction, Asher tucked up his knees and shoved the mage back with his feet. Splayed on the floor, Menvin's body twitched and frothy spit gathered in the corners of his mouth. The assassin looked on at the extreme display and realised that the mage was the first person, besides himself, ever to touch the gem. More questions about the black crystal and its origins were mounting, but they would have to wait. The Ironsworn were coming.

Having heard the crash of the body, the door burst open as the three Ironsworn dashed into the gloomy chamber, their haste given pause when they discovered Menvin convulsing on the damp floor. Asher had dropped his head into his chest prior to their sudden arrival and feigned his unconscious state, his body hanging limply.

"What in all the hells happened 'ere?" one of the thugs queried, before crouching down beside the mage.

"Is he dead?" another asked, though Asher couldn't be sure who the man was referring to.

"How should I know?" a third voice responded.

"Well check 'im," the first insisted.

Heavy footsteps approached the assassin and he guessed it to be the short but incredibly stocky man who had been guarding the door. *Good*, he thought. He could do with the extra weight.

Feeling two fingers briefly touch his lips - the Ironsworn checking to see if he was still breathing - Asher took this moment knowing it might be his only chance to escape. His eyes snapped open, shocking the stocky guard back a step, though he never made it further before the assassin's legs coiled around his midriff and pulled him in. Then, with every ounce of strength he had, Asher picked the Ironsworn up and pulled down on his chain with his arms.

The manacles dug into his wrists and his shoulder joints burned with the ache of holding the extra weight. Asher drew on his reserves, a well of stubborn strength that demanded he survive and endure the strain.

The well-muscled thug instinctively snatched at Asher, but the water thrown over him had created a slippery sheen that prevented the Ironsworn from attaining any kind of grip. By the time he decided to throw a punch it was too late, their combined weight just enough to pull out the bolts in the ceiling. Both came crashing down and the chain landed around them.

Asher recovered faster and planted a bare foot in his opponent's face, violently whipping the man's head back. By now, his comrades had overcome their surprise and were moving towards the assassin, who was already rolling backwards to come up on his feet. His wrists bloodied, bound, and still attached to the long chain, Asher decided to make a weapon out of it.

The first Ironsworn came at him with only a dagger in hand, the quickest thing he had been able to retrieve during his charge. Asher dodged the incoming thrust and looped the chain around his enemy's attacking hand at the same time. Grabbing the slack on the other side of the Ironsworn's arm, he was able to reverse the swing of his foe's arm until the angle was so high the pain gave him no choice but to let go of his dagger. Asher's reflexes were such that he was able to drop low and catch the falling blade. Small as it was, the dagger proved just enough to deflect the sword of the other, though the impact sent a jarring wave down Asher's arm.

The first thug, whose arm was now significantly lower than it should have been, turned on the assassin with pain fuelling his blind rage. This was a mistake to be sure, his rational mind no longer capable of making calculated attacks. The result was a wild swing with his only working arm, a swing that Asher had already anticipated based on the man's stance. His adopted dagger went straight through the Ironsworn's forearm, a precursor to the elbow he slammed into the man's face.

As he hit the floor, his resting place for the next few hours, Asher returned his attention to the last Ironsworn who was coming at him with another attack, this time a thrust followed by two successive strikes. The assassin evaded all three, his footwork enough to keep him beyond the reach of the sword. His dagger still protruding from his previous opponent's arm, Asher resumed his use of the chain as a weapon.

"I'm going to gut you!" the Ironsworn threatened, bobbing from side to side on the balls of his feet, his sword pointed at Asher's chest.

"You're going to try," Asher corrected, slowly wrapping a portion of the chain around one of his hands.

The swordsman came in with his angle of attack - another thrust. The assassin danced to the side and batted the blade away with the chain around his knuckles. The Ironsworn was fast, to his credit, and he lashed out again before Asher could deliver his counterattack. Rolling away, he pulled the chain taut from its mooring on the wall. A leg either side of it, the thug tripped and cracked his jaw on the floor.

Taking no chances, Asher jumped to his feet and throttled his foe with the remainder of the chain. After feeling the fight leave the man, Asher dropped the Ironsworn's head back to the floor.

Sweating, his breath ragged, the assassin slumped beside the man and lazily rolled onto his back. It had been a long time since he had been forced to fight his way out of a situation with manacles on - which, in itself, was the next obstacle he needed to overcome.

In his attempt to sit up again, he was reminded by a wave of nausea that he had recently suffered an injury to the head. So close to his target now, there was no question about using the gem to heal the wounds that limited him. He tugged it from the necklace and slipped it over his right index finger. He was racked with guilt over the strength returning to his body, a privilege Thomas Murell would never even have the opportunity to experience.

As he relived that sickening moment, he also imagined the same thing happening to Esabelle Murell. It was an image that hastened his recovery and rise from the floor. With speed and efficiency, he began to pat down the fallen Ironsworn in search of the keys to his manacles. With no luck, he turned to Menvin, who had remained oblivious to the fight that had taken place around him.

A single key, no bigger than his little finger, was tucked inside the tight band of the mage's belt. As he recovered it, however, the mage's hand clamped around his wrist. There was no fight left in him. He simply looked at Asher with bloodshot eyes, a single tear running down the side of his face.

"How long have you done your master's bidding?" Asher asked rhetorically. "How many lives have you taken because the lord of Skystead commanded it? In this, we are alike," he admitted, picking up the mage's wand as he rose to his feet. "Men like us shouldn't be allowed to exist." He pointed the wand at Menvin and took a moment to recall the spell he had previously uttered. "*Vala.*" The word gave life to the spell and the wand tip glowed a white-orange.

Menvin's eyes went wide, though his body was unable to move while Asher touched the tip to his robes, setting them alight. The flames reflected in Asher's blue eyes as he truly considered his own words.

His mind snapping back from reverie to action, the assassin freed himself of the manacles and went about retrieving his gear and weapons. Once his leathers were fitted and his weapons strapped to his person, Asher relieved one of the Ironsworn of their long coat and even wore their sword on his hip. It was about as much as he could do, with the time he had, to make himself appear as one of them.

A short passage led to a spiral staircase that took Asher from the small tower into the fort proper. For the most part, the hallways were clear, the soldiers and Ironsworn stationed on the ramparts and at the doors that led in and out of the fort. A pair of soldiers bearing the lion sigil of King Merkaris passed him as he moved from the west wing to the east wing, but his appearance alone was apparently enough to grant him unlimited freedom. In fact, he noted the northmen avert their eyes upon spotting his approach. The Ironsworn had certainly made their mark on Skystead.

The real test came in the form of an actual Ironsworn, a balding man who strolled through the fort like he owned it, a half-eaten sandwich in hand. Asher had already flicked the collar up on his coat, concealing half of his face. Tempting as it was to lower his head, he had to embody the cocky nature of an Ironsworn and walk as if he belonged. Going one step further, he even offered the passing thug a nod of the head. He was given a nod in return, though a flicker of uncertainty crossed his expression.

Asher was sure to take the next passage and get out of the man's sight as soon as possible. With every step, his mind moved through the map in his memory, recalling the various levels of The White Citadel. It was getting late, but not late enough that the lord had likely retired yet. There were several places he could be spending his evening, be it in the throne room, the library, or even his bedchamber if the company was right. Before the assassin could decide on any one place to investigate, the fort was dropped into chaos.

At first it was a single bell ringing out, but it was soon joined by two more, adding to the cacophony that brought the fortress alive with activity. The sound of rattling armour echoed down the stone walls as soldiers mobilised. The obnoxious cries of Ironsworn were hollered from the ramparts, not far from Asher's position.

The bodies had been found.

For a younger, less-experienced, Arakesh, this might have signalled the end of their mission or at least their first attempt at killing the target. For Asher, however, it was an opportunity to be seized. Mirroring the excitable energy of the Ironsworn running down the connecting passage, the assassin fell in behind them. They were met by another group of thugs at the intersecting hall, a meeting that brought them all to a skidding stop.

"Celric," the Ironsworn in Asher's party addressed. "What's going on?"

"Menvin's dead," Celric answered, already returning to his run. "We need to protect the boss!"

"Menvin's dead?" came a tone of disbelief from another in Asher's group.

"That assassin they brought in," Celric continued as they dashed from passage to passage, "he's escaped!"

"You mean he's in here with us?" another asked with a hint of apprehension.

"We need to lock this place down!"

"No. We need to lock the *boss* down," Celric determined. "Let the soldiers watch the stone. Tolvin says he's in the library."

"Good," came the response. "There's only one way in and out of there."

Asher kept his mouth shut and simply trailed them. Orders were barked at soldiers as they passed each other, commanding the armoured men to take up particular stations. Seeing the arched library doors up ahead, Asher took advantage of the chaos and instructed two northern soldiers to accompany them. Only after the Ironsworn had entered the library did Asher turn around at the doorway and give the men a specific mandate.

"Guard this door," he said in his gruff voice. "No one else comes in, not even our lot. Understand?" Both men, if they were old enough to be called men, nodded their helmeted heads. "Oh, and whatever you hear, don't come in. The boss is going to be in a foul mood and you know how he likes to break things." Again, with just a note of fear in their eyes, the northmen nodded their heads.

Entering the library, Asher was sure to close the doors and turn the key before pocketing it. While Celric explained why the alarms were ringing, though he struggled through Lord Kalben's expletive responses, the assassin slunk around the edges of the room, doing his best to blend in with the towering shelves of leather-bound books. The other Ironsworn, of which there were four beside Celric, had clearly put themselves into a loosely protective circle, if a little distant from their violent boss.

Kalben roared at the news of his mage's death and upturned the nearest table, launching a dozen books into the air. "How could this have happened?" he fumed. "He was chained up and guarded by four men! Four! And for the sake of the gods, one of them wielded magic!"

"The fort is being locked down as we speak," Celric explained again, having subtly taken a step back. "They'll find him, boss. We just need to stay here until they do."

"Why?" Tarn snapped. "Because we're safe in here? That man we had locked up in the tower was an Arakesh, you dithering fool!" The lord kicked a chair over, sending Celric back another step. "I'm surrounded by morons! Menvin was our only real defence against the assassin. He's probably already in here with…"

In the light of so many torches, Asher had known his presence could only be masked for so long, his face known to Kalben. That's why, while leaning against the end of a bookcase, he had been planning every step of his attack while the lord wittered on. By the time his target had scanned the library and landed on Asher's familiar face, the Arakesh had taken three of his flat throwing knives in hand, all concealed by his long coat.

As the alarm broke out on Tarn's wide-set face, Asher exploded into action. All three knives were given flight, one after the other. Static as they were, the Ironsworn were easy targets. While one was destined to bleed out and die over the next few minutes, the other two were dead before they hit the floor. Asher was also moving before they hit the floor. He slid across the nearest table and whipped one foot across Celric's jaw, twisting the man around before he collided with Kalben Tarn.

That left one Ironsworn still on his feet, his sword scraping out of its scabbard. Asher continued his momentum into a dive and roll that allowed him to pick up a fallen book on his short journey. As he came out of the manoeuvre, the assassin flicked his wrist and sent the book spinning into his enemy's face. The corner took him in the eye and knocked his head back, exposing his throat. Asher put all his weight behind the fist that collapsed the man's windpipe and assured his end.

Behind him, Celric was recovering and retrieving the two axes from his belt. Asher shrugged off the long coat and unclipped the sword belt, favouring the hourglass blades instead. The feel of those short-swords was almost enough to make him feel invincible, their weight and balance having been with him since his first day in Nightfall.

The Ironsworn in front of him was naught but a brute, a man who had relied more on the threat of violence than violence itself. And so, without the proper training, he was just a child playing with tools he didn't know how to wield. This was evident after the assassin batted the very first attack away and countered with a swift double strike, cutting an X across his enemy's chest. Falling away, Lord Kalben filled Asher's view.

"How do you justify the death of so many to save one life?" the larger man asked, an edge of desperation in his voice.

Asher had already challenged that very question, able to recall now the moment he had taken their lives. Gone was the comfort of that switch in his mind, his violent actions laid bare for his memories to soak up. The truth was, killing men like the Ironsworn was almost enjoyable, an outlet his many years of training demanded. But that was all too hard to put into a sentence that Kalben Tarn could understand, so Asher put it simply.

"You're all monsters. Killing monsters is easy."

The Ironsworn boss sneered and removed his waistcoat. "You will soon discover that some monsters are harder to kill than others."

Asher lunged at his unarmed target, his blades coming down from high to low. Lord Kalben, however, was quicker than a man of his size could usually boast, a remnant of his years in the fighting pits no doubt. His bear-like hands wrapped around the assassin's wrists and halted his attack mid-strike. His meaty fingertips then applied enough pressure to the tendons beneath Asher's wrists that the assassin lost his grip on both hilts.

As they fell to the floor, the lord of Skystead threw his head forward and struck Asher across the nose, sending him reeling. The next thing the Arakesh knew, he was being thrown onto a table, there to be pounded by heavy fists. He took three to the gut before reaching up and yanking his enemy's head down and into his thrusting knee. Kalben staggered backwards while Asher rolled over his own shoulders, bringing him back to the floor and perfectly in line to deliver a side kick. Again, the blow staggered Tarn back a step, where he then snatched at a chair and swung it into the assassin, halting his immediate charge.

Knocked to the floor, Asher took one of the broken chair legs in hand and drove it into Kalben's leg. The lord growled before dropping a hammer-like punch into the assassin's face, ridding him of his grip on the chair leg. After yanking it free, Tarn discarded the makeshift weapon, preferring his hands when it came to the kill.

Asher was subsequently lifted to his feet and hurled from one book shelf to another. Amidst the tumbling books, the assassin threw one punch after another into his foe, but Kalben Tarn, it seemed, had spent a lifetime absorbing such blows. He simply shrugged the attacks off and continued to use Asher to rearrange the order of books.

Deciding that he needed to change tactics, and quickly if he was going to end the fight, Asher grabbed the greatest weapon in all of Verda - knowledge. He couldn't say what book he had managed to clumsily pull from the closest shelf, but it fitted neatly in one hand and the leather felt particularly hard.

Gripped in both hands, the assassin thrust the book upwards, severing Kalben's hold on his leathers. Taking the end of the book in one hand, he shoved it straight into his opponent's face, breaking the nose in the process. Another identical attack cut the lord's cheek and pushed him back into the seating area. A backhand cracked his cheekbone and sprawled the bigger man flat across a table. Kalben wasn't out of the fight yet though, his back arching as he corrected his stance and came at the assassin with a strong punch. Presented with the flat of the indomitable book, however, the lord of Skystead broke at least two knuckles and then received the spine of the book to his groin for his efforts.

His chest heaving from the exertion, Asher lined the end of the book up with Kalben's throat and elbowed it, a blow that sent both men to the floor. Tarn's hand grasped at his neck, his face turning alarmingly red. The assassin pulled himself up on to all fours and straddled his enemy's chest, the book still in hand. He looked the man in the eyes, bulging as they were.

He wanted to really feel this one.

Calling on his last reserves of strength, he raised the book high in both hands, the ridged spine facing down. Then, to save Esabelle, Asher slammed it into Kalben's face. He did this repeatedly, not even bothering to count the blows he delivered. He just beat his enemy until the spine was coated in gore and the body beneath him grew still. Asher knew a dead person when he saw one, and Lord Kalben Tarn was most certainly dead.

Tossing the book aside, the assassin crumpled to the floor beside the corpse, rolling onto his back. He turned his head and looked upon his work. This had not been the assassination style of an Arakesh, at least not one of his calibre. This was a massacre, a frenzy of killing orchestrated by a man on fire. Thinking back, there had been several options available to the assassin, options that would have ended the fight and Kalben's life much sooner. But he had wanted to cause as much pain as possible. And he had wanted to feel as much pain as possible.

The pain kept Thomas Murell at bay.

CHAPTER 12

END OF THE ROAD

*Forget all that you believe you know of pain. Over the course of your
training it will be redefined.*
*A true Arakesh embraces pain as an old friend. It will remind you that
you're still alive and, if you're still alive, you can get back up. You must
learn to push through all manner of pain and always get back up. Nothing
can be allowed to keep you down or hold you back.*
*Your will is to be one of iron, iron forged in the flames of agony. Accept this
and move on, for you must survive.*

The Night Codex, A Life of Pain, Page 37.

Master Enteari, 442 of the Third Age.

A muffled argument brought Asher back to his senses. A groan
was forced from deep in his chest as he rose unsteadily to
his feet. He was surrounded by mayhem and death, the

blood of his victims staining every surface. His own blood was smeared across his face and matted into his hair.

Beyond the library doors the argument was intensifying. From the choice of words, more expletive than not, he built the image in his mind of multiple Ironsworn trying to gain entry, the way barred by the two soldiers. They could only hold off the thugs for so long. Soon, seconds perhaps, they would shove their way through and discover the corpses.

Asher scrambled to retrieve his two short-swords before putting on the long Ironsworn coat again. He knew how he was going to escape for it was the only obvious route and his instincts demanded he evade detection. What he was purposefully not doing, however, was giving that particular route any more than a passing thought. Instead, he worked to put one foot in front of the other and make his way to the back of the library.

A set of glass doors, tall and slim, provided entry to a small balcony that overlooked The King's Lake, behind the fort. The key was already in the lock, making his exit all the easier. He even locked the door from the outside and tossed the key away, a small effort that might prevent any immediate pursuit.

Continuing his stride, every step a welcomed moment of pain, Asher didn't hesitate to throw himself over the railing. The icy lake was deep enough to take the brunt of his fall, though his back still knocked against the bottom before his head followed suit. His focus was unravelled in an instant. Thoughts came and went, his mind struggling to hold on to any one of them.

Weighed down by his weapons and heavy coat, the assassin remained there, in the darkness of the water's embrace. There was no effort made to save himself and swim to the surface. He had meant what he said to Menvin. Monsters like them shouldn't be allowed to exist. All he had to do now was let the water take him and the world would be rid of another murderer. It would all be over soon.

Nightfall, however, had not spent over two decades training the

Arakesh to greet Death with open arms. Every fibre of his being had been honed to survive and return to the Father, there to await another kill. To that end, the moment Asher choked, trying to take his first breath, his eyes snapped open, his heart pounded in his chest, and his instincts set his limbs to moving. His conditioning prevailed as he broke the surface and gulped a mouthful of air.

Fuming with himself, the assassin swam to shore and made his way east until The White Citadel was hidden by buildings. Under the cover of darkness, he climbed a ladder built into the stone wall and ascended to the raised foundation of the city. There he slumped in the alley, his knees folded up into his chest. The shock of the icy water, and now the cold wind, turned his attention from pain to simply getting warm again.

"This is ridiculous!" came the complaint of a young man.

"So you've said," an older voice replied, the tone one of exasperation.

"It's the middle of the night!" the younger man continued. "Why can't this wait until morning?"

"The delivery was supposed to be in Kelp Town *this* morning. If you leave now, it will be there early tomorrow evening."

"Or I could leave in the morning and get there by tomorrow night," the younger man argued.

"Letterman's won't be open tomorrow night, which means you'll have to wait until the next morning. I'm already having to give a discount for the late delivery as it is! Not to mention the cost of putting you up in Kelp Town if you stayed overnight."

"You're going to have to do that anyway if I'm not getting there until the evening."

"The hells I am. You're delivering the supplies and then turning straight around. You can sleep in the wagon; I've thrown some supplies in."

"I really think—"

"You'll do this, boy," the older man interjected, "or your brother will get the lion's share of the inheritance."

"What inheritance?" the son muttered as he ascended the wagon.

"I heard that!"

The young man cajoled the horses into a steady trot and put Skystead behind him, unaware that a stranger had crept into the back of his wagon.

Surrounded by stacks of bound parchment, some of which had been spoiled by the water dripping off his body, Asher was knocked awake by a rut in the road. His head felt heavy, filled with thick soup, for what else could explain the grogginess and disorientation.

Indistinct voices filtered through the narrow gap in the fabric of the wagon's rear. There was also some natural light, though not so much as to be considered day time. It all added to the assassin's discomfort. The last thing he remembered was sneaking into the wagon in the dead of night. Soon after that, his eyes had closed and the nightmares had begun.

"You're late." Those words belonged to a disgruntled man.

"My apologies," the rider offered before his own yawn interrupted him. "I have journeyed through night and day to get here as fast as possible."

Asher sat up, placing himself in Kelp Town now. He could only blame his wounds for such a long and deep sleep.

"That doesn't change the facts," the aggravated man responded. "I've had to turn customers away, cancel orders, offer refunds."

Asher didn't care for their issues - he still had one last task to complete. Making no effort to conceal himself, the assassin climbed out through the back of the wagon and sighed into the bitter air, his breath clouding before him. He rolled his shoulders and cracked his back in the process, his every movement awakening one of his injuries.

"Who in the gods' names are you?"

Asher turned to see the young man, a bewildered expression on his face. Behind, the shop owner looked from the assassin to the wagon and back, a degree of surprise creasing his brow.

"What's going on here?" he asked.

Asher flashed them his best *I've killed people* look and flicked up his collar. Neither man offered another word as he walked away, taking the street to the main road. He heard them exchanging numerous questions in his wake and a brief mention of the town watch. Let them report him, he thought. Kelp Town would be far behind him by the time the watch came looking for him.

Without food or water, the assassin took the southern road out of town and simply kept walking. As fatigue began to settle in, he gritted his teeth, thought of that little boy, and kept his feet moving. He walked and walked, adding his own indentations to The Selk Road. To his right, the southern edge of The Vengoran Mountains dominated the landscape. They towered over the road and eclipsed the stars like dark gods watching wayward travellers.

His journey, however, had but one end. Asher knew what that was - he had spent his every waking moment imagining it. Yet he had failed to find the courage to meet that end.

As the sun rose on a new day, Asher veered from the road and wandered into the woods that lined the base of the mountains. Two of the trees had come together over time and formed an arch of sorts, as if the woods had an entrance. He didn't know why he had chosen this place or even this time to leave the road behind. Perhaps, he pondered, his thoughts had finally amassed into something so over-whelming he could do naught but give in. Had he not been such a coward he would never have made it this far.

Trampling through dozens of ferns, Asher finally came to a small clearing. The rising sun cast shafts of light through the gaps in the branches, lending the area a warm glow. This would do. In one motion, the assassin discarded the long coat, retrieved his short-swords, and dropped to his knees in the damp grass. He plunged both weapons into the ground and left them standing either side of him. With one hand he unbuckled the straps around his chest and let the quiver and bow fall to the ground behind him.

And so here he was. The end of the road. His final task was all that remained. This moment had been set in stone, much in the same way the death of Lord Kalben Tarn had been, or Jorgan before him. Monsters all.

After one calming breath, Asher slowly drew the longest dagger he possessed from the sheath on his belt. This was not the death he deserved, peaceful as it was to be. The assassin knew he should have endured so much worse before the sweet release of death took him away. He also thought, if fleetingly, that a better punishment would be to live with the pain and shame of what he had done. After all, this was to be the coward's way out, an escape from the memories.

But no. Monsters like him shouldn't be allowed to exist.

Placing the dagger on the ground before him, Asher went about freeing himself of the leathers that protected his chest. His dark shirt, already torn almost in half, was kept together by a few strands of material at the bottom. He ran his fingers over the skin and felt his beating heart therein. The black gem caught his eye, the ring resting over his chest. He was to die without the answers, his past and that of the gem a mystery to all.

Images of Menvin's convulsions flashed before his eyes. The gem, it seemed, did not care for the touch of others and devastatingly so. Asher then imagined the poor soul who came across his body. What would happen to them if they tried to retrieve the ring? A part of him tried to declare that he simply didn't care, but he knew in his heart - that cold wretched thing that had recently found new life - that he didn't want anyone else to suffer because of him.

Granting himself a few more minutes of life, Asher rose to his feet and scanned the area. He found what he was looking for a little further into the woods, where a landslide had forced its way between the trees. The scree protruded with varying sizes of rocks from pebbles to boulders that could flatten a horse. Navigating the jagged protrusion, the assassin progressed twenty feet before lowering his aching body into a crouch. He removed the ring from his necklace and gave the gem one last scrutiny. Like him, it would never hurt another person.

Small as it was, the ring slipped neatly into a gap between two of the larger stones. Sealing it in, Asher placed a rock no bigger than his palm into the gap behind it. He looked twice upon seeing the flecks of blood that now stained the pale stone. An inspection of his hand showed two recent cuts had split open, the wounds oozing blood. Paying them no heed, the assassin wiped his hand over his trousers and returned to the clearing, a place that Fate had called him to.

On his knees once more, Asher steadied his breath and picked up his dagger, the blade forged with just the hint of a curve in it. With no leathers to protect him and no gem to heal him, this was truly to be the end of Asher the Arakesh. Gripping the blade in both hands, he positioned the tip directly over his heart and applied just enough pressure to pierce the skin and draw blood.

"Just do it," he muttered to himself.

Asher took a breath and braced himself, ready to plunge the dagger through his chest. Yet more blood was forced from the wound but the steel failed to threaten his life. The assassin tensed his jaw and took another deep breath. He was going to do it this time. His arms began to shake, as if the blade was fighting him. But it wasn't the blade. It was his conditioning, the work of his masters that bade him to always survive, never to give up.

A frustrated growl tore its way free of his lips and he raised the dagger in a bid to thrust it home. Still he lived, the tip pausing before it even touched his skin. Asher roared and stabbed his leathers on the ground.

"Just do it, you coward!" Asher had hoped his rage would fuel his strength and see the deed done.

Instead, he heard Kalben Tarn's words echo in his mind. *"You will soon discover that some monsters are harder to kill than others."*

The lord of Skystead had been referring to himself but, right now, Asher felt those words applied only to him. It sickened him all the more to think of the ease with which he had slain so many people, but found it so difficult to take this one last life, one of the few who actually deserved to meet his blade.

He decided there was only one way he was going to find the courage to stick that dagger where it belonged. On the exhale, he recalled the moment Thomas Murell had gasped, the last thing he ever did. It was a haunting memory, one that took the fight right out of him and made the whole affair all the easier. With one hand gripping the hilt, he placed the other over the pommel and took *his* last breath.

He felt the sharp pinch of intruding steel as a harrowing cry cut through the woods, halting what was to have been his final action. Asher turned his head to the south, sure that it had originated from a man. Still, it wasn't his concern. Returning his attention to the grim task, he renewed the strength of his grip around the hilt and braced himself for the end. But the distant holler came again, only this time it sounded more akin to a battle cry than that of an injured man. It then sounded as if the man was hacking at something, his every blow accompanied by gruff exertion.

Asher shook his head, determined to keep to his task and see it through. But then came another sound, a terrible roar that thundered through the woods. What followed was a yelp from the man before the very trees rustled from some form of collision.

The assassin sighed, his chin dipping. Again, that cold wretched thing in his chest had discovered something new to beat for.

Dropping the dagger, Asher cast his pain aside and took his short-swords in hand as he dashed to his feet. His focus narrowing now, the pain grew ever distant and, before he knew it, he was sprinting through the trees and homing in on the monstrous noises. He found it alarming that the man had yet to make another sound since the beast had let loose its ear-splitting roar. Drawing closer, however, he heard the fight continuing, the man rushing about and swinging some kind of weapon.

"You should have kept well to yourself!" the stranger warned his foe.

Asher put more power into his calves and propelled himself up a tall mound of haphazard boulders. It gave him the required height to come down on the monster with both short-swords inverted in his grip. Where once he might have stopped at the top and surveyed his environment and assessed his enemy, Asher now leapt without thought or care.

Free of the rock and given over to gravity, the assassin had a mere second to take in what awaited him. Unaccustomed to the world of monsters that roamed Illian's surface, Asher couldn't identify the foul creature he was hurtling towards, though foul it was.

A nightmare of nature, the hunched beast was twice the size of a human. Its exterior was more akin to that of a tree than anything else, its back layered in broken branches. A gaunt head, resembling the skull of a goat, was crowned with sharp antlers. Standing on two legs, the monster swiped at its prey with two gangly arms that ended in a trio of claws.

Asher was unable to make any kind of real assessment on those individual elements, his second of flight coming to a crashing end atop the monster's hunched back. The twin blades drove down almost to the hilts, securing his place among the awkward branches. Some of those branches snapped under his weight and his feet, which he dug in to find purchase. All the while, the tree-like fiend thrashed about, swinging its hulking shoulders from side to side.

The assassin pressed himself flat as the beast staggered into the surrounding trees in a bid to shake him free. Claws came up over its shoulders to rake at him but only succeeded in tearing through its own rough exterior. It was then that Asher realised the tree-like elements to the monster were in patches, like a suit of armour on a man. Between the bark was a black musculature and it was this softer biology that his short-swords had pierced.

Somewhere below the chaos of its swinging claws and spinning orientation, the stranger on the ground was lunging in and out, his sword flashing high and low. The monster eventually stopped its thrashing and backhanded him, launching him into the cluster of rocks Asher had leapt from. The monster straightened its back and roared, its voice a distorted and unnatural sound. Looking up, the assassin could now see its neck clearly, a break in the creature's armour.

The killer in him knew exactly how to end the fight.

Leaving one blade lodged in the tight bundle of muscle fibres, Asher yanked the other out and began to ascend his enemy's back. He used the protruding hilt as a firm step to gain ground and reach up for the left antler. From there, he pulled himself up to again seek the advantage of the high ground. The monster tilted its hideous head to better see the pest balanced on its shoulders and, in the process, stretched its neck, exposing the tough but penetrable hide.

Asher hammered his blade down and stabbed the creature repeatedly, only half aware of the sharp antlers cutting his skin. The roar that escaped its maw quickly lost its edge until it was closer to a moan. Its two legs, each a bundle of roots, wobbled under the weight of the dying body. It pushed away from one tree and twisted on the spot before collapsing on its back.

Asher would have been more aware of this had he not fallen with the beast and struck the back of his head on an unforgiving branch.

In the darkness that followed, a perfect oblivion, he found sweet release from the familiar nightmares.

CHAPTER 13
A TWIST OF FATE

Skalagat - A mistake of nature to be sure. These monsters are often referred to as forest knights or knights of the wood. They are not so noble as knights, however.

Their black hides produce a sticky substance that binds whatever they can find to their bodies. Most commonly, they are found to be using bark from the trees, lending their exterior a look something akin to a suit of armour - hence the reference to knights.

It should be noted that Skalagats will use anything they can find, not just parts of the forest. They have been seen to wear the skulls of their victims like masks or even utilise the claws of other animals.

If you can get close enough to bring your sword to bear, they are vulnerable between these makeshift plates of armour. Getting close can be difficult though. Fully grown Skalagats can reach twenty feet in height, a fact that allows them to blend in with the trees.

A Chronicle of Monsters: A Ranger's Bestiary, 12th Edition, Page 35.

Margotta Elysabef, Ranger.

. . .

As his eyes fluttered against the pale light of the sky, Asher's consciousness steadily rose through the layers of his mind. Dazed as he was, the assassin was still able to build a picture of his situation. He was lying flat on his back and covered in his long coat and furs, but he wasn't on the ground. This particular revelation sent a jolt of alarm through him.

He hadn't intended to groan as he sat up but that's exactly what sound escaped his lips. He was in a topless wagon, exposed to the air, where he could see everything around him, including the large man guiding the horse.

"Still with us then, little man," he remarked, his voice a rich timbre that spoke of experience and age. "I was beginning to wonder," he continued. "That was quite the knock to the head after all."

Asher worked furiously to recall recent events, his hand reaching up to investigate the back of his head. His probing brought pain and the memory of fighting a monster in the woods.

"Where are my things?" he demanded, his focus shifting between their environment and the contents of the wagon, most of which were concealed under a tarp.

"Back there with you," the stranger reassured.

Asher pulled back the coat and furs, happy to see that he was still dressed, if caked in mud. Even his red blindfold was knotted around his belt. Lifting the tarp, he discovered one of his short-swords, his dark leather cuirass, and the dagger he had intended to use on himself. His hand naturally pressed to his chest where the black gem had sat for most of his life. It took an extra moment to recall the rocks where he had hidden it, now long behind him. Perhaps that was for the best, he thought.

His belongings weren't all he discovered under the tarp.

The assassin liked to believe that he wasn't easily shocked, but he was taken aback upon sighting the severed head of the monster.

Within its skull-like exterior, he could see a pair of lifeless eyes staring into the abyss of death.

"Sorry about that," the stranger called back. "Had nowhere else to put you."

Asher put his questions concerning the decapitated monster to one side. "Where's my other sword?"

The stranger turned to look briefly over his shoulder, his shaggy black hair giving just a glimpse of one eye. "A thank you wouldn't go amiss, fella. I had to track your steps back to that little clearing to gather your belongings. And that was after I put you on my wagon and covered you in *my* furs."

"My other blade," Asher said flatly. "Where is it?"

"I'd forget about it if I were you - it's lost."

The assassin frowned as he could remember exactly where he had left it. "Lost?" he echoed.

"Well," the stranger considered, "it might as well be; it's buried under two tons of Skalagat."

"A what?"

"Skal-a-gat," the big man enunciated. "The creature you stabbed to death," he went on, with some amusement. "You're sharing a wagon with its head."

"I can see that," Asher muttered, feeling naked without both of his blades.

"That was an impressive display back there," the stranger complimented. "An interesting approach at the very least," he added more under his breath.

"Where are we?" Asher questioned, his irritation mounting under the piling disorientation. "And who are you?"

"You've got quite the wicked tone for someone who was saved from being left for dead."

"I would have been fine," Asher said, as he went about fitting his leather cuirass.

"Not in those woods you wouldn't, and especially not lying next to the corpse of a Skalagat. The body would have drawn in all kinds of other beasts and you, my new friend, would have made for a tasty starter."

"You didn't save me," Asher insisted. "If anything, *I* saved *you*."

"I had the whole thing under control," the stranger countered confidently. "That wasn't to be my first Skalagat."

"You still haven't answered my questions," the assassin pointed out.

The big man pulled hard on the reins and brought the horse to a halt. The leather of his own cuirass creaked as he turned in his seat to face Asher. His portly face was hard to make out through his bushy black beard and unkempt hair.

"The name's Geron, Geron Thorbear." As well as his name, he offered a hand in greeting.

Asher didn't take it. "And where are we?" he repeated.

Geron closed his fist and retracted the arm. "We're in The Ice Vales, though you must have known that - you were south of Kelp Town in those woods."

Asher leaned to one side and looked ahead of their route. "And where are we going?"

"This is The Selk Road," Geron explained.

"I know what it is," Asher interjected. "Where were you taking me?"

Geron licked his lips as a smile cut through his beard. "You've got some trust issues, fella." When Asher didn't respond, he continued. "Grey Stone is my destination. I thought to get you some aid," he added, tapping the back of his own head. "It's the capital in these lands - plenty of healers to be found there."

"I'll be fine," Asher replied without thought of thanks.

"Aye," Geron agreed. "I think you will. There's not many who could bring down a Skalagat without knowing what it was. Without knowing its weaknesses. Who are you to do such a thing?"

Asher's instinct was to lie. "I'm nobody," he said instead.

"Does nobody have a name?" Geron enquired.

After putting the Ironsworn coat on, Asher sheathed his dagger and picked up the remaining short-sword. "No," he answered simply. With that, he hopped over the side of the wagon and splashed down in a puddle. As he did so, a crack of thunder split the heavens in the east and rumbled across the sky. A storm cloud was approaching, heralding the night.

"Come now," Geron suggested. "It's another day to Grey Stone and the weather's about to turn. You can camp with me. I've got enough food for us both."

Unaccustomed to the generosity, Asher had no ready reply. "I'll walk," he said with a shake of the head.

Geron turned his small brown eyes to the darkening sky. "Suit yourself. Good luck to you, *nobody*."

By the time the rain arrived, Geron Thorbear and his wagon were lost to a bend in the road, the path taking the big man round the mountain. Asher trudged on as the temperature dropped and the rain picked up. Soon, the sound of it bouncing off his coat was deafening. Not long after that, the last of the daylight disappeared. Still, the assassin walked ever onwards, mindlessly putting one foot in front of the other.

Where was he going? Was Grey Stone his destination now? The road would lead there before all else. But what was he to do there? He was supposed to be dead. Feeling the dagger knocking into the base of his back, he began to wonder if he should choose another location to finish his task. That was if he could.

A flickering light caught his attention and prevented his thoughts from spiralling. Wiping the matted hair from his face, Asher narrowed his eyes through the rain. There, under a natural shelf that had formed out of the mountain, Geron and his horse were camped around a fire, the wagon left to one side.

Asher turned away from the scene, determined to keep going, pointless as that felt. He took one step before the smell of cooked pork gave him pause. It was as if he had struck a wall, his body demanding that he investigate the origins of the smell and consume his findings. It felt like a weakness, and he had learned long ago to dispel such things. He took another step on his journey to nowhere when the sound of singing reached his ears. He looked again and saw Geron singing a melody between every bite.

There was something welcoming about it all. Asher couldn't recall ever seeing such a thing, place or person that invited him by appearance alone. He had only ever known the dark and those who would kill him given half a chance.

Without really considering it, the assassin found himself approaching the camp. It was an immediate relief to step under the rocky canopy and be free of the relentless rain. Then there was the warmth coming off the fire, the flames slowly cooking a joint of ham. He didn't know what to say - there was no training for this.

"There's plenty of room," Geron pointed out, gesturing to a spot beside the fire.

Asher simply nodded and took the offered space. He put his hands out to the flames and wondered if he was ever going to get any feeling back in his fingers.

Geron nodded beyond the assassin. "There's dry furs in the wagon."

Again, Asher replied with a silent nod of the head before retrieving the furs. He removed his coat and laid it by the fire while the dry furs cloaked his shoulders. Geron removed a second tin plate from his pack and tore off a few strips of pork for him. There were no words exchanged while Asher ate and drank the water passed to him.

A flash of lightning illuminated the night, followed a second later by an almighty crack of thunder. Geron's horse was rattled by the weather and looked as if it was about to rise to its hooves and bolt.

"Easy, boy," Geron bade, stroking its dark mane. "Hector here is something of a coward when it comes to... well, everything actually."

His laugh was hearty, speaking of genuine amusement and affection towards the animal. "I don't think the same could be said of you though," he continued, side-eyeing Asher. "There's not many who would throw themselves at a Skalagat. Even fewer who would survive such a hare-brained idea. Why *did* you do that?"

Asher finished his plate of meat and gave the big man a glance before focusing on the flames. "I heard the fight. Heard you getting thrown about," he specified. "I just... reacted."

"For the record, I wasn't getting *thrown about*." Geron paused to consider his words. "I was using the environment to my strategic advantage, that's all. Had you arrived a few moments later, you would have discovered an adolescent Skalagat with my axe in its head."

Asher caught Geron's eyes flit to the axe strapped to Hector's saddle. It was bladed on one side while the other possessed four small hammer heads. It was big enough to be wielded in two hands, but Asher had no trouble picturing a man of Geron's size using it one-handed.

The assassin averted his gaze from the weapon, catching himself slipping into a familiar thought pattern. He was assessing the potential threats that surrounded him, chiefly the weapons available to Geron.

"That thing wasn't fully grown?" Asher asked the question to steer his mind in a different direction.

"It wasn't far off," Geron informed him casually. "The one you slew was a male though, so it maybe had another five feet in it. The females are another matter."

"You know a lot about them," Asher commented.

Geron nodded along, stoking the fire as he did. "Skalagats, Gobbers, Sandstalkers... Hells I even know a few things about Vorska. It's my job."

The latter piqued Asher's interest, thawing some of his mental numbness. "Your job? You're some kind of hunter?"

"Hunters seek game," Geron explained. "Monsters be my lot!

Folks call me a *ranger*, though I'm not alone. Our numbers are few and our life-expectancy is short. But our work is valued. People will pay good coin to keep the monsters from their door."

Asher absorbed every word. "Is that why you..." He had turned to take in the wagon.

"Aye, that's the reason you were sharing my wagon with the Skalagat's head. The contract came out of Grey Stone. Cities always pay more coin, though the contracts are rarer. There aren't a lot of monsters attracted to the noise of large populations. But, when a contract comes up somewhere like the capital of The Ice Vales, you can bet me and mine will show up to collect. That particular Skalagat was causing some grief, snatching folk from the road. Once it disrupted supplies, orders came from on high to have the monster taken care of." Geron held out his arms. "And here we are."

Asher raised an eyebrow. "But you didn't kill the Skalagat."

Geron's broad grin fell away. "No," he drawled. "But its head is in *my* wagon. Besides, if I hadn't distracted it you would never have killed it."

Asher was surprised to hear a quiet laugh from himself. "Perhaps you are right. I have no intention of claiming your coin," he added as a reassurance.

"You couldn't claim it if you wanted to, fella. The ink is dry and it's my name on the contract. The captain I dealt with wouldn't pay good coin to just anyone."

"Good to know," Asher replied as his cup graced his lips.

"I know a lot of things that are *good to know*," Geron told him with a sly grin. "It's what you know that interests me. For instance, where did you learn to fight? Wielding two blades is damn hard. Or, better yet, where did you learn to take such a beating and still get back up? From the looks of you, someone gave you a thrashing before you jumped on that Skalagat."

"You should see the other guy," Asher uttered, wondering just how badly bruised and cut he looked.

Geron relaxed back into Hector. "Something tells me there wouldn't be much left of him to see."

A flash of Lord Kalben's bloodied face crossed Asher's vision, his head caved in by one of his own books. "You're not wrong."

Geron folded his arms and tapped his fingers against his elbow. "You're entitled to your secrets," he finally said. "I'd settle instead for your name."

Asher hesitated. Outside of Nightfall, he had only ever used aliases when moving about the realm. It felt unnatural to offer his real name, as if he was offering up a part of himself that could be used against him. Whether he liked it or not, however, his time as an Arakesh was at an end. He could never return. Without title or home, his name was the only thing he truly possessed.

"Asher," he said, if quietly.

"What's that?"

"My name," he said a little louder. "It's Asher."

Geron leaned forward and, again, proffered his arm. "Well met, Asher."

Asher looked from the offered hand to Geron's eyes and back. "Well met," he echoed, grasping the man's forearm.

Taking his arm back, the ranger returned to his relaxed state. "Can I ask what you were doing in those woods? Before you stole my kill that is."

Asher swallowed, his sight fixed on the dirt between him and the fire. "I was going to kill myself."

He heard the words come out of his mouth though he couldn't quite believe he had said them. Was that how honesty worked? Did one truth beget another? Or was it the company? There was something undeniably strange about Geron Thorbear. His relaxed demeanour seemed to pull Asher in and make him feel safe.

He didn't like it.

"Oh," the ranger replied, taken aback. "But you decided to put that off and kill a Skalagat?"

"I didn't know it was a Skalagat," Asher reaffirmed.

"No. You just thought you were helping someone…"

Asher knew there was something further to analyse in that statement, something profound about his choice of action, but he continued to hone his focus on the ground, a blank canvas from which there was no input.

Geron cupped his thick beard. "Why would you want to kill yourself?"

Asher was already shaking his head, regretting his lapse in secrecy. "It's a long story."

Geron held out a hand to the rain beyond their shelter. "This storm isn't going anywhere."

Asher remained perfectly still, his lips sealed. How could he speak the words? It tore him to pieces just thinking about Dunwich.

Geron eyed him across the flames. "You don't look like a man who's lost something. You look like a man who's *done* something."

Asher met the ranger's scrutinising gaze. He had to wonder if Geron knew that look in a man from experiences of his own.

"If there's one thing I've learned in this life," Geron told him, "it's that we're all caught between running away from something… and chasing something. Hells, that's why I enjoy being a ranger so much. Keeps me on the move, puts coin in my pocket, and I get to kill some things along the way. I'm forever putting somewhere behind me while journeying towards somewhere else."

"Sounds like honest work," Asher said for lack of anything else to say.

He was still chastising himself for sharing the truth with Geron. Perhaps, he thought, the truth had come out because he wanted someone, anyone, to know that he was gone.

After the crackling fire filled the void for a while, Geron tentatively asked, "Will you try again?"

It shouldn't have been a question for Asher - of course he would try again. Like the Skalagat, he was a monster that had plagued the realm of man and required putting down. Yet he couldn't answer, fuelling his belief that he was naught but a coward at heart.

In the absence of a response, Geron passed him some more meat. "Well," he began, "if you can delay such a grim deed a while longer, you should accompany me to Grey Stone."

"Why should I do that?" the assassin asked evenly, genuinely curious.

"I haven't been pitching you this ranger business for nothing," Geron replied with some humour. "You're clearly a man of skill, though I would say your bravery walks hand in hand with stupidity. But, as I said, our numbers are few. You would make a great addition to the charter."

The idea of a career change, if it could be described as such in its simplest form, was unfathomable to Asher. He didn't deserve his very next breath, let alone a second chance and a new job.

"I know nothing about monsters," he confessed by way of dismissing Geron's offer.

"Neither did I," the ranger admitted. Reaching into one of the saddle bags, Geron produced a leather-bound book that had seen better days. "Here," he said, tossing the book to Asher.

"A Chronicle of Monsters," Asher read aloud. "A Ranger's Bestiary."

"It's not got everything in it," Geron explained, "but it's got the essentials. There's a more comprehensive archive back at The Ranch."

Asher flicked through the book, giving no one page more than a glance. "The Ranch?"

Geron thumbed over his shoulder. "We're based out of Lirian. And it's not exactly a ranch," he added, holding his meaty hands up. "The name just stuck - it's been around since before our time."

Asher nodded along and closed the book. What use did a dead man have for new information?

"At least accompany me to Grey Stone," the ranger tried to persuade. "It's a big city. Lots of opportunities there. You never know, you might find something that suits you." He gave a short sharp bark of a laugh. "Suits you better than death anyway," he said, lending words to his amusement.

"You don't need to save me," Asher said quietly.

Geron's mouth twisted out of shape, bringing a pause to his response. "It's the least I can do for the man who... saved *me*."

Asher tilted his head, a question in his expression.

The burly ranger sighed. "That Skalagat might... *might* have got the jump on me."

An unexpected smile ruled Asher's face before he caught himself.

"Careful there, little man," Geron jested, "don't want to ruin your grimace."

"There's no debt," Asher assured, moving on from the moment.

"Still," the ranger persisted, "I would appreciate the company. I would split the coin with you," he offered, trying to sweeten the deal.

"You can keep your coin," Asher told him, keeping his voice light so as not to sound ungrateful.

Geron looked pained. "Well," he began in a defeated tone, "if it's only death that interests you, there's plenty of ways to die in Grey Stone. Big cities come with big troubles. Though..." The ranger let his word hang in the air between them for a time. "There must be a reason why you're sat round my fire. You woke up from that knock to the head some time ago." The big man shrugged. "Not fancy dying in the rain?"

Asher's blue eyes swivelled on the ranger. It would have been easy to believe that Geron was calling him a coward, his accusation hidden between his words. And, indeed, Asher felt the fire rising in his veins in response to the veiled insult. He wanted to take his dagger in hand there and then and show this man of the wilds that his will was one of iron, a will that would see his suicide completed.

But there was something disarming about the ranger that extinguished that fire. Asher was adept at reading people and understanding what they were about. Geron was a man of truths, his words honest and always spoken from the heart. It was there to be seen on his face, plain as day. He wasn't calling him a coward. He was, in fact, trying his damnedest to keep him alive.

"Perhaps I will accompany you," Asher finally said, ignoring the ranger's comments and question.

A broad grin pushed Geron's beard up the sides of his round face. "I hope you like singing, fella! The road brings it out in me!"

It was hard not to get carried away in his jovial laughter.

CHAPTER 14
GREY STONE

*Spider - If you can squash it with your boot, it's not the breed of Spider
I'm writing about.*

*There are parts of the world where Spiders grow and grow until they could
stand side by side with a horse (see A Charter of Monsters, Page 22, for
known locations).*

*If possible, bring a mage into the contract; they're worth their weight in
coins when it comes to Spiders. You see, Spiders hate the light, despise it.
Now don't be thinking you can just take a torch into a nest - you're going
to need a weapon in both hands. A mage can bring light to the hunt and it
could mean the difference between life and death.*

*Your next advantage will be to keep moving. If you remain in one spot,
which will be tempting when faced by waves of the fiends, you will be
overwhelmed. See below for extensive list of strengths and weaknesses.*

***A Chronicle of Monsters: A Ranger's Bestiary, 12th Edition,
Page 391.***

The knight with no name, Ranger.

. . .

A very long day had awaited Asher on the back of that wagon. When Geron wasn't singing, which wasn't often, the ranger would talk incessantly. He cared little for responses from Asher; the assassin was simply another set of ears besides Hector's, his horse. Adding to the experience, the foul stench of the Skalagat's head intensified with every mile.

Continuing south-west, along The Selk Road, the temperature refused to be anything but freezing, as if they were still in the colds of the north. Asher draped the furs over his shoulders and tucked his knees up into his chest.

"A strange place, ain't it?" Geron called back. "They don't call it The *Ice* Vales for nothing, I suppose. Legend has it the entire region was cursed by the magic of the elves, if you believe such tales."

"I've been here in the summer," Asher rasped. "I can believe it."

Geron glanced back over the wagon. "I thought you were asleep," he said with a laugh.

"Then why have you been talking to me?" Asher queried.

The ranger shrugged. "I like talking," he asserted. "Words are what connect us to the world, to *people*. Perhaps such things don't interest a man of your breed."

Reinforcing the point, Asher pulled the furs a little higher around his neck and kept his words to himself. If he was lucky, they would cover the last few miles in silence. Any hope of that was dashed, however, when Geron broke into a new song about a scullery maid from Velia.

Asher sank further into his furs and wondered what he was doing in the wagon. Why had he agreed to travel with this ranger to Grey Stone? The assassin had no future, so what need did he have of the city? Seated against the side of the wagon, he could feel the dagger hilt pressing into his back, reminding him of the deed he was yet to complete.

It had to be soon, Asher decided. He couldn't endure another night's sleep and the dreams that haunted him. Not only was he seeing Thomas Murell, but also the faces of every person he had killed since his teens. Though he recalled every kill in his sleep, the assassin had believed their faces were lost to him. How wrong he had been. His conditioning was in ruins and, with the collapse of those mental walls, his memories came flooding back.

No, he thought. He could not sleep again.

In the twilight of dusk, Geron's wagon rounded the southern curve in The Vengoran Mountains and slipped into the shadow of Grey Stone. Built into the sheer cliffs, it was a city of stark divides. On top of the cliffs, where a vast plateau offered a great deal of flat land, King Gregorn of house Orvish ruled from The Black Fort, surrounded by the numerous manors of The Ice Vales' high borns. His people, however, dwelled within the mountain stone in a maze of streets and alleys that had been carved out of Vengora.

Looking beyond Geron's considerable frame, Asher settled on the single fissure that cut down the middle of the cliff, the only entrance to the city. At the width of thirty men abreast, it wasn't a particularly grand entrance, but the sheer walls either side towered over the land at just under a thousand feet. Amidst the zig-zagging stairwells that had been dug into these walls, a network of bridges, both wooden and stone, connected one side to the other.

Inside the stone city, under the boots of the king and his high borns, the socio-economic hierarchy was simple: the higher up you were, the better off you were. The poorest of Grey Stone lived on the ground levels, the furthest from their king, while the wealthier merchants owned homes built into the lofty tiers of the interior cliff.

There ended Asher's knowledge of the city. He had no real idea how the people lived or what they did from day to day - their actual lives had always been background noise to him. As with everywhere else, he just knew how their culture worked and the best way to penetrate it, depending upon his needs.

"Grey Stone!" Geron announced from his seat. "It's certainly an intimidating beast! Never been successfully invaded," he added as a point of interest. "And without gates!" he said incredulously.

The ranger waffled on in this manner as he brought the wagon in line with a number of merchants and visitors on the road. Asher barely took a word in. Instead, he was scanning all the new faces and the contents of the carts and wagons. Would he know another Arakesh if he saw one? He hadn't met or even seen every assassin in Nightfall and they were all trained to blend in, utilising the highest levels of detail.

This led Asher to questioning what he would do if he did cross paths with an Arakesh. Did they all know he was a traitor? Were they even tracking him yet? And then, of course, the most important question of all crossed his mind: did it matter? Coming face to face with an Arakesh would mean death, the very thing he sought. Then why, he wondered, was he so focused on trying to spot one? Was it merely instinct? Or did he truly wish to live?

Asher's thoughts were dashed when the wagon rolled over a stubborn rock as Geron guided Hector off the road. The ranger was taking them towards the collection of buildings that hugged the outer wall, beside the looming entrance. There, Asher could see, were clusters of soldiers huddling round fiery braziers, the flames blowing wildly in the wind. Besides the spears they wielded and the swords resting on their hips, they all bore the sigil of house Orvish, a roaring bear's head. For Asher, it was a natural feeling to be wary of soldiers, those who upheld the laws he so regularly broke.

"Well met!" Geron's voice boomed over the wind, his great girth unsettling the wagon as he jumped into the snow.

"State your business, big man!" one of the soldiers replied with some caution.

Geron's size put them all on edge, it seemed. Of this particular cluster, every soldier broke away from the warmth of the fire and presented the ranger with a wall of trained fighters.

"Come on, fellas!" the ranger beseeched. "It's me, Geron Thor-bear! Ranger! Monster hunter! Don't any of you have a memory that goes back further than your last meal?" he muttered so that only Asher could hear him. "Just fetch Captain Wrenly. He and I have business."

One of the soldiers raised an eyebrow of disbelief. "And what business is that?"

Geron flashed the man a smile before pulling back the tarp. Every man bearing the Orvish sigil stepped back in fright upon seeing the decapitated Skalagat. Their reaction made the ranger smile all the more.

"Now go fetch him," he commanded, his tone firm. "And make sure he brings his coin purse too."

The mouthy soldier struggled to tear his eyes away from the horror inside the wagon. "Captain Wrenly is seeing to a matter in the upper tiers."

Geron craned his thick neck and considered the distance between them. "Well, you had better get to it then. Skalagats have been known to grow their bodies back," he added mischievously. As two of the soldiers were set at a pace, the ranger whipped his head around to face the man who had questioned him so much. "My friend and I can be found in The Mason's Lounge. Come and get me when your captain arrives."

Without waiting for a response from the soldier, Geron gave Asher a nod to follow him into the city. Hopping over the side, the assassin naturally kept his features hidden with his head tilted and his collar high. He left the furs behind as they belonged to Geron and a part of him knew he wasn't going to see Hector or the wagon again.

Passing between the two walls of the entrance, the city closed in on the pair and the warmth washed over them like a wave. Market stalls lined the walls for a hundred feet before the shops carved into the stone lent the street more space. The alleys and side streets were all tunnels, short and long, that wormed deeper into the city's warrens.

There was activity in every direction, with people traversing the bridges overhead and journeying up and down the stone steps either side. Asher was used to weaving his way through dense crowds, with or without his blindfold on, but no such skill was required when walking side by side with Geron. The ranger was a head taller than everyone and his width parted the swarming citizens of Grey Stone.

"Prepare yourself, fella," Geron was saying, his gaze never wandering from their path. "You're about to taste the finest mead in all of Illian. I've frequented just about every bar, inn, and tavern the six kingdoms have to offer, so trust me when I say that."

"Is it on the ground level?" Asher asked, sure that such a fine drink could only be served in the upper tiers.

"Of course!" Geron answered, as if it was obvious. "All the best places in Grey Stone are down here. The air gets a little stuffy up there if you ask me."

As the ranger went on to list more admirable qualities of The Mason's Lounge, Asher was calculating. He had already noted the alleyway coming up on his right. To the left, on Geron's side, a young man was hauling several crates of vegetables on top of each other, while simultaneously staring at a pretty woman passing him by. The coming calamity was clear to see and every fibre of Asher's being demanded that he take advantage of the situation.

Inevitably, the young man walked into the barrel he would have seen were it not for his wandering attention. The weight of his load saw him tip right over the barrel and land in a crash of vegetables and broken crates. A passing couple cried out as they jumped aside to avoid the debris and the young man's employer barked a stream of profanities at his incompetence.

As expected, Geron turned his head of bushy black hair to look at the harmless incident. At the same moment, Asher slipped further to his right, allowing a group of six nuns to come between him and the ranger. Before the group of gods' maids had completely passed them by, Asher vanished down the alley he had spotted and left Geron Thorbear behind.

It was for the best, he believed. The assassin realised now that being with the ranger was simply a way of distracting himself. The big man had a way of derailing his dark thoughts and keeping him focused on the present. As long as he was with him, he would never find that state of mind that would commit to suicide.

As night drew over Grey Stone, slivers of starlight reigned overhead, defining the web of fissures. Asher had kept on the move for some time to ensure that Geron never caught up with him. There was every chance though that the ranger had made it all the way to The Mason's Lounge before realising he was alone.

Keeping to himself, the assassin was brought to a halt when he heard the familiar sound of a good tussle. Turning on the spot, he looked down the lane to his left, where the fissure split and the roads led to different districts. A door burst open further along and a dishevelled man was tossed out of a tavern with a threat if he was to return. Asher turned his eyes to the sign nailed high on the wall: *Turner Street*, it read. From memory, he knew Turner Street was the entrance to the Olding District, an area where even the king's soldiers didn't dare tread.

Without thought, Asher started down Turner Street.

The atmosphere was almost instantly different to the rest of the city. The lanes and passageways weren't nearly as packed, every crevice was filthy and littered, and the residents who called the Olding District home appeared to have led a much harder life, their clothes worn and their skin aged.

There was also the criminal element that Asher couldn't miss. It took the assassin an extra moment to recall the guild that ruled Grey Stone's underworld, but the name Grey Faces eventually came to him. The Olding District, however, was a melting pot of various factions and guilds who all vied for the throne that the Grey Faces currently resided on. It was this constant warring that made the area as run down as it was, as well as the perfect place to hide if you were an assassin passing through. This time, though, Asher wasn't looking for a bed for a night.

One tavern stood out from the rest, its occupants a breed of man that clearly had a penchant for violence. Asher had often found himself proficient at profiling, a talent he had always used to his advantage in the past. Tonight, he intended to use it against himself.

With confident strides, he announced himself to every patron inside The Rattigan. He was halfway to the bar before the doors slammed shut behind him. Predators all, their collective gaze fell on this potential lone prey that had so arrogantly entered their midst. Ignoring them, the assassin proceeded to lean over the bar, his arms folded, while his mind spiralled.

Asher knew exactly why he was there. He had given it as little thought as possible in the hope that he wouldn't be able to talk himself out of it and, now, he was standing in a place where he wasn't welcome. Still, no one made a move on him. He deliberately made eye contact with several patrons, sure to display some challenge in his look, but none took the bait.

The assassin sighed, and not because he was destined to die in this crummy bar, but because he was going to have to work at it. Reaching out to his right, Asher snatched the tankard of beer from its place in front of its owner and proceeded to down the contents in one. The barkeep witnessed the event as the patron turned on Asher with murder in his eyes.

"Another," Asher ordered, hammering the tankard down. "On him," he added, with a nod of the head.

The barkeep gave the assassin his best crooked smile. "Oh, you're going to get more than Big Billy's coin, mate," he quipped.

Asher slowly turned his head and lazily looked Big Billy up and down. "Why do they call you *big*?" he asked, as if blind to the man's hulking frame.

Big Billy sneered, a prelude to his violent outburst.

Asher closed his eyes, aware that if he saw what was coming, his conditioning might take over. From there it was all muscle memory and, ultimately, a very dead Big Billy. So he kept his eyes shut as the thug picked him up, slammed him down on the bar, and rammed to the other end. His journey came to a sudden stop when he flew off the counter and crashed into a table and chairs, shattering most of the furniture in the process.

Groaning with new injury, Asher rose unsteadily to his hands and knees. "Damn it, Bill, you've got a good knife on your belt," he uttered. "This could have been over by now."

Big Billy's bear-sized hands seized Asher from the floor and easily yanked him to his feet, where he enjoyed a vertical existence for all of one second. The fist that collided with the assassin's chest launched him across one table, where his body swiped every tankard away, before he finally hit the floor and tumbled into a seated patron. That same patron was not too happy about having their chair taken out from under them.

Asher opened his eyes in time to see a new, smaller, fist coming at his face. He spat blood across the floor and saw Big Billy's enormous boots storming towards him.

"I think it's his turn now," Asher croaked.

Indeed, the smaller man backed away in Billy's shadow. Again, his overly large hands grabbed at Asher's coat and dragged him up to his feet. This time, however, Asher forgot to close his eyes. He saw the obvious punch, angled towards his jaw, and his muscles simply reacted, his instincts always triggered by pain. Big Billy's fist found naught but air, the assassin having freed himself of the hand holding his coat and side-stepped the incoming attack.

What followed was an all-out assault on his opponent's nerve clusters - a counter attack that lasted no more than two seconds. The first was a strike to the nerve under his wrist, devastating his closed fist and numbing most of his arm. The second was a slap to the back of his jaw, a blow that dazed the man and rendered him mute. The third and final counter was a sharp elbow to his left pectoral, sending enough pain through Big Billy to put him on his knees.

Asher frowned, aggravated by his own response. "I didn't mean to do that," he began, holding his hands up to a stunned room. "It was just...." There was no explanation he could give that The Rattigan's patrons would understand. Instead, he leaned down and removed Big Billy's knife. "Just use this," he suggested, presenting it to the man hilt forward.

Big Billy coughed and spluttered before rolling onto his side. He wouldn't be doing anything for a while.

To the assassin's right, The Rattigan's owner chopped a meat cleaver into the bar, drawing all eyes to him. "Free drinks for the rest of the week to the man who puts this fella in his grave."

The tavern paused as every patron weighed up the task and the reward. Then they charged. Asher's muscle memory reacted to the threat, causing his wrist to flick Big Billy's knife towards the closest thug. The pommel struck the fool in the head and knocked him to the floor with a pulsing welt for his troubles. That was one down, twenty to go.

Asher shut his eyes tightly and clenched his fists, desperate to fight the punctilious conditioning that Nightfall had instilled in him. It would be the difference between his death and all of theirs.

The mob rammed into him with the force of a bull. The assassin was on the floor without being able to say exactly how he got there. Next came the beating from the kicking feet and pounding fists. Asher naturally curled up into a ball, a defensive measure to protect his vital organs and head. The pain brought back memories of his youth, in lessons under Nasta Nal-Aket's well-attuned senses. Enduring a decent beating was seen as good character building in Nightfall, a way of introducing an initiate to pain so that they might hold it close throughout all their days.

At some point, Asher knew he was going to have to unfurl his limbs and expose his vulnerable areas. As he was, he knew he could hold out longer than most of these unfit men could maintain their attack. Then, one by one, the blows lessened. The cacophonous shouts of aggression were replaced by yelps of surprise and then pain. Asher was sure he could feel bodies hitting the floor beyond the kicking rabble that surrounded him.

One of the closest attackers was dragged away from the assassin and subsequently thrown over the bar, where his flailing limbs broke a dozen bottles. The gap left in his wake gave Asher a glimpse of the tavern and the green cloak that swished from side to side. Only seconds later, the men beating Asher were turning away and taking part in a new fight.

Bloodied and bruised, the assassin slowly adjusted his position on the floor and looked upon a giant among men. Geron Thorbear moved like a dancer, impressively fast for a man of his size. His encompassing hands took men by the face and thrust them into the nearest solid object, reducing them to limp bodies on the floor. A backhand here and a headbutt there dropped his foes with brutal efficiency. In fact, his entire fighting style was one of brutality and decisive movements. He even took their retaliation with all the stoicism of a punch bag.

When only a handful of The Rattigan's patrons remained on their feet, including the barkeep, the brawl ground to a halt, their courage dissipated. "Well if that's to be it," Geron declared, sounding somewhat bored, "I'll be taking my friend and leaving you to your evening."

Asher held on to his pain as the ranger picked him up and partially dragged him out of the tavern. Outside, the night air had settled between the high walls of the mountainous city. It was refreshing after being thrown around the hot and stuffy Rattigan, though not refreshing enough to give Asher his second wind. Released from Geron's support, he collapsed to the stone and rolled on to his back, his breath laboured and heart pounding with fury.

"Why?" he rasped.

Geron was standing over him and using a kerchief to wipe blood from his knuckles. "Why indeed, little man?" he echoed patronisingly. "Did you really go in there to die? In *there*? Plenty of people die in these streets every week, but The Rattigan is so foul I'm not even sure the gods would come to collect your soul."

Asher sighed. "Stop calling me that."

"What - little man? I can't help it if you're both little and a man."

Asher doubled down on his sigh. "How did you find me?"

Geron crouched down beside him. "I'm a ranger; tracking comes with the territory."

The assassin rolled aside to get away from the man's pungent breath and began the arduous journey back to his feet. "You shouldn't have come," he stated, furious to still be alive.

Geron rose with him and reached out to put a hand on his shoulder. "I don't know why you want to die so badly—"

Asher lashed out with one arm and freed himself of the ranger's comforting hand. "It's *my* business!" he growled. "Not yours. This has nothing to do with you. Leave me be," he finally uttered, staggering away.

Geron sidestepped, placing his mountainous frame directly in Asher's path.

The assassin stopped and gave the ranger his most threatening glare. "Move. Or be moved."

Geron folded his arms, lending him the thickness of a tree.

Asher sneered. "Fine." He went to shrug off his coat, ready for the fight to come, when the pain of lifting his right shoulder gave him pause and a pinched expression.

"You've still got a lot of fire in your veins for a man who wants to die," Geron observed.

Every part of Asher sagged with exhaustion, including his will to pursue death. "If you knew what I had done, you would run me through yourself."

Geron raised his chin, perhaps considering what a man had to do to warrant an execution from his own hands. "The Mason's Lounge never closes," he said. "Why don't I buy you a drink and you can tell me all about it. If I so decide, I'll ride you out of the city and chop your head off myself. Sound good?"

Asher wasn't sure he wanted any of that, but he nodded his head as he had nothing else to say.

~

Since Geron didn't easily fit into any of the booths at The Mason's Lounge, the pair had been seated at a table on the second floor, giving them a view of the bar and layout below. It suited Asher who was always more comfortable with a lofty vantage of his surroundings.

Geron clapped his hands together and licked his lips when the barmaid brought them their frothing tankards. "Duke's Mead!" he hollered with delight. "Brewed right here in the city. It's even said that King Gregorn favours the stuff!"

Despite the surreal feeling that he was actually sat in a tavern, sharing a drink with another person, Asher put the mead to his lips and sampled the lauded liquor. It was bitter, with a surprisingly sweet aftertaste. "Not bad," he praised.

"Not bad, he says!" Geron announced to no one in particular. "Coming from you I'm to take it that you love Duke's Mead. Another!" he ordered before finishing his own.

Asher eyed the coin purse Geron dumped on the table. It was notably larger than when they had arrived at the city.

"It's not all mine," Geron told him, catching the assassin's lingering scrutiny. "Fifteen percent goes to The Ranch."

Asher looked at the purse again. "Captain Wrenly paid you," he concluded.

"He did indeed!" the ranger confirmed with a swig of his mead. "Not that he wanted to," he added with a burp. "Happens all the time," he continued as if Asher had asked a follow-up question. "There's always a reason why they don't feel they should pay the full amount. Rich or poor, they all have that in common."

Against his better judgment Asher gave in to his curiosity. "Why does The Ranch get a cut?"

Geron shrugged. "Upkeep and the like," he answered vaguely. "The fifteen percent is never more than I would end up paying for supplies from elsewhere between contracts. And the archives are a big help - not every monster can be slain with a good swing of steel. There's beds for the night too. And a swordsmith!" he added with a finger in the air. "You're going to love it," the ranger assured. "That is unless I'm to chop your head off first!" he exclaimed cheerfully, seeing Asher's protest coming.

There was a natural pause while the barmaid returned with two fresh tankards of Duke's Mead, though Asher retained most of his first.

"Go on then, little man," Geron coaxed, ignoring Asher's dislike for the nickname. "Why should I taint my axe with the likes of you?"

The assassin opened his mouth to speak the words, words that would condemn any soul on Verda's green earth, when his lips sealed shut again. Like the coward he was, Asher fell on his lies, regardless of the truth therein.

"I killed someone," he said quietly, his words left in the air between them.

"Haven't we all, fella," Geron replied before lifting his tankard to conceal half of his face.

Asher gave the big man a hard look. Unlike most people whose paths he crossed, the assassin couldn't fathom this ranger of the wilds.

"Who did you kill that demands your own death?" Geron probed.

Thomas Murell came to the forefront of his mind, as did the gasp he made before he died and the brief expression of horror on his young face. "It's the number of people I've killed," Asher specified, weaving the truth he wished Geron to hear. "Have you heard news out of Skystead?"

"News from the north does not idly make its way south," the ranger remarked. "Though there have been some nasty rumours, if you're the sort to believe in such things. Folks are saying something about Lord Kalben. Apparently he was killed in The White Citadel, which I find hard to believe. That place is locked up tighter than The Dragon Keep."

"I killed him," Asher stated, causing Geron to choke on a mouthful of mead.

"Oh," the ranger said simply, wiping his beard dry.

"And several others," the assassin explained. "I can't even count them all," he confessed, his gaze dropping into his tankard. "I've been killing people for nearly two decades. So many faces and names... So much blood."

Geron's left hand attempted to casually drop down and grip the hilt of his hunting knife. "You're a murderer then?"

"That's one word for what I am," Asher agreed. "But I never did it for fun or personal gain. They were just... a job," he described for lack of a better word.

"A job?" Geron repeated. "You mean to say, you were paid to kill people? Are you a..." The ranger checked the proximity of those around them before leaning in. "Are you an assassin?"

Asher nodded his head.

Geron sat back and blew his cheeks out, his grip relenting on the hunting knife. "That's heavy work for the soul, fella. It's no wonder all those lives are weighing on you."

It wasn't the reaction Asher had anticipated, giving him cause to scrutinise the ranger again. "Is this not cause enough to bring your axe to bear?"

Geron tilted his head in thought. "I don't know. Were any of them good people? I mean, everyone knows that Skystead is corrupted to the eyeballs. That's got to start with the house of Tarn. You might actually have done some good there."

"I haven't done good anywhere," Asher insisted, his knuckles whitening around the handle of his tankard. "As for the people I've killed..." He stopped himself from entering the dark halls of his memories, where so many bloody faces awaited him. "I have no idea if they were good or bad. I didn't care. After I was given their name, they were as good as dead. It doesn't matter either way. They were people. Ordinary men and women going about their lives before I tore through them."

Geron grew serious, hunching over his elbows on the table. "I've heard the lord of Skystead is... was a little rough around the edges. Most said he never needed the protection of his station. How did you, you know... How did you kill him, if you don't mind me asking?"

Asher licked his lips, the memory close to the surface in his mind. "With a book."

Geron blinked. Then he laughed, putting Asher all the more off balance around him. "With a book?" he repeated, his laugh increasing. Seeing the unease his reaction had triggered in Asher, the ranger settled down and wiped his face from top to bottom. "How did you get in to that ugly business then?" he asked, his tone returned to a level of seriousness.

Of all Asher's conditioning, refraining from talking about Nightfall and his training was, perhaps, the most cemented in his bones. "My father was an assassin," he offered instead.

"*My* father was a farmer," Geron replied, his tone lightening. "Who would have thought the children of such men would end up sharing a drink, eh?"

Again, Asher found himself looking at the ranger with some disbelief. "Most people wouldn't continue to sit here and share a drink."

"Most people would have you locked up in chains and publicly executed," Geron corrected. "But most people are boring," he quipped as an afterthought. "The way I see it, it's simple. You've killed people for money because you were raised to do so. Not great, but what can you do about it? Do you now regret it? It seems you do. Do you deserve a second chance? Many would say *no*, to the gallows with you. But I'm not the many." The ranger paused to lower his voice and add a touch of sincerity to it. "The Ranch is full of people in search of redemption, Asher. The broken have long been attracted to the life of a ranger - it suits us."

"I told you," Asher replied, "I don't know anything—"

"I know what you said," Geron interjected. "You also said you haven't done good anywhere. I'm inclined to believe you," the ranger added before finishing his drink. "What I want to know is: would you like to? Would you like to do some good? Get a taste of the other side.

I'm not saying you get to start again. Hells, none of us do. What we've done stays with us; it's why we keep doing what we do."

Asher appreciated Geron's attempts to lend some kind of value to his life. "There is but one conclusion to my tale," he said, feeling the pressure of that dagger on his hip again.

"As I said," Geron persisted, "the life expectancy of a ranger is short at best. You could do some good before you die, something that *matters*. What's the worst that could happen?" the big man questioned, enticing him to commit. "You die trying to kill some monster? Problem solved!"

Asher opened his mouth to renew his argument against the idea when the prospect of atonement finally struck a chord. *No*, he thought definitively. No amount of lives saved or monsters slain could make up for the people he had murdered, especially the murder of Thomas Murell.

Dying in battle, however, would be easy given that his conditioning - that iron will to always survive - could hold no sway over the actions of a monster that simply bested him.

He looked at Geron Thorbear and gave his answer.

CHAPTER 15
A LIFE SAVED

Lech - To the common folk, these monsters are known as Mudslugs. It's an apt description, though Lech are closer in size to a large dog.
Typically found in bogs and marshes due to their preference for wet environments. If you can't see through the water and it's past your knees, take a care. The bite on these beasts is almost as painful as it is strong. Once they've got you in their maw, you're going to need fire to make their fangs retract.
Thankfully, they're easy to kill. They have no outer shell or any natural protection beside their ability to blend in with their surroundings.
They don't taste too bad either.

A Chronicle of Monsters: A Ranger's Bestiary, 12th Edition, Page 66.

Dane, son of Heslin, Ranger.

There was no such thing as silence to Nasta Nal-Aket. Even standing in a room in which no one was talking or moving, there was always noise.

Of the six young men and women, adolescents all, he could hear their hearts pounding, bones rubbing together, and saliva running down their throats. Added to that, he could feel their lungs expanding and contracting as their collective breath filled the chamber and touched his skin. He could taste the sweat gathering and subsequently absorbed by their clothing.

There was one in particular, however, whose heart was beating faster, whose sweat was twice that of his peers, and whose breathing rate was increasing by the minute. The young man - stripped to his waist - stood in the middle, surrounded by the other five.

The Nightseye elixir fuelling the initiate's heightened senses informed him that his peers were wielding a pair of wooden batons each. Their focus was sharpened to a point and directed at him, like a pack of wolves that had surrounded their prey.

Nasta entered their circle, his bare feet padding against the cold stone. "This is a test of control," he uttered, facing the initiate in the dark. "The world is full of noise. You must learn to home your senses, even under duress. Through pain and threat of death, you must always remain on target."

The Father left the inner circle and began to pace the perimeter. "Should any of you reach my age, you will discover the consequences of a violent life, the toll it takes on your body; especially your bones. I now possess the ability to crack every one of my knuckles on command." To demonstrate, Nasta closed his fist one finger at a time so that the initiates recognised the sound. "I'm going to crack three knuckles on my left hand," he continued. "My left hand," he emphasised. "You must indicate when you hear the crack. Only after you have heard all three, will the test be at an end."

Nasta continued to circle the initiates, pleased to hear that the young man in the centre had finally begun to get his breathing and heart rate under control. Stopping by the open archway, the Father simply instructed, "Begin."

The stillness of the chamber was upended on a word. Three of the five initiates moved in while the other two stepped back, ready to attack as a second wave. In the heart of the violence, the young man was forced to defend himself against a brutal beating and with no weapons of his own.

Nasta heard the wooden batons impact the initiate's limbs, the percussive force rippling through skin, muscle, and bone. Those who scored hits to his midriff sent crippling waves of sheer force through his internal organs. Within seconds there was blood splattered on the floor, smeared up the batons, and speckled across their young faces.

As the initiate being tested scored a successful counter attack against two of his opponents, Nasta cracked one of his knuckles. The young man opened his mouth to count the first of three when he stopped himself and ducked under two incoming strikes.

"Very good," Nasta praised through the chaos, satisfied that the initiate had sense enough to know he had used his right hand instead of his left.

Running steps drew the Father's attention to the archway at his back. Another initiate, younger than those fighting behind him, dropped to one knee and held out a length of string. The small girl remained in her kneeling position while Nasta's fingers ran over all the knots. Incidentally, one of the knuckles on his left hand cracked and the initiate called the number out, his mouth full of blood.

After reaching the end of the message, Nasta wrapped the string around his hand. "What are you doing, boy?" he asked aloud, his thoughts clouded by Asher. The young girl at his feet turned her face up, her brow furrowed questioningly. "Have a message dispatched to Dunwich at once," he instructed her. "The patron is dead. They are not to spill blood. Have them await further orders." The initiate darted back into the hallway and disappeared with her orders.

It dawned on him then, however briefly, that he had just given an order that would save a life. In all his tenure as Father, he had never been given cause to issue such a thing.

The thought barely stuck before he squeezed the string in his clenched fist, his mind lost to events in the north. What was Asher doing? He had an opportunity to get lost in the world and make a new start. Why was he leaving a trail of bodies across Skystead? Of course, killing Lord Kalben spoke clearly of Asher's motives, though Nasta would never have predicted his prodigy would go so far out of the way to ensure the other child's survival.

A scream returned some of his attention to the test and he clicked another knuckle on his left hand. Unfortunately, the initiate didn't detect it, prolonging his beating - and it had become a beating. His arms were so bruised now that he couldn't keep the wooden batons at bay. The result was multiple blows to his face and chest. In his favour, on the other hand, he had succeeded in knocking two of his opponents into slumber.

Feeling the knots on the end of the string, his mind was cast to distant Skystead once more. It wouldn't be long before the entire realm heard news of the brutal killing, the victim being a lord. It would make for good gossip, gossip that would end up being heard by the court of assassins. They would pick up the hunt in Skystead and track him down.

Nasta considered all that he had taught Asher when it came to evasion. Always stay on the move was lesson one. People who put down roots made connections and, ultimately, became memorable to the locals.

Lesson two came straight from lesson one: blend in. Nasta had told Asher that just as every song has a tempo, so too do environments have a baseline. He was sure that, right now, Asher would be imitating those around him, be it in their dress or the way they talked.

Lesson three was simple: don't make friends. Friends require trust and no one can be trusted. Nasta had no doubts where this particular lesson was concerned. After all, of the many things Nightfall had drummed into its Arakesh over the years, trusting no one was a fundamental truth of life.

There were numerous lessons beyond these three - and he had spent years ensuring Asher kept to them all - but as long as he stayed true to the first three, he would always stay ahead of the court.

There was a crack of bone and it wasn't his knuckle this time. The Father tilted his head and detected the four broken ribs that dropped the initiate to his knees. One last baton to the face laid him flat and very still. Nasta could still hear his pulse, but the young man wouldn't be getting back up anytime soon. A better man would have felt a pang of guilt for his lapse in attention, but Nasta wasn't that man.

CHAPTER 16

THE RANCH

Stravakin - So wicked and foul a creature could only have been born of nightmares I tell you. Bone eaters our ancestors called them and rightly so. The first one I came across had left a bear carcass in its wake. Can you imagine finding a dead bear with all but its bones? A more unnatural thing I never saw.

The bite on these beasts is next to none, their jaws capable of reducing bones to splinters. And, as large as their pointed maw might be, don't bother attacking it - those jaws will blunt your blade. Fire is your best bet. Set your trap and make certain you've plenty of oil about it. Don't hang about to watch it burn, mind you. Something in its gut gives off poisonous fumes when put to fire. Those fumes, however, are the perfect lure for the mate, and Stravakin always have a mate they're paired with until death.

A Chronicle of Monsters: A Ranger's Bestiary, 12th Edition, Page 236.

Welek Tysarion, Ranger.

The journey from Grey Stone to Lirian was a transition from black and white into all the colours of the world. Gone were the towering dark mountains of Vengora and the seemingly endless vales of ice and snow. Returned truly to spring, the trees and fields came alive around them, the vibrancy a stark contrast, and a welcome one.

Asher enjoyed the sun on his face as the rhythm of the wagon carried him along. He couldn't remember the last time, if ever, he had appreciated anything about the weather. It had always been just another aspect of his environment, no more interesting than a table or a door.

The cursed land put behind them, Geron soon left The Selk Road in favour of a short cut that crossed the wilds, a path that would take them to the lush kingdom of Felgarn, nestled inside the tall trees of The Evermoore.

Before they could arrive at their destination, however, there were many miles to cross and, much to Asher's dismay, an awful amount of Geron's talking to get through. The ranger seemed to enjoy words more than anything and, when he wasn't speaking, he would simply fill the silence with singing or humming. For the first leg of their journey, having listened to the big man's voice, Asher felt exhausted around their first camp fire and offered barely more than a handful of words in response.

By the second day, Geron had begun to tease more from him. The topics remained relatively light, covering likes and dislikes where food was concerned or varying techniques in hunting while off the beaten track. By the following week, when the boundary of The Evermoore was a distant line on the flat horizon, the ranger was comfortable enough to criticise the assassin.

Geron gestured at the hourglass short-sword resting on the log beside Asher. "You're going to need more than that toothpick if you're to be a ranger, little man."

Asher glanced at the weapon. "I killed a Skalagat with that *tooth-pick*," he pointed out, tearing his flat bread into edible strips.

"It's dumb luck you didn't die," the ranger opined. "You weren't just close to the beast you were bloody on top of it," he added with a laugh.

"I've never liked axes," Asher replied, sighting the handle poking over the top of the cart. "Too unwieldy."

"An axe has its moments," Geron defended. "But it's not my weapon of choice."

Asher could see that the ranger's smile was leading to a reveal, one he was eager to share with the assassin. Heaving his bulk from the ground, Geron moved a portion of the tarp and brought a sword back to the fire with him. The weapon was no surprise to Asher, who had made a comprehensive survey of all his companion's weapons, supplies, and tools since the first time he stepped into the wagon.

"Now this," Geron began, presenting the blade in its scabbard, "is a monster killer!" With one hand he drew the steel from its sheath and held it up so that the firelight might dance across its surface.

"It's a claymore," Asher remarked as a matter of fact.

Geron discarded the scabbard and took the blade in both hands. "Don't be saying that as if it's some simple sword," he said with an expression of hurt. "If you know what you're doing, you can cleave a Vorska's head clean from its neck with one of these. Two-handed grip for a stronger swing," he commented, displaying the hilt. "Sturdy pommel for when things get a little up-close," he continued, raising the weapon to show off the detailed head of a bear. "And then there's the blade," the ranger said admiringly. "Tempered steel, double-edged to give *you* the edge."

Asher eyed the big man while taking a swig from the water skin. "Are you a ranger or a sword salesman?"

Geron responded with his usual laugh, the noise distorted as he returned to the ground, his back to one of the wagon's large wheels. "Oh, I'm not trying to sell it to you, fella. This one is all *mine*. I can't even guess at the number of times this girl has seen me through certain death. When she comes out, monsters die."

Asher scrutinised the enormous sword now resting across the ranger's lap. "Does it have a name?" He regretted his question immediately upon seeing Geron's smirking face.

"The sword?" he queried, his tone close to mocking.

"I thought you monster-killers did that sort of thing," he elaborated, trying to sound casual about it.

Geron chuckled. "No, my sword doesn't have a name. It's a *sword*. I've found that the men who name their swords are usually overcompensating for something."

Now it was Asher's turn to laugh, an unfamiliar sound to both men.

~

The next day, after their journey had begun anew, Geron turned his head over his shoulder. "I'll tell you what you do have that interests me," he said, as if their conversation from the previous night had never ended. "That bow of yours," he specified, turning all the more in his seat so that he might lay eyes on the weapon.

Asher looked to the quiver and folded bow, the pair leaning against the side of the wagon's interior. "What of it?"

"Well, I've never seen anything like it," the ranger explained, his attention returning to the east. "Looks dwarven to my eyes."

Asher sighted the back of the ranger's head. "You've met a dwarf?"

"Aye, there's a particularly cantankerous one who runs a forge just outside of Darkwell. Damn good smith."

"I didn't think they were seen outside of Dhenaheim," Asher said more to himself than the ranger.

"It's rare," Geron stated. "I take it that bow isn't dwarven then," he reasoned.

"No," the assassin responded. "It isn't."

The ranger glanced over his shoulder again. "Have it your way," he said, seeing no forthcoming explanation.

And so on they rode, putting mile after mile behind them until the ranger finally steered Hector back onto The Selk Road, bringing them before the imposing wall of trees that made up The Evermoore.

The merchants and travellers they passed on the road appeared more jovial in this part of the realm, their lives yet to be troubled by the bleak weather and terrain that awaited them in The Ice Vales. Geron spoke to them all, much to Asher's irritation. Some he would simply offer a friendly greeting, while others he would engage in conversation about the wares they were selling or just enquiring about their destination. Like Asher had been, the travellers were quickly taken in by the ranger's pleasant and cheerful demeanour.

For all of these exchanges, the assassin would keep to himself in the back of the wagon, his head down and eyes averted. Of course, there wasn't much to look at in the back of the wagon, save for the stinking Skalagat's head.

"Why have you not dumped the head?" Asher had asked upon their departure from the city. "You've received your coin."

"That I have," Geron had replied over his shoulder. "But the head still has its uses. You'll see."

The road cut through the forest, weaving gently north and south as it took them ever eastward, to the heart of The Evermoore. It was there, sprawled at the base of the forest's only mountain, that Lirian, the capital of Felgarn, came to life under a midday sun. As always, Asher's mind bypassed the aesthetics of the city and, instead, ran through the facts that applied to his survival.

He knew there were three roads in and out of the city: one to the north, that took travellers directly to Wood Vale, a second in the south, that passed through the city of Vangarth and out onto The Moonlit Plains, and the third, which he was currently travelling along. Lirian boasted no walls, the city and its people protected by the natural enclosure of the forest itself, though The Everhold - the palace and home of King Uthain - was fortified, its ramparts built out of the mountain stone.

Since the armies of Felgarn were situated some miles away, in a clearing that could manage their numbers, Lirian was well patrolled by the city watch, a collection of mostly retired, if fit, soldiers. They were capable fighters and more than efficient when confronted, but it was easier, and far less messy, to simply outrun them if it came to it.

Geron took in the city with a warm smile. "Beautiful, isn't it?"

Asher looked from the ranger to the city once more, tasking his eyes to try and see what Geron did. That was harder than it should have been. The assassin naturally scanned the people who lived on the outskirts, profiling them for threats or those he could take advantage of. He began counting windows and doors, alleyways that ran into dead ends, and buildings that would offer the fastest way to the roof.

The effort of seeing the city any other way was beginning to give him a headache. "It is," he lied, answering Geron's question. "Are you from here?" he asked.

The ranger barked a laugh. "Days and nights out in the wilds together and you finally ask a question about me. No, little man, I'm not from here."

Asher waited expectantly only to find silence for the first time since meeting the ranger.

Geron cast one eye back at him. "Now you know how that feels," he said with a snigger.

Offering naught but mystery, Geron guided Hector further into the bustling streets of Lirian. Here and there, folks gave the ranger a nod or a pleasant greeting, some even calling him by name. Though he didn't hail from Lirian, it seemed the big man had certainly made an impression on its people.

"Hmm! You smell that, Asher?"

The assassin winced at the sound of his own name being spoken so loudly. "I can only smell this rotting Skalagat," he complained gruffly.

"That's the smell of Mrs Fairden's bakery," he went on, his nose turned to the sky. "Best sweet meat pies in all of Illian! And the spiced cake!" Geron licked his lips. "We'll make time, don't worry. First things first..."

The ranger steered Hector to the east, navigating the constant stream of people that crossed the roads. Half way down Ruskin Street, they came to a stop outside a single-storey building that stood out for its lack of designation. Most of the roof shingles were in need of repair and every inch of the paintwork was chipped.

Climbing out of the wagon, Asher searched for any kind of sign to indicate the purpose of the building. There was nothing. It could easily have been a large house, detached on either side, the chimney expelling smoke like every other dwelling in the area. There were, however, a handful of horses hitched to posts outside the porch and a couple of wagons in the alley.

Geron patted Hector on the neck after binding him to a vacant post. "Good boy," the ranger praised, before clapping his hands together and turning to Asher. "Home!" he exclaimed. "Follow me."

Asher ascended the steps onto the porch, noting the numerous barrels and crates of supplies stacked on top of each other. The Ranch certainly seemed well-equipped. Geron walked right on in - no key or secret knock required.

"Anybody home?" the big man called.

Asher looked left and right, taking in the open plan flooring that made up the ground level. Its size reminded him of something similar to a tavern. The interior, he realised, was in a similar state of disrepair to the outside. Everywhere looked intact, capable of keeping out the cold and the rain, but not an inch of it had seen any care for many years. In the most spacious area, to Asher's right, rested a long table with a dozen chairs around it, the only things not covered in dust. And, mimicking the porch, crates and barrels of supplies lined the walls.

"That fifteen percent goes a long way," Asher remarked.

Geron looked from Asher to the supplies and back. "Aye, we make it work for us," he replied cheerfully. "Don't worry; you'll see the benefits before long."

"Is that you, Geron?" The question turned both men to the left, where a lithe and hooded figure was seated at a small round table, his feet propped up on another, while a slender pipe hung limply from his mouth.

Geron beamed at the man. "Do you have to ask?"

The glow from the end of the pipe brought some illumination to the shadows inside the man's green hood, revealing dark eyes and darker skin. "True enough," he said. "There are few who can fit in your boots." The stranger's head tilted to one side, his nose expelling a stream of smoke. "Bringing home strays again?"

"Where are my manners?" Geron chastised, stepping aside. "Asher, this is Artem Gorinson, a fellow ranger and the best damned archer Illian has to offer. Artem, this is Asher, soon to be a better ranger than yourself," he added with a mischievous grin of amusement.

If Artem saw any humour in the jest he failed to show it. Instead, he rose to his feet, his movements fluid and easy, and pulled back his hood. There wasn't a hair on his head, not even a hint of an eyebrow. The whites of his eyes were islands on a dark palette: eyes that scrutinised every inch of the assassin as he made a slow circle around him.

Asher was doing exactly the same thing.

He counted three identical small blades sheathed across Artem's chest, each a flat piece of steel that made for perfect throwing knives. This informed the assassin that Artem was a precision fighter, his skills requiring years of honing. Compounding that was the bow and quiver the ranger had left standing against the table. Here was a man who took down his opponents from a distance. Failing that, he clearly wasn't afraid to get into a sword fight. Resting on his hip was a one-handed scimitar, the type of sleek weapon seen in The Arid Lands - Artem's likely place of origin.

"Artem's got a good eye for folk like us," Geron said, trying to sound encouraging. "His measure of a man ain't never been wrong." He turned to the hairless ranger. "Well, Artem? What do you think?"

"*I think,*" he replied in a dialect known only to the people of Ameeraska, "*that he's bound for a monster's stomach.*"

Geron raised an eyebrow. "In the common tongue, if you don't mind."

Asher, on the other hand, had understood every word. It was tempting to respond in the same language and put Artem off balance, but that would be tipping his hand at a stage when he needed to collect more information about these people and where he was.

"I think you've got your work cut out," the archer said instead. "No one is killing a monster with so short a blade," he jibed, his dark eyes flitting down to the hourglass short-sword which Asher carried in his hand, his grip half way up the scabbard.

Geron laughed. "That's what I said! Killed himself a Skalagat though..." he told the ranger, his sentence falling away so that Artem might make up his own mind about that fact.

The slim ranger gave Asher one last look up and down. "He will have to do more than that to get his name on the charter."

Geron rolled his eyes. "Come along," he bade the assassin. "I'm afraid not everyone is as welcoming as me." He shot Artem a frown of disappointment as they left him to his seat and plate of cold meats.

Geron led the way, taking them through the door on the far left and down a set of narrow steps that required the big man to twist his shoulders in order to fit. Beneath The Ranch was an entirely different dwelling, a place where good coin had clearly been put to use. The stairwell opened up to a room half the size of the one above, the space dotted with armchairs and low tables. The wood and fixtures appeared new and the rugs that decorated the floor were clean. Seated in a wingback armchair, a red-headed woman was enjoying the heat coming from the hearth while sipping a cup of something hot.

"Kalantha," Geron called, ending their discussion. "Have you seen Vask?"

The female ranger eyed Asher before answering his question. "In his office last I saw."

"Much obliged," Geron replied, taking off down the only corridor that led from the room.

Asher ran his eyes over Kalantha, her position making it hard to assess anything of real worth. What he could see in her was the look of someone who had been pressed upon by the weight of the world and found a way to survive, however that might be. Kalantha's edges were hard and her eyes windows to a soul that had borne witness to nightmares.

He knew the feeling.

In tow behind Geron, Asher passed several doors suggesting the basement was more akin to a labyrinth and possibly even larger than the plot upstairs. The corridor made a sharp right but the big man came to a stop outside the door on their left, his hairy knuckles rapping against the smooth cherry wood.

"You in there, Boss?" he hollered through the door.

"There's no avoiding your nose, is there, Geron?" came the response.

The ranger took that as an invitation and opened the door. Natural light flooded the room from a narrow window set high into the back wall, where Lirian's foot traffic provided a constant flicker in the shadows. All else was illuminated by candles and a blazing fireplace behind a considerable desk, the detailing of the finest craftsmanship. It all added to the growing contrast between The Ranch's two floors.

Behind the desk, set to the task of pinning small pieces of parchment to the wall, was a man of hardened stock by the look of him. He kept himself in shape, something easily deduced as he wore a dark cotton shirt, unlike the tough leathers all the other rangers wore. A strong jawline was still visible through his white beard and his well-trimmed hair did nothing to hide the three claw-like scars that marred the right side of his face. He turned to look at Geron, but his focus was quickly taken by Asher's appearance. He assessed the assassin with eyes of both blue and green, though his blue eye was a shade darker than Asher's.

"What do we have here?" the boss asked, replacing a pile of notes on the desk so that he might give this newcomer his full attention.

"This is Asher," Geron introduced, gesturing at the assassin with his massive hand.

"Asher," the boss repeated, testing the name on his lips. "Is that it? Just *Asher*?"

"Just Asher," the assassin confirmed, sighting more scars on the boss's neck and one that disappeared beyond his hairline.

"Just Asher is *good*," the older man complimented, walking around the desk. "My name is Rolan Vask," he offered with a welcoming grin and an outstretched hand.

Asher hesitated with a glance at Geron. The big man, however, gave him an encouraging nod and he met Rolan's greeting by clasping the man's forearm.

"Well met," Rolan said, increasing his grin. "Won't you have a seat?" he suggested, nodding at the chair in front of his desk.

Asher didn't like sitting down with people he didn't know. Sitting was a compromising position to be in, limiting his responses. But he was still holding his short-sword, bow, and quiver, neither weapon taken from him. Adding to his security, Rolan was unarmed, his nearest weapon the sword resting horizontally on the wall beside him. Should he reach for it, Asher was confident he could get to him first and even kill him with the quill lying on the edge of the desk, saving him the time required to draw his short-sword. Geron was another matter.

Before Asher could begin to contemplate the level of threat posed by the big man, he caught Rolan's questioning look thrown Geron's way and he realised he had remained standing for too long. Without a word, he placed his weapons down on the floor and took the offered seat as Rolan took his own on the other side of the desk.

The so-named boss took a few extra seconds to size Asher up before sharing a silent exchange with Geron, who stood in the back corner where the assassin couldn't see him. "So Geron here's talked you into the life of a ranger, has he?"

"All he does is talk."

Both Rolan and Geron laughed at the statement. "That he does," Vask agreed. "What has he told you about what we do?"

"You kill monsters for coin," Asher replied.

"That we do. Our profession has been around since the time of old king Gal Tion himself. There's a thousand years of history where our business is concerned."

"I bet there's a thousand corpses too," Asher remarked dryly.

Rolan skipped over his next words to respond to the statement. "You're not wrong, Asher. There's not many who have retired to the peaceful life. But that's up to you to make your savings and know when the time is right to walk away. I'm not going to lie to you though: it's an addictive life. Most rangers keep at it, not realising that they're getting older and slower."

"And how long have you been in the ranger business?" Asher enquired, building his knowledge of the man before him.

"Since I was younger than you," Rolan answered cryptically. "But then I got old and slow," he said, pointing to the three lines of scars across his face. "I was lucky. After that, however, I decided a desk was better than a sword," he added, his finger flicking up towards the mounted weapon. "Now I run The Ranch," he explained with open arms.

"Vask turned this whole place around," Geron chipped in from the back. "The ranger business was dying before he—"

Rolan flexed his fingers from their place on the desk and silenced the big man with a polite smile. "I'm sure Asher's more interested in where we're going rather than where we've been. And trust me, Asher, we *are* going somewhere. Now is the time to get into this business. Every ranger who joins our charter is entitled to a share in the profits at the end of the year, including part-ownership of this very establishment. That aside, we're close to setting up another ranch in Velia."

"Expansion," Geron announced eagerly.

Rolan gestured at the big man. "Exactly. I've already legalised our business here in Felgarn with the local notaries at Baron and Sons. I intend to take the rangers to every kingdom, even Dragorn."

Asher doubted that latter of Vask's desires - the kingdom of Dragorn didn't even accept Graycoats on their island. He kept his opinion to himself along with any other reply for the moment. He had often found that silences put people off balance, right where he liked them. "That all sounds like quite the prospect. I just have to live long enough to see any of it."

Rolan briefly raised his hands from the desk. "You look like a survivor to me, Asher."

"If I might, Boss," Geron interjected. "I think Asher might be more interested in the job itself."

"Of course," Rolan said almost apologetically. "I get a little carried away with the possibilities. How, might I ask, did the two of you even meet? You must have done something to convince Geron here that you're up to the job. And it's not every day we get new recruits."

"I was in the right place at the right time," Asher told him, trying to take control of the narrative before Geron could butt in.

"Is that so?" Vask said after Asher failed to go on.

"It is."

The boss gave a half-hearted laugh. "You don't give much away, do you?"

"He killed a Skalagat!" Geron inevitably blurted.

Rolan's interest was immediately piqued. "A Skalagat? Or *the* Skalagat? The one *you* were contracted to slay, Geron."

"It... *might* have taken me a little by surprise," Geron confessed. "Asher heard the fight and jumped in without a care." The big man shrugged his mountainous shoulders. "He saved my life to be sure," he said seriously.

"Skalagat's are notoriously hard to put down," Rolan opined. "That's why *Geron* took the contract."

Asher's expression remained as hard as stone. "Like I said: right place, right time."

Rolan relaxed back in his chair, struggling, perhaps, to understand the mysterious man on the other side of his desk. "Do you have experience killing any other monsters?"

Asher thought of Jorgan, Lord Kalben, and the other Ironsworn thugs he had put into early graves. "A few, but none worth mentioning."

Rolan nodded along. Every now and again he would share a look with Geron. "What's your history?" he asked outright. "It must be interesting given your ability to slay Skalagats on a whim."

Asher saw how naive he had been now. He had never been questioned like this before - why would he have been? But of course they would want to know about his past career before giving him the job. Unfortunately, he didn't have an answer right away, himself the one put off balance.

Naturally, Geron stepped in. "He was an assassin," the ranger articulated, garnering a scornful look from Asher as he turned to spy the man over his shoulder. The ranger shrugged. "There's no point in hiding it here, fella. And there's certainly no judgement. Those be skills we can seriously—"

"Geron." Rolan's tone was enough to stop the ranger in his tracks. "Why don't we leave it to Asher to decide how much he would like to share?" Geron held up a hand by way of an apology and bowed his head, signalling his departure from the conversation.

Feeling uncomfortably exposed, Asher began to fidget in his chair. He was weighing up his options, be that to stay or simply walk out and disappear into the world.

"Though he spoke out of turn," Rolan continued, "Geron is right: there's no judgement here. Rangers have always come from all walks of life. Many have seen it as a second chance, a new start. Putting down monsters and saving lives is honourable. I truly believe it can redeem anyone."

Asher desperately wanted to share that belief, though he still felt that death would be his only release. "I was an assassin for a long time," he admitted. "I would like to... I would like to do some good. So where do I sign?" he asked, eager to be done with the formalities.

"Sign?"

Asher glanced at the parchments and books piled on the desk. "You said something about a charter."

"Oh, yes." Rolan directed Asher's attention to an open book displayed on a stand in the corner of the room. "I'm sure you have all the makings of a ranger," he praised. "And I'm sure you will fit in with the others," he added confidently. "But even arriving at my desk beside Geron doesn't put ink to paper. Every ranger must prove themselves in the field first. Complete a contract to the client's satisfaction and return here with the coin as proof. *Then*, you can sign the charter."

Asher couldn't count how many times he had proved himself over his lifetime. What was one more? "Where do I find contracts?"

"We have a system of couriers, far riders, who bring news to us from across all of Illian. Of course, the time between these nuggets of information can be lengthy. You'll find most jobs on the road, moving from town to town, city to city. Ask around, keep your ear to the ground. You'll soon learn what you need to be listening for. Though," he added with some thought behind his words, "I wonder if you would be better suited working alongside the Mendals."

Geron cleared his throat.

"Yes, Geron?"

The ranger licked his lips. "Though well-equipped to work with the Mendals, I think he might be better working with me. For a little while longer at least."

Rolan nodded in agreement. "Of course."

"Who are the Mendals?" Asher asked.

"The Mendal brothers," Rolan explained. "Born rangers. Though their approach is an acquired taste. You'll meet them in time," he assured. "For now you should simply learn the ropes and continue to accompany Geron here." Vask turned his full attention to the big man. "Take the night to rest, there are rooms available. Then see that Asher is ready for the road. And make sure you take him to see Bail." Rolan stood from his desk, a gesture in itself to inform them the meeting was at an end.

Asher picked up his weapons and found himself in Geron's shadow once more as he slapped him on the shoulder. "When was the last time you slept in a bed, little man?"

Asher couldn't rightly recall.

CHAPTER 17
GEAR UP

Basilisk - These are likely to be among my last words, certainly my last written words. I have recently returned to Lirian after taking a contract in Longdale.

It's a miracle of the gods that I made it back. I slew the Basilisk plaguing the outer villages, but not before it sank its fangs into my arm. There is no cure for their venom save for a touch of magic perhaps. A simple ranger, I possess no such talents.

I was able to make a small amount of Selvin paste (see Nature's Secrets, A Ranger's Companion, Page 88) with local resources. This helped with the pain and slowed down the deadly venom.

Now for what might help you. I found that luring the Basilisk was made all the easier using a blend of Gorsk oil and sheep fat. If you can also get your hands on a vial of Weet Green, add this to the bait. It will make the monster gag until it spills the contents of its stomach. This will be your moment to—

A Chronicle of Monsters: A Ranger's Bestiary, 12th Edition, Page 212.

Amaya Hawkyns, Ranger.

Geron's boulder of a fist hammered Asher's door, rousing him with a start. Before his eyes had even snapped open, the assassin's fist was closed around the slender dagger that usually rested at the base of his back. As always, he had slept with it.

Sat upright, his chest heaving, he scanned the room to find that the chair he had wedged against the door was still in place and the scattered old breadcrumbs lay undisturbed on the floor.

"Wakey, wakey, little man!" Geron bellowed through the door. "Lots to do before we hit the road again!"

Asher ran a hand through his hair, collecting the sweat as he did. Only seconds ago he had been in Palios, disguised as one of the scholars in the All-Tower. He blinked hard and relived the moment he murdered the Grand Scholiost, strangling the man with his own chain of letters, a ceremonial piece of jewellery given to all who held his title. He remembered the man's eyes bulging with fright before he died.

"Asher!" Geron called.

"I'm coming!" he snapped, pinching the bridge of his nose.

Meeting the ranger on the other side of the door, he had the Ironsworn coat in one hand and his weapons and quiver in the other. Geron was exactly as he had left him, attired in his leathers and green cloak, a claymore strapped to his back, and a broad grin on his round face.

"You can keep the gear," he instructed. "Leave the coat—you won't be needing it anymore."

Asher dumped the coat on the floor and fell in beside the ranger. They passed through the comfy seating area, now devoid of rangers, and ascended to the decrepit shell that most believed was the entirety of The Ranch. Artem Gorinson had moved on, though that didn't stop Asher from scanning the shadows twice.

"Through here," Geron directed, taking him through a set of double doors opposite the main entrance.

The room beyond was much smaller, its every inch of wall space occupied with rails and stalls of clothing and armour. Asher paused to finger the closest piece of armour, a leather vambrace that had been lined up with dozens of others. It felt old, the leather tough and curled with raggedy straps and half-rusted buckles. He wasn't impressed.

"I know it's not exactly the best," Geron said, picking up and throwing down one of the other vambraces, "but it's what we've got. There's a reason we don't live long," he added with a laugh.

Asher remained unimpressed. "This is where you get your armour from?" he asked, scrutinising the other tables and rails. "This has holes in it," he pointed out, poking his finger through a hole in a leather cuirass. "And blood..." The assassin removed his finger and looked back at Geron. "Did these all belong to previous rangers? Dead rangers?"

"Some, aye," Geron answered without hesitation or shame. "Other bits we've scavenged or traded for. We're not exactly a well-funded operation here."

Asher's brow furled into a tight frown. "That's not what I saw downstairs."

"The coin goes where the coin goes. That's all Vask's business. And, like he said, we're focusing on expansion right now." Geron clapped his hands together. "So, what do you fancy?"

"You mean what do I fancy dying in?" Asher quipped.

"I thought that was the plan." Geron's response teetered on the edge of being a question, a question that Asher didn't want to dwell on.

"This one, I suppose," the assassin finally said, handling one of the cuirasses on the rail. "It has the fewest holes in it." Noting the growing amusement on Geron's face was enough to give him pause.

The big man broke out in a thunderous laugh that turned his face red. "I'm just messing with you! These are just spares, you know, in case you need something before Bail can make it for you. You can put in orders over there," he said, gesturing to a dusty roll of parchment pinned to the wall, "and Bail will see to the replacements for you."

Asher understood the system, grim as it was, and found it hard to see himself stopping by to replace his boots with those of a dead man. Still, he knew from memory that he had worn worse.

The large ranger crossed the room with meaningful strides, leading Asher to a closed wardrobe and chest in the far corner. "*This* is what you need," he announced.

Asher stood back to give the ranger the room to open the wardrobe doors and lift the lid on the chest. The wardrobe housed three cloaks, all the same dark shade of green as the one on Geron's back. Beside them were two studded leather cuirasses and matching leather pauldrons of the same brown - none of which had any holes in them. On the other side was a single quilted gambeson to put on under the leathers, its length long enough to cover his thighs, though what protection it would offer against monsters remained to be seen.

The chest boasted four pairs of boots, all in different sizes, two pairs of leather vambraces with elements of steel laced into the design, a knot of belts, and variety of gloves.

Asher took one of the cloaks from the rail and shook the dust from it. He then noted that *everything* inside the wardrobe and chest needed dusting down.

"It's been a while since we've had any new recruits," Geron admitted. "But it's all in good order," he assured. "Of course, you could keep the leathers you've got."

The assassin hesitated - he had worn the black armour like a second skin for most of his life. "No," he said at last. "They have to go. Do you have somewhere I can burn them?"

Geron was taken aback. "You don't have to burn them. I'm sure we can find good use for them if you don't want to—"

"No," Asher cut in. "They need to be destroyed."

"Fair enough," Geron conceded. "We can have them destroyed if that's what you want." The big man nodded at the gear. "Get this lot on and I'll introduce you to Bail. You're going to like him. Well," he considered, "you'll like what he has for you. There's not many that can say they actually like Bail."

Asher brushed down the ranger gear before replacing the various parts. He felt Geron's eyes roam over the scars that formed horrific patterns across his back and over his ribs. They had all been wounds inflicted in the sight of others, preventing him from using the black gem to heal. That thought led him to the unusual relic, its absence weighing on him for the first time. He had never liked to entertain the idea, but he couldn't deny that he had relied on the gem, often aware that he could afford to throw himself into a dangerous situation and emerge whole again.

The gem had been life, or at least a tether to life. As far as he was concerned now, there wasn't much left of his life and, therefore, there was no need to miss the relic. Asher massaged his finger where the ring had been before fitting his vambraces and moving on.

After kitting himself out in brown leathers and even replacing his boots, Asher attached his quiver, bow and short-sword over his back. There was only one thing missing and Geron held it up in both hands, presenting him with the green cloak. While looking at the assassin like a proud father, the larger ranger helped him to latch it over his shoulders.

"It looks good on you," Geron complimented, brushing his hands over the cloak on Asher's shoulders. "You'll really look the part when it's all covered in blood, eh!" Asher nearly choked as Geron patted him on the back. "Oh! That reminds me." The ranger moved to the east wall and slid a door-sized panel to one side to reveal a small alcove. "You're going to need one of these."

Asher accepted the book, one of a few dozen that lined the shelves inside the alcove. He already recognised it as the Ranger's

Bestiary Geron had shown him on the road to Grey Stone, only it was in far better condition.

"This is the archives you spoke of?" Asher needed only a glance to take in the entirety of the book collection.

"Getting these scribed ain't cheap," Geron replied. "But, believe me, the words within are worth a fortune."

Asher hefted the book and gave the ranger a nod of thanks. In truth, he knew he would commit himself to the information therein, for there was nothing more important to an Arakesh than knowing your enemy.

Geron took the lead again and opened the door set into the far left corner. Sunlight streamed in and revealed the currents of dust that glided through the air. The light was accompanied by the sound of hammer on anvil and the hissing of fire and steam. Following Geron outside, into a small courtyard, the atmosphere was thick with the smell of sweat and smoke. The edges of the courtyard were under cover, an extension of The Ranch's roof, and it was there that a naked man worked a forge.

"Bail!" Geron called.

The smith turned from his labour, his front covered by a long black apron. He sighted both men on approach, though his expression was hidden behind a thick layer of ash and soot. What could not be hidden was his rippling muscles, his back akin to the open wolds of the Westlands. Asher guessed the smith to be half a head shorter than himself, almost a dwarf in Geron's eyes. What he might lack in height, however, he had certainly made up for in strength - evident in the graceful strokes of his hammer.

Walking under the shelter of the surrounding roof, Asher got a better look at the man. His greying hair was a knotted mess, suggesting he had tended to his work for some time in favour of bathing. And, though the ash and soot covered his face, the assassin estimated the smith's age to be somewhere between forty-five and fifty.

"What do you want?" Bail grumbled, his attention still fixed on the blade resting over his anvil.

Geron stood in the orange light of the forge and hooked his thumbs into his belt. "We've fresh steel for the forge!" he declared.

Bail glanced at Asher. "Doesn't look fresh to me," he remarked, before returning to his work.

Geron nudged Asher's elbow. "He likes you," he said with some disbelief, to which Asher could only respond with a quizzical expression.

"What do you want?" Bail repeated, a note of impatience added to his irritation this time.

"Asher's here to be a monster killer," Geron informed. "He needs something to kill monsters with."

Bail halted his hammering, looked at both men, and then looked at the numerous weapons that lined the courtyard. "Well what are you talking to me for?"

Geron folded his arms and gave the smith a judgemental look. "Come on now, Bail, new rangers don't walk through that door every day. Help a fella out - I'm trying to give him the full experience."

Bail sighed and a low grumble accompanied it from deep in his throat. He placed his hammer down with more care than would have been expected from a man of his disposition and walked out under the blue sky.

The smith beckoned them with a gesture and a contorted face, as if thinking caused him real pain. He scrutinised Asher in a variety of ways, his gaze regularly flitting to the weapons around them. He muttered under his breath while a dirty hand wiped more filth down his cheeks. Without obvious reason, he approached one of the stands that housed a row of swords and retrieved one of the blades, the muscles in his forearm coiling like pythons.

"Try this," he said, tossing the weapon to Asher.

The assassin caught it easily enough, though the weight and length were immediately cumbersome. He gripped it in two hands and hefted it from left to right, getting a feel for the balance. It still felt wrong.

"No," Bail uttered, shaking his head. "The longsword's not for you. You look likely to hurt yourself before any monster."

Asher refrained from rolling his eyes as he handed the longsword back. Bail returned it to the rack and continued his search for the ideal weapon. He picked up an axe resting against one of the pillars supporting the roof, his eyes darting between the weapon and Asher. At last, he shook his head and discarded the axe.

"You're a sword man," the smith said mostly to himself.

"He needs something with a bit of reach," Geron suggested, though Bail appeared less than pleased at the comment.

"Have you ever wielded a sabre?" Bail asked, flipping one over in his hand.

"Yes," Asher replied.

The smith looked back at him, considering, before shaking his head again and moving on. "How about a scimitar?"

"Yes," Asher said again.

Bail didn't even bother to pick the scimitar up, his finger merely touching the pommel. "Could you use a falchion?" The smith's tone betrayed some of his curiosity.

"I could and I have," Asher answered simply.

The smith stopped his search and met the assassin's blue eyes. "You've used a lot of swords it seems," he observed.

"When the moment called for it," Asher responded cryptically.

Bail ceased his search among the weapons and approached Asher instead. Without asking, he carefully took the assassin's arm in his hands and raised it for inspection, unaware that Asher's other hand had just grasped the hilt of the dagger at the base of his back. Strong fingers began probing his muscles, working their way down to his hand, where the smith turned his palm over.

"You can handle the weight," Bail stated. "You've got the posture of a dancer too," he pointed out, his head tilted to take in Asher's stance. "You haven't just used weapons - you've been *trained* to use weapons." The smith clicked his fingers and thrust one into the assassin's face. "You need something with balance. Yes... You're all about balance, aren't you?" He cupped his jaw and resumed his scan of the courtyard. "Something with reach. Something with balance. Something that straddles the line between elegance and blunt force."

Without another word, the smith took off, cutting a path between Asher and Geron. The light caught the sweat glistening on Bail's back before he disappeared under the shadow of the canopy. He began to rummage through a large chest on the floor and, when his hunt came to no avail, he moved on to sift through two racks of swords and axes.

"Where is it?" he questioned over and over again.

Geron chuckled to himself. "I love it when he does this."

"*This*," Bail began, returning from behind one of the pillars, "is *your* sword." The smith presented the weapon in both hands. "A broadsword of my own making. The blade is shorter than a longsword or a claymore, perfect for that balance you require."

Asher accepted the weapon and held it up in one hand, impressed with the weight, size, and balance.

"Tempered steel, of course," the smith explained, coming alive as he described his work. "Double edged. Simple cross-guard. I can't be doing with those fancy bits the high borns love so much. A two-handed grip, unusual for a broadsword I know, but you're going to need a two-handed swing, trust me. The leather strapping around the hilt is Basilisk hide - killed it myself some years ago." Bail gestured to the pommel. "Now for the brute force I mentioned."

Asher tilted the blade to better see the pommel, a ball of steel layered in small spikes. It should have been enough to put the entire weapon off-balance, yet Bail must have forged the blade and the pommel with each in mind for the overall design.

"It'll do," Asher affirmed, much to Geron's disappointment.

Bail grunted in agreement. "I like this one," he commented on his way back to the forge.

That returned a grin to the big man's face. "Told you," the ranger said with a wink and a nudge to Asher's arm.

"You'll need a scabbard," the smith called back, his thumb directing the assassin to a pile of scabbards by the far wall.

"I'm taking this!" Geron hollered at the smith as he hefted a spear from one of the racks. Bail didn't bother responding, his attention already captured by the blade on his anvil. "And burn this, would you?" the ranger added, tossing the sack of Asher's assassin gear across the courtyard floor.

After sizing up the right scabbard and strapping the new sword to his belt, Asher was ready to accompany Geron back inside The Ranch. Returning to the foyer, another ranger had taken up residence at Artem's table, though she possessed an exasperated look about her.

"Kalantha!" Geron greeted cheerfully.

Kalantha's response was not so cheerful, her focus devoted to the knife she was repeatedly stabbing between her fingers and thumb at the expense of the table. It was a task that required much practice and no shortage of patience. The scars on all of her fingers revealed something of her persistent nature.

"Allow me to introduce Asher," Geron continued as if Kalantha had replied to his greeting.

The ranger stood up with such force that her chair scraped back, the sound exaggerated by the large empty room. With one hand she placed a scroll on Geron's chest, her hand slapping against the hard leather.

"From Vask," Kalantha informed bluntly, her predatory eyes taking in Asher from head to toe.

"What's this then?" Geron asked, unrolling the parchment.

"A job," Kalantha told him, her gaze never wandering from the assassin. "A far rider's not long stopped by. There's a possible contract in Velia," she elaborated as Geron perused the parchment. "Something ate a butcher and two of his employees. Gruesome stuff if the details are true. I was going to investigate but the boss wants you to take the *pup*. See if he lives," she added, her smile as wicked as the look in her eyes.

Asher kept his distance from Kalantha while quietly assessing the ranger. With her scalp shaved on either side, only a strip of copper hair ran over her head into the ponytail that touched her neck. Thick tattoos decorated the shaved areas of her head, curling around the backs of her ears and down beneath her collar.

A pair of single-handed axes rested on her hips, the blade of each showing signs of regular battle. Asher's eye caught her hand gripping the head of one of those axes, though it wasn't her action that had focused him - it was another tattoo.

"You never seen one of these before?" Kalantha enquired with disbelief.

"I've seen them before," Asher replied evenly, seeing clearly now the black ring that had been tattooed around her wrist. He didn't need to look to know that an identical tattoo had been etched into her other wrist.

Kalantha touched her wrists together as if they were manacled and stepped closer to Asher. "Got them in The Peak," she began, naming the nightmarish dungeons used by the kingdom of The Ice Vales. "Ever passed through yourself?" the ranger asked.

Asher pulled down the leather strap of one vambrace to reveal no such tattoo. "Can't say I have," he replied, aware that the prison was built high into The Vengoran Mountains, above Grey Stone. "From what I've heard," he continued, "you're lucky to have ever got out."

Before she could reply, Geron patted the woman on the shoulder. "Our Kalantha is one tough nut! She served her time and found a better way to live. Ain't that right?"

Kalantha lowered her arms and let her sleeves conceal the markings of a prisoner. "That's right," she agreed, moving away from their small gathering. "Hanaghan wants the Skalagat head," she told Geron on her return to the table and chair.

The ranger placed an overly large hand over his round face and sighed. "I completely forgot. We're going to have to do that before we make for Velia."

Leaving Kalantha to her dangerous game, Asher assisted Geron in the grim task of heaving the rotting Skalagat head through The Ranch, downstairs, and round the corner, past Rolan Vask's office.

"He's not going to like this," Geron whispered, as he shouldered his way through the door.

Asher's curiosity had been mounting since the big man had told him the head still had its uses. "What in the hells are we doing with this thing, Geron?" he demanded, twisting the awkward head and horns to fit through the door.

"I can smell that thing from here," came a call from inside the room, "and I can tell you now it will be of no use to me!"

Asher searched for the origin of the voice but his focus was taken in every direction by the contents of the long room, its size comparable to the seating area round the corner. As considerable as it was, every inch of the space was well used, occupied by long tables, both high and low, covered in vials and jars, all filled with viscous fluids of varying colours. What the majority of these vials and jars housed couldn't be easily identified by the assassin.

The largest table that ran through the middle of the room also had an abundance of exotic equipment on it. Glass tubules, connected by long and winding pipes, were stacked next to bubbling cauldrons, each with its own hourglass pouring sand from one chamber to another. A set of brass scales caught Asher's eye when he noticed that they were comparing the weight of two different organs - though whether they were human organs or not remained to be seen.

"I hope there isn't a line of Skalagat innards from your cart to my door, Geron," that same voice berated.

"It's all good, Hanaghan!" Geron assured, coming to a stop in front of a white line painted across the floor. "Though I'll admit, it's a little on the old side." He motioned for Asher to drop his half of the head.

At last a small man appeared from behind a mountain of equipment - at least Asher assumed it was a man. Such a distinction was hard to make through the voluminous robes and an encompassing leather mask. Through tiny holes, a pair of dark eyes roamed over the Skalagat until they landed on Asher. Geron slowly put his arm out and directed the assassin to take a step back. The suggestion put Asher immediately on edge, sending his hand in search of steel.

"Hanaghan," Geron drawled, placing himself between the small man and Asher.

The masked man darted forward without a sound, his hands coming up to display ragged nails and dirty fingers. As the small man dashed towards them, a chain rattled throughout the room until it became taut, at which point Hanaghan was thrown face down inches in front of the white line Geron had refrained from crossing. Flat on the floor now, Asher could see the shackle around the small man's left ankle.

"What is this?" the assassin hissed, his hand firmly gripped around the hilt of his new sword.

"He didn't mean it," Geron reassured with his hands up.

"My apologies," Hanaghan muttered as he slowly picked himself up. "New faces," he added with a hint of shame.

Asher looked to Geron for a better explanation. "Hanaghan here isn't your typical fella," the ranger addressed.

Hanaghan dusted himself down and took a few steps back. "That's a very nice way to put it, Geron. Thank you."

"Is he a prisoner?" It felt the only logical conclusion to Asher, given the shackle and chain.

"Not exactly," Geron attempted before Hanaghan raised a bony hand.

"The moment has passed, Geron. I can speak for myself, thank you." The unusual man glanced at Asher through those tiny holes in his mask, but he quickly averted his gaze and busied himself with some instruments on the nearest table. "Please don't take it personally..."

"Asher," Geron informed happily.

"Asher," Hanaghan repeated. "I'm afraid that happens with every new face I see. I'm also sorry to say that it will likely happen again, when next we meet."

"Why is that?" Asher asked him directly.

"If you ask Bail, he will tell you my head was used as an anvil during my time in The Peak."

Asher turned his look of confusion on Geron, who replied, "Hanaghan and Kalantha were in The Peak together. In fact, Kalantha is the only one who can cross the line," he said, indicating the strip of white paint.

"You've met Kalantha," Hanaghan concluded. "She's a fiery one," he added, with obvious affection.

"*She* isn't the one chained up," Asher observed.

"Quite," Hanaghan agreed, his continued speech suggesting he was a learned man. "The things that were done to me in The Peak were done over a very long time, so long that I can hardly recall most of it. This is the only life I have ever known," he said, taking in the walls. "And down here I am a threat to no one. In fact, my work can *help*!"

Geron rapped his knuckles against the antlers protruding from the Skalagat's head. "Hanaghan here researches every monster we hunt down. His work adds to the archives."

Hanaghan stared at Geron for a moment. "Quite," he said at last, his voice curiously quiet. "Welcome to our little brotherhood, Asher. I hope you survive long enough for me to grow accustomed to your face. Do you know where you're going next?"

"Velia," Geron informed, tapping the rolled up parchment tucked into his belt.

Hanaghan nodded. "Ah... The Scudders. Should prove easy enough."

Geron paused, his mouth twisted into the shape of a possible word, yet he was unable to speak. He clutched the end of the parchment in his belt. "You've seen the message from Velia?" he enquired of the small man.

Hanaghan paused before catching up. "Indeed," he replied casually. "Rolan consulted with me on the potential monster in question. I thought Kalantha was taking the job."

"The boss wants *us* to look into it," Geron corrected.

"What are Scudders?" Asher asked, with suspicion creeping into his bones - though he couldn't say exactly why.

"Cousins to the Lech," Hanaghan explained from behind his leathery mask. "Mudslugs to you," he specified. "Except Scudders are the more aggressive of the species. It's all in the bestiary."

Geron clapped Asher on the back. "Looks like you've got some reading to do."

"Here," Hanaghan called, having moved on to rummage through a set of drawers. "Take this." He placed a thin vial of yellow fluid onto a tray and pushed it down towards Asher, his eyes always averted. "Drawn from the glands of a female Scudder," he explained. "The males will be attracted to it but, more importantly, another female Scudder will seek it out - they don't share territory well."

"Why do I want to lure the female?" Asher asked, holding the vial up to the torchlight.

His head bowed, Hanaghan answered, "If you're dealing with a nest, killing the female will be the only way to get on top of it. Otherwise, she'll just keep spawning more Scudders if the environment is right."

Geron raised a calming hand. "I don't think we're dealing with a nest. If the report is accurate it's just a few rogue Scudders. Speaking of which, we should get moving - Velia's not exactly around the corner. Be seeing you, Hanaghan."

"Good hunting," the small man called back, disappearing into his work once more.

By the time they loaded up the wagon, including Geron's new spear, and readied Hector for the journey, a light drizzle of rain had beset the forest kingdom. The big man turned his face to the sky and opened his mouth, a wide grin forming there.

"Every journey should start with rain," he insisted. "A sign of good luck from Lady Lethia," he decided, naming the goddess of fortune. "Are you riding up front with me?"

Asher considered the available space on the bench. "I think I would be more comfortable in the wagon. Or on my own horse," he muttered as he climbed in.

"Horses don't grow on trees," Geron grunted over his shoulder. "Get a few contracts under your belt and you can buy one."

Asher placed his new broadsword next to Geron's spear and rested his elbows on his knees. "Noted," he remarked.

Geron paused before guiding Hector down the road. "Contract or no contract, little man, you're wearing that green cloak now. That means you're a ranger. *That* means you're an assassin no more."

Asher gave a short sharp nod in response. He raised his hood to keep the rain out and bowed his head, his thoughts chewing over Geron's words.

CHAPTER 18
A TALE OF THE PAST

Scudder - Just because you've killed yourself a Lech or two, don't be thinking you can tackle a Scudder. These beasts are faster and far more aggressive than Mudslugs.

And when I say fast, I don't just mean in the water - they're equally fast out of it. And when I say they, I do mean they. These buggers do naught but eat and breed, increasing the size of their nest as they go.

Thankfully, they're prey to a number of other monsters who help to keep their numbers down, but should they encroach on civilisation, they need rooting out as soon as possible.

There's always a female at the heart of the nest and she's the one you want if you're to put a stop to the nightmare. She's no fiercer than the males, though she is somewhat larger.

Now, there's nothing special required to kill the wretches. You just need something sharp and a strong swing behind it. (Read on for known sources of natural bait).

A Chronicle of Monsters: A Ranger's Bestiary, 12th Edition, Page 73.

Handor Grain, Ranger.

The light drizzle that had started in Lirian had followed the rangers on their journey south, and then increased to heavy rain by the time they were turning east, towards The Shining Coast. After nearly two days of it, Asher was thankful to be looking upon Whistle Town, a place no one looked upon with thanks. Yet it provided an opportunity to have something other than a piece of fabric between him and the relentless rain. Perhaps, he dared to dream, even a wall to separate him from Geron's voice for just a night.

"What do you mean we aren't staying the night?" Asher questioned as Geron led them into The Green Hag, a tavern that had seen better days, much like the rest of the town that surrounded it.

"We've got limited coin until we make good on that contract," Geron replied as if the answer was obvious. "Who knows what we might need between now and then. We might even need to purchase supplies to help with the hunt. Sleeping in beds is costly, little man. The wilds will do us just fine." The ranger breathed in as he slid his girth into one side of a booth.

"Then why have we stopped here at all?" Asher demanded, pushing his soaked hood back as he took the bench opposite.

Geron beamed, glad, it seemed, to have been asked that particular question. "Because though the wilds of the world might provide us with ground to sleep on, it does not serve the best Golden Ale in all the realm." Catching the barmaid's eye, he raised two stocky fingers in the air before pointing at the table.

Asher noted the staircase at the other end of the tavern. "They likely have rooms, *cheap* rooms—"

"Of course they do," Geron chuckled. "And of course they're cheap - this is Whistle Town! But it changes nothing, little man. I want us over Barden Bridge before we get some shut eye."

Asher sighed when the two tankards of Golden Ale were placed on their table. Geron was quick to get his lips around the rim of the tankard and consume his first mouthful, all the while lifting one finger to keep the barmaid where she stood. The big man had a look of great satisfaction about him, leading to a repeat order of drinks and a hot meal.

Asher was loath to admit that he enjoyed the taste of the Golden Ale and so he continued to merely sip it while producing the bestiary. He searched for page seventy-three, as he had several times on their trip, and renewed his education on all things Scudder-related.

"You've had your head in that thing since we left Lirian," Geron commented. "I'm not complaining," he added with his hands in the air. "It's damn good that you're getting to grips with it all. You're just not making for much of an interesting travel companion. In fact, I'd go so far as to say I get more conversation out of Hector, and that bugger's scared of his own shadow."

Asher didn't much care for any of that. "Back in Lirian, you said it was likely just some rogue Scudders—"

"Because it probably is," Geron interjected, swigging another mouthful.

"According to this," Asher countered, swivelling the book side on, "that's very unlikely. This talks of a nest. There's always a female," he read aloud. "The males go out and bring back food for it."

Geron waved a hand through it all. "Can't a man be optimistic? Hmm? A few rogue Scudders is easily dealt with. If there's a nest..." He shrugged. "If there's a nest we're probably about three rangers too short. But that isn't the case," he reaffirmed. "It's just a few rogue Scudders who wandered too far from the nest. You'll see."

Asher closed the book and sat back, unconvinced and unsure how Geron could be so certain. Still, he had to accept the fact that he was the less experienced of the two, not a concept he was familiar with. Nasta Nal-Aket had pushed him to be the best at everything Nightfall put him through and he had never felt arrogant in considering himself one of the best, if not *the* best, Arakesh of his generation. It was an odd feeling to be on the bottom rung again.

The tavern door opened and the sound of rain filled the room. Asher, as ever, was discreet in his observations, though he needed no more than a second to register the fact that two Graycoats had just entered The Green Hag. As was his habit, the assassin immediately broke the pair down into a list of knowns and unknowns.

The shorter of the two was a young woman, her strong jaw line suggesting she was possibly from the north. Her coat was relatively new, unblemished by the rough lifestyle of their order, indicating that she was either still in training or recently bestowed with the title of Graycoat. Asher was instantly confident that he could kill her in three moves or less.

The taller of the two was growing a little old in the fang, his beard and ponytail traced with grey hair. Crow's feet ringed his eyes and a crooked nose told of a lifetime of having it broken, reset, and then broken again. Like all those of his order, however, he was still in good shape, his strength displayed in his walk alone. Five moves, Asher decided. Perhaps six.

"Are you still with me, little man?"

Geron's question broke the spell of Asher's conditioning and summoned his conscious mind to the present. He blinked hard, turning his face towards the inner booth as he did so. *Will I ever stop thinking like an assassin?* he wondered. He was a ranger now. That meant very little, however, when the deeds of his new life were put side by side with those of his previous life.

"Are you ever going to stop calling me that?" he asked as he leaned his head against one hand, concealing his face from the rest of the tavern.

"I don't know," Geron mused. "Are you planning on getting any bigger?"

"There's no correlation between size and skill," Asher quipped, much to Geron's amusement.

"That's what all little men say," the big man countered with an obnoxiously loud bout of laughter, attracting more attention than Asher would have liked, though he did enjoy their moment of camaraderie. He buried that thought when he realised the Graycoats were among those who had turned to look at them. "If we're to make it beyond Barden Bridge before nightfall then we should be off," he suggested.

Geron scowled. "First you want to stay. Now you want to go. Which is it?"

Asher was about to insist they leave immediately when the barmaid placed two steaming meals down on their table. There would be no moving the big man now.

Another hour went by before they finally returned to Hector and the cart, and another two hours before Barden Bridge and Whistle Town were put behind them. The entire time they were inside The Green Hag, Asher had been convinced that it could only end in violence, as it so often did with the knights of West Fellion. The whole affair had, ultimately, been rather normal - another concept he wasn't familiar with.

Using a rare break in the rain, the two rangers took the opportunity to set up camp under the shelter of an ancient oak tree. Long after the fire had been lit and Geron's constant chatter had died down to singing and then humming, Asher found himself with a question for his companion, though its personal nature kept his mouth shut for some time beyond the birth of his curiosity.

"You don't say much," Geron remarked. "But you've got a look about you now that suggests you've got something to say. Spill it, *Ranger*."

Asher disliked being read, and so accurately at that, but he shrugged it off and asked his question. "How did you get into this life?"

Geron stared at him for a brief moment before his laughter broke the tension. "How much time have we spent together, side by side? You've asked me what? One question perhaps? Is that wall starting to come down between us?"

"Forget I said anything," Asher was quick to retort, happy to busy himself with cleaning the cogs of his bow.

"You say so few words it's hard to forget any of them," Geron jested. "And it's a perfectly good question. Just a little late I'd say."

"You don't have to tell me anything," Asher said without looking at the man.

"But you want to know and I want to tell you," Geron reassured. "Though, I must warn you, mine is not an easy tale to hear."

Asher was confident there were worse things in just one of his nightmares than whatever Geron was about to confide, but he didn't say as much. Instead, he put his bow down and turned his attention on the big man, content to listen to the hardships of another for a change.

"Before this life," the large ranger began, "I was a bounty hunter, and a damn good one. My father didn't approve, of course; he wanted me to plough the fields, as he had done, for the rest of my life. But look at me! Do you think a farm could contain me? I needed the world. The life of a bounty hunter suited me, rewarded me even. I found a good wife, Lavinia." He said her name wistfully and with a warm smile. "We bought a good home in Longdale and... well, the gods never blessed us with children. But Lavinia and I were happy. Then, one day, a new bounty comes my way - a *big* one. The kingdoms of both Alborn and Felgarn wanted a man named Kradamir Damakas."

The name meant nothing to Asher. "Who was he?"

"A slaver," Geron said with clear disdain, "and a wicked one at that, which is saying something for his ilk. As you know, slavery down in the south is a way of life: they exchange people down there like coins. But Kradamir specialised in procuring slaves from *outside* The Arid Lands. He would come to the northern kingdoms and take all manner of folk, snatching them from their lives and selling them to the lords of the desert - to those who fancied a more exotic slave."

"Sounds like a piece of work," Asher opined. "You took the bounty then?"

"Aye. I thought he was scum, and I enjoyed hunting down scum. The bounty was mighty big too. So large, in fact, that it would change our lives. So I accepted the job, kissed Lavinia goodbye for what I knew would be some time, and made Kradamir Damakas my life." Geron tapped his leg, his thoughts navigating a memory he clearly found hard to put into words.

"I started in Karath," he continued. "I figured the capital would have the largest slave trade. I picked up a few leads, ended up in Ameeraska, knocked a few heads together - that led me to Calmardra - and then I got my first glimpse of him. He had a number of men on his payroll so he was rarely alone. I watched how he operated for weeks, even followed him across the desert, back to Tregaran - which is where he was based as it turned out."

"That must have taken some time," Asher surmised.

"Months, near on a year in fact." Geron was shaking his head at the thought of it. "But there was no way I could get to him. He was a cautious man and always surrounded by thugs." The ranger leaned forward. "Until he came north that is. To avoid suspicion in places like Velia and Lirian, he would only be accompanied by two lieutenants. I tracked him across The Moonlit Plains, all the way to Vangarth." He sighed. "That's where things got messy. I bungled the grab, killed one of his men, and was left half dead in the gutter, lucky to be alive at all. But three poor souls were still put in Kradamir's cart and condemned to slavery."

Geron paused, perhaps considering whether he really wanted to go on with his tale.

"It all got very personal after that," he said, at last. "I eventually recovered and renewed my hunt, but this time I had some fury in my veins. Upon my return to Tregaran, I started to set Kradamir's life on fire. It became a crusade of sorts. I spent over a year in those hot lands, my every waking moment devoted to making Kradamir's life a miserable hell. I freed slaves, gutted his men - I couldn't even guess at the number of men I left in my wake - and worst of all, I cut *deep* into his pockets. He was losing coin with my every breath." Geron laughed softly to himself. "There were entire months where I forgot about the bounty. The reward was to simply leave him naked in the streets with nothing but the skin on his back."

"What happened?" Asher pressed, genuinely curious.

"Exactly that, in time. He got into debt trying to keep me off his back and he was already dealing with some serious debt. Then there were the various high borns of The Arid Lands who held grudges against him - I'm talking about the worst humanity has to offer," he added gravely, "and they never forget. But his little empire had kept him safe for years. Once it all started to come down, he was prey to them all. As it turned out though, without a single coin to his name and nowhere to call his own, the slippery bugger disappeared on the streets - another faceless beggar."

Asher knew from experience how easy it was to disappear in plain view when you could blend in with the filth of the streets. "So what did you do?" he asked.

"The only thing I could do," Geron replied. "I went home, to Lavinia. She had every right to be less than impressed with my return, empty handed as I was. But, gods bless her, she was just happy to have me back." The big man sat in that moment for a while, his memory transporting him back to another life.

"But that's not how it ended," Asher assumed, his voice low.

"No," Geron uttered. "That is not the end of my tale. I never forgot about Kradamir. I just thought he was a world away. I never thought... I never thought he would come looking for me. But, of course, he wasn't the same man I had been tasked with hunting down. No. After I was done with him, Kradamir was a broken and desperate man. And I mean desperate. He had nothing, Asher. *Nothing.* He had been living like a rat, scurrying from town to town, city to city, surviving on scraps and sleeping in the dirt. He was fuelled by revenge."

"He found you in Longdale?" Asher pictured the positions of both Longdale and Tregaran in his mind and knew that almost all of Illian's length lay between the two.

"Aye... but not before he found Lavinia." Geron's hand squeezed the leather straps around his claymore's grip. "I was out hunting in the woods. I've no idea how long he had been watching us for, waiting."

Asher could see the strain put upon Geron by his recounting. "You don't have to say any more," he told him.

The big man nodded his head in thanks. "I'm alright," he reassured. "By the time I returned to our home, Kradamir had spent the day in my house. Lavinia... Lavinia was dead, though he did not grant her a quick death. In my sorrow, the wretch attacked me from the shadows." Geron tilted his head to show Asher a scar that cut up through his jaw line and across part of his cheek, most of which was hidden beneath his beard. "We fought like men with nothing to lose," he said, his eyes glazing over, taken by the flames of their fire. "I killed him with my bare hands."

Asher had never cared for the misery of other men and so, when the emotion struck him, it was all the more profound. "I'm sorry, Geron," he offered, unsure what else to say.

"She was pregnant," Geron announced with hardly a breath in his lungs. "I didn't know... until after."

Asher didn't know what to say, his training useless. He felt the impact on his emotions but he didn't know how to translate them into words, especially meaningful words that would be an appropriate response. So he remained silent.

"No laws were brought against me," Geron continued, "but I couldn't stay there. A copious amount of drink and violence followed after that. I ended up in the cells in Galosha at one point. To this day I'm not even sure what I did. Before I knew it, I was living that same desperate life that Kradamir had known in the end. I had nothing but my grief for company. Then he found me - Rolan Vask. He turned me around, gave me a second chance at life. It wasn't a quick process but here I am." The smile on his face didn't quite reach his eyes.

A heavy silence sat between them for a while, the only sound the crackling of the fire and Hector's sleeping breath. Asher was tempted to share something of his own past, something other than the curated truth he had told Geron so far. But what could he say? And where would he even start? The practices of Nightfall were foreign to all but those who had passed through and emerged as Arakesh.

"I'm going to get some shut eye," Geron declared, breaking the silence. "I suggest you do the same."

Asher laid out his roll and lay down to face the fire, the light enough to keep the Nightseye elixir in his blood from enhancing his senses. Geron's tale played through his mind once or twice before sleep finally claimed him. Then the real nightmares began.

CHAPTER 19
ON THE JOB

Werewolf - *'Tis a curse, simply put. How this began is up for much debate, though talking about it makes little difference. Werewolves are real and they are among us.*

Contracts concerning these beasts should be left to the most experienced of our kind. I don't just say that because these beasts are seven feet tall with claws as long as your fingers. I urge the young among our ranks to leave these contracts because a wise ranger knows you don't hunt the wolf. You hunt the poor soul who received the cursed bite. They're stronger than the average person but they're weaker in their human form. Still, it's going to feel like killing a person. A deed like that will weigh on a good man.

Oh, and don't stock up on silver, it's a myth most likely started by a werewolf. You can kill it the same way you kill anything - with a good swing of steel.

A Chronicle of Monsters: A Ranger's Bestiary, 12th Edition,
Page 49.

Arnathor (the old hunter), Ranger.

. . .

Velia, the capital of Alborn and the crowning jewel of The Shining Coast, stood tall on Illian's eastern shore. Its grey walls curved amid flat plains, rising high to protect the city. Higher still were the four kings of old, their towering statues built out from the walls to loom over the land: silent watchers from the past.

Asher couldn't name any one of the kings, nor could he name the reason they had been chosen by the people to be so immortalised. Yet, though he cared little for name or reason, he stood in the middle of the road and stared up at them.

The lower town, a village of sorts, that sprawled across The Selk Road outside Velia's walls, was busy with activity, including the constant traffic of merchants in and out of the city. There were people everywhere, creating an environment that should have set Asher on edge. Instead, he remained rooted to the spot, his neck craned, and his eyes locked on those ancient kings.

"First time in Velia?" Geron asked, pulling Hector by the reins to stand beside him.

"No," Asher replied absently. "I've been here many times. I've just never stopped to look up."

"Grand old boys, aren't they?" The big man joined him in his observation. "They cast long shadows. A little judgey for my liking," he opined. "Let's leave them to their business, I say. We have business of our own to conduct!" he added, dropping a heavy hand on Asher's shoulder.

The former assassin picked up his feet and accompanied Geron down the road, the view now entirely lost behind the surrounding lower town. There was only the enormous archway before them, the thick doors open and the portcullis retracted to allow ease of movement in and out of the city. Velian soldiers stood guard on the ramparts above, while a few milled around the inner courtyard.

Passing through, Asher scanned a table of four soldiers playing a game of Galant, not one taking any notice of those who moved through the city.

Then they were inside, back to back with one of the towering kings, and confronted by one of the largest and most densely populated cities in all of Illian. The elven presence in the city had been absent for a millennium, leaving little of their culture still to be seen. Velia now stood as a spectacle of what humanity could achieve: a great feat Asher thought, given that every human had been an Outlander living in The Wild Moores only a thousand years past.

Geron tapped the edges of the rolled-up scroll tucked into his belt. "The butcher's shop is in the Garden Quarter," he said, nodding at the street to their left.

Walking through the city, Asher couldn't help but see the handholds and uneven brickwork where he knew he could scale the buildings. His instincts were always calling him to the heights of the world, places where he could look down from safety and assess the environment. He was simultaneously laying out the city in his mind, seeing the streets and alleys that connected and led to new areas and districts. He knew where all the shadows were and how to move unseen.

Yet here he was, brazenly walking up Sailor's Way under a clear blue sky and blazing sun. They entered the Garden Quarter, an ironic name given the lack of gardens, and continued to navigate the branching streets until they reached the butcher's in question. It was easily spotted since a single board had been nailed into the door frame, barring entry. Added to that, the door itself had a red X painted over it, put there by the city watch no doubt.

Geron tied Hector up to a nearby post and retrieved the claymore from the wagon. "What do you reckon?" he asked, strapping the sword to his hip.

Asher raised an eyebrow before looking back at the butcher's shop. "What is there to reckon? It's boarded up. Not much to see from out here."

"That, my friend, is rarely the case." Geron looked beyond Asher, directing him to a tanner's shop further up the street.

Asher frowned in disbelief - how could he have missed it? "The tanner's is boarded up too," he said, seeing the same red X painted over the door.

"Aye," Geron replied with a sigh. "It seems the Scudders have been busy," he added while rubbing his hands together.

"This pleases you?"

"Of course not," Geron quickly retorted. "But it does mean that local authorities have failed to get the situation under control. That gives us more bargaining power."

Something about the whole affair struck Asher as wrong, though he couldn't articulate it yet, his own sense of morality a largely grey area. And so he nodded his head in agreement - more bodies would drive up the price of their skills, something any professional would want. Perhaps, the ranger thought, there should have been more consideration for the people those extra bodies had once been.

Then again, there was little that could have been done for them. It took time to traverse the realm and monsters were always going to do what monsters do. Their concern should now lie with potential future victims.

"Asher." Geron said his name as if it wasn't the first time. "Get your head in the game, little man. We're on the hunt now."

The ranger nodded both his understanding and apology. His growing conscience, it seemed, was becoming something of a distraction, shattering the intense focus he had honed over his lifetime.

"Are we going inside?" he enquired.

"That would be against the law and land us in the cells," Geron told him as if it was obvious. "First, we have to actually get the job. In order to do that, we have to talk to the people who are willing to pay and can also afford us. In this case, that would have to be the city watch as the butcher is already dead. The same can likely be said of the tanner. Come along," he bade.

Arriving at the local chapter house for the Garden Quarter's city watch, Geron walked right on inside as if he belonged there. Asher followed him inside, confident that no one knew his appearance. In fact, the last target he had killed in Velia was three years past and he had ensured it looked like a suicide, eliminating any suspicion that could have clung to the new stable hand with a black fang tattoo under his left eye.

Six members of the city watch were inside, mostly crowded around their captain's desk, their attention fixed on a large piece of parchment that had been weighed down at the corners. Of course, Geron's size stole the attention of any in his vicinity.

"Well met, fellas!" the big man began with his usual grin. "We hear you've got yourself a monster problem."

"And who in the hells are you two?" one of the watchmen demanded, folding his arms across his iron cuirass.

"Easy, Kail," the captain said from the other side of the desk. He made his way around the men to face the rangers, his experienced eyes taking them in from head to toe. "We aren't saying things like *monster*. Such things do not plague us inside the walls."

"That's not what we've heard," Geron responded as he scratched his beard.

"And who are you exactly?" the captain asked more diplomatically.

"Geron Thorbear," he declared, thumbing his broad chest. "This here is Asher. We're *rangers*."

A touch of revelation flashed across the captain's old eyes. "Monster hunters," he translated. "Well, my name is Captain Palan. The Garden Quarter is my district."

Geron took a big breath, increasing his size momentarily. "I'm sorry to tell you, Captain, but your district has a monster infestation. We had already heard of the incident at the butcher's shop, but I see your tanner has been hit too."

"And what have you heard, Mr Thorbear?" Captain Palan asked.

"The butcher and two of his staff are dead. I believe the word *eaten* was in the report."

"A rumour," the captain countered. "No such report came from my chapter house. They could easily have been killed by a person."

Geron looked down at the man and tilted his head. "I'm willing to bet that whatever horrors you found in the butcher's are exactly the same as you found in the tanner's."

"Sadly, you are correct, though that doesn't mean monsters are responsible, Mr Thorbear. We could be dealing with a mad man."

"True enough," Geron conceded. "Let us take a look at the bodies and we can give you a definitive answer. It's what we do."

"And what fee accompanies such consultation?" Captain Palan asked suspiciously.

Geron held his hands up. "No fee. But if you agree we're dealing with monsters, the city will pay us the required fee to deal with them." The big man held out his hand, waiting for the offer to be accepted.

The captain narrowed his eyes, his mouth twisting out of shape while he considered the deal. "Kail. Run ahead and make sure that last body hasn't been destroyed." After giving his man the instruction, Palan clasped Geron's forearm. "Your services will be rewarded should they be required."

Geron gave a simple nod. "What's this about bodies being destroyed?"

"Come with us," the captain ordered, making for the door.

Asher remained quiet for their short journey through the quarter. He listened to the captain's explanation concerning the bodies of the victims - all to be burned before burial.

"Is that normal practice?" Geron asked as they arrived at the waiting hall, a place for the dead before burial rites could be arranged.

"No," Palan replied, if somewhat begrudgingly.

"Then why burn them first?" he pressed.

The captain's eyes shifted to one side, meeting Geron's knowing smile, though he declined to answer the question. To Asher, the answer seemed obvious - they had suspected monsters and decided to destroy the bodies before burial.

"Why won't they face the truth?" Asher enquired in a whisper.

Geron leaned down. "Rumours of monsters can cause a panic. Never a good thing in a city this crowded. Also," he remarked with some amusement, "it makes the lot of them look a little incompetent, what with all these high walls they live behind."

The waiting hall was dank and gloomy, a place well suited to the dead. There were no windows in the main chamber, a large room that arched from one side to the other. The torches on the wall and candles in the alcoves flickered when the door opened and some of the outside world got in. Kail was already inside, standing beside one of the three bodies that lay in waiting.

"Scheduled to be burned this afternoon, Captain," he reported.

"There's no reason for that to change," Palan replied, coming to a stop at the bottom of the stone slab. "Begin your investigation, Rangers."

Geron motioned for Asher to go round to the other side of the body as he pulled back the heavy sheet. There was nothing about a dead body that either shocked or frightened Asher, though he was unaccustomed to being around a body that had been dead for so long. This particular body was that of a man, his features severely bloated beyond what his skin had been used to in life. And the skin itself was discoloured and waxy having turned to an off yellow on the front and a deep purple on the back, where the blood had settled after death.

Then there was the smell.

Asher had succeeded in maintaining his stony expression upon entering the chamber, but the already pungent odour was intensified now that the sheet had been pulled back. He tilted his head, as if angling his nose away would make any difference.

"Who was this?" Geron asked, scrutinising the edges of several lacerations that had been carved into the corpse's limbs before he died.

"The tanner," Captain Palan informed. "His wife met the same end."

"And what an end it must have been," Geron muttered under his breath. "What do you make of it?" His question was directed at Asher.

The ranger glanced at the numerous watchmen crowded around the captain before turning his full attention to the body. "The cause of death seems clear," he began, gesturing to the bloody gash in the man's abdomen. "Though gut wounds are typically slow and painful deaths. People who die from this type of wound are commonly left with an expression of agony, but this man looks to have died in a state of shock, suggesting his death was quick."

"Very good," Geron praised, his tone genuine. "What else?"

Asher pulled the sheet back a little further and discovered mangled stumps where the hands should have been. There were also deep cuts to his forearms and evidence of broken bones.

"He saw his killer coming and raised his hands to defend himself," Asher continued. "He lost his hands in the process." The ranger crouched down to better see the wounds. "The skin is jagged, torn. A blade didn't do this. The same can be said of the wounds up his arms."

"I agree," Geron said. "His hands were chewed off." That statement alone turned some of the watchmen pale. "What's been ruled as the cause of death? For all of them?"

Captain Palan licked his lips, his discomfort mounting. "Blood loss. It was decided that the killer - or killers - cut the victims open and let them bleed to death."

Geron nodded along, his mouth pursed. "And was there a lot of blood on the floor?"

"There was blood everywhere," Kail interjected.

"Aye," Geron agreed. "I bet it was splattered up the walls and what not. But was it pooling on the floor? The human body holds a lot of blood. I would have expected the body to be caked in it."

Palan swallowed. "Not particularly."

Geron nodded knowingly. "Asher," he said suddenly. "Stick your hand inside the body, tell me your findings." Asher looked as hesitant as the captain looked shocked. "Go on now," the big man encouraged. "He's dead, he's not going to bite."

Asher cleared his throat and repeatedly clenched his hand before lining it up with the gruesome abdominal wound. Then, trying to give the deed as little thought as possible, he plunged his hand in and began a more tactile investigation. One of the watchmen excused himself and jogged out of the chamber while a couple of the others had to turn away.

"Is this necessary?" Captain Palan demanded. "This was a good man."

Geron held his arms out. "And doesn't a good man deserve to have his killer found and brought to justice?"

"That's exactly what me and my men are doing."

"You're burying your heads in the sand," Geron argued. "You know this isn't the work of a man."

"There's no organs," Asher announced, ending the argument before it could go any further.

The captain scowled at him. "What? No organs?"

Asher removed his hand and flicked some of the gore off. "Not a one. The heart, liver, kidneys - all of them. They're all missing."

"They're not missing," Geron corrected. "They're currently inside the gut of a *Scudder*."

Captain Palan took a calming breath and straightened his back. "And what is a Scudder?"

The big man shrugged. "I suppose you'd classify it as... a *monster*." A smile crept over Geron's face as he enunciated the last word.

Palan folded his arms and tapped his finger incessantly. "You are certain?" he finally asked.

Geron opened the flap on his satchel and retrieved A Chronicle of Monsters: A Ranger's Bestiary. He turned to the page pertaining to Scudders and swivelled the book for the captain's benefit, displaying the information. Beside the section that specified a Scudder's appetite for internal organs, there was also a drawing of a dead body that looked very similar to the tanner's.

"Like I said: this is what we do."

The captain rubbed his eyes before pinching the bridge of his nose. "What would you need to take care of this?"

"We've got all the supplies we need," Geron assured. "What we don't have is the coin."

Captain Palan took a moment to consider the position he was in. He held up a finger to silence the quiet, if persistent, advice of his men, taking only his own counsel on the matter.

"I hate to press you, Captain," Geron stressed, "but Scudders like to eat often. Your next victim could show up this very day..."

Palan raised his chin. "How much?"

The large ranger didn't miss a beat. "Three thousand," he stated.

The captain's expression cracked in amusement. "How preposterous!" he exclaimed. "My men and I don't make three thousand between us for a month's work."

"And yet three thousand is the price," Geron insisted.

"You're serious?"

"Given the company we're in," Geron replied, his head tilting down to the tanner's body, "I wouldn't like to jest."

A deal of irritation and discomfort came over Captain Palan. "That's extortionate. People are dying, man. If you have the skills to help them then you are obligated to do so. For a *reasonable* price I might add."

"I'm *obligated* to value our skills," Geron told him. "We might very well die trying to rid your city of Scudders. Who knows how many we're dealing with? I know it's more than one. If you can't pay our price you're welcome to hunt them down yourself. How was that going by the way?"

Palan was taken aback by the insult, though he had no response that spoke in their favour for the tanner and his wife were testament to their failure. "I do not have the authority to sign off on that amount," he said with tight lips.

"Fair enough. I suggest you go and find whoever does have the authority and come back to me with something I can put ink to. Once we're squared away, we'll hunt and kill your Scudder infestation."

Captain Palan shot the rangers a severe look before spinning on the spot and storming away, his entourage close on his heels. Asher didn't bother to watch them leave, more concerned with the gore clinging to his hand.

"That was a nice piece of theatrics," Asher remarked, washing his hand in a nearby bowl of water.

"Theatrics?"

Asher looked from the abdominal wound to Geron. "You already knew it was Scudders - Hanaghan told us as much. What did it say in the report?"

Geron frowned. "The report?"

Asher gestured at the scroll poking out of his companion's belt. "The one brought by the far rider."

"Oh." Geron patted the parchment. "It was the death wound," he said, wagging his finger over the bloody gash. "Scudders love them some organs - they always go for the gut. Don't worry, little man, such details will stand out to you soon enough. Though you do need to practise your own *theatrics*," he advised. "Most city folk don't grasp the need for us and our skills. We need to remind them. Also, it always helps to drive up the price."

The morning soon disappeared and midday was upon Velia by the time Captain Palan returned with a contract that met their terms. Geron and Asher signed it before accepting half of the coin as a deposit, some of which would secure them somewhere to sleep the night... should they survive till then.

The details behind them, the rangers were escorted back to the butcher's shop and granted access. The smell of death struck them as physically as any solid object. The meats had been left to spoil and no effort had been made to clear up the blood and gore that marred the walls, floor, and even the ceiling.

Asher wafted the flies out of his face and stepped over three severed fingers to walk past the counter. Judging by the blood splatter that ran up the wall, the ranger guessed one of the victims to have been standing behind the counter when the Scudder fell upon them. And, just as Geron had pointed out, there was not enough blood on the floor to support a simple stabbing.

"There's nothing by the door," Asher commented, looking back at the way they had entered.

"No," Geron agreed with a light chuckle. "Scudders aren't known for using doors. Let's keep looking."

They ventured into the back, where customers weren't permitted. There was only a store room and a kitchen to inspect, but both were decorated with blood. Geron entered the kitchen first and crouched down to examine a butcher's knife.

"Which body was in here?" he asked aloud.

"One of the assistants," Kail replied gruffly.

"Well they succeeded in stabbing the beast," Geron explained, picking the knife up between two fingers. "See the slime?" He pointed to the thick goop mixed with the blood around the top of the handle. "Scudders are coated in the stuff."

Asher turned his attention to the floor and followed the thick trail of blood that wormed round the corner and into the shop front. "It was definitely bleeding," he remarked.

"The second one wasn't," Geron said, pointing to a set of red dots that traversed the room.

"Second one?" Kail questioned.

"Aye. The second one was a little late to the party and walked through the blood of its friend. See all the dots. Scudders have fifty little pincer-like feet. Quite sharp if I do say so."

Asher left the kitchen, his eyes still on the blood trail that had created a chaotic pattern from one room to another. The blood loss from the monster suggested it had been stabbed in the kitchen, moved to the shop front, and then returned to the store room. Walking inside, the smeared blood streaked across the floor and disappeared where a square hatch interrupted the stone slabs. There were also two bloody hand prints on the floor.

"Geron," he called.

The big man came in behind him, quickly coming to the same conclusion. "What's down there?"

"Another store room," Kail answered. "That's where we found the other assistant."

Geron turned to Asher. "After you," he insisted with a bemused grin.

The ranger crouched down and lifted the hatch door by the brass ring. More death awaited them in the dark if the foul odour was anything to go by.

"I need a torch," Asher stated.

By the time Asher climbed down the ladder, Kail had supplied a large candle, the best he could find in such little time. It was no torch, but the single flame illuminated the cold storeroom, revealing three pig carcasses hanging from meat hooks and a stack of crates, all of which were covered in flies and maggots.

Geron descended next, his bulk filling out the room to complement the shadows. "I reckon this is where they entered," he said.

Asher held the candle low and followed the gutter that ran down the middle of the room. "Over here," he directed, the light banishing the darkness that enveloped the arched grate bolted to the wall. "Two of the bars are bent," he observed.

Geron crouched down to investigate. "Scudders aren't strong enough to bend iron. The bars must have been damaged some time ago. Still, they're opportunistic little buggers. Where does this go?"

Kail, who remained halfway up the ladder, replied, "The catacombs most likely. There's a few streams that run under the city too. Everything connects to the sea."

"They must have heard the assistant down here and just followed the sound," Geron reckoned. "They've no bones to speak of, except for their jaws. Must have squeezed through the broken bars, killed their prey, and slithered back into the sewers."

"What about the tanner's?" Asher asked, looking to Kail.

"The tanner's place has a store room just like this," the watchman explained. "He wasn't really using it, mind, but there's still a grate like that one.

"Were the bars bent like this one?" he queried.

"They were as a matter of fact."

That irked Asher. "What are the chances of that?"

Geron rolled his broad shoulders. "Slim, I'll admit, but not impossible. These grates are centuries old after all." The big man noted Asher's continued intrigue. "Well, what's the alternative? Someone bent the bars deliberately? Come on," he cajoled. "People and Scudders don't work together. They probably tried to get into a dozen other places just looking for a way in. Speaking of which," he added, turning to Kail, "where can a man of my size enter the under city?"

"I can show you," the watchman assured.

"We're also going to need that map of yours," Geron asserted.

"What map?"

Geron flashed him a broad smile. "The one you were all looking at on your captain's desk of course. I believe it was a map of the old tunnels. Though why you'd all be so interested in them when you weren't looking for a monster is beyond me."

Kail averted his gaze and climbed back up the ladder to the sound of Geron's gentle laughter.

Asher held the candle up between them. "The old tunnels?"

"Aye," Geron beamed. "The real fun's about to begin!"

CHAPTER 20

HUNTING MONSTERS

Dragons - *The addition of this creature is a point of contention among my fellow rangers and for more than one reason at that.*

Firstly, no one has seen a dragon since the time of the elves, a thousand years ago. Some say they're extinct, others say they migrated to lands unknown. The truth is beyond this humble ranger.

Secondly, what legends there are speak of intelligent creatures of innate wisdom. Of course, we're still talking about an animal that has the power to level cities and torch entire forests.

Should you meet one, as unlikely as that is, pray to the gods that your death is swift and worthy of history's note.

** I would also add that more than one report has come from The Shining Coast in years of late. Rumour has it the mages of Korkanath have one under their spell, a pet of some sort perhaps.*

A Chronicle of Monsters: A Ranger's Bestiary, 12th Edition, Page 377.

Fenrid Arlvark, Ranger.

. . .

On the outskirts of the city, where the outer wall blocked all but the sky, Asher looked into the darkness of a long-abandoned tunnel. A trickling stream flowed from somewhere out of sight and followed the curve of the wall before vanishing into the cracks beneath the street.

"We're going in there?" he asked, the exasperation audible in his voice.

"Oh aye," Geron replied cheerfully, giving the map of the catacombs and sewers one last inspection. "You might as well learn now that a ranger's job is not a glamorous one."

"That had occurred to me already," Asher replied, jumping down the small drop and into the stream.

Geron tucked his bow and quiver under the tarp of his wagon and retrieved his newly acquired spear. "This ought to get the job done," he commented, hefting the weapon in one hand. With his claymore strapped to his belt and an axe slung over his back, there would be little to stop him getting any job done.

"We're not coming in there with you," Kail voiced from the side, speaking on behalf of his fellow watchmen.

"Of course you're not," Geron agreed. "That's why they pay us the real coin," he taunted, joining Asher in the shallow stream.

"Kail!" came a barking call from the steps cut into the city's inner wall. Captain Palan was making his way down towards them, his blue cloak swishing from side to side behind him.

"Captain?"

"You're going in there with them," Palan instructed, his tone not to be trifled with.

"But, Captain—"

Palan held up a hand to silence Kail. "We're paying them three thousand bits to kill the wretches - you're going to make sure they don't simply take off with half."

"I'm standing right here," Geron complained.

Captain Palan flashed him a look before addressing Kail again. "You are not obligated to assist them. Just make sure they do what we're paying them to do. Stavish, Grimil, go with him." Both men appeared about as disheartened as Kail.

"Torches," Asher requested, beckoning two of the watchmen over. They handed the rangers a flaming torch each and backed away, happy to have nothing to do with the ugly business.

"If we haven't returned by sunrise," Geron called up to the captain, "we're dead. In that case, you're going to need an army to clear them out." He gave the watchmen a wink and proceeded to turn his back on the light of the world. "I hope you're not afraid of the dark," he called back to Asher.

There were a number of quips that Asher could have responded with but, as always, he fell upon his actions to speak for him. The ranger confidently drew his broadsword and gave the blue sky one last look before following the big man into the tunnel.

The labyrinth beneath Velia stretched out in all directions, a web of tunnels and abandoned chambers that touched the furthest boundaries of the city. Here and there, narrow shafts of light would find their way through the cracks in the foundations and illuminate the way. For the most part, however, the rangers and the watchmen relied on the light of their torches to show them the way.

After several hours of trekking through the dank and musty tunnels, encountering blockages and impassable passageways, the sunlight ceased its intrusion, informing the hunting party that night had fallen upon the world beyond the under city. Every now and then, Geron would pause and consult the old map, searching for the area that corresponded with the Garden Quarter.

At the back of the group, Asher would routinely look over his shoulder and make certain they hadn't become the hunted. He had never seen or heard a Scudder before, a fact that convinced him every foreign noise must be one of the monsters. More than once he discovered his hand feeling for the fabric of the red cloth tucked into his belt. If he could only shut out the light, the Scudders' whereabouts would become obvious, ending the tedious hunt.

"This way," Geron said, for, perhaps, the tenth time since the sun had set.

"We should split up," Asher finally suggested. "We could cover more ground."

Geron was already shaking his head. "Those without the map would be stuck down here. Besides, this is your first hunt and you've never encountered Scudders before. I'm not leaving you to face them on your own."

And so their journey through the under city continued, taking them through hewn chambers and rocky caverns, all connected by narrow passages and putrid flooded channels.

"This should be it," Geron announced at last, coming to a halt in front of an arched tunnel. "We're at the Garden Quarter. Now I reckon there's only a couple of them, but they're likely to be sticking together. They'll blindly seek out a female until they die. When they're together, their tactics—"

"I'm aware," Asher cut in, raising his torch in case the beasts were clinging to the ceiling of the archway. "One will attempt to consume an arm, thereby holding the victim down, while the other feeds." His description had a physical effect on the three watchmen, all of whom shared looks of concern.

"Aye," Geron replied. "And it'll take all your fingers in the process. Scudders are more mouth than anything else; their jaws take up half of their body. If one of them does get a hold of you, be it your arm or leg, don't struggle - you'll only hasten the loss of your limb. Strike at the body and kill it - then remove yourself from its mouth. Got it?"

The watchmen nodded as one, their hands holding tight to the hilts of their swords. "Don't expect us to do your work for you,

Ranger," Kail blurted. "Just do your job and we won't need to worry about our limbs."

Geron's cheerful nature fell from his face as he took one stride that left the watchman looking up at his chin. "You need to knock your captain's words right out of your head, fella," he said gruffly. "You're in it now. Down here, the monsters aren't going to tell us apart. You and your friends here are just food, same as us."

Kail visibly swallowed, his lips sealed.

Something further up the tunnel disturbed the water, ending the disagreement and turning every head towards the darkness that awaited them. Geron's broad smile returned and he pointed his spear down the tunnel.

Asher held his torch out in front and angled his broadsword from high to low, the tip positioned to thrust down. Geron stalked beside him, their approach one of caution. Again they heard the scurrying sound of pincer-like legs dashing through the puddles in the dark.

Together, the rangers rounded the first corner, their weapons ready to strike anything that moved. Indeed, the shadows were moving, and fast. Lowering his torch, Asher laid his eyes on dozens of rats running towards them and scattering into the main tunnel. All three of the watchmen yelped in surprise and immediately began lashing out at the rodents.

Geron watched the rats as they disappeared through small holes and cracks in the walls. "Now where are you lot running off to?" he pondered.

"They're not running," Asher corrected. "They're *fleeing*."

Geron's gaze never quite found Asher, his attention held by the tunnel beyond. "I think you might be right," he muttered.

Asher whipped his head around to see a Scudder unfurling from the ceiling, its thick worm-like body dropping down to the wet floor. Proving the bestiary right where their speed was concerned, the moment all fifty of its feet touched the floor, the monster was flitting through the shadows until it reared up into the light of their torches. Two dozen circular rows of black teeth greeted them in the tunnel, each subsequent row decreasing in size. There were no eyes to speak of, only a hungry maw.

Geron didn't hesitate to thrust his spear with one hand, shoving the weapon all the way to the monster's throat and beyond. Those razor-sharp teeth instantly closed around the haft of the spear and would likely have shattered it had Geron's initial thrust not pierced through its body and taken the fight out of it. Refusing to die, however, the creature writhed on the end of the spear. The big man dropped his torch and took the weapon in both hands. Utilising his considerable strength, Geron heaved the Scudder into the air and slammed it into the wall and ceiling before hammering it into the floor at Asher's feet.

"Kill it!" he urged.

Asher was already swinging his broadsword, the edge brought down along the Scudder's midriff. The steel sliced through its ridged body and split the monster in two, spilling the contents of its gut across the floor.

"Nicely done," Geron complimented, yanking his spear free.

Asher moved his torch over the slime-covered carcass. The creature's skin was a light pink, run through with dark red and purple veins. Its deep mouth did, as Geron had said, account for half of the Scudder's length, which was comparable to a large dog.

"Satisfying, isn't it?" Geron gave the monster a nudge with his foot. "Nothing beats chopping through a Scudder." The big man nodded his chin down the tunnel. "The other one must be around here somewhere. Take point."

Asher resumed his full height and stepped over the dead Scudder. He could see the particularly slimy patch above him where the monster had been resting, the thick goop dripping down and mixing with the dirty water. The tunnel opened up into a chamber with a high ceiling and a black pool to one side, where the floor obviously sloped down. The ranger recalled a section from the bestiary that spoke of wet environments, often in enclosed places, where a female liked to breed.

Geron and the watchmen soon joined him in the chamber, their added torches revealing more of the space and the tunnels that extended from it. The watchmen in particular were searching every dark corner, their backs always together.

"I don't see it," Kail reported from his huddle.

"Hmm." Geron eyed the still water. "Asher, have you got that vial Hanaghan gave you?"

The ranger tapped the pouch on his belt that contained the vial of yellow liquid, drawn from the gland of a female Scudder.

"Good." Geron rested his torch against the stone wall. "Splash a little on the floor, would you. Let's see if we can't get the other's attention."

Asher moved to the edge of the water and crouched down. He placed his torch on the floor and made to retrieve the vial when he noticed something poking out of the water. Tilting his head, to better make it out, the ranger decided it was the corner of something man-made. Rather than produce the vial, he reached over the water and found purchase on the object.

"Asher?" Geron enquired, his view blocked by the crouching ranger.

"There's something in the water," Asher told him before dragging it out. He quickly realised it was a box of some sort, though the sides and ends were fitted with bars rather than wood. One of those ends was open, the bars slightly bent out of shape.

"What is it?"

Asher wanted to tell his companion that it was a box, but a more appropriate word came to mind. "It's a cage..."

The water's flat surface exploded beside Asher and the other Scudder launched itself at him mouth first. The ranger abandoned his investigation of the cage and his torch in favour of rolling aside, thereby evading the gaping maw coming for him. The fire from his torch gave the monster reason to halt its pursuit and rear up. All three of the watchmen stepped back despite the distance that already existed between them and the Scudder.

Asher came back up to his feet. The creature was scurrying around the torch. He slashed and waved his broadsword, keeping it at bay while he considered the best way to exterminate the beast. Off to one side, Geron was satisfied to merely watch the fight, though he still appeared ready to intervene with his spear should he be required.

The Scudder changed its approach and came for Asher's leg, hoping to consume the entire limb and render him harmless. He swung his sword from low to high, taking with it a chunk of the monster's flesh. Its mouth knocked aside, Asher stepped in beside it and twisted his blade to point down. He immediately dropped into a crouch and drove his broadsword down through the middle of the Scudder.

Pinned, the monster screeched in agony and hurried away from the ranger, its multitude of legs moving with all haste. It was the last act of a foolish creature that could summon no more intelligence than its simple desire to feed, for fleeing the blade only served to split its body down the middle. Along with its own guts, several human organs poured out of the fiend before it finally lay still.

"That's what happens when you've got more mouth than brain," Geron commented as he poked the Scudder with his spear tip. "That was well handled." Asher stood up and gave a nod of appreciation. "It's not a bad way to earn a ton of coin, eh?"

Asher's reply was drowned out by the shrill scream of Grimil. The ranger didn't need to see the watchman to know that there was more than just fear in that scream - there was also pain. Moving past Geron, Grimil came into view. As did the Scudder, its mouth having consumed the man's arm almost to the shoulder. Grimil thrashed about but the weight of the Scudder inevitably dragged him down. It was then that another of its wretched kind emerged from the shadows and attempted to bury its mouth in his gut.

"Kill it quickly!" Geron yelled over the screams.

Kail and Stavish swung their blades with all the finesse of a child playing at being a Graycoat. Wild as they were, their swords gave the second Scudder enough to think about that it detached from Grimil. Kail succeeded in chopping one down, delivering a blow that separated its mouth from its body. Stavish was too clumsy in his attacks and only succeeded in pushing the monster back, along with most of Grimil's shredded arm. Geron threw his spear with great accuracy and pinned the Scudder down, lending him enough time to draw his claymore and cleave the fiend in two.

Asher came to stand over Grimil, watching as shock robbed the man of his senses. Given the state of his arm, the ranger decided it was a mercy for now. If he was to survive such a wound the entire arm would need to be amputated and quickly before the blood spoiled.

"So much for there being two," he remarked.

Geron only offered a deep rumble from his throat. It was the most unhappy he had ever seen the big man.

"Help him!" Kail snapped, holding Grimil in his arms.

"We're rangers," Geron told him, "not healers."

"He might survive if you take the arm," Asher offered. "We can use a torch to seal the wound."

"You want me to cut my friend's arm off?" Kail fumed. He looked up at Stavish for support on the matter, only to find the man visibly shaking, his whole body taken by fright.

Both Geron and Asher slowly turned back to the inky pool, following Stavish's look of terror. Both men swore and raised their swords as numerous points on the water's surface broke, each one a hungry Scudder.

CHAPTER 21

SCUDDER HELL

Golem - The first thing to know about these brutes is that they aren't natural. Golem aren't born, they're made out of pieces of the dead. Make no mistake, this is dark magic, necromancy work, crude as it may be. The most important thing to keep in mind is that they cannot be killed. Burn them, break them, cut them into bits - nothing stops them except a command from their maker.

That leads me to my next point, so be sure to read it twice. You're looking for people, not the Golem itself. Be it a mage, wizard, witch - whatever you want to call them. They're the key. You either trap the monster in something it can never get out of (good luck with that) or you convince the wretch who brought it into the world to stop it.

But be warned; a Golem will protect its master, and most Golems can rip a man in half with their bare hands. Trust me, I've seen it.

A Chronicle of Monsters: A Ranger's Bestiary, 12th Edition, Page 400.

Hamish Lancet, Ranger.

. . .

As the first six Scudders reached the water's edge, a larger creature began to rise in the middle of the pool, its mouth wide enough to swallow one of the Scudders whole. A single strip of spikes lined its sinewy body, identifying it as a female if Asher had read the bestiary correctly.

"Do you know what that is?" Geron whispered.

"*It* is the thing you said it couldn't be," Asher replied sarcastically, his frustration forming the foundation of his words.

Nearly twenty more rose from the water, some even scurrying over the female before plunging back into the depths. The first to have left the water were creeping ever closer to the hunting party.

Kail laid Grimil down and brought his sword to bear. "What... What do we do now?"

"Now?" Geron's knuckles cracked as he tightened his grip around the hilt. "Now we really earn our coin. *You* get to fight for your city," he added dryly.

Stavish let loose an unintelligible sound and turned on his heel. He burst into a mad dash for the nearest tunnel, his courage having long fled. He made it as far as the threshold before a previously unseen Scudder lowered its mouth from an alcove in the ceiling and wrapped its mouth around his head. The monster had only to drop the rest of its weight to the floor and the watchman was taken down with it. As Grimil had done, he forgot Geron's advice and thrashed about in a bid to free himself. It was impossible to declare him dead, but he soon stopped moving.

Excited by the kill, the rest of the Scudders charged their prey.

There was no time for words. Asher allied himself with his new sword and wielded it as an extension of his body. He leapt over the first Scudder and came down hard on the second, his two-handed hammer-stroke slicing its head down the centre. His back muscles worked to assist him in swinging left then right, each strike a different height and a confirmed kill.

One of the fiends attempted to engulf his foot and leg, but the ranger managed to lift his boot and stamp on the creature's head before driving the point of his sword down through its body. His left hand deftly retrieved the dagger from the back of his belt and whipped the blade out straight as a Scudder tried to consume his arm. It tasted steel for its trouble and received a broadsword across the midriff for good measure.

Only feet away, Geron was dicing up Scudders on all sides. It seemed they had decided he possessed the best organs. The big man booted them away and flicked his claymore high, spraying blood into the air. Despite the bodies mounting around him, one incorrigible Scudder mounted its dead brothers and jumped at the ranger. Geron thrust his claymore and speared the beast through its mouth before hammering it to the ground, there to be crushed under his boot.

While Stavish was having his insides sucked out of his gut, Grimil had been taken by the legs and dragged through the fray. Kail fought to save him, his blade hacking and slashing at the fiends, but there was no getting to him before he was pulled under the water. Unfortunately, he came to his senses only a moment before the water claimed him, stealing his last scream. The female curled her body and dived under to meet him.

"There's too many!" Kail shouted, before crying in pain as a Scudder bit into his leg.

Asher rolled across the floor and brought his broadsword down over the monster's head, immediately freeing the watchman. "Run!" he bellowed, pointing at the closest tunnel. Kail didn't need telling twice and limped away as fast as his injured leg would allow. "Geron!" Asher side-stepped a leaping Scudder and turned on the spot to cut it in half mid-air. "Geron! We need to get out of here!"

Geron roared, his mind set to a frenzy as he brought both his axe and sword to bear. The big man was only given pause when the female pushed up from the pool, its longer legs stretching over the edge.

"This way!" Asher waved his companion towards him.

Geron turned to run and lost his claymore in the process, the blade gripped in the maw of a Scudder. With the female advancing from the water, the ranger took his axe in both hands and hacked his way to Asher, who managed to scoop up one of the fallen torches.

"Run!" Geron urged.

Asher led the way, his torch held out as far as he could. The path ahead was blocked by ancient debris but the light revealed a narrower passage to their left. "Through here!" the ranger guided.

Geron was forced to angle his shoulders to one side in order to fit. It claimed some of his speed and gave the pursuing Scudders the chance to catch up. His leathers scraped against the stone as he finally broke free of the passage and found ample room again. Asher was already to one side, waiting with his broadsword held high. The first Scudder to emerge tasted steel, and the second scurried over its carcass and met Geron's axe.

"Keep going!" Asher spat, pushing the big man on.

They ran through the web of tunnels with no thought given to their direction or destination. It was through the cracks and fissures that they heard Kail running for his life, his sword knocking against the stone as he stumbled through the dark.

"Help me!" he bawled.

Asher felt the need to find the watchman but there was no telling where exactly he was or how to reach him. It was tempting to call out to him and give the man a chance to try and find them, but the Scudders relied heavily on sound when it came to hunting their prey.

"Hold up," Geron cautioned, grabbing Asher by the cloak. "Back here." He directed them to an old rusted gate that had been left partially open decades or even centuries earlier. It squeaked terribly as they opened it, but the bars of the gate would form a natural barrier against the Scudders.

"Where does this lead?" Asher posed, gazing into the darkness ahead of them.

Geron sniffed the air. "Salt," he detected. "Fancy a stroll down the beach?"

Asher could smell it too now, the salty water of The Adean breaking against The Shining Coast. "Why go to the beach," he replied, "when it's so lovely down here?"

Geron chuckled. "I didn't know you could be funny, little man."

"When the occasion calls for it," Asher explained, his torch illuminating the way.

They eventually found themselves in a rocky cavern that looked to have been in the process of improvement, some eons past. Sections of the natural rock had been smoothed and attempts had begun at tunnelling new passageways, but there was only one other way out on the far side, where a rotting cart had long been forsaken.

Geron found himself a perch and planted himself down upon it, a heavy sigh deflating his chest.

"We should keep moving," Asher insisted.

"I've got fifteen hard years on you," Geron told him, yanking a single Scudder tooth from his thigh. "I just need a moment's rest, fella."

Asher walked back to Geron, his eyes never straying from the way they had come. "We cannot linger here," he warned.

"They're not hunting us," Geron reassured. "They'll be following that loud idiot."

Even now, Asher could hear the distant echoes of Kail's living nightmare. "How does a whole nest come to be under a city like Velia?" the new ranger pondered, suspicion in his tone. "Every reference to them in the bestiary has them living in the wilds - they prefer it."

Geron's shaking head was hanging between his knees. "There are any number of reasons. Their territory could have been invaded and the female sought out new ground. Perhaps they ran out of food. You saw the size of that nest. Scudders upon Scudders. They need a lot of prey when they reach a certain size."

Asher came to stand directly in front of Geron, where he waited until the bigger man turned his head up at him. "Or the female was brought here," he intoned.

Geron's eyes shifted back to the doorway. "The cage…"

"It was big enough to fit an adolescent female," Asher remarked.

Geron looked up at him. "You have been reading, haven't you?" He sat up and wiped Scudder blood from his face. "But you're not wrong. And it didn't look particularly old either," he added.

"Have you ever seen anything like this before?" Asher asked him.

"I've seen beastly men lure people into monster territory," Geron answered. "They were usually robbers though, hoping to come in after the fact and take the victims' belongings. I don't see the gains in capturing a female Scudder and releasing it in Velia's under city."

Asher had come across every type of man during his time as an Arakesh and knew the driving force behind the majority was the opportunity to increase their wealth. "An increase in deaths would decrease the value of an area… of a district."

Geron wagged his finger. "You might be on to something there, little man. If people keep showing up dead in the Garden Quarter, not only are their establishments going to be up for sale but they'll likely be sold at a low price." Geron waved the idea away. "It doesn't help us down here. Our problem is the Scudders, specifically that bloody large female. She's probably birthing new sprogs as we speak."

Asher took to the rocky outcropping opposite Geron and sat down before planting the torch in the soft dirt at his feet. "What are the chances of her leaving the nest?"

"Slim to none," Geron grumbled. "She's got everything she needs in that rank pool. And even if we did find a way to slay her, there's still the matter of her numerous children. The job ain't done until every Scudder is dead."

Geron's choice of wording set off a pang of guilt within Asher, penetrating his focus and bringing up images of Thomas Murell. Without thinking, he rubbed his face with both hands, blocking out the light long enough for the Nightseye elixir to come alive in his veins. He could hear hundreds of pincers tapping incessantly against stone as distant Scudders tracked their prey. Much closer was the sound of heavy footsteps and laboured breath.

"Someone's coming," he announced from behind his hands.

"Eh?" was Geron's confused response.

One intake of breath through his nose brought an odour of sweat, both his and Geron's. Sampling the air beyond that, he detected an enormous amount of fear.

"What are you talking about?" the big man pressed, one hand reaching for his axe.

Listening to the pattern of the stranger's approach, he knew from the clumsy advance - caused by an injured leg - that it was none other than Kail, the watchman lucky enough to have found his way to them. He heard the man's hands slapping against the stone as he felt his way along the walls, though they soon gripped around the bars of the gate.

"It's Kail," Asher uttered, trying to put Geron at ease.

Before the big man could ask any further questions, the hinges of the old gate squeaked. Soon after, Kail's footsteps could be heard by ordinary ears.

"Praise Atilan," the watchman panted seeing the rangers in the torchlight. "I thought I was lost to the darkness," he moaned, limping towards them.

Asher removed his hands from his face and accepted the disorientation that accompanied the transition. Suddenly, the encompassing shadows of the cavern felt very oppressive.

Geron was eyeing him from his perch. "I wouldn't be so certain you hold favour with the gods," he said, slowly turning to greet the watchman. "A nest of Scudders lies between you and the way out of this hell and we're not leaving until it's cleared out."

"We can't stay down here," Kail argued. "There's too many of them. We need to find a way around and return to the city."

"That's not an option for us, fella," Geron told him. "We're rangers. We don't walk away from the hunt. Besides, I really want the rest of that reward," he continued in a lighter tone. "It's been a long time since my body has enjoyed a few suds, and there's an exquisite bath house on Gendry Street that can see to such a thing."

"How can you speak of such things?" Kail spat. "Two men are dead! Good men! And we will be next if we don't get out of here."

"I don't appreciate the tone," Geron said, rising to his superior height. "And I *really* don't appreciate the volume of your voice," he whispered.

"You have a choice," Asher interjected calmly. "Stay and fight with us or take your chances out there on your own."

"But the map and the torch stay with us," Geron dictated.

"What choice is that?" Kail countered, his voice lowered now. "Both will spell my end."

Geron looked past the watchman, to the doorway from which he had come. "Then you're going to have to decide whether you want to die running for your life in this rat-infested darkness," he posed, hefting his axe in both hands, "or facing your enemy with the gods at your back and your sword swinging." The big man was already moving before he had finished speaking.

Asher narrowed his eyes and looked to the doorway where a lone Scudder had crept into the cavern. In a flash of steel, Geron's axe flew through the air and split the Scudder almost clean in half.

"Any more?" Asher asked, rising with his broadsword in hand.

"You tell me," Geron replied, his tone laden with suspicion.

"Is there another way out of here?" Kail was turning on the spot, his fear laid bare.

Geron retrieved his axe and spat on the dead monster. "We're not looking for a way out, remember? We've a job to finish. That female needs to die."

The watchman's face screwed up. "So we're to just wait here until it finds us?"

"No," Asher said evenly, his mind cast back to his last hunt, among the streets of Skystead. "We can't attack the Scudders in their nest - it's too well defended and they know the terrain. We need to lure the female out, to somewhere that serves *us*."

Geron clicked his fingers, his grin visible in the flickering light. "Hanaghan's vial."

"What's that?" Kail asked impatiently.

Asher produced the vial of yellowish liquid. "Bait," he answered simply. "The female will be drawn to it, believing another female has entered its domain. Supposedly," he added with a look thrown at Geron.

"Hanaghan's never wrong about these things," the big man defended.

"So why can't we stay here?" Kail continued with his line of questioning.

Asher gestured at the doorway on the far side, where they had yet to venture. "Two points of entry; means we could be ambushed. Also, the female won't fit through either one."

Kail blinked hard. "You mean to say we have to lure that monster into a chamber with only one way in or out?"

"Sounds like a damn good plan to me," Geron concurred. "Let's be off then, I wouldn't mind being done by breakfast."

"No," Asher disagreed, stopping the big man from leaving. "We'll be slower and louder if we go together," he pointed out, looking briefly at Kail's injured leg. "I will go alone, find the right environment, and come back for you both."

Geron looked pained by the strength of the argument. "You're sure?"

"This is what we do," Asher replied, echoing Geron's own words.

The big man groaned. "To the hells with it. Tear a strip of your cloak off," he instructed the watchman. "We're going to need another torch."

"Keep it," Asher cut in, bewildering both men.

Geron watched his companion make for the old gate. "Keep it?" he repeated incredulously. "I know you've got a death wish, fella, but I could really do with your help seeing this job through."

"I *will* return," Asher promised. "Stay here," he bade before walking away.

"So he's a dead man," Kail could be heard saying as the ranger passed beyond the old gate.

The pitch black of Velia's under city wrapped itself around Asher and, in so doing, revealed to him its secrets. Dripping water informed him of a multitude of tunnels, while scurrying rats helped to build a picture of the cracks and broken walls that connected everything together. The stench of mould was everywhere, having long assumed dominance throughout the catacombs. Mixed in with it was the foul odour of the Scudders, their collective scent guiding him to the tunnel on his right.

Since they required a larger space to lure the female, he stood still and felt for the cold drafts that breezed through the tunnels. They took him on a short journey through the maze, leading him to one such chamber that clearly resided beneath a popular tavern. With his hand to the stone, the ranger could feel the vibrations of their ruckus, picking out distinct hollers and cheers. The chamber itself, however, wasn't fit for their purpose, the doorways and arches too small or collapsed.

Continuing through the dark at a pace no ordinary man could hope to manage, Asher followed the hewn stone, staying away from the areas that had been left as they were. Entering a new chamber, closer to the heart of the city, the ranger immediately felt the open space around him as his moving body had less of an impact on the air pressure. He clicked his fingers and heard the sound disperse to fill out the chamber, confirming its expanse.

He could taste iron in the air, and rusted at that. He rubbed his fingers together and felt the shape of an iron portcullis resting high on the wall behind him. The chains holding it up felt weak to him but, more importantly, the passage beneath the portcullis was wide enough to accommodate the female Scudder and it was the only way in or out.

Confident he could remember the way without the benefit of the Nightseye elixir, Asher returned to Geron and Kail with news of the perfect trap. They followed him through the under city, ever wary of their shadowy surroundings, and finally entered the chamber as one.

"What was this?" Kail asked, holding the torch high.

"Most likely a store room of some kind when they were building the foundations." Asher pointed out the portcullis. "They didn't want the workers stealing food and supplies."

"What are you thinking?" Geron enquired, his fingers running along one of the ancient chains.

Asher gestured to the space in the centre of the room. "We use Hanaghan's vial to lure it here. Let it see us. As it crosses the threshold, one of us breaks the chain and drops the portcullis on it. If it survives that, it'll be pinned down. We can finish it from this side."

"We'll make a ranger of you yet," Geron beamed.

Kail held up a hand. "What about the others? There were dozens of the smaller ones."

"The female won't bring them with her," Geron explained. "She'll be too afraid they'll like the look of the other one. No, this is a fight for queens alone."

Asher nodded in agreement. "I'll get its attention."

Leaving them once again, the ranger headed out into the tunnels and began to leave droplets of the viscous gland liquid on the floor and walls until he had created a trail that took him back to the chamber. Standing side by side with the watchman, he smashed the remains of the vial on the stone and gave Geron the nod as he waited out of sight, his axe primed to come down on the chain.

The wait felt like a lifetime. Geron had, inevitably lowered his axe and even slumped down against the wall. The watchman had been the first to sit on the cold floor, his wounded leg getting the better of him. Asher paced, his sword twisting round and round in his hand. He was accustomed to waiting for his prey to be in the perfect position, but this felt different somehow, as if the line had blurred between predator and prey and, for the first time, he wasn't sure which side of that line he was on.

His sword froze mid-spin. No one moved. All three had heard the same sound. It grew in volume from a constant clatter to distinct legs tapping against the floor and walls beyond the portcullis. Kail and Geron picked themselves up and assumed their former positions, though the watchman was notably further back than Asher.

Before its hideous form emerged from the shadows, its ragged breathing preceded it, piercing the chamber with the smell of death. As it came into the light of the torch, its mouth and clicking teeth dominated the width of the passage. The Scudder hissed and spat as it approached, thinking, perhaps, that it was threatening another female.

Asher fell into a fighting stance, his knees bent and shoulders hunched. "Come on," he muttered, before tapping his sword against the stone.

The female's monstrous thoughts were its own as the beast interpreted what really awaited it inside the chamber. Its pincer-like legs picked up speed, bringing its slug of a body over the threshold. Geron didn't hesitate to chop the chain and drop the portcullis. With a mighty crash, the ancient gate fell upon the female, the iron spikes leading the way.

Asher was on the verge of propelling himself across the chamber, ready to finish the monster off, when he witnessed his plan fall to pieces. The iron gate failed to penetrate the strip of spikes that lined the female's back and was ultimately ripped from its rusted tracks, its tumble to the floor adding to the cacophony. It hadn't even slowed the Scudder down.

Kail leapt to one side in a bid to evade the open maw charging right at them. Asher went on the attack. He swung his broadsword and caught the Scudder on the side of its mouth, its steel edge splitting the thick tissue. The female hissed and lunged forward in an attempt to ensnare him, but the ranger was quicker on his feet than the prey it was used to. Dancing to one side, he spun around to put as much strength as he could behind his next swing. The blade carved a red line along the monster's body and splattered blood up the wall.

Not to be left out, Geron exploded into action and literally jumped into the fray, his axe coming down from on high. The curved steel was buried deep in the Scudder and even chipped a portion of its spikes. Like an experienced woodsman, the big man deftly removed his axe and struck again, as if he was felling a stubborn tree.

The female twisted her body at some speed and knocked both rangers down. Proving he still retained some courage, Kail darted in with a thrust of his sword and occupied the Scudder long enough for the hunters to get back up. The monster defied its hulking size and reared up, just as the smaller males did. In the process, Kail was robbed of his sword, the weapon flung away. Now, the watchman looked up at a circular jaw of several hundred teeth, a portal that would take him straight into the afterlife.

Geron thundered into him, his broad shoulder more than enough to launch Kail out of the way. In his place, the experienced ranger faced the looming Scudder with a bloody axe. As the monster came down on him, he raised his weapon high and dropped to one knee, using his considerable size and strength to brace himself between the Scudder's maw and the cold floor. Blood rained down on him as the axe bit into the roof of the female's mouth, the pain of it enough to keep the beast from bringing its jaws together around him.

Tempting as it was to simply hack and slash at the monster from the side, Asher attacked with precision. Using two hands, he plunged his broadsword deep into the Scudder's body and began to move the blade like a saw, splitting the tissue open. The beast reeled and abandoned its attack on Geron. Lurching to the side, it pushed Asher back and off his feet, his weapon left inside the creature's guts.

"Move!" Geron bellowed.

Asher rolled to the side and evaded the incoming mouth and its complement of teeth. The female tossed her head and flung the ranger away in the process. Then its legs went to work, hurrying it across the chamber with an open maw. Geron hurled his axe and caught the Scudder part way between its spikes and thick skin, slowing it down just enough for Asher to retrieve the short-sword from over his shoulder.

"Get out of the way!" Geron warned.

But Asher did the opposite and thrust his arm out, the short-sword held vertically in his hand. The female naturally moved to bite his extended arm off but only succeeded in wrapping its mouth around the blade. With the tip lodged in the roof of its mouth, the beast could no longer close its jaws around anything without driving the steel further into its own body.

In its distress, the creature's movements became erratic and wild. Asher darted in and grasped a firm hold on the hilt of his broadsword. He had only to brace himself and the Scudder's thrashing parted its body from the weapon. The sword grasped in both hands now, the ranger moved in for the kill, confident that his foe could no longer bite him.

Steel flashed again and again in the torchlight and dark blood sprayed across the chamber. Geron moved to assist him but his axe remained buried in the spikes. Asher, however, didn't need the help. Killing was the one thing he was good at, be it monster or man. Proving such a point, he soon stood beside the still carcass of a female Scudder, its body ravaged by his blade.

"That'll do it," Geron remarked. The big man placed a large boot on the side of the beast and yanked his axe free. "Good kill."

Asher grunted and sheathed his blade so that he might retrieve his short-sword from the Scudder's mouth. The weapon required some wiggling before it came loose.

"Is it over?" Kail was lying on his side, exhausted from his brief clash with the monster.

"Aye," Geron replied. "Sent to Scudder hell now."

Kail gestured to their surroundings. "Isn't that where we are?"

Geron chuckled and bandied words with the watchman, but the rest of their exchange was lost on Asher. That sixth sense that most assassins would claim to possess informed him that he was being watched. He turned away from his companions and set his gaze beyond the broken portcullis, to the darkness of the tunnel. There was nothing to see, but he was sure there were eyes out there, boring into him. In a burst of action, he scooped up the torch and threw it into the shadows.

The torchlight revealed a pair of boots before the owner spun on their heel and sped off into the tunnels. Without explanation, Asher gave chase, leaving his companions behind. It didn't take long for the darkness to consume him and the Nightseye elixir to amplify his senses. The sudden transition - at speed - caused him to clip the corner of a wall and stumble further down the tunnel. By the time he had regained his footing, the figure was disappearing down another tunnel.

Asher renewed his pursuit and even leapt off the corner wall to maintain his speed. He could hear the distant footsteps slapping through puddles, while ragged breaths left warm air in their wake. Their scent, however, continued to elude him, lost as it was among the stench of Scudders and filth. Soon, though, he was breathing in the sea air as they ran ever eastward, towards The Adean.

The last corner he turned brought an end to the effects of the Nightseye elixir, the glow of the morning sun illuminating the end of the passage. The man he was chasing had become a silhouette against the dawn. The easing shift from darkness to light allowed Asher's senses to adjust without issue and he maintained his speed.

The tunnel opened up onto the sandy beach and the crashing waves of Illian's Shining Coast. Clumps of long reeds lined the edge where the beach rose up to meet the city. Asher turned continuously on the spot, searching the dunes, reeds, and the path that rounded the city wall. Nothing. There was no sign of the stranger who had been watching from the shadows.

It occurred to Asher then that it had been no stranger at all. How could it have been? The assailant had fled through the same darkness he had and required no light to do so. There was only one suspect as far as the ranger was concerned - an Arakesh.

How had they found him? And why track him through Velia's under city and make no move to kill him? Had the assassin hoped the

Scudders would do the job for them? Asher swore with the lack of answers he possessed.

He walked back towards the tunnel, a sense of defeat upon him despite his victory over the Scudder. He was almost over the threshold when a gleam of light caught his eye. He paused to investigate and crouched down to inspect the object half-buried in the sand. It was a small glass vial, the cork already popped and contents drained. He brought it to his nose and sniffed the interior. The ranger knew immediately what had recently occupied the vial.

Nightseye elixir.

Or, at least, a more human variant of the elven potion. It was missing a few ingredients that Alidyr Yalathanil had included from the teachings of his people, but the main odour was exactly the same. Asher couldn't think of the name humans gave the elixir, but he knew it could only grant the consumer temporary vision in the dark. It was not something an Arakesh would have need of.

The ranger stood up and pocketed the empty vial. If not an assassin of Nightfall, then who? More questions. No answers. Though he suspected they had something to do with the Scudders and the cage he had found.

"Asher!"

Geron and Kail approached from the darkness of the tunnel, their inquisitive expressions visible in the light of the torch. Kail limped all the faster to reach the light of the day, while Geron's focus remained firmly on Asher.

"What was all that about?" the big man asked.

"There was someone else in there with us," Asher told him confidently.

Geron frowned. "Another person?"

"Yes," Asher said with no lack of irritation. "Likely the same person who put that female Scudder down there."

"What?" Kail looked from ranger to ranger.

Geron held up a hand to calm the watchman. "We don't know that for certain. Though it wouldn't hurt to inform your captain of the matter, as it's not *ours* to investigate," he added with a look at Asher. "In fact," he continued, "you might as well go on ahead and find good old Captain Palan and tell him to have our coin ready."

"Why?" Kail asked. "Where are you two going?"

Geron rested his axe over his shoulder and thumbed down the tunnel. "To finish the job."

The watchman peered into the dark beyond them. "You're going back in there?"

"There's still dozens of Scudders to put down," the big man reminded him. "Rangers earn every one of their coins. Now best be on your way, Watchman Kail. You can tell your captain you and your company fought bravely."

Kail nodded absently before limping off down the beach.

Geron waited for him to be out of earshot before turning to Asher. "What's between your ears? We hunt monsters and people who *be* monsters. Everything else is watchman business - *kingly* business for all I care!"

"He needed to know," Asher insisted, holding his ground. "Hells, we should know. The person who did this might not be a monster but they share responsibility for the deaths."

"Monsters kill people every day," Geron countered. "If it hadn't been these people it would have been others, somewhere else." The big man waved the whole argument away. "You shouldn't focus on the deaths. Think about the lives you've saved, about the deaths that won't happen because of what we've done here. There's no more to our business than that. It's simple."

The involvement of a person rather complicated the matter for Asher. "How can the job be done if the one who instigated it is still at large?"

"Well aren't you a well-educated assassin," Geron remarked on Asher's use of vocabulary. "We should be thanking the one who *instigated* it. Because of them our purses are going to be three thousand coins heavier."

Asher's stony expression finally cracked, revealing some of his shock. Geron didn't miss it and his entire demeanour shifted in an instant.

"I'm sorry," he said. "I'm sorry. I didn't mean that. It's good to earn the coin, but I would never have wanted anyone to die for it. When the job's finished, we'll tell the captain everything we know. Hunting people is their territory. Though," he countered himself, "we can offer our assistance should he require it."

Asher nodded his agreement, still unsure about his companion's motivations. Trust didn't come easily to him.

Geron scratched the side of his head, clearly uncomfortable. "And I'm sorry about the assassin comment. It wasn't right of me to bring that up."

Asher shrugged, intending to break the tension. "You're not wrong; I am a well-educated assassin."

Geron cracked up and offered his familiar hearty laughter. "Come on then, little man, let's see this through. I want my sword back."

The ranger drew his broadsword and accompanied the big man back into the darkness.

CHAPTER 22

THE FINE PRINT

Troll - There exist variants of this creature, both big and enormous (read on for the breakdown of all types). They are brutes all and of limited intellect at that.

Solitary beasts, they are rarely found in any numbers, though, be aware, their breeding season runs through winter. These areas can be found by following the sounds of recurring landslides.

Weak spots for most variants include the face, in particular their large eyes, and their softer midriff. I would advise using a surprise attack and with a spear, utilising the distance of such a weapon. If possible, coat the tip in Oylish poison (see A Ranger's Guide to Alchemy, Page 97) so that you might slow the Troll down first.

A Chronicle of Monsters: A Ranger's Bestiary, 12th Edition, Page 27.

Gallad Corsair, Ranger.

Some time after midday, Asher and Geron stood before Captain Palan's desk, their shoulders sagging and every inch of them coated in Scudder slime and gore. Asher did his best not to lick his lips and taste the innards that had splashed across his face. There was nothing he could do about the smell - there was nothing anyone could do about that.

Captain Palan, along with Kail and all his watchmen, winced at the odour permeating their chapter house. The older man looked the rangers up and down with disgust deepening his wrinkles. Asher awkwardly glanced back over his shoulder and saw the mud and filth they had trekked in with every step.

"I'm sorry about the men you lost," Geron offered.

Palan nodded. "Kail has informed us of the details. You slew the rest of them, I trust."

Geron looked down at Asher before taking in his own gruesome appearance. "I'd say so, aye. It took half a day, mind you, but there ain't a Scudder left alive down there."

"Very good," the captain replied, his attention momentarily captured by the thick slime dripping off their fingertips.

"You have our coin?" the big man pursued, his eyes roaming the desk.

Palan flicked a single finger and Kail produced a small chest and a large pouch. "It's all there," the captain assured.

Geron grinned. "I'm sure it is."

Asher nudged his companion's arm.

"Oh right," Geron said, his hands refraining from picking up the chest. "We have no proof exactly, but it would seem your monster problem was a deliberate action."

"Indeed," Captain Palan interjected. "Kail reported your findings - something about a cage and a man."

"Aye. We didn't catch the fella—"

"Nor did we see him," Kail cut in.

"I saw him," Asher stated, drawing all eyes to him.

"Asher's got no reason to lie," Geron said, backing his claim up. "And that cage suggests at least one Scudder was released down there. I'd say you've got a murderer on your hands."

"And I'd say you only solved half of our monster problem then," the captain deftly responded, one hand pulling the chest of coins back.

Geron tensed. "How's that then?" he demanded, his tone down several octaves.

"Since you didn't catch the one responsible for this infestation, there's no reason why it can't happen again. I think, if you read our contract, you'll find it states, quite clearly, that you would eliminate the root, that is to say the *cause* of the infestation." Palan held out his hands. "I am not so wicked as to withhold *all* of your earnings. Take the purse and be on your way, rangers. Your service to this city is at an end."

Geron was disturbingly still, like a snake before it sprang. Asher intervened and snatched the purse from the desk, his quick movement enough to cast slime and blood across the captain's desk and stack of parchments. With a firm hand on Geron's chest, he guided the big man out of the chapter house, pausing only to flash Palan an ominous look. Kail, he noticed, looked upon their departure with guilt. Still, the watchman had no other place to stand and Asher wasn't going to hold his silence against him.

The door closed behind them and Geron was anything but silent. He swore and cursed the gods before kicking the wall of the chapter house. "I'm of a mind to go back in there and shove that chest down his throat!" he fumed. "He's no right to take our coin!"

Asher thought of suggesting they take the matter to the local notaries, but the odds were stacked against them when facing the city's own watchmen. "I'm sorry," he said instead. "I shouldn't have..." He couldn't bring himself to say it, as he knew informing them of human involvement was the right thing. Though they had been dismissed, the captain would likely keep a suspicious eye over events unfolding in the Garden Quarter now.

Geron sighed, oblivious of the woman who gave him a wide berth due to his odour. "There's no apology to be had, fella. We did the right thing *and* we did our job. That's a damn sight more than any of them can say. He's just twisting the words of the contract. And you know what? He'll keep that bloody coin!"

Asher nodded, having already come to that conclusion. "What do you want to do now?"

Disheartened by the whole affair, Geron waved his arms, sending Scudder guts everywhere. "I want that damned bath," he growled. "Gods know I need it."

"I wouldn't say no," Asher replied.

Side by side, weary and dismayed, the rangers walked down the street in search of well-deserved comfort and a much-needed wash.

Asher couldn't remember the last time his whole body had felt so good. The steam from the hot water seemed to carry his ailments away, allowing him to forget, for a moment, about his injuries and aching joints.

The large tub easily accommodated him, though he rested his feet on the rim to keep the pressure off his feet for a while. He had already scrubbed himself down before getting in, a lengthy process that had failed to remove all the Scudder innards. He didn't like to think about the layer of grime that sat over the water's surface.

Propped up against the side of the tub, he could see the hilt of his broadsword and knew that the rest of his gear was close by. Only his clothes had been taken to be thoroughly cleaned - part of the service they had paid for.

Asher didn't need to open his eyes to know that the heavy foot-steps were those of Geron. The big man walked down the centre of the long room with nothing but a towel draped over one shoulder. He took to the bath opposite Asher's, or, at least, Asher assumed it was the bath opposite his own - he refused to open his eyes until the hulking ranger was submerged.

Geron sighed with relief. "Now that's what these old bones needed." He immediately plunged his head under the water and came back up with his thick mane slicked back. "The matron says our clothes should be ready by morning. Our rooms are already prepared."

"Can we afford all this?" Asher enquired.

"Well, it would have been much more affordable if we had all the coin we were owed, but there's no worries here, little man; we can afford it. What's the point of it all if we can't treat ourselves to a bit of luxury every now and then, eh?"

"Won't Vask be expecting more from The Ranch's fifteen percent?"

"Rolan has no idea how much we were going to negotiate," Geron explained. "But I'll tell him what happened with the captain. I'll also tell him about the fella who put the damned Scudder down there in the first place. It's good to know for any future jobs that might pop up in the city."

Asher accepted the explanation and adopted Geron's relaxed attitude towards the loss of coin. He was also pleased to hear that his companion was going to pass on the information concerning the stranger in the tunnels. It all helped him to settle down in the bath and enjoy what he could of the luxury while he relived the fight with the Scudder and analysed his performance.

"How does it feel then?" Geron asked.

"It feels better than being covered in Scudder slime," Asher quipped.

Geron laughed softly. "Not the bath, you fool. How does it feel to have done some good? There's no denying that Scudder nest would have grown and grown. Who knows how many people we've saved - maybe the whole city," he pondered loftily.

Asher didn't respond straight away, taking the moment to truly reflect on what they had done. "It feels good," he said.

Geron groaned. "Is that it? I was hoping for some kind of revelation, an epiphany, anything."

"It feels *good*," Asher repeated, his tone implying that his words were enough. He eventually opened his eyes and discovered Geron looking right at him.

"It should feel good," the big man said seriously. "This was just one job. There's always another. There's always more lives to save, more deaths to avenge. I don't expect clearing that nest to have tipped the scales for you. Just know that every job you do, the weight starts mounting in your favour. It also mounts against the past. Just keep swinging, fella."

Asher nodded his head, appreciating the advice. With every day that had passed since he murdered Thomas Murell, the urge to kill himself had, indeed, begun to fade. He hated it.

But now there was something in front of him that he couldn't possibly have imagined: hope. Hope that he might atone for his misdeeds. Hope that he might save lives with his skills instead of taking them from the world.

One day at a time, he told himself. He closed his eyes again, wondering now if his new-found hope was a manipulation of his own mind, his instilled instinct to survive rearing its head and convincing him that he had grown a conscience.

Geron spoke up again before his thoughts spiralled. "Are you going to tell me how you did it?"

Asher didn't bother to open his eyes. "How I did what?"

"How you found that chamber in the pitch black. Or how you chased that fella through the dark. By all rights, you should still be down there, lost to your last breath."

"No," was all Asher said to that.

"No what?"

"No, I'm not going to tell you," he specified.

Geron harrumphed. "Fine, little man. Keep your secrets if you must. You'll crack eventually."

"No I won't," Asher assured.

Geron chuckled to himself. "We make for Lirian tomorrow," he said, changing the subject. "Get some rest tonight. You've earned it."

Asher inhaled slowly and sank beneath the hot water, shutting out the world and Geron's humming. It was going to be a long journey back to The Ranch.

CHAPTER 23

ONWARDS AND, UNFORTUNATELY, UPWARDS

__Mer-folk__ - The darkest depths of The Adean are said to be home to numerous creatures of intelligence, some even equal to our own (though that's entirely debatable), but it is those who dwell closer to our shores that move my quill this day. They be real monsters.

Depending on when you are reading this, you may or may not know of Haven Run, a fishing village on The Shining Coast, just north of Velia. The creatures of the sea came in the night, slithering across the beach like snakes. All but myself were dragged from their homes into those murky waters, reducing the village itself to a lifeless husk.

I found no weakness in them other than with the swing of my sword, a skill the fishermen did not possess. Should a contract be posted concerning these monsters, share the coin with your fellow rangers - your only hope is in numbers.

***A Chronicle of Monsters: A Ranger's Bestiary, 12th Edition,
Page 101.***

Olav One-Eye, Ranger.

. . .

Besides the constant sound of Geron's voice, be it in the form of song or incessant chatter, the return journey to the kingdom of Felgarn and its capital, Lirian, was relatively pleasant. Spring was bringing out the colours of the world and the tall trees of The Evermoore had offered welcome shade from the strengthening sun.

Lirian was just as they had left it, bustling with activity and life, unaware that the two men riding into the city had just saved Velia from a Scudder infestation. Just like the first time, Geron mentioned the smell of Mrs Fairden's bakery, a scent that he apparently used to navigate the city and find his way to The Ranch.

The pair were soon standing before Rolan Vask's ornate desk with fifteen percent of their reward between them. "Good haul, boys," the boss praised, peering inside the purse. "I'm glad to see you both returned to us. Was it Scudders?"

Asher could still see the inside of the female's mouth when he closed his eyes. "It was," he answered, nothing in his tone to hint whether the job had been easy or hard.

"Big female," Geron reported, his arms outstretched. "Asher took care of it like a seasoned ranger though."

Rolan appeared impressed, if a little caught off guard. "A female? That's a mean swing you've got there, Asher. Those beasts aren't always the easiest creatures to slay."

"There's more," Geron said, before the boss could go on. He turned to Asher. "Why don't you go find a replacement for your bracer," he suggested, eyeing the vambrace on the ranger's right forearm, the tough leather poked through by Scudder teeth. "I'll give the boss our report and then we can find some food. Sound good?"

Asher wasn't one for talking if it wasn't necessary. "Suits me."

Closing Vask's door behind him, the ranger took a single step before pausing in the corridor. He looked to his left and laid eyes on Hanaghan's door. It felt unwise to go before the unpredictable man without a chaperone, someone he was more familiar with, but Asher had a question he had wanted answering since they departed Velia.

There came no response from his knock on the door so the ranger let himself in. "Hanaghan?" he called after resetting the latch. "It's Asher," he informed.

"You will understand this time if I don't look at you," Hanaghan finally replied, appearing from behind the large work bench, at the other end of the chamber. His masked head was facing the ranger but, this time, an extra piece of fabric was covering the small eye holes.

"I understand," Asher said, letting go of the sword resting on his hip.

"The Scudders proved easy enough then," the diminutive figure assumed.

Despite Hanaghan's lack of vision, Asher habitually gestured to the numerous vials and ingredients scattered across the central work station. "Your vial proved essential," he told him.

"As did your sword, I'm sure."

Asher wasn't going to deny that. "Both had their moments," he admitted.

"Is there something I can do for you?" Hanaghan asked. "I'm brewing a solution that might conceal your scent from a Vorska and the cauldron requires regular tending to."

Asher removed the empty glass vial from his belt and lightly tapped it against the side bar, letting Hanaghan hear the glass. He proceeded to place the vial in the tray, careful to stay on his side of the white line. The masked man held out his hand and felt for the edge of the side bar before his fingers searched for the rope attached to the tray. He dragged it down the bar towards him and picked up the vial. He required no instruction to begin his investigation.

"Why have you brought me an empty vial of Darkest Night?" he enquired, after inserting the vial into his mask where he might inhale the remnants of the contents.

"Darkest Night," Asher muttered to himself, the absent name

having plagued him since discovering the dropped vial. "You know what it is then?"

"Of course," Hanaghan said, his fingers running over the ridges crafted into the vial. "One dose, such as this, would allow for two, perhaps three, hours of perfect night vision."

"Where could someone acquire the elixir?" Asher pressed.

"You won't find many places that sell Darkest Night - it's illegal in every kingdom. It tends to be a favourite of robbers and the like. There isn't, however, any law against selling the ingredients. You just have to know the method of brewing to create it."

"And you could purchase these ingredients anywhere?"

Hanaghan shrugged, lifting his robes enough to reveal his grubby bare feet. "Most cities have apothecaries who stock the required ingredients, though they won't instruct you on the brewing method."

Asher nodded his understanding, though Hanaghan would never know. "Thank you. I'll leave you to your tasks."

"Asher," Hanaghan called after him. "You need not waste coin on an apothecary, nor waste the time trying to brew the elixir. I can whip you up a batch of Darkest Night before you leave for your next job," he offered.

Asher kept his hand on the door latch. "*You* can make Darkest Night?"

"Of course," the smaller man replied innocently. "Rangers hunt monsters, monsters like the dark. It's been some time since I made any but I have the list of ingredients written down somewhere. Would you like me to make you some?"

"No. No thank you," he added politely. "You've told me all I needed to know."

With that, he left Hanaghan to his experiments and rested his back against the door after closing it. Asher knew he should have left the mystery surrounding the man in the under city to the watchmen of Velia, but it gnawed at him. Unfortunately, Hanaghan had given him nothing that would help track the man down. Anyone in the city with enough coin could find a way to get their hands on Darkest Night.

His concerns for Velia were snatched away when the sound of an argument reached his ears. There was no missing Geron's booming voice nor the sudden scrape of a chair as it was pushed out of the way. Asher hurried down the corridor, quickly discovering that the argument was coming from the larger room directly under The Ranch.

Geron's broad shoulders and green cloak concealed those he was arguing with, though Asher spotted a pair of boots resting on a foot stool in front of the hearth. Off to one side, Rolan Vask looked to be mediating the tense exchange, ready to step in and stop any violence. Upon sighting Asher's entrance, the boss announced him with a hint of surprise in his voice, enough to bring the argument to an end.

Geron whipped his head around, his face flushed red. "I thought you were upstairs."

Asher crossed the room, still trying to assess the situation he had walked in on. "I was talking to Hanaghan," he said.

Geron blinked. "On your own? Don't be daft, fella. He might be small but he'll rip your face off given half a chance."

Asher was finally close enough to see the other side of the argument - two men, one standing, the other sitting comfortably with his feet up. Both wore long coats of black hide, their tattered green cloaks draped over the top. A number of hooks, small blades, and stuffed pouches lined their belts, and both wore more than one belt around their waist.

The one standing up was an inch shorter than Asher, but their builds were similar. His muddy green eyes looked Asher up and down, clearly unimpressed with what he saw. His seated companion turned his head up at the new ranger, a pick fixed between his teeth. Neither man was easily intimidated. If anything, they appeared bored in the fuming shadow of Geron.

"Is there a problem?" Asher asked.

"Why?" the standing ranger retorted, shifting his coat around the hilt of his sword. "Would you like one?"

"Royce," Rolan cautioned.

The world closed in around Asher's sight, his focus drawn to a single point. "Where did you get that?" he demanded, his blue eyes roaming the black cuirass Royce had exposed when moving his coat aside.

Royce rapped his knuckles against the tough leather. "You've got to earn the good stuff," he replied with a wicked grin.

Asher gripped the hilt of his broadsword. "Take it off."

His action was enough to see Royce's seated companion leap to his feet. More impressive was the speed with which he drew a curved dagger from the scabbard on his chest.

Royce, however, had remained perfectly calm in the face of the obvious threat. "What are you going to do with that then?" he asked with some amusement, his eyes flitting over Asher's sword. "My brother here'll run his blade across your throat before that sword even leaves its scabbard."

Asher lifted his weapon an inch, his teeth clamped together. In the same moment, Royce's brother flicked his hand out, bringing the curved dagger within an inch of Asher's neck. Mimicking Royce's confidence, Asher didn't so much as flinch, his gaze fixed on the man wearing his old cuirass, a cuirass that should have been destroyed.

Somehow, Geron made himself even taller. "Put your knife away, Davin." His tone was firm enough to give the most hardened of warriors reason to rethink their actions. Only when Royce gave him the nod did Davin actually lower his weapon, though he did not sheath it.

"Take it off," Asher repeated.

Geron raked his hand across Royce's chest, dragging his coat away to expose the leather cuirass. "That was Asher's," he pointed out, a portion of his previous aggression returning.

Royce's confusion made him appear uncomfortable for a moment, but his bravado was soon to return. "Then he's stupider than he looks," he jibed, shaking Geron's hand away. "This is better than anything we keep around here."

"It was supposed to be destroyed," Asher stated, his blade still an inch removed from its scabbard.

"Even Bail's thick skull could see the folly in that," Royce spat. "I'm putting it to better use."

"Take it—"

Royce stepped closer to Asher, cutting him off. "If you tell me to take it off one more time, I *will*. And then I'll make you *eat* it."

If Royce could have seen inside Asher's mind, he would have known that the previous assassin had already constructed multiple scenarios that ended with the obnoxious ranger struggling to walk and talk for the rest of his days.

Geron's bough of an arm came between them and pushed Royce back before any of those scenarios came to be. "I've already got cause to put you through the wall," the big man said ominously. "Don't add to it."

Royce finally tore his eyes from Asher and looked up at Geron with a taunting grin. "How many times have we done this, half man? I'm not afraid of you. And I'm pretty sure I could put you in the ground without breaking a sweat."

There wasn't a man in that room who didn't hear Geron's knuckles crack as his fists closed into hammers.

"I don't want holes in my walls or blood on my floors," Rolan declared, attempting to diffuse the situation. "Asher, you discarded the cuirass leaving Royce to claim ownership - there's no more to that matter."

Royce spared Asher a smug expression. "Do as you're told like a good little—"

"Shut it!" Rolan barked, silencing the ranger. "I don't want to hear another word come out of your mouth. Geron..." The big man was staring at Royce, caught up in his own murderous thoughts perhaps. "Geron," Vask said again, getting his attention this time.

"As for your argument," he continued, his finger connecting Geron to Royce, "it's done. Finished. Move on."

The big man slowly nodded his head. "As you say, Boss."

"I do say," Rolan reinforced. "I want you to take Asher to the notaries so they can get his description on file. Congratulations," he offered in the same even tone, "you're joining our charter. Come and see me after you've got some rest." And with that, the boss strode away, his words the entirety of any celebration Asher might have received.

"Come on," Geron grumbled, making for the stairs.

Asher maintained his rigid posture for a moment longer, his attention lingering over the cuirass. Geron beckoned him again and he dropped his broadsword back into its scabbard.

"Be seeing you," Davin uttered from the side, his dagger rolling endlessly in his hand.

Asher gave no response. If he did anything other than walk away he was likely to be responsible for the death of them both.

Passing through The Ranch's green door and out into Lirian's streets, Asher came to a stop in the middle of the road. Geron continued another ten feet before realising his companion was no longer keeping up.

"What's the issue?" the big man questioned.

Asher didn't give him an answer. Instead, he slowly turned on the spot and scanned every face, every movement, and every high perch from which he might be observed unnoticed. It had just occurred to him, now that he was exposed, that Royce had provided a link between the Arakesh and his whereabouts.

There were dozens of people walking up and down Ruskin Street; too many for him to see them all. He couldn't define exactly what he was looking for in them but he would just know an assassin of Nightfall if he saw one.

"Asher?" Geron called.

Nothing. He hadn't laid eyes on any that drew his suspicion. But they were out there, he had no doubt. Besides those who were on assignment, the Arakesh who wormed their way through the six kingdoms, there was also the *court*. They would be actively hunting him down and there would be no mistaking his work in Skystead. Tracking him from there to Grey Stone and then on to Lirian would be more difficult; the impression he had left on the world far softer.

But no Arakesh would miss a man boldly walking around with one of their cuirasses on. "Where were Royce and Davin before they returned to The Ranch?" he asked suddenly, taking Geron by surprise.

"What?" the big man replied, scratching his head.

"They were obviously here shortly after us," Asher ploughed on, "otherwise Royce wouldn't be wearing my cuirass. Where did they go after that, while we were in Velia?"

Geron looked back to The Ranch. "I think they were in Palios," he said.

That calmed some of Asher's nerves. Palios was in the east, nestled within the kingdom of Alborn, like its capital, Velia. It was on the other side of the realm to Skystead and Grey Stone. He reminded himself that the court would likely be in the west right now, trying to discern the manner in which he departed Skystead after killing its lord. That meant the chances of coming across Royce were slim.

"What's this all about?" Geron queried. "Listen, don't let them fools get in your head."

"The Mendal brothers, I assume," Asher reasoned, his eyes still moving from person to person.

"Aye," Geron grumbled. "They have their uses, though I wouldn't pay either of them a compliment right now. Come on," he bade. "Let's be getting to the notaries."

Asher fell in beside him, struggling to be anything but on edge. "What were you arguing about?"

"Eh?"

"You were arguing with the brothers," Asher reminded.

"Oh, aye, that I was. I get into an argument with them every time one of them opens his mouth. I wouldn't worry about it, though I do appreciate you having my back..."

Asher was brought to a standstill, the conversation taken right out of him as his eyes rested on a small boy in the middle of the road. The noise of the city faded away as the ranger focused on the pale, deathly figure of Thomas Murell. The boy was staring at him, through the gap in the walking traffic. The sight of the boy and his blood-stained clothes stole Asher's breath away.

"Oi!" Geron cajoled, his heavy hand coming down on Asher's shoulder and breaking his moment with the dead. "You still with me?"

Asher sucked in his first breath in several seconds and clenched the hilt of his sword until the knuckles were white. "Sorry," he mumbled. "I thought I saw..." The ranger shook his head and cleared his throat. "Why did Royce call you *half man*?" he asked, moving the subject on as quickly as possible.

The big man groaned, continuing their journey. "They've been telling me my mother was a Giant since the first day we met."

Asher looked his companion up and down. "They might be right."

Geron eyed him before breaking into laughter, a sound that had become a familiar background to Asher's new life. "Now then, what were you doing going to see Hanaghan by yourself? It's going to be some time before he doesn't want to rip your face off at the mere sight of you."

Asher shrugged, giving himself an extra second to conjure a lie. "I was just thanking him for the vial he gave us. If not for that, we might still be down there trying to reach the female."

"That was damn fine of you," Geron replied. "There's not many who think to thank Hanaghan for his efforts. He's a troubled man to be sure, but he's making amends, just like the rest of us."

Asher nodded along, thinking back to his conversation beneath The Ranch. "Have you ever used elixirs on a hunt?"

Geron's expression soured. "It's all a little too close to magic for my liking. Spells and such don't do it for me; feels unnatural. Why? Has Hanaghan asked you to try one of his new concoctions? Always say no," he added firmly. "He gets it right... in the end. But it ain't worth your trouble being the first."

"Good advice," Asher noted, satisfied to leave the subject there.

After meeting with one of the notaries and having his name and likeness scribed to record, Asher enjoyed a small pie from Mrs Fairden's bakery and returned to The Ranch with Geron. The big man was excited for him to finally put his name to the charter, though he happily paused along the way to introduce Asher to another ranger he had never met before.

"Dunkan!" Geron said everyone's name like they were long lost family. "Where've you been hiding, you old dog?"

"Geron!" Dunkan's beaming smile was refreshing after the batch of rangers Asher had come across so far. "I hear you made good coin in Velia. Something about a female Scudder."

"Word travels fast - we only got back today. Oh, this is Asher, the newest member of our little family. He's about to sign the charter."

Dunkan held out his hand and clasped Asher's forearm. "Well met. You'll learn much with Geron at your side."

Asher took in the new ranger, his dark complexion suggesting a southern origin, yet that assumption clashed with an accent that spoke of a northern upbringing. He had to be older than Geron, though such a distinction could only be seen in Dunkan's grey eyebrows and goatee. He possessed a solid build, though not so broad as Geron, his strength felt in the grip of his hand.

"Well met," Asher greeted. "Have you just returned from a job?" he asked, for lack of anything else to say.

Curiously, Dunkan glanced at Geron before answering. "Came across a contract in Bleak of all places. The whole town had to save up to afford my services mind you, but they preferred to part with the coin than any more folk."

Geron looked very interested. "What was it?"

"A pack of Gobbers," Dunkan informed. "They'd carved out some territory on the very edge of The Wild Moores. They considered Bleak to be inside their hunting grounds and started picking people off in the dead of night."

"You got them all?" Geron sounded a little impressed.

"It took me two damn months but aye, I killed them all."

Geron gave a hearty laugh and patted Dunkan on the arm. "Good man! We should get a drink while we're both here."

Dunkan smiled. "It's your round if I recall."

Geron started away. "I think you must have hit your head fighting them Gobbers," he remarked mischievously. "Come on, Asher; let's make this official."

Asher offered Dunkan a friendly nod before accompanying the big man downstairs. The Mendal brothers were both leant over a low table, playing a game of Galant by the look of the cards they were holding. The four exchanged brief looks before the corridor to Vask's office separated them.

Soon after, he was scribing his name on the charter and receiving a pat on the back from both Geron and Rolan. "You're one of us now, Asher," the boss declared. "You officially own a little bit of all this."

Asher wasn't much interested in owning anything he couldn't carry. "Is there another job?"

Rolan looked at Geron with some amusement. "I need a hundred more like this one. Eager to get back on the road are we, Asher?"

"There's always another job," Asher said, echoing Geron's words from the bath house.

"Unfortunately there is." Vask appeared somewhat downcast at that fact. "Ever had cause to visit Hogstead?"

It took Asher a moment to recall the name and place it on Illian's map. "Can't say I have," he answered honestly.

"It's a village just east of Longdale, across the river." Rolan lazily gestured to a curled up sheet of parchment on his desk. "Our very own Artem Gorinson is there as we speak. He sent that."

"He's got trouble?" Geron asked.

"It would seem so. A far rider brought news of missing livestock. A few sheep disappeared, then a couple of goats, even a horse. By the time Artem got there, the village claimed two of its people had gone missing."

Geron cupped his beard, intrigued. "Troll?" he presumed.

"Or Giant," Vask offered. "Artem isn't sure. His letter doesn't go into detail on his investigation, only that it's one or the other and he could do with an extra sword at his side."

Geron raised a curious, if bushy, eyebrow. "Hogstead is a sleepy little village. I'm surprised they can afford three rangers, let alone one."

"They can't. They can barely afford one of us, in fact. That's why they're only getting one and a half rangers." Vask picked up a bound scroll from his desk and handed it to the big man. "I have a different contract for you. Asher will assist Artem alone."

Geron frowned and unfurled the parchment. As he scanned the words his frown deepened. "Sounds like a job for the Mendals," he grunted.

Rolan shook his head. "They have a contract in Snowfell to deal with. This needs seeing to, Geron. You more than have the skill to get the job done, *alone.*"

"What's the job?" Asher enquired, unsure by the tension if he was even to be privy to such information.

Geron rolled the parchment up and stuffed it into his belt. "Some rich bloke in Dunwich wants the monster experience," he grumbled.

"The monster experience?"

"Aye. No one gets bored like the rich. I've got to escort some lofty coin bag into the wilds and help him track down and kill a monster." Geron eyed the boss. "Unbefitting of a ranger if you ask me."

"Needs must," Roland insisted. "We cannot expand and help

more people if we don't have the coin to do so. Just hunt down some Gobbers and make him feel like a warrior."

"At least it's in Dunwich," Geron said with a little cheer returned to his voice. "We can still travel together."

Asher lost his focus for a second as he realised the path that lay ahead of him now. By road, he would have to pass through Dunwich in order to get even further north, to Hogstead. He hadn't planned on returning to Dunwich for years; perhaps never if he could help it. The local authorities wouldn't be looking for him there, his features unknown even to Esabelle Murell, the only person to have actually come face to face with him on that wretched night.

His palms became clammy just thinking about walking those streets again. Perhaps, the ranger considered, he could go around Dunwich and simply keep The Black Wood on his left. If he continued north he would eventually come across the road again and that would lead him to Merrybuck Bridge. But that would also mean forgoing the supplies he would need to replenish in Dunwich if he was to see his journey through to Hogstead. That would be a very foolish thing to do in northern territory.

"What do you reckon, Asher?" Rolan posed, breaking his discreet moment of panic. "Up for the challenge of taking on a Giant or a Troll?"

Asher swallowed and attempted to regain his composure. "I'll leave at first light," he said.

"Good man," Rolan praised.

Geron patted Asher's shoulder. "Come on, let's treat ourselves to a good meal before we meet the north. Everything tastes like potato up there." The big man paused on their way out and turned back to Rolan. "And he's no half ranger," he remonstrated before shutting the door with some force.

CHAPTER 24

A FAMILY MATTER

Vorska - These monsters have gone by many names over the centuries. Your great grandparents likely called them Vampeer or Vampire. Before that, they were Gorgers and Blood Fiends. Whatever you wish to call them, know this: they are the real hunters. They have been preying on humanity since the dawn of time.

Should you cross them in the light of day, you will see their true appearance and what a monstrosity they are, their nightmarish features forged in the pits of the lowest hell. But, by night, they will appear as the most beautiful person you could imagine. They will charm their victims into seclusion before their beastly tongue drains them of blood.

Silver, my friends. They abhor its touch. Use this to reveal them, then take their head with a good piece of steel.

A Chronicle of Monsters: A Ranger's Bestiary, 12th Edition, Page 46.

Dobrin Vansorg, Ranger.

For most who wished to travel from Lirian to the north, they would first have to take the road either west or south before their path eventually turned to Orith. It was a lengthy journey as The Evermoore itself required navigating if the rest of the realm was to be seen. Thankfully, Geron knew how to get everywhere from anywhere without having to rely solely on the roads.

Leading them with Hector's reins in his hand, the big man cut out through the eastern trees of The Evermoore, his songs filling the great forest. After breaking its outer edge, they continued across the plains and fields, always travelling into the numerous sunrises.

Their camps were relatively quiet affairs, though Asher couldn't understand why Geron had so little to say for a change. Asher knew, of course, why his own mind had retreated into a sanctuary of silence, his turbulent thoughts always ahead of them, to Dunwich. The ranger told himself that his time in the northern town would be brief. He had only to resupply and then he could be on his way again.

That wasn't enough to stop Thomas Murell from haunting his every waking moment.

Sitting in the wagon for the entire trip, the ranger had often found the curved dagger in his hands, the weapon twisted over and over again as he visualised what it would look like buried up to the hilt in his own chest. That was where it belonged, he reminded himself. As with every other moment of torment, however, Asher lacked the conviction to see it through.

"There's always more lives to save, more deaths to avenge." Geron's words had stuck with the ranger and continued to weave a new future for him. Perhaps, he often thought, it was a more befitting punishment that he live with his deeds for the rest of his life, a life that would be filled with atonement, whether it was enough or not.

On The Selk Road now, and journeying north, they passed The Vrost Mountains that dominated the western horizon. Beyond that, the rangers were quickly struck by an icy gale, extreme even for this part of the world. Though the men might have pushed on, Hector was less enthusiastic about the growing winds and continued to slow them down with his protests. Deciding to make an early camp of it, and let the winds settle, Geron guided them to a spot by a tree line, just off the road.

"We're exposed here," Asher commented, eyeing the road from their position. "We should sleep in shifts, lest we be set upon by robbers."

"More fool them I say," Geron replied with a short laugh. "And I think that's the most you've said since we left Lirian. Something stuck in your head, little man?"

"I could ask the same of you," Asher countered.

"You could. I suppose you'd get out of answering my question then, wouldn't you?"

Asher looked down at his hands, where the curved dagger turned end over end between his fingers. "I would have avoided Dunwich if I could," he said, his words almost a mutter.

"You've got history there," Geron reasoned.

Asher took a breath, his reserves required to say any semblance of the truth. "My last target was in Dunwich."

Geron stopped running a piece of cloth down the blade of his claymore. "I thought you killed that fella in Skystead, Lord..."

"Kalben Tarn," Asher reminded. "He was not my..." Another breath was needed to compose himself and find the right words, but they would not come. "It's complicated," he settled on.

"Fair enough," Geron accepted with a solemn nod.

Asher finally sheathed the dagger at the base of his back. "And why have you been unusually quiet? I've grown accustomed to your voice replacing my thoughts."

Geron shrugged. "I would have liked to join you taking on the beast plaguing Hogstead. And I hate jobs like this one," he added, throwing his head to the north.

"You've taken on contracts like this before?" Asher asked.

Geron kept his eyes on his sword. "Aye," he uttered. "I'd rather be hunting a monster that's earned the edge of my blade." The big man sighed. "I'm making an early night of it," he declared, ending any further discussion on the matter. "You take first watch. Wake me when the moon's up there," he requested, pointing at the spot directly above them.

Asher rested back against a tree and pulled his blanket tightly about him, content to watch the world go by for a while. A cloudless night crept over the world and an ocean of twinkling eyes opened up to peer down on the realm of man. The fire needed tending to every now and then and Hector grew ever more restless as the dark encompassed Verda, requiring Asher to rise periodically from his perch and soothe the horse.

There were no more caravans, travellers, or merchants on the road after dark. That didn't mean they were alone, however, as predators always preferred the dark, lurking just beyond the light of the fire. Asher sat very still, his hand gripped around the hilt of his broadsword, as he attuned himself to his environment. In the dead of night, several hours after Geron had started snoring, there was a new sound that captured the ranger's attention. He whipped his head to the left, sure that he had just heard his own name being whispered over the crackling of the fire.

His name was called again, only it originated from his right this time. The ranger was on his feet now, his broadsword pulled an inch from its scabbard. Moving away from the tree, Asher put the fire between him and the wood, making him harder to spot through the dancing flames. There was nothing out there, to his eyes at least. He reached for the red blindfold tucked into his belt.

"That won't be necessary," came the voice again, halting Asher's hand as he touched the red fabric.

The ranger tensed all the more upon recognising that voice. "Show yourself," he whispered.

The shadows loosened their grip on the lithe figure that stepped out of the wood. Clad in the black leathers of Nightfall, a red blindfold covering her eyes, and a pair of short-swords strapped to her back, Demry Stormwell ignored her training and allowed herself to be seen. He quickly decided that was absurd - being seen was likely all a part of her plan to kill him.

"Demry," he greeted quietly.

"Asher," she replied evenly.

The ranger raised his elbow to draw his sword. "Make a sound and he dies first," Demry informed him.

Asher's eyes shifted to one side to take in Geron's sleeping form. "What now then?" he asked.

Demry removed her blindfold and cracked her neck as she adjusted to the low light. "Now you follow me."

Without further explanation, the Arakesh turned around and walked into the wood, her footsteps barely audible. Asher regarded Geron, weighing up his need of the big man. For all the help Geron could offer, Demry possessed the skills to kill him with the flick of her wrist and he believed her threat to be the truth of his companion's fate. Leaving him where he slept, Asher entered the wood and followed the assassin.

Under the glow of the moon, he stepped into a small clearing with a fallen log cutting it in half. Demry's sun-kissed face was just as pale as his under the cold moon, her eyes dark orbs that tracked his every movement. Though he couldn't see it from this distance, he knew there was a scar that ran up one side of her neck and stopped at the base of her left ear. She had received it during the sparring matches in their teenage years in Nightfall, though he couldn't recall the name of the one who had inflicted the wound.

Asher half turned, as if he could see the camp they had left. "You could have waited until I was asleep," he suggested. "That would have been much easier."

"Is that what you would have done?" Demry posed. "Killed me in my sleep?"

Asher considered the scenario for a moment. "I suppose not," he decided. There was no honour among their kind, but growing up in the same cohort was the closest thing any of them had to family, twisted as it was. He would have given her the opportunity to face him and fight for her life.

Demry nodded along. "So this is what you left us for? Hunting monsters for something as trivial as coin?"

"It's a life," Asher said, offering the only defence he felt like giving.

"A pitiful one," Demry quipped.

Asher didn't much care for her opinion. "You're a member of the court then?"

"Of course," she replied casually. "'Tis an honour. Decades slip by in between, but the hunt is always recorded in our archives."

Asher maintained his nonplussed demeanour. "How many others have the honour of hunting me?"

"Four of us have been set to the task," Demry told him. "Though I will see to it that you're never troubled by the other three."

Asher didn't respond to her easy threat, surprised by the number of Arakesh sent to kill him. He was sure that he had broken far more than four of Nightfall's sacred rules. "And who do you share this task with?" he asked, mimicking her casual tone.

"That would be telling," Demry said through her wry smile.

"What does it matter if you're going to kill me in a moment?"

Demry's wry smile became one of amusement. "That was a nice angle to try, but I'm ever the pragmatist. Should you survive this night, the court will see to your end."

"That's if they can find me," Asher pointed out, turning his body so that the hand gripping the dagger behind his back was concealed.

"I found you," Demry boasted.

"That you did," Asher conceded. "How, might I ask? Settle a dead man's curiosity."

Demry's lips pouted and twisted as she considered her course. "I'll answer your question if you answer mine."

Asher pulled on the dagger, exposing a portion of the steel to the cold air. "Sounds fair."

"You were among the best of us," she began. "You even had the Father's favour. His title was inevitably to be your own one day. Why would you risk your life and walk away from all that you've known?"

"To save the girl," Asher told her simply.

Demry blinked. "You turned your back on Nightfall to save the target?"

"The target was a *child*, Demry—"

"They're all *something*," the Arakesh snapped back. "*Their* world is full of names and attachments," she continued, gesturing into the dark. "We are Arakesh. We are unborn of the world and given to shadow and dust. We are the blade in the dark, a companion to Death itself. We may be of flesh and blood, but we are as ethereal as the gods themselves, our every action an extension of fate."

Asher recognised most of her words from The Night Codex, but every one of them rang hollow now. "I couldn't hide behind that any longer," he replied. "*Their* world is the *only* world. We were all a part of it once. Nightfall just stole us away, threw us into the dark, and told us the truth that suited them. Then they *beat* us until we believed it. If you held on to the real world you were as good as dead. Even now, can't you feel the sting of every hook, blade, and hammer brought to bear against you in those halls? How many times were we dragged from our beds and tormented until we rested on the cusp of death? All for what? So we would make for better murderers? So we could kill children in their sleep without a thought?"

Asher shook his head. "Whatever they did to me, it's broken. For the first time since Nasta found me my eyes are actually open - not hiding behind a blindfold."

Demry maintained her serious expression a moment longer before she giggled to herself. "Never would I have expected such nonsense to come from *your* mouth. You're supposed to be *the* Arakesh. There wasn't one among our brothers and sisters who didn't want to be you."

"That isn't me anymore."

"Clearly." Demry's disappointment wasn't missed.

Asher took a breath, his eyes narrowing. "Your turn."

Demry's features lost their harshness as she ascended the fallen log, taking to it like a child at play. "There was no missing your handiwork in Skystead. So many bodies. You had only to kill the patron to save the target you know."

"I was working through some things," Asher said darkly.

"Indeed. How unfortunate for The Ironsworn that Asher discovered his feelings. You've set their entire operation back a couple of decades for sure."

"Knowing I was in Skystead doesn't explain how you tracked me to the side of the road in the middle of nowhere."

"Well, I knew that if any of your training was still driving your actions you wouldn't have left a trace leaving Skystead, so it seemed like a long way to go when all you left was a pile of corpses. Killing the patron with a book by the way - how very *you*," she said with an approving grin.

"You haven't answered my question," Asher reminded her.

Demry performed a playful spin on the log. "Patience, Asher. Anyone else would do their best to continue this conversation in the hope of prolonging their life."

"It's the curiosity that's killing me," the ranger assured, bringing out a soundless chuckle from the assassin.

"Do you still hear Nasta's voice in your head? He always gave our cohort more attention than the others. I suspect that was because of you."

Asher remained stoical, awaiting the real answer to his question.

"*Distance*, he always said," Demry continued. "Get out of the kingdom at least and put as much distance between you and your work. Then *disappear*. His words have always been like guiding stars, haven't they? So I heeded them and simply looked at a map. I thought where would I go to disappear? Well, the entire width of the realm sits between Skystead and Velia, and Velia has one of the largest populations in all of Illian. So I did what any good predator does - I chose my hunting ground and I waited. There's only one way in and out of the capital too, the perfect place to keep my eyes on."

"You saw me in Velia?" Asher thought of a dozen opportunities to kill him in the bustling city, yet here he was.

Demry laughed out loud this time. "You were actually *in* Velia? I was right?" she beamed with self-satisfaction. "I didn't see you. Apparently, I just missed you."

Asher couldn't hide his confusion. "If you didn't see me, how have we arrived at this moment?"

"Picture it," Demry said, her hands coming up to set the frame. "I'm there looking for you, the traitor of our generation, when I see this repugnant excuse of a man striding out of Velia's gate with all the boldness of a king... wearing *your* cuirass."

A low growl of annoyance rumbled from Asher's throat. More than anything, right now, he wanted to get his hands around Royce Mendal's throat.

"Of course," Demry continued, "I didn't know it was yours exactly, but people don't just go walking around wearing the garb of Nightfall. I didn't peg the man as being capable of besting an Arakesh either, which led me to assume he had a potential connection to you. So I followed him all the way to Lirian." Demry was almost within striking distance now, her smile broadening with every word. "I couldn't believe my luck. You were just strolling around the city with that Giant back there."

Asher drew his dagger another inch. "It looks like I didn't cover my tracks well enough."

"It looks like you've abandoned everything Nightfall taught us," the assassin retorted, her grin turning predatory.

"Not everything," Asher replied, a prelude to launching his dagger.

Demry twisted her body, pivoting on the ball of her foot, and narrowly avoided the spinning blade. At the same time, Asher dived away from the fallen log and simultaneously reached around for his folded bow. By the time he was coming up on one knee, the bow had unfurled and his free hand was nocking an arrow. Demonstrating her own lightning reflexes even further, the Arakesh was already leaping towards him with both of her short-swords in hand. The arrow was set free, its aim true and deadly, but the fine shaft was chopped down mid-flight by the edge of Demry's blade.

There was no time to nock another arrow, forcing Asher to drop the bow and retrieve the hour-glass blade from over his shoulder. He brought it to bear with hardly a second to spare, their weapons clashing with a ring of steel. Their dance set to a quick pace, the warriors collided in the manner of coiled snakes. Every strike was precise, targeting areas of the body that would deliver a mortal blow.

With two blades, Demry maintained the advantage, making Asher work twice as hard to parry, evade, and counterstrike where he could. Her footwork was almost identical to his own, a testament to their shared time together in Nightfall. Try as he might, there would be no out-manoeuvring her to work the best angle. He needed to even the fight.

Where he could, Asher threw out a punch, elbow, or kick to put his opponent off balance, but Demry took every impact and adapted her next attack to fit with it. In order to avoid a spinning back kick to the jaw, Asher dropped to the ground and rolled aside, swiping as he rose again. The Arakesh, however, raised her boot and evaded the swing. She used the shift in her weight, instead, to come down on the ranger with a chopping blow.

Seeing the feint for what it was, Asher predicted her real attack, the one she intended to skewer him with. He parried high to block the incoming sword and their blades met. As steel collided, the ranger reached out with his free hand and grasped Demry's other wrist. He succeeded in halting the plunging attack of her second blade, though the tip still pierced his leathers and cut into his skin, just below the ribs. There they remained, frozen in a moment of wills.

"This is the only honour you get," Demry hissed through a clenched jaw.

Asher wasn't one for speaking while his life was on the line - that's what his weapons were for.

Freeing his blade from its locked battle, the ranger spun the short-sword round in an arc. The weapon was now swinging from low to high and cutting a line between their bodies. The movement required less than a second to execute, leaving Demry with no choice but to yank the tip of her second blade back or lose her entire hand. Her sudden movement was enough to break Asher's vice-like grip and present his short-sword with naught but air to slice.

Changing the angle of his attack at the last moment, however, the ranger rolled his shoulder and slammed his elbow into Demry's face. The Arakesh was taken from her feet as she stumbled backwards and fell to the ground. Not one to stay down, Demry turned her momentum into a backwards roll and came up on her feet again. Her top lip was cut, the blood running over her grimace and onto her chin.

"I'd say that killer's still in there," she said wickedly, wiping the blood away. "You could return to Nightfall. Beg the Father for forgiveness. There would be punishment, of course, but you could be allowed back into the fold. It's where you belong."

Asher tilted his head. "Are you pleading for your life?"

Demry's grimace turned into a snarl, leading her to lunge with her one and only blade. Asher reversed his grip on the hilt of his short-sword and met his foe with a flurry of strikes and counter-strikes. They flitted across the clearing, stepping and jumping over the log to continue their battle. Asher scored a series of shallow cuts but never managed to sink his blade in and finish the job. Demry proved the more acrobatic of the pair, twisting her body from one unorthodox position to another in a bid to confuse the ranger.

One such display of flexibility saw the assassin lock Asher's sword arm in her grip before her entire body spun end over end. Asher had no choice but to flip with her or suffer a broken arm. It was a choice, however, that laid him on his back beside his enemy. His attempt to recover was dashed when Demry's leg whipped up and caught him in the jaw, preceding the tip of her blade, angled down at the ranger's chest.

There was nothing he could do about it, no angle he could exploit, and no defence he could muster. The moment was hers and she was seizing it just as they had been trained to do. There was a glimpse of hope, however, hope that only Asher could see from his angle. Without a blindfold on, Demry's awareness went no further than any ordinary person's, and no ordinary person would have heard the slow and delicate movements of an experienced ranger approaching their prey.

Geron Thorbear broke his silent approach with a barrelling leap that took both him and the Arakesh tumbling away. Somewhere along the way, Demry had retrieved a small knife from her belt and now slashed at Geron's throat as they came to a stop, side by side. Her reach was too short, a fact that saved Geron's life but not a portion of his beard. Her next swipe was intercepted by one of his meaty hands, his grip powerful enough to make the assassin drop the small blade.

Demry's hips thrust her legs into the air, where they twisted at speed to bring her round and onto her feet once more. Incapable of such a feat, Geron remained very much on the ground. Now it was the big man looking down the length of the Arakesh's short-sword.

"No," Asher growled, rising enough to throw his hour-glass blade. It was a lazy throw, but the weapon still required redirecting by Demry, lending Geron enough time to push up from the ground and slug her round the face with a knotted fist.

Asher found his feet, half of his face covered in dirt, the other half already bruising from Demry's boot. He closed in on Geron's side, drawing his broadsword as the big man took his claymore in hand.

"What in all the hells have I walked in on?" the large ranger demanded.

Asher wanted to instruct his companion to leave, to stay well away from the matter, but it was too late for that. Demry would kill him as soon as she could, which meant Geron was in the fight now, a fight against an order as old as the Third Age, an order that had perfected the art of killing people for a thousand years.

"Use the advantage of your reach," Asher told him through laboured breath. "Don't let her get in close."

Demry cut a lithesome figure in the middle of the clearing, her pose offering no suggestions as to her next action. She had, however, risen with her red blindfold tied around her head, concealing her eyes. Two against one made no difference now - the advantage was hers.

Breaking into a sprint, Demry was upon the rangers in moments. The log allowed the assassin to leap high and split her legs, whipping a boot in each of their faces. Returned to her feet, she spun around and lashed out at a staggering Geron, who yelled out as the tip cut through his hip, pushing him back even more. The big man gave her no opportunity to deliver a second attack though, his claymore swinging round in a devastating arc of steel. The Arakesh ducked beneath the blade and came up with Asher now bearing down on her after closing the gap again.

The Nightseye elixir coursing through Demry's veins informed her of every micro-movement Asher made, declaring his violent intentions with clarity. The assassin weaved between his strikes with only the slightest of shifts in her stance. Sensing her moment to go on the attack, Demry leapt into the air and planted both feet into Asher's chest. The force of it launched the ranger clear off his feet and into the dirt.

Stretching his back to the point that his spine cracked, Geron presented the Arakesh with a look of determination and true grit. Against Asher's pained protests, the big man strode towards Demry with his claymore gripped in both hands. Geron's speed was inspiring, but it wasn't enough. The assassin knew of his every attack half a second before it landed, more than enough time for her to evade. She scored a dozen cuts across his considerable body, making a mockery of his hard leathers. Every one only served to anger the big man all the more. He came at her again and again, his successive blows growing wilder and clumsier.

His claymore, though, did succeed in keeping Demry at bay, never quite able to get in close enough to use her short-sword. An Arakesh, however, was nothing if not adaptable. In a deft and graceful move, the assassin performed a rolling handstand as she advanced on the ranger. As she came out of the flip, her hand bowled a rock she had collected on her way up, her momentum and strength behind it. Big as he was, Geron's very human skull could not stand against the stone that impacted it, just above his right eye.

He staggered one way, then the next, like the mast of a ship caught in a storm. As blood began to trickle down his face, his legs finally buckled and he collapsed to the ground, struggling to hold on to consciousness.

Demry wasted no time, moving in to finish the kill. The assassin paused after a single step, her senses informing her of a new development in the fight. She cocked her head and knew immediately that Asher was on his feet again, sword in hand... and eyes covered behind red cloth.

The ranger could hear Demry's heart quicken. He could smell the blood oozing from her various wounds. The air was foul with the taste of her sweat - and her fear. It wasn't fear of death, Asher knew, for there was no escaping such a fate, not even for the Arakesh. No. Demry was afraid of failing.

And now, despite the battlefield having evened out again, her quarry had settled back into the mindset of a true killer, his senses just as heightened as hers.

"You should have killed me in my sleep," he said, keeping his feet rooted.

Demry's chest heaved as her shoulders bobbed up and down with her rapid breathing. For all her training, and that voice that had been nurtured inside of her to reinforce her predatory nature, the assassin knew there was a good chance she would never see the dawn. As she herself had said, Asher was *the* Arakesh. Submerged into his heightened senses, he was Death incarnate.

That didn't stop her from trying, that drive to not only eliminate her target but also to survive, putting her muscles to action. The assassin crossed the clearing at a sprint, yet Asher remained where he stood, not to be moved by the imminent threat.

He could feel the impact her every movement had on the environment. Her rushing limbs pushed the air around her, informing him of direction and speed. Subtle shifts in her balance and micro tensions in her muscles screamed her intentions. When she was finally upon him, Asher tossed his broadsword at her feet, forcing her to make predictable adjustments to her attack. He then twisted his shoulders to one side so that the edge of Demry's blade skimmed his leathers and pushed on into air alone.

That was step one in a series of movements that, ultimately, reversed Demry's sword arm down and then up to her shoulder blade, flipping the assassin onto her back. Not a second after slamming into the ground did Asher snatch her blindfold from her eyes and drop his knee onto her neck. Pain and disorientation robbed the Arakesh of precious moments in which she might have formulated a plan to escape.

By the time her ordinary senses had readjusted to the world there was nothing she could do. Asher's full weight was driven down through his knee and onto her windpipe. With one hand he maintained a grip on her wrist, preventing her from using the short-sword she had managed to keep hold of.

Then he waited.

Demry writhed and squirmed under his pressure, her heart beating so fast it sounded as if it might burst. Inevitably, it began to slow down. Her erratic movements calmed down and she lost her grip on the short-sword. Finally, her gargling faded away and her pulse ceased its drumming.

Asher let go of her wrist and stood up. From the direction of Geron's breathing, he could tell that the big man was looking directly at him from across the clearing. He was still lying where he had fallen, though the blood had stopped trickling from the cut on his head.

"It's finished," Asher told him.

"Aye," the ranger replied with a tone of disbelief. "What *are* you?"

CHAPTER 25
A LIFE OF CHOICE

Sandstalkers - *Don't run. Never Run. Sandstalkers are among the most confident predators the world of monsters has to offer. Standing your ground will put them off balance and lend you an edge in the fight. If faced by one on its own - and this is unlikely - seek out the monster's weak spots, the softer flesh between the joints; their chitinous exterior can blunt the best of steel. That said, it is more likely you will encounter a nest. In this instance, run. Run until the heat of The Arid Lands beats you into the sand. A nest of Sandstalkers is not to be taken lightly, nor ever alone.*

A Chronicle of Monsters: A Ranger's Bestiary, 12th Edition, Page 256.

Jorven Dorn, Ranger.

Under the same starry night and cold moon that had seen Demry to the next life, Asher and Geron sat opposite each other, their tension added to the fire between them. The big man's dark eyes crossed those flames and bored holes into Asher as he waited for some kind of explanation.

"An old lover?" Geron questioned, tired of waiting.

"More like a sister," Asher grumbled, seeing no way around the conversation.

"Who was she?"

Asher stared at the flames, aware of the new injuries that began to nag at him. "Her name was Demry Stormwell," he began. "And she was an assassin, like me."

"When you say, *like you*, you mean the pair of you could kill with your eyes closed?"

Asher licked his swollen lips. "Yes," he said.

Geron nodded as he mulled it all over. "You know, there's stories, *myths* I suppose, about assassins who come in the dark and kill you with their eyes closed. Actually, most of those stories tell of assassins wearing blindfolds. Red ones if I recall the tales."

Asher didn't miss the glance at the red cloth currently wrapped around his hand. The ranger squeezed his fist - another life taken with it. He hated wearing it, but he couldn't deny the results it yielded.

"Arakesh," he declared softly.

"Aye," Geron replied. "That's the name."

"It's elven," Asher explained. "It means assassin."

Geron physically rocked back on his perch. "They're real? You're... real?"

Asher nodded silently.

"No," the big man drawled. "You're having me on. They're just legends."

"We're very real," Asher told him gravely. "Night..." The ranger caught himself instinctively, his fist squeezing the blindfold all the tighter. "Nightfall is real," he managed, pushing through the mental barriers.

"What's that then?"

"It's where they train us. They take children, usually orphans, and indoctrinate them into the order. They break you down, unmake you, undo all that the world might have taught you, and then they build you back up into a weapon."

Geron was doing his best to absorb the information, revelatory as it was. "And your father, he was an... Arakesh?"

Asher sighed, exhausted from the fight and eager to sleep more than anything, but Geron deserved some answers after what he'd just been through. "My real father was an Outlander," he answered, shaking his head as he did so. "I remember nothing of him, not his face nor even his voice. Everything before Nightfall is just smoke. The man I spoke to you of is Nasta Nal-Aket, though I warn you, Geron Thorbear," he named, making certain his companion grasped the gravity of what he was about to say, "should you ever be heard to say his name I cannot guarantee it won't reach the wrong ears. A swift death would surely follow."

Geron arched his bottom lip and slowly nodded his head. "Why'd you call him your father then?"

Asher shrugged. "It's complicated. He's the one in charge of Nightfall though, and he's also the one who sent Demry Stormwell to kill me."

"Because you walked away?" Geron posed. "I witnessed the slavers in The Arid Lands do something similar."

Asher turned the flat of his short-sword over scrutinising each side of the blade. "You don't walk away from Nightfall. Once an Arakesh, you die an Arakesh. Demry is one of four sent to kill me."

Geron's bushy eyebrows pushed up into his head, causing the big man to wince as he stretched the cut above his right eye. "Four?" he echoed with concern. "Four like *her*?"

"They will all have varying degrees of talent, but they are all killers of the highest order. Each one will have been hand-picked by the masters to form their court of assassins."

Geron did nothing to hide his dismay. "Let's say you beat these killers," he theorised. "What then? They just send more until you're dead?"

"The court has a particular set of rules. If I can survive those sent to kill me, Nightfall will stop hunting me."

"That's quite the trial," Geron remarked.

"Surviving the four doesn't make me a free man," Asher lamented. "For the rest of my days the Arakesh will kill me on sight. I'll be running till I die."

"Well, look on the bright side," Geron suggested, raising his waterskin, "it's just three now."

That was little comfort to Asher. "We should part ways," he announced suddenly.

"What's that?" Geron questioned with a scowl.

"If I stay a ranger, you, the others, The Ranch... They'll kill you all to get to me."

"They know nothing about us," Geron protested, trying to reassure him. "I mean, *she* knew, but you said that's because she followed Royce and Davin back to Lirian. She got lucky. The other three are in the dark."

"That's the problem," Asher muttered, taking the comment as literal.

"Stick with us, Asher," Geron insisted. "We've got your back." Asher considered those he had met who called themselves ranger and thought otherwise. Seeing the doubt on his face, the big man continued. "I've got your back," he promised. "You joined us to start a new life. If *I* have to fight for that life, you can bet my claymore's going to swing."

Asher nodded his appreciation, unable to articulate the thanks he truly felt. No one had ever been there to guard his back, to look out for him. Nasta was a close contender, but his motives were twisted. Before he could be taken down the dark halls of his life and the people he had been surrounded by, Geron's words came back to him, quickly followed by Demry's recounting of her hunt.

"You said the brothers were in Palios when we were in Velia." Asher did his best to keep his tone even and non-accusatory.

"Aye," Geron agreed. "That's because they were. I saw the chart with my own eyes in Rolan's office. They were dealing with a Wraith if I recall."

A flash of suspicion crossed Asher's face. "Then how did Demry follow them from Velia? They arrived in Lirian almost as we did, so they must have been in the city while we were there."

Geron shrugged. "I couldn't say what goes through the minds of those idiots. They were likely taking The Selk Road back to Lirian - they would have come across Velia from Palios. There's not many who won't stop in the capital, especially when they've got good coin to spend."

Asher couldn't argue with that logic and it soothed the dark questions that had been rising to the surface. Though he still couldn't say what he was going to do when he saw Royce Mendal again.

"So." Geron drew the word out after Asher had remained silent for some time. "What can I expect should I run into another of your old pals? Can they all..." The big man covered his eyes with one hand.

"They can all fight with their eyes closed," Asher elaborated. "In fact, they're much harder to kill with their eyes closed. If you can, remove the blindfold. I'm not saying that will make them easy to kill, but it might even the odds... a little."

"How can you fight *better* with your eyes closed?" Geron asked, dabbing the cut on his head with a wet cloth.

Asher's instincts continued to tell him to keep his mouth shut, that pain would follow if Nightfall's secrets spilled out. But Geron was in it now, an oath taken to fight by his side. He needed to know what he was up against.

"It's called Nightseye elixir," he began. "It's an elven potion similar to Darkest Night. The effects are more potent and, if you consume it daily for a long time, those effects become permanent."

Geron looked at him across the fire in disbelief. "Permanent?"

Asher raised his hand to display the red blindfold. "All we have to do is shut out the light - *all* light. The elixir is sensitive. If there's even a speck of light pressing against your eyelids it won't work."

"So that's how you were able to make your way through Velia's under city," Geron concluded.

"Without sight, my other senses are heightened. They build an image of my surroundings in my mind, only its clearer than anything my eyes could ever see."

"That sounds incredible," Geron opined wistfully.

"It can be addictive," Asher admitted. "Nothing compares to the feeling of superiority it instils in you. It connects you to the world in a way you can't imagine. Everything touches something else. You can taste without putting anything in your mouth. You can feel the vibrations of someone's voice on your fingertips. I can smell how many people have touched you since you last bathed. I can even smell the fear that comes out in your sweat. And you hear *everything*. Your bones grinding. Your heart beating. I can hear the hairs in your nose moving with every breath. Nothing escapes an Arakesh in the dark."

Geron opened his mouth before blowing out a cloud of hot air. "Maybe I'll just leave killing them to you," he finally said.

"The Nightseye is only one of their tools," Asher went on. "Every Arakesh is trained to blend in. We're taught every language, every belief, and we've spent time in every culture in all six kingdoms. You could have walked past one of us already and never known it."

"Do you know the other three who are coming for you?"

Asher shook his head. "Demry wouldn't say."

"Would *you* know them if you saw them?"

"Possibly," Asher suggested. "Some are better than others at blending in. And I don't know every assassin in Nightfall."

Geron remained quiet for a time, mulling it all over. "Is it such a good thing that you visit Dunwich?" he eventually asked. "If that's the last place they knew you to be."

"They know I was in Skystead after Dunwich," Asher explained. "They also know I won't go over my own tracks until they're stone cold. They won't be expecting me to return to Dunwich so soon."

Geron nodded, accepting Asher's knowledge where the Arakesh were concerned. "What happened there, in Dunwich?" he asked softly, and for the second time that night. "What did you do?"

Asher looked up to see his companion but his eyes were drawn beyond him, to the image of Thomas Murell standing in the snow. "I took one life too many," the ranger whispered, his eyes never straying from the small boy. "I never stopped to think for myself. Or think at all, for that matter. My conditioning was like a blanket, shielding me, *blinding* me, from what I was really doing." He took a breath, determined to say it out loud. "I killed a child."

As the last syllable left his mouth, the contents of his stomach rose with some force into his throat. The ranger threw his head to one side and vomited on the ground. A groan escaped his lips as he straightened up again. Thomas Murell was gone, leaving only Geron's dark eyes to see across the flames.

"Someone paid for the death of a child?" the big man posed with disgust.

"Not someone," Asher said. "Lord Kalben Tarn."

Revelation crossed Geron's features. "That's why you killed him."

"He had to die," Asher insisted. "He had paid for the death of two children, brother and sister. Only his death would end the contract with Nightfall and save the girl."

"Good riddance," Geron sneered.

Asher nodded absently, his gaze stolen by the flickering fire. He was slipping into a dark place inside his mind, a place that determined his punishment should be death. Perhaps he should have let Demry kill him - at least it would have been over in a heartbeat.

"It's like you said," Geron spoke up, cutting through his bleak thoughts, "you didn't know what you were doing."

"It's no excuse," the ranger replied, his throat dry.

"No," Geron whispered. "I suppose it's not. But you know what you're doing now. You *can* think for yourself. You *chose* to kill Kalben Tarn. So you have to choose again. Will you take that dagger of yours and drive it through your heart? Or will you keep that green cloak on and do some good in the world? And, the truth is, you might have to make that choice every day for the rest of your life."

Asher absorbed those words, taking them on as a foundational truth about his life. Perhaps one day he would choose the former and end it all. But he knew that wasn't this day. Not yet.

"You don't feel like killing me yourself?" Asher questioned.

Geron could only give him a glance while he contemplated his response. "No," he said, after some thought. "At least not tonight," he added wearily. "Ask me again in the morning."

Asher's mouth attempted a smile but contorted into something else instead. "I'll keep watch," he volunteered.

"Good on you, little man," Geron replied, getting comfy on his bed roll. "Should any more of your friends turn up, leave me be would you?"

Pained as it was, Asher found a brief smile. Then he was left to the flames and his thoughts.

CHAPTER 26
A DARK DAWN

***Gobbers** - Gangly creatures of muscle and claw. What they lack in intelligence I have found they make up for in ferocity, a feature that is amplified all the more by their pack-like behaviour.*
They have speed on their side and you won't see them coming until they have you ambushed. Their scales are tough but not impenetrable - nothing a good axe can't deal with.

A Chronicle of Monsters: A Ranger's Bestiary, 12th Edition,
Page 112.
Kel Kregor, Ranger.

Spring in Dunwich was no different to winter in Dunwich - cold and bleak. What it lacked in physical warmth, however, the people made up for in their good nature and general busyness. The markets were out in full force with throngs of merchants and customers in constant flux as the rangers made their way through to the inner town.

Asher was hesitant to climb out of the open-top wagon, his eyes darting about from the concealment of his green hood. He took in every person and counted the number of watchmen that crossed their path. Here and there were a few of King Tion's soldiers, lingering, no doubt, after the assassination of the lord's son.

Geron had no such hesitation and jumped down from his perch behind Hector. "You've no need to accompany me," he said. "And I think it best if you get back on the road as soon as possible," he added in a quieter tone. "You know where's good to get supplies from here?" the big man asked.

Asher simply nodded, having already planned out where he was going to go and exactly what he was going to purchase for the remainder of his journey to Hogstead.

"Now, when you get to where you're going," Geron continued, while unharnessing Hector, "Artem will be waiting for you. He'll be expecting anyone but you, so prepare yourself. As you already know, Artem is something of a *harsh* man. He won't be thinking much of you and he'll say so. Harsh as he is," the big man countered himself, "he knows what he's doing. He's read that bestiary more times than both of us, so listen to his advice. Troll or Giant, either is going to be big trouble."

Asher, at last, climbed out of the wagon, one hand under his quiver to keep it steady on his back. His feet slid into the mushy snow and sank into the mud of Dunwich's streets. "I can handle Artem," he assured.

"I've no doubt," Geron quipped, his eyebrows jumping briefly into his forehead. "Take Hector," the big man insisted, holding out the horse's reins.

Asher looked from the mount to his companion. "You're sure?"

"Of course," Geron replied, gesturing for Asher to take the reins from him. "You don't want to trek to Hogstead on foot and then face a monster. Though, I warn you: if Hector sees a monster, or his own shadow, he's definitely going to bolt, so always keep him back."

"Understood," Asher said, taking the reins in hand.

"Meet me back here when you're done," Geron told him, slinging his axe over one shoulder. "Oh, and take the spear," he added, thrusting his jaw at the wagon. "A weapon with a bit of reach is no bad thing when it comes to Trolls and Giants."

Having read most of the material regarding both fiends on their journey north, Asher wasn't about to disagree. Keeping the spear upright, he strapped it to the back of the saddle before removing an empty satchel he intended to fill with supplies.

Geron held his arm out and waited for Asher to take it, the pair embracing the wrist of the other. "Between now and your return," the big man said, holding him in place, "be sure to make the right choice every day. I expect to enjoy a hot meal and a drink while you regale me with the details of your hunt."

Asher nodded his understanding. "Good hunting yourself," he offered.

Geron let go of the ranger's arm and shrugged the comment away. "It's hardly a hunt," he grumbled. "Now be off with you, little man. The people of Hogstead are in need of you."

The rangers parted ways, taking opposite directions. Asher paused to look back, but the big man was already gone. Deciding it was important to keep his feet moving, he towed Hector through the streets and moved from shop to shop, stall to stall, collecting what he needed for the journey. He hardly bartered for a single item, eager to just pay the required coin and be on his way.

Pushing on, his supplies packed and attached to the saddle, Asher guided Hector on foot and made for The Selk Road north out of the town. The ranger was brought to a halt in his tracks, however, his attention captured by a familiar sign swinging in the wind: Bellman and Sons. The undertaker's office appeared quiet from the outside with only the flicker of a candle seen through the window.

Asher tightened his grip around the reins in one hand while the other reached down and rubbed the red cloth of his blindfold. *Keep going*, he told himself. He had no business in there nor ever again. Turning away, he fully intended to put one foot in front of the other and be on his way. But his feet remained rooted. A spiralling thought entered his mind, its hooks digging deep. He didn't know for sure that Esabelle Murell was still alive. There was a chance the under-taker still had a message in there for the assassin that had been sent to replace him.

Keep going, he urged himself.

Against his better judgement, Asher was already tying Hector to a nearby post. He double knotted the reins and sighed, aware that he was making a mistake.

Ignoring his instincts, the ranger entered the undertaker's office, once again feeling the red string wrapped around the neck of the door handle. He kept his hood up, lending him a menacing appear-ance in the gloom of the office. Like the last time he had stepped inside, the old Bellman was looking over parchments on his tall desk. He didn't miss Asher's entrance this time.

"Can I help you?" he asked, clearly concerned.

Asher paused, licking his lips. "A dark dawn this morning," he replied, giving the coded phrase.

The undertaker's concern slipped into confusion. "I don't have anything for you."

Asher took that in, standing perfectly still for a moment. His finger then began to tap incessantly against his leg, his thoughts racing ahead. He was about to leave when a question found its way out of him. "Have any others been here? Recently?"

The undertaker was caught somewhere between terror and bewilderment. "I'm not sure what I'm supposed to say," he muttered. "You don't normally ask questions."

Already feeling impatient, Asher stepped right up to the desk and pressed one finger onto the surface. "Have any others like me been in here recently? Have you received any messages?"

The undertaker glanced nervously to the side, leading Asher to the open door behind the desk, where another, smaller, office could be seen. Without invitation, the ranger rounded the desk and strode into the smaller room. The undertaker raised a hand as if to protest at the intrusion but he quickly lost his nerve and lowered his arm.

This desk was a mess of scattered paperwork and sundries, most of which Asher swept aside. "Where is it?" he demanded.

The old Bellman swallowed and looked nervously at the fireplace fixed into the wall beside the desk.

Asher knocked over a chair in his haste. Crouching by the flames, he examined the ashes and used his dagger to move the debris. There it was, a small length of knotted red string no longer than his finger tip.

"You burned it," he growled.

"I'm supposed to," the undertaker stuttered.

Asher clenched his fist around the remaining piece of string, the message lost to him forever. "How long ago did you receive this?" he questioned without looking at the old Bellman.

More panic overcame the man. "I'm not sure. A week, maybe two. Maybe *more*. All the days have blended into one of late."

Asher tossed what remained of the string into the flames and marched out of Bellman and Sons, shouldering his way past the undertaker as he did so. He could learn no more from this place and, if he stayed a moment longer, he was going to cripple the old Bellman with his bare hands.

Returned to the cold air, where his breath was all the more visible, Asher untethered Hector and turned down the street that would take them to The Selk Road. Again, his feet refused to move in the intended direction.

He needed to know.

Instead of going left, he went right, a path that would take them to the manor of house Murell.

By the time the grand house was in sight, the ranger's heart was thundering in his chest. He knew a handful of techniques that would slow his heart rate down and grant him a more level head, but none of them came to mind in the shadow of the manor.

Keeping his face in the shade of the hood, Asher guided Hector down the street, past the front of the house. There were twice as many guards outside the front gate, none of whom looked to be distracted by a game or even light conversation. Behind them, over the walls, the ranger could see that the window he had leaped from had been replaced and bars fitted to the outside. That was all he had seen by the time the manor was behind him, its inhabitants locked away inside.

Again, Asher ignored the warning in his mind and tied Hector to another post, outside a carpenter's workshop this time. Leaving the horse, he quickly made his way down the nearest alley, sure to check over his shoulder for any watchers. Confident he had entered the alley unseen, the ranger pulled back his hood and began to climb the side of the building. He was crouched low and hurrying over the rooftops in less than a minute, working his way back to the Murell's manor.

Returned to the same perch he had occupied after fleeing the grounds, Asher had the perfect vantage over the manor and its surroundings. Like the gate, the interior courtyard and lawn had twice the number of guards on patrol. Narrowing his vision, he tried to see through the windows and actually spy Esabelle with his own eyes. To see her, to know truly that she was living and breathing would relieve but a portion of the burden and worry that had beset him since that fateful night.

Alas, the light of day reflected off the windows and prevented any penetrating gaze. Asher knew it was unwise to linger, his presence on the roof alone more than enough to have him brought before the lord in chains. Then there was the matter of the other Arakesh, who might or might not still be in town somewhere. But, he *had* to know.

Giving it no further thought, Asher tied the red blindfold around his eyes and submerged himself into the details of the world. The ranger focused until the ruckus of the street was reduced to whispers in the back of his mind. Concentrating on the house, he detected the rich wood of its external doors and pushed on, searching for the vibrations that rippled through the floors. There were servants, though notably fewer than before his attack. He could feel the subtle shifting of weary feet carrying the weight of a guard and all their armour: a soldier posted at almost every internal corner.

There was but one voice inside the manor and it possessed the light and playful tones of a child. Homing in on it, Asher found three guards stationed outside the room and one more inside with the child. Wooden toys were being knocked together and towers of small blocks pushed over, the latter of which caused the child to giggle.

It was Esabelle.

Asher sighed with relief. The ranger slumped against the chimney and removed the blindfold - he didn't deserve to intrude on their lives any further. Esabelle was alive and that was all that mattered.

Retracing his steps, Asher climbed down to the alley floor with all the stealth he had employed on his ascent. He checked the street, left and right, before emerging to reclaim Hector. Of the faces who passed him by, Asher could confidently say he had never seen any of them before, and he always remembered the faces that crossed his path.

Mounting Hector right now felt too much like standing out, leading Asher to simply guide the horse to the north road on foot, his head bowed and returned to the shadows of his hood.

It was time to go on the hunt.

CHAPTER 27

HOGSTEAD

Wraith - This foul creature is not of this world, but that of the Shadow Realm, a nightmarish place that only the most experienced mages can access (see Monsters of the Deep World).

Half in this world, half in another, most folk call them ghosts but, as we all know, there's no such thing. Though, fighting these beasts can sometimes feel like fighting smoke.

Killing the mage who conjured the Wraith won't change a thing; once it's here it's here to stay. Studying Wraiths is near impossible due to their hyper-violent nature, so we have no idea what they crave. We only know that their victims are drained of vitality and life: a painful process from all reports.

While magic is the best weapon against a Wraith, they can be killed with traditional means, including an unusual weakness to salt. For reasons unknown, salt disrupts their ethereal nature and reveals more flesh and blood. Good hunting.

A Chronicle of Monsters: A Ranger's Bestiary, 12th Edition, Page 50.

Gudvig, son of Gendervig, Ranger.

Putting Dunwich and The Old Well behind him, Asher took The Selk Road north until he arrived at a fork - west to Namdhor or north-east to Longdale and its surrounding villages. Astride Hector now, he had taken that north-easterly path, known as The Icing Road, and journeyed the days and nights required to bring him to Merrybuck Bridge. Besides the handful of merchants and their small caravans, the road had been his, much to the ranger's dismay.

The silence had not been kind to him.

Absent Geron's constant noise, Asher's mind had struggled to leave Dunwich. Though he had heard the laughter and play of Esabelle, he had also detected the silence of her father, locked away in his study, there to be consumed by his grief. Then there was her mother, motionless yet awake in her son's bed, her knees tucked up to her chest with his blanket bundled between her arms.

He had broken their family, shattered it into a thousand pieces that would never be put back together as they once were. How many times before had he done just that? How many lives had been ruined and families torn apart because of his actions?

Such were his thoughts for the duration of his travels, thoughts that followed him into his sleep and robbed him of rest. It was only after crossing Merrybuck Bridge, a wooden and rickety structure, that his mind began to turn towards the hunt that awaited him. It had been a solitary footprint that had caught his attention and finally allowed him to leave some of his past behind.

The print in question lay across his path, sunken into the snow and mud beneath. Of course, had it been the foot of any man or woman, the ranger would likely have missed it. But it could not be the foot of any human. Bringing Hector to a halt beside the print, Asher looked down to scrutinise the shape and size. It was easily the length of his own legs and perhaps a touch wider than the width of his shoulders. By his reckoning, that placed the being who had made the impression at somewhere between twenty and thirty feet tall.

Further examination defined the three stubby toes on the end of the foot, though, according to the bestiary, this wasn't enough to determine the owner as either Troll or Giant, as there were variants of both species who possessed three toes. Still, the size of the print led Asher to believe he was dealing with a Giant rather than a Troll, which were typically smaller than their Giant cousins.

Continuing his journey, he followed the path until it curved to the north to run parallel with The Adanae River. The most eastern tip of The Vengoran Mountains dominated the distant horizon now, their final end just kissing the frozen edges of The Shining Coast. Asher's destination was not so far as that, however, his time on the road brought to an end as he reached Hogstead.

Smoke rose from every chimney in the small village, their rooftops covered in thick layers of snow. Almost every dwelling had a fenced-off pasture that housed livestock of some description, these constant animal sounds the loudest noise in all of Hogstead. There were people here and there, though they moved quickly and lightly on their feet, hurrying from view upon spotting Asher riding in.

The assassin in him knew it would be hard to kill a person here, a place where strangers stood out. And there would be no utilising the straw rooftops in Hogstead, the gap between buildings too far for any man to jump. And that's if the thick snow didn't trip him up first. After a couple of minutes, keeping Hector to his slowest pace, they were already half way through the village.

"Best be stating your business!" came a holler from behind.

Asher was in no hurry to look back, more than confident that he was the most dangerous thing in Hogstead. Instead, he took an extra moment to look over his surroundings and commit the layout to memory.

"Oi!" came that same voice. "I said—"

"My name is Asher," the ranger interjected, turning Hector around.

There he saw not one man but seven, all of whom were brandishing rakes, hoes, and pitchforks as if they were effective weapons against this well-armed stranger. Their ages ranged from late teens to late fifties, their bodies toned from years of hard labour in a harsh land. Not a one of them was a threat in Asher's eyes.

"And what be your business in Hogstead, *Asher*?" the oldest among them demanded.

"He's a ranger," came the answer, though not from Asher's lips. "At least he thinks he is," Artem Gorinson added in his southern accent.

Artem's recognition of Asher put the men at ease. "He's with you?" the older villager queried.

"It would seem so," the archer replied, his tone conveying his disappointment.

"I hear you have a Giant problem," Asher pointed out.

"I have a *numbers* problem," Artem corrected. "I need more rangers and you barely count as one."

"Is this going to cost more?" one of the villagers questioned with some concern.

"No," Artem told him reassuringly. "Asher will not be staying."

"I won't?" The ranger's voice was especially gruff from lack of use, but his tone of surprise could still be heard.

"No, you won't. Take the road to Dunwich and have a raven or far rider sent to The Ranch. Tell Vask I need a *real* ranger." With his bow in hand, Artem turned around and walked away, his sudden departure creating a disturbance amongst the villagers.

Asher gave them an awkward bow of the head and directed Hector to catch up with the stubborn ranger. "There is no one else," he told Artem. "Geron has taken a job in Dunwich and by the time your message reached Rolan the Giant plaguing these people will have taken more lives."

"You keep saying *Giant*," the archer retorted without looking up at him.

"Judging by the prints I came across on my way in I'd say it's a good guess - too big for a Troll."

Artem tutted under his breath. "If guesswork is the best I can hope from you we're all doomed. And don't tell me about Trolls until you've actually faced one," he added. "They can get bigger than anything you've read about in that book." The archer glanced over the gear attached to Hector's saddle. "Did you even bring any Oylish poison?"

The questioned stumped Asher for a second. "Oylish poison only affects Trolls."

"It slows Trolls down," Artem countered, "but it really irritates Giants - distracts them. The bestiary can only tell you so much. The rest you must learn yourself. And since you didn't know whether you were dealing with a Troll or Giant, you should have come prepared for both."

Asher's jaw tensed with the condescension he was receiving. "Troll or Giant," he continued, climbing down from Hector before the horse had come to a stop, "there's something big out there and your message said it had started killing people. I'm all you've got out here, so you can either work with me or I'll hunt this monster myself."

Artem finally stopped in his tracks and turned to face Asher, though all but his eyes were concealed by his hood and a cloth mask. Still, those dark eyes bored into the ranger. "Bold words for one whose blade has never known the blood of Troll or Giant." The archer took a breath and looked Asher up and down. "But if you're all I've got... I suppose you would make for suitable *bait*."

Asher nodded in agreement before Artem's last word caught up with him. "Bait?"

"Come," Artem bade, without bothering to explain himself.

The archer entered the largest building in the village - its only tavern. After securing Hector in a nearby stable, Asher noted that the seven men who had confronted him were moving to join them inside, their wariness replaced by curiosity now. Inside, a central and blazing hearth kept the cold air of the far north out and, indeed, the flames gave the tavern a warm and cosy atmosphere. A number of animal skulls decorated the walls while the main chandelier appeared to have been put together using antlers.

"At last," said the man from behind the bar, on the other side of the hearth. "Do we have another monster slayer in our midst, Artem?"

The archer glanced at Asher. "He's going to help me kill the beast," is all he said. "He's going to need somewhere to sleep, Felick."

The tavern owner blew out his beetroot-coloured cheeks. "There's only your room, I'm afraid. There's the store room," he offered apologetically. "It ain't going to be comfy but it's big enough for a man to lie down."

"He'll take the store room," Artem volunteered for him.

"I'll sleep by the hearth," Asher said firmly, if only to remind Artem that he wasn't in charge of him. "If that's alright by you?" he added, looking to the owner.

"I never let it die," Felick replied cheerfully. "I could put down some furs for you."

"I appreciate that," Asher said, though his eyes never left Artem - showing that he had won that one.

"Sleep where you like," the archer responded with little care in his voice. "Just be sure you're ready at dawn."

Asher frowned. "It's still light."

"Not for long," Artem pointed out.

"It goes dark up here real fast Mr Ranger," Felick added. "Then it gets cold."

"*Then* it gets cold?" Asher echoed in disbelief.

Felick chuckled. "Oh aye, it's a summer's day out there."

"You have journeyed far," Artem reminded him, making his way to a door beside the bar. "Get your rest. You're going to need it."

As the archer disappeared behind the door, Asher sighed and let his head fall onto his chest for a moment. He didn't want to sleep, he wanted to hunt. Turning around, those same seven men were staring at him, their hands gripped to their farming tools.

The oldest among them looked from Artem's departure to Asher. "Do you want to see it?"

Asher raised an eyebrow. "See what?"

"What it done - the *beast*."

A hungry smile pushed at the ranger's cheeks. "Show me," he instructed eagerly.

Following the men back into the icy streets of Hogstead, the ranger was now walking under a light sprinkling of snow.

"I'm Abe, by the way," the older man announced. "Abe Hammersmith."

"Well met, Abe," Asher replied, catching glimpses of women and children spying him through their windows.

"We're all mighty glad you could reach us up here, Mr... Asher was it?"

"Just Asher is fine," the ranger said, entering the north-east corner of the village.

"When Mr Gorinson said he'd need help with the beast, we started to lose all hope you see. But he assured us that when help arrived you'd see to its end. And here you are! Soon to put our troubles to death."

One of the younger men among their group broke away, dashing ahead to discourage a pair of children playing in the yard of a near ruin house. "This is it," Abe pointed out, though he needn't have.

Asher craned his neck to scrutinise the roof. Whatever had forced its way through had been powerful enough to knock the entire house to one side, leaving it standing at an awkward, and most certainly dangerous, angle. Judging by the direction the straw and struts were punctured inwards, it had definitely been attacked from the outside.

"Can I go inside?" he asked.

Abe swallowed. "Aye, but be warned: it ain't safe. We're going to have to knock it all down soon and start again before it blows over in the wind. Oh, and it ain't for the faint of heart either."

Asher had a plethora of memories he could have recalled, all far worse than anything he was about to see inside that house and all caused by him no less. Rather than terrify the locals with a tale from his past, he simply nodded his head and thanked Abe for the warning.

The door was severely cracked and hanging from the top hinge at a slanted angle. Asher was tempted to simply rip it from the house, but he too easily imagined the entire building dropping with it. Instead, he heaved it aside and ducked under the broken frame to enter. The first thing he noticed was the circle of snow falling through the hole in the roof, blanketing the wooden floor.

As quickly as his eyes took in the scene, his nose took in the scent of death. There was no mistaking the smell of a person's insides, especially after they appeared to be everywhere, decorating the walls. Opting to breathe through his mouth alone, Asher pushed on into the dwelling, careful where he planted his feet among the debris.

The central beam that ran from floor to ceiling was cracked, the whole piece only kept together by splinters of wood. A single hand print, made with blood, streaked up the beam, as if someone had been sucked out of the hole in the roof. That was only a drop of blood, however, when compared to the pile of gore on the floor beside the broken beam. Added to the human mess was a pair of frozen legs, though there was no sign of the torso that had once been connected to them.

Asher looked up at the hole in the roof and thought he had a pretty good idea where that torso had gone.

On the other side of the small home, the wall was smeared from end to end in blood. Approaching the gruesome scene, Asher narrowed his eyes to examine the details of what could only have been an horrendous death. Plastered along the length of the wall were fragments of bone and organ parts that could never be identified.

The ranger ran his hand through the air, over the wall, where a web of deep cracks threatened its integrity. Following the trail of blood along the wall again, Asher could see that the victim had been wrenched from the house like the other.

"Parqin and Gregor," Abe said from the front door. "Brothers," he continued. "They grew up in Hogstead; known them since they were babes. They lived here together after their parents died some years back. Good lads they were..."

Asher accepted the information despite its lack of relevance. Though he did begin to see things inside the house that he had overlooked before. He now knew who had slept in the beds and eaten at the table. The ranger couldn't help but notice the stack of books beside one of the beds. There were also a number of small wooden objects that had clearly been whittled by one of the brothers - a hobby perhaps. These weren't just two dead men, they were people who had enjoyed their lives right up to the moment some monster shoved a hand through their roof and murdered them.

"What are you thinking?" Abe asked.

Asher tilted his head as he took in the scene as a whole, his findings building a picture of events in his mind. "I'm thinking *Giant*," he began. "It shoved its hand through the roof and grabbed..." Asher wanted to refer to the legs by name but even if the head had remained he still couldn't identify one brother from the other.

"Parqin," Abe told him. "It's the boots..." he offered quietly, by way of an explanation.

"I think the Giant grabbed Parqin first. It either got excited at the catch or it had no concept of how fragile humans are. It crushed Parqin instantly, separating..." Asher simply gestured at the legs. "It pulled the rest of him out and likely ate him. That's why there's nothing left." The ranger turned to look at the wall. "But Parqin wasn't enough to satiate the Giant."

"Eh?"

"The Giant was still hungry," Asher rephrased. "With all the finesse of a boulder, it put its hand back through the hole and rummaged around trying to find Gregor. Again, it overestimated the strength of its prey. Gregor was pushed into the wall with enough force to... Well, he would have been killed as quickly as Parqin was. Those cracks were likely made by either the Giant's knuckles or finger tips as it dragged Gregor along the wall. Then it pulled him out and..." The ranger left it there.

"Gods bless their souls," Abe uttered from the doorway.

"These men were not blessed," Asher muttered to himself.

"What's that?" Abe queried, turning his ear to the interior.

"Were the brothers the only victims?" the ranger asked, his opinion his own.

"Sadly no," Abe replied.

Curious to know more, Asher stepped over the debris and entrails and made his way outside, where the icy wind was beginning to pick up. The ranger was just glad to inhale fresh air. "Who else met this monster?"

"Salandra Greary," Abe informed, his sorrow mirrored in the others behind him. "She was a lovely lass. She liked to pick the dendrun flowers north of here - sturdy things they are; give no care for winter... a bit like Salandra really."

"What happened?" Asher looked around, sure that he would be able to see where the Giant had attacked.

"We heard her scream," Abe reported. "It were getting late, the sun was low and the shadows were about. Salandra was on her way back from picking the dendruns and it... grabbed her, I suppose. By the time we got out there," he continued, glancing at the north, "there was nothing but blood in the snow."

Asher moved to see straight through the heart of the village and on to the pass that led to the edge of The Vengoran Mountains. From what he had read in the bestiary, the ranger knew that the majority of Giants preferred to live in the mountains, their size requiring a large cavern in most instances. It stood to reason that this particular

Giant hailed from the north then, where the mountains could offer it the best shelter.

A blast of wind swept through the village and picked up Asher's green cloak. Indeed, the weather was turning and the sky darkening at quite the pace. The ranger was sure he could continue his investigation in the dark - to the benefit of the investigation, in fact - but he wasn't immune to the plummeting temperature, and he didn't want to meet a Giant if his limbs were sluggish.

"Thank you for showing me this," Asher said to Abe. "Artem and I will hunt the beast at dawn."

"Very good!" Abe said enthusiastically.

Asher began the short journey back to Hogstead's only tavern when he paused, wondering why the group of men were still following him. He shot them a questioning look, eager to be rid of them and returned to the tavern's hearth again. The cold was quickly taking the fight out of him.

"Oh, the village'll be joining you," Abe told him as a matter of fact. "They do every night," he added cheerfully.

Asher considered their opportunity to frequent anywhere else. "Of course they do," he said dryly.

By true dark, Hogstead's tavern was bursting with its people, all jostling the unsociable ranger to get a spot at the bar. And, hospitable as they were, they still charged him for his hot meal and drink, desperate, perhaps, to recoup some of the coin they had spent on the services of monster hunters.

Looking back at the spot beside the hearth, where he was meant to be sleeping, Asher watched as patrons sloshed their drinks over the floor. He groaned into his tankard. Rest would have to wait, it seemed.

CHAPTER 28
A GIANT PROBLEM

Giant - Not to be confused with Trolls. Their heights might cross over, especially where the Mawclaw Giant and Mountain Troll are concerned, but the Giants are, as their name suggests, the largest of Illian's monsters. Their level of intelligence varies across the subspecies. Through all my travels and all the contracts I've taken, it is my strong belief that the Ice Giants of West Vengora are the smartest and, therefore, the deadliest. Regardless of the subspecies, however, all Giants appear to suffer from bad hearing. Either that or they can't hear us tiny folk. Keep this in mind when springing your trap or ambush.

A Chronicle of Monsters: A Ranger's Bestiary, 12th Edition, Page 420.

Bragen Durth, Ranger.

The piercing crow of a rooster awoke Asher with a start. His hand instinctively retrieved the curved dagger from his belt and, before Felick could utter a sound, the ranger was pressing the cold edge of the blade against the tavern owner's neck.

Asher took a breath and composed himself, retracting the dagger as he did. "Apologies," he offered.

Felick, still in the throes of being terrified, simply nodded with a meek smile. "None necessary Mr Asher," he replied, his voice catching in the middle. "I should have known better than to just approach a sleeping monster killer," he added with a light chuckle, though it did nothing to take the terror out of his eyes.

The ranger absorbed his environment, dismayed to find that he had fallen asleep at the bar, though that explained the pain in his back. He didn't even remember the villagers leaving the tavern. Sheathing the dagger on his belt, he glanced over his shoulder to find three other patrons hanging off their chairs, asleep. A fourth was staggering out through the door with naught but a weary wave for Felick.

"Good day to you Bjorn!" the tavern owner called after him. "Some among our folk got mighty excited that a couple of rangers such as yourself have come to our aid. As you can see, you've had company overnight. I best be sending these fellas on their way."

Asher squinted at the light streaming in from the open door, a stark contrast to the narrow shafts of morning light spearing the warm gloom. "I should be going," he croaked.

"Getting to the hunt, eh?" Some of Felick's good nature had returned to his tone.

"Something like that," Asher managed, standing and stretching from the bar stool. Making his way down the bar, the ranger knocked on Artem's door and even attempted to open it. "Artem?" he called, unable to get past the lock on the other side. "Artem, we need to be going," he cajoled to no avail. Again, the ranger attempted to turn the handle and enter the room. "Artem!"

Asher eyed Felick from across the bar, his flat stare enough to rob Felick of his good nature again. "Have you seen him?"

Felick shifted nervously on his feet. "I ain't seen Mr Gorinson since he introduced yourself to me yesterday."

"He didn't leave at first light?" Asher questioned, knocking on the door again.

Felick shrugged. "I haven't seen him, Mr Asher. Though... his door can only be locked from the inside."

Asher produced a few coins from the purse on his belt and planted them on the end of the bar.

"What's that for?" the owner asked.

Asher slammed his boot into the flat of the door and shattered the lock in the process. He was stepping through into Artem's lodging before the door had even impacted the wall. The room was empty. The bed had been made and the ranger's belongings and supplies had been tidied to one side.

Felick came up behind him, but said nothing regarding the broken door. "How's he managed that then?" he said instead.

Asher couldn't say, though his suspicions were growing as he paid closer attention to the details. Crouching down, he ran two fingers across the wooden planks - they were damp. So too was the bedside table and the framework of the bed itself. That led Asher back up to the closed window, a wooden panel that slid to one side.

The ranger stood up, his conclusion made. "He left via the window," he explained aloud. "The snow got in and made every-thing damp while he climbed out." Asher slid the window aside and discovered a quiet alley between the buildings, allowing Artem to slip away unseen if he wished.

"Why would he do that?"

Asher held on to his answer, as well as the word choice he was going to apply to Artem himself. "I have to go," is all he said.

Marching across Hogstead's main road, Asher saddled Hector inside the small stable and rode the horse out of the village, heading north. Once he had ridden a little further, the various foot prints in the snow petered out until only one fresh pair remained. They were the tracks of a horse; Artem's most likely since his was missing from the stable. The hoof prints were moving north, suggesting that the archer had come to the same conclusion that the Giant hailed from somewhere closer to the mountains.

"Fool," Asher hissed, spurring Hector on.

After putting a mile behind him, the ranger began to wonder if this had been Artem's plan all along. After all, the archer had told him to his face that he would make for suitable bait. Did Artem know that Asher would come looking for him? Had he set up a trap for the Giant and Asher was no more than a lure?

Tempting as it was to chalk the questions up to paranoia, Asher couldn't deny the fact that he had stayed alive all these years because he listened to his paranoia. Nasta Nal-Aket had told him every day during his training that he was to trust no one and he had taken that edict as fact. Of course, it was just as likely that Artem had struck out on his own because he believed Asher an incompetent ranger.

After riding through a white meadow with blue dendruns and a snow-capped thicket, Hector rounded the edge of a cliff face and entered a rocky valley that, if followed, would lead into the depths of Vengora. Those mountains loomed tall around the valley, but Asher's gaze was brought down by the enormous footprint stamped into the frozen ground. There were more up ahead and further apart than the ones he had come across on his way into Hogstead. The Giant had been running.

The ranger conjured an image of the Giant running towards him, a rushing wall of unstoppable muscle and bone. He considered the spear Geron had loaned him and wondered how such a weapon, regardless of its reach, could stop a Giant.

"Everything is flesh and blood," Nasta used to say. *"Everything bleeds. Everything dies."*

Those words used to bolster him, remind him that there was no foe that could withstand a knife to the heart. He wasn't so sure if his old mentor's words applied anymore, his new foes unlike anything Nightfall trained their Arakesh to fight.

Another hour drifted by while Hector covered more ground

inside the valley. Caves dotted the cliffs on either side, but none of them seemed large enough to accommodate a Giant. A dark cloud floated across the heavens and let free a light shower of fresh snow on the world before continuing on its journey and leaving a pale sky in its wake. Any trace of Artem's horse had disappeared over a mile back, leaving only the monster's trail to follow.

Asher had Hector weave between the boulders and rocks scattered across the valley floor, the horse's pace brought down to a slow walk. Craning his neck, the ranger scrutinised the cliff face from which the boulders and rocks had once fallen. He imagined a Giant climbing the cliff with ease, its ascent knocking much of the frost-shattered wall loose.

Sensing his hunt was coming to an end, the ranger raised a leg and jumped down to the ground. He offered Hector an apple to keep the mount satisfied and still while he moved ahead on foot, his spear now in hand. Sure to keep the weapon braced in front of him, Asher tilted his head this way and that to look around the largest of the boulders before progressing any further.

A disturbance on the cliff above him brought the ranger to a sudden halt.

Investigating that top ridge, where so much ice clung to the rock, Asher witnessed a handful of pebbles tumble over the side. A moment later, Artem Gorinson revealed himself. His hood and mask concealed all but his eyes, though the ranger was too far away to be anything other than a man clad in leathers and a green cloak. Of course, Asher thought, the archer was always going to take the high ground.

Using a hand gesture, Artem directed Asher to continue navigating the fallen rocks while he mirrored his movements from the ledge above. Hector, it seemed, was more than happy to stay back and let his rider meet the monster alone.

Eventually, the restricting boulders and rocks cleared enough for him to lay eyes upon that which they hunted.

A Giant.

Asher had never seen one before and, for just a moment, his mind tried to convince itself that it was being tricked by the light, for no being could grow to such a height, and it was sitting down. With its back resting against the cliff, the Giant was busy tearing the branches off a small tree it had previously uprooted. To Asher's eyes it was starting to look like a club.

Its head was hidden behind a curtain of matted black hair, unlike the rest of its grey body that had nothing to conceal it nor protect it from the northern chill. Taking shelter behind a small boulder, Asher narrowed his gaze to further understand this new enemy. Its skin looked to be coated in dried mud, the cracks weaving a web across every inch from its three stubby toes to its four hairy fingers.

All four limbs had thick ropes haphazardly wrapped around them, though Asher couldn't fathom their use. To consider that the Giant wore them out of choice was to let madness in, for the creature was naught but a monster. It was more likely, the ranger reasoned, that the Giant had recently been captured by the men of the north and subsequently escaped, the ropes the vestiges of its bindings.

Looking back up at Artem, the archer was signalling for Asher to advance again. The ranger was starting to think he was to be the bait after all. Moving from cover to cover, he approached the Giant with a level of trepidation he had never known before. Nightfall had spent a long time stripping back his fears where an opponent was concerned, but this was no mere opponent he could tell himself was the lesser fighter. In fact, the Giant didn't need to know anything about fighting to kill him, it had only to bring its foot down and that would be the end of Asher the ranger.

Above him, Artem was still making his way along the edge of the cliff, his form hunched into a crouch. When, at last, he looked down at Asher, the ranger gave a shrug as he had no idea what Artem's plan was. Since the experienced ranger had withheld everything thus far, Asher had to assume his lack of knowledge was all a part of the archer's plan.

If they survived this, Asher decided, he was going to share more than a few harsh words with the ranger.

Artem retrieved an arrow from his quiver and nocked it onto his bow, his head flicking towards the Giant. Asher envisioned their combined attack from high and low and knew immediately who would perish first out of the two rangers. Aggrieved by the unfolding of events, Asher adjusted his grip on the spear, readying it to hurl. It had been a long time since he had had cause to launch a spear, but there was little chance of missing today.

Moving on again, a sinking feeling began to churn in Asher's gut. This didn't feel right. Attacking in daylight rarely did to the assassin in him, but their lack of a unified plan spelled their doom in the ranger's opinion. Not to mention the fact that, at this distance, the spear would do little damage. Added to his list of potential troubles, there was only one way out of the valley and that was back the way he had come, through the narrow path that weaved between the boulders. If it came to that kind of retreat, the Giant had him beaten on speed every day of the week.

Artem waved his hand in an attempt to draw the ranger's attention to the rise, but his sudden movement knocked loose a handful of stones from the edge.

Asher looked back at the Giant though, concerned that the beast had heard the falling debris. Proving the bestiary right in some way, at least, the Giant didn't flinch at the noise, oblivious to Artem's mistake. His heart still hammering in his chest, Asher finally gave the archer his attention once more. Artem motioned with one hand for Asher to throw his spear and aim for the side of the Giant's head, pointing specifically at his own ear to indicate where he should target.

Nodding his understanding, limited as it was, Asher slowly rose from his hiding place and hefted the spear up to shoulder height. He took a steadying breath and visualised the spear leaving his hand and sailing right into the side of the Giant's head. The wind was beginning to pick up now, filling the valley with its howl. It would make his throw all the harder.

The ranger couldn't say why, but he gave Artem one last glance before committing himself to the task of battling a Giant. Fleeting as that glance was, it was enough to save his life.

Artem Gorinson was aiming his bow at Asher.

The ranger kept hold of his spear and leapt wildly to the side, a heartbeat before Artem's arrow struck the spot where he had been braced. Before meeting the ground, Asher tucked up his knees and turned his fall into a roll that brought him back up to his feet. Artem, however, maintained the advantage on the cliff and had already nocked another arrow. Asher decided against launching his spear in favour of throwing himself behind another boulder. As he landed, so too did the arrow, only a few feet away.

Gripping his spear, and with limited movement behind the cover of the rock, Asher peered over the top of the boulder to spy the treacherous ranger. Another arrow skimmed the surface of the stone and bounced over the ranger's head. Asher ducked and growled with frustration. He wanted to replace the spear with his bow and fire back at Artem, but the time it would take to stand up, draw the bow string, and launch the arrow would be more than enough for the skilled archer to kill him.

A shudder ran through the earth and the distant sound of something akin to a landslide kept Asher rooted to the spot. He slowly turned his head to the north and looked through the strands of his hair. The Giant was on its feet. It was also looking right at him.

Asher swore in the gaze of those black eyes, devoid of any familiar detail.

The Giant sniffed the air using the two slits that sat pitted into its face where a nose should have been. Judging by the crooked smile that tore through its severe features, the monster was pleased by what it found. Before Asher could do anything about his predicament, the Giant advanced and was upon him in four steps. It reached down with one hand, easily capable of picking him up and dropping him into its mouth of jagged teeth.

Asher made certain he wasn't there when that hand scooped in.

In his mad dash to evade the Giant, however, he had thrown himself into the rounded wall of a much larger boulder, its size preventing him from escaping further. The behemoth whipped its head around to spot him again, anger creasing its brow. This time it brought the tree-club down on him. Fortunately, its actions had been terribly obvious and had alerted Asher to the incoming attack. Again, he dived to the side as the club impacted both the boulder and the ground, breaking the end and showering the ranger in splinters.

Catching a glimpse of that same club rising high into the air again, Asher rolled aside and survived the next impact by a hair's breadth. He had also just stopped short of another arrow fired from Artem's bow. If there had been time to curse the archer he would have. As it was, the Giant had decided that stamping on its next meal was its best course of action.

The ranger scrambled to his knees and did the only thing he could: he raised his spear. Bracing the weapon against the base of rock, he angled the tip to meet the Giant's sole before *it* met him. The massive foot still hit the ranger, knocking him flat to the ground, but the spear pierced the monster's foot and caused enough pain that it retracted the limb almost immediately, sparing Asher's life.

The Giant wailed and hopped back, striking the cliff edge with its club. Artem's next arrow went astray as he was faced with a wave of loose rocks and ice.

Taking a sheet of the cliff with it, the Giant slid down the side until it was sitting on the ground, where it could pluck the spear from its foot. It roared with pain again when the bloody spear came free, no more than a stick in its large hand.

Asher wiped the blood from his nose and blinked hard in an attempt to focus his vision. He might have avoided being squashed, but being kicked into the ground by a Giant didn't come without its consequences. Ignoring the pain in his back and ribs, the ranger skidded and tripped on his way back to his feet, though it was this clumsy rise that saved him from his own spear, launched his way by a fuming Giant. He dared to steal a glance at the rise in the west, searching for any sign of Artem. If he was to have any luck that day he hoped it was that the Giant had already swatted the archer into the next life.

The ground shook under him as the monster picked itself up, though it staggered upon placing weight down through its injured foot. The Giant growled, baring its crooked teeth and spilling a mouthful of drool over its chest. Asher was too busy navigating the valley of boulders to pay the beast any heed. The pain in his head was a constant throb, robbing him of his sharp focus and forcing him to push off every rock he met.

The scattered boulders and rocks were awkwardly positioned for the Giant, who struggled to fit its feet between them. Instead, it scrambled and squeezed its way through, climbing over them where needed, to try and keep sight of the ranger.

Battered by the wind, his hair and cloak blown out behind him, Asher decided he was in a maze. Perhaps, the ranger feared, he had been turned around. That would certainly explain why the Giant was gaining on him. He cursed the injury to his head and the way it had taken the hard lines of the world away.

A Giant-sized hand came down beside him as the monster attempted to snatch at the ranger. The large fingers clawed at the ground and knocked loose rocks about, but only succeeded in pushing Asher to one side, taking him from his feet. The Giant roared and hammered the end of its make-shift club down between the boulders.

Asher crawled on his hands and knees to avoid the blows. He searched out the more cramped areas where the boulders had fallen into each other and created narrow passages and tunnels. One such path brought him to a crevice at the base of the cliff side, where the sheet of rock sheltered him from above. Peering out, through the gaps in the rocks, he saw the Giant moving over the boulders on all fours, its black eyes shifting in its enormous skull. It didn't know where he was.

The ranger let himself relax for a moment and catch his breath.

Despite the icy chill, he was hot and sweating under his leathers. He retrieved the small waterskin from his belt and took a swig before splashing his face with the rest of it. The feel of it on his skin sent a refreshing jolt through him. It was only then that he realised he had lost sight of the Giant. He couldn't even hear it.

Moving slowly, and remaining in his crouch, Asher edged away from the safety of the crevice and investigated the immediate area. There was no sign of the Giant, neither amongst the valley of fallen rocks or up on the adjacent rise. Taking a few more steps, the howl of the wind bombarded his ears, robbing him of an essential sense. He turned this way and that, his disbelief mounting. How could he have lost sight of a Giant?

The ranger stopped moving. There was a new sound added to the wind. It was a whistling sound. It was a...

Asher dropped to the ground before an arrow bounced off the rock behind him. A second later and he would have been far more acquainted with that arrow than was healthy for a person. Cautiously rising, he was dismayed to hear the increasing pitch of yet another whistling arrow. Where was it coming from? Listening to his instincts, he shifted his shoulders just in time and the arrow sank into the ground at his feet.

The crevice offered him shelter once more, though a third arrow struck the shelf after he ducked under it. All three shots had been uncanny, none of them giving Artem's position away. They certainly spoke of the archer's skill. Asher had never known any but an Arakesh so easily use the wind to manipulate the flight of their arrow. That thought was followed up by a fourth arrow that managed to enter the crevice and skid along the gravel. The arrowhead nicked the outer edge of Asher's hand, drawing blood and a pained growl from the ranger.

That had been an impossible shot.

There was no convincing Asher otherwise. He had no doubt that Artem Gorinson was an exceptional archer, but that arrow had been fired from the rise by someone who knew exactly where the wind was moving, its ebb and flow an extension of their own body.

Keeping almost flat to the sloping ground, Asher crept closer to the edge of the crevice and set his eyes to the adjacent cliff rise, just visible over the highest boulders. Like the Giant, the archer was nowhere to be seen. But that didn't stop the archer from finding him. A fifth arrow careened off the rocks and nearly cut a line across Asher's face, sending him back into the shelter again.

At a disadvantage and with few options left to him, Asher lay flat on his back and tied the red blindfold around his eyes. His enhanced senses were consumed by the lingering presence of the Giant. Its foul odour - a mixture of its own filth and rotting flesh - was carried in the wind, clinging to the valley.

Thunder boomed overhead. No, not thunder. There was a rhythm to it, a beat. The Giant's heart, Asher knew. The beat pulsed through its body and down through the stone to his waiting ears and sensitive skin. The monster was above him, waiting for its prey to reveal itself. Judging by its motionless state, the Giant was unaware of the archer on the opposite cliff. Perhaps, the ranger considered, the arrows and the noise they made were too small and too quiet to be noticed by such a being.

It also meant the archer was hiding from sight, meaning his accurate shots were being fired blind. The ranger's suspicions were growing into surety - this was an assassin of Nightfall. It had to be.

Asher licked his lips and tasted the world. Blood. It was on the air and fresh, unlike the stench that accompanied the Giant. Turning his head to the right, he inhaled the air whipping through the crevice.

He could smell the archer on the rise and the blood on his gloves. The scent on the clothes was that of Artem Gorinson, though Asher strongly suspected the blood on the gloves was also that of Artem Gorinson. The ranger was undoubtedly dead, his body stripped and buried somewhere no one would ever find him.

"This is somewhat elaborate," Asher declared at his normal volume, confident his enemy would have no trouble hearing him.

He felt the Giant's hands tense around the edge of the cliff above him, its dull ears detecting the noise but not nearly well enough to track it back to the source.

"You've gone to a lot of trouble to put an arrow in my back," he went on. Hearing no response, Asher continued to bait the assassin. "All this so you wouldn't have to meet me face to face. Perhaps you should just give up now and return to Nightfall."

"You would speak of our home so openly?" came the angry response, the hiss amplified in Asher's ears.

Asher wasn't the only one to hear the Arakesh's response. The Giant grunted quizzically and raised its chin to the air, likely running its black eyes over the adjacent cliff and wondering if its prey had moved unseen. It pounded one fist into the cliff, raining dust and fragments of ice down on Asher's position.

"So there is some fire in your bones," the ranger provoked. "And here I was thinking you were a coward too terrified to actually fight me."

"My face will be the last thing you ever see, traitor," the Arakesh promised, followed by the twang of his bow. The arrow skidded across the gravel, at least two feet away.

"Not even close," Asher goaded, a hint of amusement in his voice. "Don't take it personally. It's the cold; makes the fingers numb."

"You're not leaving this valley," the archer threatened, ignoring the ranger's words.

"You got a name?" Asher enquired, while retrieving the folded bow from his back.

"What does it matter to a dead man?" the assassin countered.

"Perhaps I will take it to the next life," Asher suggested, as he awkwardly removed an arrow from his quiver. "You will be welcomed with open arms when *your* time comes."

"You and I both know we are destined for the lowest of hells," the Arakesh replied. "The dark things that await us down there welcome all with open arms."

Asher was barely paying any attention to his foe's response.

Instead, he was tracking the voice back to its origin by following the various echoes that bounced off the valley walls. Simultaneously, his skin was feeling for the direction of the wind, sensing the currents that lifted, curved, and dropped.

There...

The archer was hiding behind a pointed rock, set back from the edge of the cliff. It was a difficult shot and made all the harder with the limited time he would have to make it. But it might just be enough to get him out of the crevice and back into the fight. After all, he knew what he was dealing with now.

"Try it," the archer said, giving Asher pause as he nocked the arrow.

Not to be put off, and with the set of his jaw showing grim determination, Asher rolled onto one knee and let loose his arrow at the highest possible angle. Then he moved, and fast. The ranger kicked up gravel and chips of ice on his way out of the crevice. He made a sharp right, around one of the larger boulders, and darted from cover to cover. Even over the sound of his own boots and rapid breath, he still heard the assassin's arrow knock his own from its path in the sky. The second arrow he fired hit the stone a few inches from the ranger's face.

"The name's Rendal," the Arakesh announced, his confidence boosted.

"Doesn't ring any bells," Asher said, letting fly another arrow, soon to be caught by the wind and directed towards the assassin.

Irked by the ranger's response, Rendal was slower to respond, but he still managed to fire an arrow of his own to intercept Asher's mid-flight again.

Skidding to another rocky cover, Asher held his breath - the Giant was on the move. The ranger had been careful to time his retaliations against Rendal with the monster's turn of the head, but it was entirely possible the creature had caught his scent in the breeze. Either way, Asher wasn't moving any time soon.

The sound of the wind was accompanied by the Giant's slitted nostrils inhaling between every gap in the boulders. It was going to find him. There was no avoiding the violent and inevitable conclusion. Since killing the beast was not only his job, but his only way of surviving to see anything beyond this frigid valley, Asher decided to do exactly what the ranger's bestiary told him to.

He sprang the trap.

In one fluid movement, he dropped the bow and retrieved the hourglass short-sword from over his shoulder. Supernaturally aware of his surroundings and the positioning of every ridge on the scattered rocks, Asher rounded his cover and leapt from one boulder to another, increasing his height with every jump. This would have got him nowhere had the Giant not been lowering its head into that exact spot at that exact moment.

The ranger's free hand gripped the monster's matted hair, giving him purchase directly in front of its glaring right eye. That black orb widened in surprise, its mouth agape. It was then that Asher introduced it to his steel. The blade sank to the hilt in the corner of the Giant's eye and sent the beast reeling, its agony renewed.

Using both hands, Asher held on as if his life depended on it. The Giant stumbled and tripped over the rocks, often knocking the ranger into its face. As the roaring creature whipped its head about, Asher took what might be his only chance at survival and let go, his momentum directing him over the lip of the adjacent cliff.

The rocky ground met him with a hard welcome but the ranger did his best to turn his landing into a roll before exploding into a flat out run. He had only a second to reach the assassin. Indeed, Rendal was already rising from his cover as Asher was coming to his feet. Predictably, the archer took his close-range shot, the arrow on course to strike Asher in the heart. The ranger, however, had already envisioned his attack and there was nothing Rendal could do to stop it.

Asher left the ground while twisting his body around, allowing the arrow to sail past him and cut harmlessly through his cloak. Not to be left idle, his right leg was coming up, sprung tight and ready to be unleashed. When the distance between them was just right, he kicked out and took the Arakesh in the chest. As one man flew from the ground, the other was landing.

His bow abandoned amidst the violent tumble, Rendal came up on one knee with a hand reaching for the previously concealed short-sword on his back. Asher would have removed his own were it not giving the Giant so much grief that it continued to trip over itself in blinding pain. As it was, he took his broadsword in hand, relishing in the sound the steel made as it left the scabbard.

"You did well tracking me this far," Asher managed through laboured breath. "The court was chosen well."

"I'm not on the court," Rendal told him, racing out of his crouched position.

The unexpected response delayed Asher's defence by half a second, bringing Rendal's blade a few inches closer to his face. Still, it was nothing the larger broadsword couldn't keep at bay. The ranger pushed his foe back and brought to bear a swing of his own. Their swords collided in the warrior's lullaby of clashing steel. Their elegant footwork then turned the affair into an elaborate dance of death.

Asher saw his opening not once but twice, a weakness in his enemy's fighting style that left his right leg exposed after every back-handed swing. He refrained from taking the opportunity to slice his opponent's artery, though, and smashed his spiked pommel into Rendal's knee instead. He would have his answers.

The Arakesh cried out in pain and immediately lost his footing. Driven down to his good knee, Asher planted a solid boot in the back of his enemy's head and sent him face-first into the ground. The next time he lifted his foot it came down on Rendal's wrist, splaying his hand open so the tip of the broadsword could fling the hourglass blade away.

"If you're not part of the court," Asher began, keeping one eye on the flailing Giant in the background, "how have you tracked me into this frozen hell?"

Rendal tried to get up but found Asher's boot in his back and the ranger's sword pressed against his neck. Without either to hinder him, the assassin would still have fallen prey to his own dislocated knee.

"You got sloppy," the Arakesh spat. "Who would have thought you'd return to Dunwich so quickly? I couldn't believe my eyes." Rendal attempted to laugh but the pain in his leg stifled the amusement. "You walked right past me and into the undertaker's office. And there I was thinking you were the Arakesh of *all* Arakesh."

Asher applied a touch more pressure to the assassin's neck. "You should have used that confidence and killed me on the road to Hogstead. You're a fine archer - you could have killed me from a distance." The ranger put all of his weight down on Rendal's back, eliciting a groan from the injured man. "I guess you were just too afraid."

Something close to a growl punched through the Arakesh's lips and he turned his head to lay a single eye on the ranger. "I'm not afraid of you!"

Asher brought his face a little closer to Rendal's. "Is that why you set up such an elaborate trap to put an arrow in my back?" To that the assassin had no reply, his face sinking into the snow and gravel. "Would you have done it?" the ranger questioned. "Would you have murdered that little girl because a piece of string told you to?"

"I would have murdered every child in Dunwich if it was the Father's will," Rendal fumed.

Asher's expression twitched, a brief sneer crossing his face. He considered the manner in which he would dispatch the Arakesh, for death was his only fate now - and deserved it was. But there was a more immediate issue coming right towards him and it was much bigger than Rendal. With blood streaking down its face, the Giant had finally sharpened its focus past the pain and found the one responsible for its torture.

The ranger sighed. "Now I have to kill a Giant."

Placing all his weight down through his foot, Asher used Rendal's back like a stepping stone to approach the edge of the cliff.

The assassin's yelp of pain was drowned out by the sudden burst of energy Asher put into his short sprint. The Giant, unfazed by the tiny human charging towards it, roared until its lungs emptied and lunged towards the cliff, its chin just in line with the jagged edge.

The inferior mind of a Giant is hard to comprehend, its structure of thinking simply... *simple*. Asher had to wonder what the monster thought was going to happen in the next moment. Perhaps it thought the tasty human running towards it would leap directly into its mouth. Or, the alternative, that he would slam into the Giant's thick head and fall dead from the impact. Whether it truly considered either of these outcomes was impossible to say, though, what it clearly did not consider was the defiant human leaping broadsword first into its good eye, a black pool of soft and vulnerable jelly.

His feet clear of the edge, the ranger thrust ahead and drove the full length of his sword through the monster's eye until most of his arm was buried in the creature's head. The blow not only surprised the beast but rocked it back, dropping it to lay strewn over the boulders.

The Giant was dead.

Its left hand twitched, an after-effect that Asher had witnessed in humans too. Giant or human, the ranger knew the dead when he saw them. At least this wasn't in his dreams.

Unfortunately, the impact took the hilt from Asher's grip and the sword sank deeper into the Giant's head, though he was more dismayed to have his own face plastered against the torn surface of the eyeball. Aching all over from the fall, he slowly yanked his arm out and stood up, one foot extended into the sunken pit of the monster's would-be nose. He was exhausted. But he needed that sword back.

Keeping his groan to himself, he moved across the Giant's face and retrieved the short-sword lodged in the corner of its other eye. Then he went about the gruesome job of butchering the eyeball concealing his broadsword until he was able to reach inside. The hilt was slippery and near-impossible to grip, frustrating the tired ranger all the more.

By the time he had reclaimed the Giant-slayer, he was coated almost head to toe in monster gore. He climbed down from its head, falling the last few feet, and stood up again to crack his back. His blindfold still intact around his eyes, he was constantly aware of Rendal's sluggish movements up on the cliff, his strenuous grunts travelling in the wind.

Asher made his way back to the place where he had dropped his bow in favour of the short-sword. Wiping some of the slime from his hands, he handled the bow and removed an arrow from his quiver. He tilted his head to the side, getting a feel for his environment and the currents that dominated the valley. Then there was Rendal, who had succeeded in crawling back to the pointed stone where he had been previously hiding.

Time to end it.

The ranger aimed high and away from the area where the assassin was concealed beyond the cliff edge. It was up there that he could feel the wind funnelling up and back on itself, running past Rendal. Whether the Arakesh knew his end was coming or not, there was little he could do about the arrow twisting and gliding to find him. It struck him in the spine, splaying him out against the flat of the pointed rock, there to take his final breath.

It was a satisfying sound and made all the more satisfying to know that one more killer had been wiped from the face of Verda.

Alone in the valley, at last, Asher removed his blindfold and sucked in the northern air. It was almost painfully cold inside his chest but he welcomed it all the same.

Hector was nowhere to be seen having, most likely, fled some time ago. Asher looked around for any sign of Artem's horse but there was no telling what Rendal had done with the mount, let alone the ranger's body. With a long sigh, he resigned himself to the arduous walk.

CHAPTER 29

PASSING THROUGH

Rakenbak *- If you haven't come across one of these beasts there's no mistaking them when you do. Imagine, if you can, a hedgehog and a bear brought together by monstrous forces and you have an idea what a Rakenbak looks like.*

They're fiercely territorial and their boundary grows as they do. This becomes a problem when the mother drops a litter close to a town or city, though you'll mostly find them in a woodland environment.

Now, once you've engaged a Rakenbak there's no walking away - or running away for that matter. At a flat-out run, they're faster than any man and they can climb anything you can. So don't attack the fiend until you know exactly how you're going to kill it. Read on for a list of suitable poisons and baits.

A Chronicle of Monsters: A Ranger's Bestiary, 12th Edition, Page 216.

Weylan Ganes, Ranger.

Hector had, indeed, fled the valley. The horse hadn't stopped until he reached Hogstead, where the village folk had taken him in.

"Well aren't you the survivor," Asher commented dryly upon their reunion.

The people of Hogstead were all the more surprised by Asher's return, fearing that the appearance of a riderless horse spelled his doom at the hands of the Giant. Their surprise had quickly turned to quiet disgust when they discovered the odour that accompanied the ranger.

His pungent arrival killed the merriment inside the tavern. "It's done," he declared. "The Giant's dead." Though most heard his good news, they all found it rather difficult to get past the smell.

Since the people of Hogstead would never understand the events that had led to Artem Gorinson's death, nor the added complication and now corpse of Rendal, Asher informed them that the other ranger had simply died fighting the Giant and left the Arakesh out of it. This was accepted by the people without question and they willingly handed over the remaining coin previously negotiated with Artem.

A portion of the coin was recouped by the village after charging Asher for another night's stay in the tavern. Then there was the charge for having his clothes and leathers washed and another charge to have them dried over a fire so that he might leave the next day. After purchasing a few supplies to see him to Dunwich, the ranger departed Hogstead with a meagre purse - a pittance for the job he had performed.

It helped that he cared little for the coin, a means to an end. If anything, he felt guilty that The Ranch had lost a good ranger for almost nothing. It reminded him what Geron had told him about a ranger's life expectancy. Wasn't *he* supposed to be dead by now? So far he had survived a nest of Scudders and taken on a Giant, and alone at that. How many more monsters would he have to face before he met Artem's fate?

He found himself presented by this question many times over as he crossed the miles from Hogstead to Dunwich. Every time he pondered such a grim outcome, he found himself thinking about the remaining Arakesh assigned to his court. Rendal's appearance had been an error of his own making, one that had cost Artem his life, but that still left three Arakesh vying for his blood. Perhaps they would beat the next monster to his death.

Leaving that frozen corner of Illian to its icy spring, the ranger made the return journey to the not quite so frozen town of Dunwich. His days on the road had felt long after battling both the Giant and the assassin and, though he would have enjoyed some comfort after returning to civilisation, Asher was keen to depart Dunwich as soon as Hector crossed the threshold.

There was a perceptible glumness about the town and it put the ranger on edge. Suspicious eyes were cast every which way and he wasn't immune to the glares; a newcomer with weapons about him. He was even asked to state his business by a pair of watchmen, who eventually accepted his reason for passing through. Trotting down the main road, Asher looked in vain for the reason of such tension. It was the tension, however, that found him first.

"What's your business being here, stranger?" one man asked, starting from his shop front.

Asher glanced back the way he had come, curious as to why he had been asked the same question twice in as many minutes.

"He's with me," came a much deeper voice, turning all to the intimidating frame of Geron Thorbear. "So get back to your own business and be quick about it," he added with a grimace. That same grimace stretched into a beaming grin once the big man looked up at Asher. "You're a sight for sore eyes, little man! What was it? Giant or Troll?"

Asher watched a few more paranoid faces disappear behind their curtains before answering. "Giant," he said.

Geron clapped his hands together and rubbed them warm. "A Giant! And here you are! Not a limb missing! Tell me everything. Wait. Where's Artem? I thought he'd be returning with you?"

Asher revealed the ranger's fate with expression alone, ridding Geron of his smile. "Is there somewhere we can talk?" he asked, making to dismount.

Geron raised a hand to stop him. "Not round here I'd say," he replied quietly. "Listen, I'd rather not hang about any longer if it can be helped and we both know you don't want to stay in Dunwich a moment longer than needed. I've got the cart stocked with all the supplies we need. If it pleases you, I say we be on our way."

Asher's curiosity was growing, but the big man wasn't wrong about his feelings towards the town. "Let's go," he agreed.

With little said between them, they reacquainted Hector with the cart and set off down The Selk Road to warmer lands. They passed a handful of travellers on the road before Asher positioned himself side on at the head of the cart, where he could face Geron.

"What happened back there?" Asher asked. "That was not the Dunwich I left."

"We'll get to that," Geron assured. "What happened to Artem?"

Asher had thought about his explanation several times on his journey out of Hogstead and already knew where he was going to begin. "It was my fault..."

Over the next mile or two, Asher told Geron all that had transpired, from his interference at the undertaker's office to fighting in the valley. The more experienced of the rangers listened to it all without interjection, absorbing Asher's every word. He wasn't nearly as downcast at hearing about Artem's demise as Asher had assumed he would be.

"I thought his death would... bother you more," the ranger opined, his recounting at an end.

Geron puffed out his cheeks and slowly exhaled as a slow shrug bobbed his shoulders. "You met the man - Artem was a hard fella to like. Truth be told, I didn't really know him; kept to himself mostly.

Never did have a kind word to say." The big man finally turned to lay his dark eyes on the ranger. "You shouldn't blame yourself. Though," he added after a moment's thought, "we won't be telling Rolan the details of Artem's passing. Let it be the Giant's work and naught else."

"You want me to lie about it?" Asher queried.

"Aye," Geron replied, as if the answer was obvious. "They won't understand the whole... *assassin* part. Don't get me wrong, there's some unsavoury pasts behind our fellow rangers, but you're right out of a nightmare most choose to believe is just a myth. As far as anyone else is concerned, little man, a Giant killed Artem Gorinson. Got it?"

Asher was a natural liar, trained to weave the most elaborate tales to navigate the world of man, but a pang of guilt struck him where Artem was concerned. After all, the archer might still be alive were it not for him. Didn't his death deserve some truth to it?

"No one cares," Geron pressed, his voice lowered to a serious tone and his gaze fixed on Asher. "That's the truth of our lives now. The same can be said of you and me. One day we'll both end up dead on the job and the truth of our doom will matter to none, not even the rangers. If we're killed by a monster, The Ranch'll send more. That's all there is."

Asher sat back and let that sink in. The same truth applied to every Arakesh in Nightfall. They were all replaceable, disposable even. It was a sad truth that Asher was, apparently, destined to live by no matter what he did.

"The takeaway from all this," Geron continued in a happier tone, "is that you single-handedly slew a Giant! Rolan's not going to believe that! And you're another assassin down on that *court* thing. What's that? Two left? You're defying the odds."

Asher swallowed and moved past the truth of his continued existence. "Three remain of the court," he corrected.

"What's that?" Geron shot back with a scowl.

"Rendal was not appointed to the court of assassins," Asher specified. "He saw me in Dunwich remember? He just followed me to Hogstead."

Geron groaned and cursed in the name of all the gods. "He just got lucky?"

"No," Asher replied. "I got sloppy," he said, using Rendal's own choice of words. "I should never have returned to Dunwich, let alone enter the undertaker's or spy on the Murells. That's what happens when you ignore your training," he complained, tying an extra knot in the blindfold around his belt. "People die."

"Well why on earth didn't this Rendal fella challenge you on the road? Why did he have to drag Artem into it? Hells, he could have killed you in the streets of Dunwich and they still wouldn't have caught him."

Asher had known the answer to that before he even killed the assassin. "I think he was afraid to challenge me openly."

"Afraid?"

Asher gave something of a humble shrug. "I might have a reputation among my peers. I fear Demry will be the only Arakesh to fight me fairly. Like Rendal, the remaining three of the court will likely set traps. *That's* why I suggested parting ways when I did," the ranger reminded, turning all the more serious. "The next trap might spell the death of another ranger, maybe even you."

Geron shook his head. "We've both survived so far, ain't we? I'd say we've got a better chance of seeing tomorrow if we stick together. Maybe we could make a thing of this, working side by side that is. It works for the Mendals. I've been telling Rolan for years we should adopt the Graycoats' way of doing things, in pairs."

Asher wasn't sure he could handle Geron on a daily basis for the rest of his days so, rather than comment as such, he turned the conversation in another direction. "How did your contract go?"

Geron drew in on himself. "I can't say I enjoyed it. Nothing makes you feel small like being at the beck and call of some rich ponce. We tracked and killed a couple of Arkilisks. That seemed to settle his bloodlust," he added with some disgust.

Asher looked across at the claymore lying on the carriage floor and noted the flecks of blood that stained the scabbard and a drop on the steel guard. He had never seen an Arkilisk - and he vowed to look them up in the bestiary later - but there was something, as Geron had put it, unbefitting about hunting an animal that hadn't posed a threat.

The ranger sighed and ran a hand through his hair. Morals, he pondered to himself. They were, perhaps, the most confusing part about being a free man.

"What happened in Dunwich?" he finally asked. "The whole town was rattled."

Geron's face twitched as if pained. "Just before dawn, a couple of dead bodies showed up not far from the lord's house."

Asher gripped the side of the cart, his gut lurching. "Bodies?"

The big man held out a hand to calm him. "Against my better judgment I looked into the matter a little, just to make sure it wasn't the Murell girl. It wasn't," he quickly reassured. "A young couple I believe. I don't know much more than that. The whole town began to turn sour and I was looking damn suspicious. I was counting the seconds to your return I can tell you that much."

"What killed them?" Asher asked, his heart rate steadily coming down.

"Who can say?" Geron replied. "But after the town's other... *murders*." The big man cleared his throat. "After all that business, you can see why they might be a bit vexed by strangers right now. Too much death for a town that size."

Asher chewed it all over, confident the deaths hadn't been the result of Nightfall's intervention - too public. Still, Dunwich felt like a black spot on Illian's map, a place he wouldn't likely return to for many years. With that in mind, he was happy to see a southern horizon ahead of them. In a few days they would be back in Lirian, and damned if he wasn't looking forward to knocking Royce Mendal off his feet and burning that cuirass himself.

CHAPTER 30

BACK IN THE FIGHT

Yarxal - *So fair a voice has never been heard, for it is like honey to the ears. How many travellers have fallen prey to this lure I cannot say, but I have discovered Yarxal nests decorated with more human bones than I could count.*

They are proficient predators that kill with admirable swiftness. This is a blessing in disguise I feel, as the beasts don't waste any part of their prey, whether it be devouring the flesh they strip from bone or using those same bones to secure their nests. These monsters prefer to hunt alone, only gathering in significant numbers for breeding purposes (don't even try hunting a Yarxal during this time).

Upright on three legs, they also possess three slender arms, their third limb protruding from their chest. Their grotesque heads will spread like the petals of flower, revealing a combination of suckers and fangs. It is also from where their unusually hypnotic voice comes from. The survivors I have encountered described the voice they heard as a lullaby, though they were all convinced it belonged to a beautiful woman.

Now, their skin breaks as easily as ours do, but I have found they suffer greatly when exposed to a particularly high pitch. I would recommend capturing a Banshee first (see page 400) and transporting it to the Yarxal nest. It's a lot of work, but a disorientated Yarxal is an easy kill.

A Chronicle of Monsters: A Ranger's Bestiary, 12th Edition, Page 475.

Gelethaine the Grey Knight, Ranger.

A few restless, and far from quiet, days on the road was all the time Asher required before he began twitching for another fight. It couldn't be helped, he decided. Violence was in his very bones, even if those bones were bruised or broken. What was he, if not putting his skills to use and spilling blood? Killing a Giant and an assassin of Nightfall hadn't done him any good by bringing the fight in him to the surface. He couldn't lie - killing the monster had felt good. Damn good.

The Giant was more than a step up from the Scudders, even the female. The idea of slaying one of the behemoths had never entered his mind as an Arakesh, nor any monster for that matter, but now that he had, the ranger was filled with new confidence in his abilities.

Confident or not, there were still three Arakesh out there who were actively hunting him. It was for this reason that the rangers merely paused briefly in Darkwell to resupply before breaking away from civilisation altogether. Backtracking their initial journey, Geron led them west across the fields and into the region of Felgarn, where Lirian held sway.

With nothing but the land before him, Asher's bloodlust cooled in his veins. By the time they reached the edge of The Evermoore, the ranger was pacified by the calm that surrounded him: the rustle of woodland creatures navigating the forest floor, the songs of the birds, and the breeze blowing through the trees. Nature, it seemed, was the perfect balm for the monster that lived inside of *him*, the creature that always wanted steel in its hands. Now he just needed to learn, as Geron had, how to cross the realm without a map or a road.

It had to end, of course. Returning to the busy streets and bustling life of Felgarn's capital, Asher's nerves returned to the edge upon which they lived. With this heightened state of existence, his hands naturally knotted into fists in the back of the cart and his eyes shifted constantly as he scanned Lirian's inhabitants. Slowly, but surely, the fighter in him was rising back to the surface, where it so loved to live.

It was then that the ranger's mind returned to the violent task he had promised himself after killing Demry. All that anger he had felt towards Royce Mendal came flooding back and, before Geron could stop him, he was leaping from the side of the cart and striding towards The Ranch.

"Asher!" Geron called after him, well aware of the encounter to come.

Rounding the corner on foot, The Ranch's green door came into view, as did Dunkan who was making his way down the steps and onto the street. He caught sight of Asher and a genuine smile stretched his face. Then he saw Geron as Hector navigated another cart in the road, the big man's alarm slowly beginning to be reflected in Dunkan.

"Well met!" he hailed, his smile faltering all the more.

Asher ignored the older ranger and stormed up the steps and ploughed his way through the door. He came to a stop in the foyer, looking left and right for any trace of the Mendals. He could hear Bail going about his laborious work out back, The Ranch's anvil always put to good use. Kalantha walked out of the armourer's room, examining a new vambrace as she did, and momentarily exemplifying Bail's rigorous work.

"What's bitten you?" she asked after seeing the scowl that had made its home on Asher's face.

Ignoring her as well, Asher made for the door on the left, where the single staircase would take him down to The Ranch's best kept secrets. He heard familiar voices as soon as he opened the door.

"Where is it now?" Rolan Vask was questioning.

"Just outside the city," Davin Mendal replied.

"It ain't going anywhere," Royce Mendal added in a reassuring tone.

"It had better not," Rolan intoned.

Asher's right fist tightened, audibly crunching his knuckles as he descended the stairs. All three men were standing in front of the fire-place, Royce specifically leaning with one arm propping him up against the mantel. His green cloak spread out, the black cuirass of Nightfall was there to be seen by all, and it had already been seen by too many.

"Asher?" Rolan narrowed his eyes at the ranger. "You've returned from Hogstead," he observed. "And in good time too. Are Geron and Artem with you?"

Rolan was added to the growing list of people Asher was ignoring. Instead of offering the man a response, he marched across the room, his intent as obvious as a Giant's attack. Davin reacted before Royce did, moving instinctively to defend his brother. That same dagger brought to Asher's neck was once again drawn from its sheath with smooth ease by Davin's delicate fingers.

"Asher." There was a warning in Rolan's voice but he was wilfully oblivious to it.

"This one's taken too many blows to the head," Royce muttered from behind his brother, straightening up beside the fireplace.

Asher was tempted to offer the fool one more chance to remove the cuirass willingly, but words had failed him last time and there was no reason why they would succeed this time. That was fine with Asher.

Continuing his meaningful stride, he advanced on Royce as if Davin wasn't even between them. The slimmer and younger of the brothers deftly twisted his blade around to bring the edge up and into Asher's throat, intending to halt him long before he reached Royce. His viper-like reflexes, however, weren't all he had come to believe they were. Before the steel was even raised to chest height, Davin's wrist was locked in the vice-like hold of an experienced Arakesh.

Asher had only to make a minor adjustment to his grip and the pain that racked Davin's hand forced him to drop the dagger before he himself dropped to one knee. It was there that he discovered Asher's knee waiting for him, the point of which thrust up into his face and broke his nose. Reeling on the floor now, there was no one standing between Asher and his cuirass.

"What in the hells?" Rolan Vask cried, starting forward.

"Wait!" Geron panted from the top of the stairs, his considerable frame bursting into the room.

Indeed, Rolan heeded the big man's words and held back from restraining Asher. That left Royce to defend himself and he seemed more than eager to do so after seeing his brother's treatment.

"You're a dead man," he told Asher with a fool's confidence.

The ranger paid no attention to his opponent's words. It was his body language that interested him. Royce had put his left foot forward and shifted his shoulders to bring his right arm back a few inches. He was a heartbeat away from throwing a right-handed punch and, judging by his gaze, he was going to slug Asher to the left of his jaw. Royce was a brawler then. This informed Asher that his foe would most likely follow up with a second right-handed attack, lowering his aim to the ranger's midriff.

It was always good to know an enemy's strategy but, in this instance, any follow up attack meant very little - Royce had only one opportunity.

Asher sidestepped the obvious punch, his opponent's fist cutting through the air an inch beside his face. At the same time, the ranger stepped in, bringing himself beside the Mendal, as his own right hand chopped up and caught the man across the throat.

Compounding his victory, Asher was sure to put a foot behind his foe's staggering back step. Accompanied by a forceful shove applied to the chest, Royce was flattened next to his brother.

The wind taken out of him and a knock to the back of his head, Royce was impotent as Asher man-handled him. Roughly, with no care given to the man, Asher removed the cuirass and left him lying in his undershirt.

"What in the hells is going on here?" Rolan demanded.

Geron put a calming hand on Vask's shoulder. "Leave it, Boss," he insisted quietly.

Rolan's jaw tensed and his tongue sat poised between his teeth. "You only get to do that once," he instructed Asher with a finger in the ranger's face.

Asher nodded his understanding, hefting the cuirass over his shoulder. "You have my word."

"Do I get to do it once?" Geron enquired innocently enough, looking over the injured brothers with mild amusement.

"Shut it!" Rolan barked, feeling, no doubt, that his authority had been undermined. "And get him out of here! I don't want to see him right now!"

Geron flicked his head, beckoning Asher to accompany him upstairs. Kalantha and Dunkan watched them go, a mixture of intrigue and awe about them both. By the time they were walking back into the streets of Lirian, Geron was laughing to himself.

"You have no idea how many of us have wanted to do that!" he chortled.

Asher didn't feel like celebrating. Just the touch of that cuirass made him feel like he needed to bathe for a week. He tossed it into the cart and dragged the tarpaulin over it; he would see to its destruction himself.

A moment later, Dunkan followed them outside and gave the ranger a pointed clap. "They've had a beating like that coming for some time now. Wasn't sure there was anyone good enough to give it to them." He peered over the edge of the cart. "You really wanted that cuirass back, eh?"

Coming to his aid and saving him from any explanation - which would have had to be a lie - Geron's indomitable cheerfulness filled the gap. "Drinks!" he declared. "Sable's Tavern is just round the corner. Why don't you two go and grab something strong and you can tell Dunkan how you slew the Giant?"

"It's the middle of the day," Asher felt he needed to point out.

"Giant?" The older ranger raised a white eyebrow, the time of day far from his concern.

"Aye!" Geron encouraged. "Besides, it'll give the brothers time to slink away and lick their wounds. Best you don't see each other for a while, I think. I'll give Rolan the report from Hogstead - you filled me in enough. I'll let him know about Artem too."

Dunkan's intrigue turned sour. "Artem?"

"Giant food," Geron said, as if it was now just another fact about the world.

"Damn good archer," Dunkan remarked, not terribly cut up about the news. "That's about all I knew of him," he added casually.

Geron gave Asher a knowing look, referring back to his own comments about his lack of fondness where Artem had been concerned. "Go on," he bade. "I'll join you after I've spoken with Rolan."

Asher took one last look at the tarpaulin covering the cart before accompanying Dunkan to Sable's Tavern. Given Dunkan's age and the years he had on Asher, the grizzled ranger had no end of stories to tell, relieving Asher of any burden to talk. Instead, he sipped his beer and listened to tales from the road. Dunkan had been a hunter by trade, before being adopted into the ways of the ranger, and had come across his own share of monsters before being paid to do so.

The circular tattoo around his right wrist didn't escape Asher's attention though. For a time in his life, Dunkan had been imprisoned somewhere in the six kingdoms and branded as such. Asher didn't enquire - it was none of his business. He simply found it curious the number of convicts employed by The Ranch. The ranger reflected on his previous career. Had he not been so good at it, he too would have been branded with permanent manacles by now. That's if he had been allowed to keep his head.

The springtime sun kept the blue in the sky where, not long ago, winter would have already heralded the night. It was around then that Geron finally entered Sable's Tavern. The first words out of his mouth were for two pitchers of the house ale. For many it would have been a day's drinking, but the big man would get through both pitchers in one round.

"Rolan's still a little salty," he informed with a shrug. "But he likes the Mendals about as much as the rest of us."

"And what of the brothers?" Asher asked.

"The boss has sent them on their way to a new job. Gods knows where."

"Good riddance," Dunkan chimed in.

And to that, the three men toasted their tankards together. Beyond that, there was no choice but to take in the band and listen to a few of Geron's stories, one of which Asher had heard twice since meeting him.

An hour or so later, Dunkan patted Geron's arm with the back of his hand. "You sure know how to pick a damn fine ranger," he complimented.

Geron expressed a prideful grin. "Told you how he killed the Giant then?" he laughed. "Right through the big bugger's eye! I must remember to try that myself!"

"Wherever you come from, Asher," Dunkan continued, "I hope they make more."

Asher and Geron made eye contact over the rim of their tankards. "Asher here's one of a kind," the big man assured. "And he's all ranger!" he cheered, raising his tankard and slopping ale across the table.

Asher enjoyed the merriment, a good distraction after instigating a fight he didn't feel had been finished. A part of him hadn't wanted to leave The Ranch before robbing the Mendal brothers of their pulses. After all, a fight was only over when the other man didn't get back up. Ever. Those were more words from Nasta's mouth to Asher's ears, there to remain for all time.

"Right," Dunkan eventually announced, hammering his tankard on the table top. "That was my last. If I stay and drink with you fine lords any longer I fear I will never leave this fair city, and I have a job to see to." The older ranger stood from the table and fingered a few coins into the empty cup.

"You've a contract?" Asher asked.

"Thankfully," Dunkan replied. "My bones are too old to go from town to town looking for work. Much prefer it when Rolan doles out the jobs."

"We should probably be getting back to The Ranch ourselves," Geron interjected before Asher's next question could leave his lips.

They squared their bill and the trio left together, making their way back to The Ranch, where Dunkan's horse was waiting for him in the stables. Geron had filled every second of their short walk with a brief tale that allowed him and Dunkan to reminisce for a time. It was only after the older ranger began to part ways from them, between the stables and The Ranch, that Asher found a moment to ask his question.

"Where's the job, Dunkan?"

The grizzled ranger thought nothing of his response. "Dunwich," he said, with hardly a turn of the head.

Asher was dumb-founded. "Dunwich?" he echoed.

"Let's be getting on with it," Geron cajoled, attempting to usher Asher up the steps to the green door.

"Aye, Dunwich," Dunkan continued. "A couple of folk have turned up dead or some such. I'll see the fiend slain," he added with a cocky grin.

"Asher," Geron tried again.

The ranger, however, had more questions and stepped further away from The Ranch. "Two deaths? In Dunwich? How do you know this?"

Dunkan finally turned around and licked his lips, his dark eyes glancing at Geron before Asher's blue orbs pulled him back in. "Some far rider brought the news as always," he said with a shrug. "Rolan gave me the job earlier today."

Asher simply nodded his head. "Good hunting," he offered by way of a farewell.

Dunkan gave a nod in return and disappeared inside the stable, leaving Asher and Geron standing in the middle of the street, a collective island the rest of the city had to navigate.

The big man scratched his cheek through his unkempt beard and said nothing for a moment. "Shall we go inside?"

"How is that possible?" Asher questioned before Geron had enunciated the last syllable.

The experienced ranger made a quizzical expression. "How's what possible?"

Asher began again, his voice low and his delivery deliberately slow. "How did a far rider beat us from Dunwich to Lirian? We cut across the land. Far riders *never* deviate from the roads."

"They're damned fast," Geron argued. "That's why they got the job in the first place."

"Geron." Asher spoke his name in the same manner he might wield a blade threateningly. "How could Rolan know to send Dunkan to investigate those deaths in Dunwich? Any such news should still be on the road. Hells, he assigned Dunkan before you even had chance to speak with him. That means Rolan knew..." The ranger trailed off as pieces of the mystery slotted into place, gruesome and wrong as they were. "That means Rolan knew two bodies were going to show up in Dunwich before they died."

Focusing on Geron once more, the burly ranger appeared somewhat larger than he had before, his shoulders squared and chin raised. Asher had more to say but he was stopped by a flash of red. The colour had crossed his vision momentarily and now drew his gaze down to Geron's belt, where a thin length of red string was blowing in the breeze. Asher reached out and snatched it from the air, his hold enough to take it from his companion's belt.

There were knots in the string.

CHAPTER 31

PRAGMATIC

Banshee - Keep your head on a swivel with these noisy buggers. They've well-earned their name and they'll use their wretched screech to disorientate you - make you look one way while they attack from the other, and always from above.

They live in swarms of up to twenty and prefer high vantages (see A Charter of Monsters, Page 107, for known locations). If you ever come across these pale predators, you'll understand why they're so well-suited to high vantages. You see, they possess a thin membrane that connects their limbs and hooked claws to the main body. Once they leap from their perch, their limbs spread out and this membrane allows them to glide without a sound.

Once they've got their hooks in your back their razored beaks will take chunks out of your head, so don't go blundering into a swarm. Locate them, then smoke them out (add Harlergrayde to the smoke and they'll get drowsy - see A Ranger's Guide to Alchemy, Page 214). Once they start dropping, get to work.

A Chronicle of Monsters: A Ranger's Bestiary, 12th Edition, Page 400.

Yurik (The Beast of Bleak), Ranger.

"What in the hells is that?" Geron questioned, eyeing the red string taken from his belt.

Asher ignored the big man for the moment and ran his finger and thumb over the knots.

The elven ruins. After sunset.

Geron was inspecting his belt. "Where did that even come from?" he asked, moving his cloak aside.

Asher immediately began to scan the streets around them, moving away from his companion to better see the people passing them by. He even grabbed at a few people, turning them roughly in his hands to see their faces. The ranger barely registered their offence and always moved on to scrutinise more Lirians.

"What's going on?" Geron demanded. "What is that in your hand?"

Asher's heart was dancing to a rapid drum beat inside his chest, his frustration fuelling the rhythm. "You didn't have this on you in the tavern," he remarked, holding the string up, his gaze never straying from the public. "That means this was hooked into your belt between Sable's and here." That fact got under the ranger's skin - how could he have missed that? They must have walked right past them and even brushed against Geron.

"What in the hells is it?" Now the big man's frustration was rising.

"This is how we talk to each other," Asher explained sharply, his finger and thumb squeezing one of the knots.

Geron frowned at the unusual form of message. "We? As in... *we?*"

"Arakesh," Asher specified.

Geron's small eyes lit up. "You mean one of them killers just..."

He was looking down at his belt before joining Asher in searching the streets. "How did they find you?"

Asher didn't have the answer to that yet, but he had a damn good idea.

Receiving no answer, Geron asked, "What does it say? The message."

"The elven ruins," Asher replied gruffly. "After sunset."

"Hmm. Sounds like a—"

"Trap," Asher cut in, suppressing his sigh for the moment. "Of course it's a trap. They don't want a fair fight."

"You could just run," Geron suggested.

Asher was shaking his head. "Whoever it is, they'll be watching me between here and there. I either fight them now or tomorrow, or the next day. I'm not running. Killing everyone on the court increases my chances of survival." His fingers took in the proposed destination again. "Elven ruins?"

"Aye," Geron answered. "If you retrace our tracks, where we cut through The Evermoore in the east, you'll come across a particularly pointed rock—"

"I remember it," Asher interjected.

"Well it's pointing south" Geron continued. "If you follow it for about two miles you'll come across some ruins left by the elves. Those are the only ruins I can think of round these parts."

Asher looked to the east, though he wasn't really looking. His mind was elsewhere, mostly to the conflict to come. He had no idea which of his brothers or sisters he would face in those ruins, but he knew only one of them would return. The question of whether he was being foolish walking into an obvious trap arose in his mind again and again. The resounding answer was yes - he couldn't get away from that. But the court of assassins was a dark cloud hanging over him and the remaining three needed dealing with.

It was time to cross another one off the list.

Geron gripped him by the arm and turned him around. "You're

not really thinking of just walking into a trap are you? You've got allies here. Use us."

"Do I have allies here?" Asher's question was barbed, his meaning not to be missed by the big man.

"You *could* have allies here," Geron told him. "You've an opportunity with us, Asher. An opportunity to—"

"Be like you?" Asher finished for him. "To be like Vask and the others?"

Geron shut his eyes and shook his head. "Just... Just forget all of them for a moment. You have an ally in *me*. At least use *me*."

"You nearly died fighting Demry," Asher pointed out. "This time you won't even see them coming."

Geron groaned. "I thought you were supposed to be a *smart* killer. Let me accompany you and we can face this bastard two against one."

"Depending on who we face," Asher said, "that might not even be enough. If I go alone, there's guaranteed to be only one death tonight."

Geron huffed. "You're a damned fool, little man. I'm not letting you stroll into an arrow. Whether you like it or not, I'm helping you."

"Why?" Asher growled, hesitant to take his eyes off their environment.

"Because... Because we're cut from the same cloth. You can't see it yet but you're one of us. You belong here, at The Ranch. You've got so much potential in this business, as a ranger."

"A ranger?" Asher echoed mockingly. "I'm not even sure that's what you are. If my suspicions are correct, none of you are rangers."

Geron waved his words away. "You don't know what you're talking about."

Asher simply nodded in return - he had somewhere to be. He took three steps towards the east and the wall of trees that surrounded Lirian when he realised Geron was in tow.

"I told you," the big man said stubbornly, "I'm coming with you."

Asher finally let out his sigh. "No you're not," he replied, an idea coming to him in the moment. "But you can help." His additional statement stumped Geron, halting his next line of argument. "You're going to need this," he began, handing over his red blindfold.

Parting ways with Geron, the big man set to his own task, Asher deviated from the east and made his way to Hanlet Street in the north of the city. It was there that he entered one of Lirian's undertaker's, its shabby exterior speaking of its reputation among the people.

With night quickly approaching, Asher didn't have time to soften his words. Or his punch. The undertaker, a man of middling age and thinning hair took the fist to his face with a sharp yelp, though his cry was cut short when the back of his head bounced off the door frame.

The ranger caught him by the collar and pinned him flat to the interior door, behind the front desk. "A dark dawn this morning," he uttered, informing the undertaker of who he was confronted by. It also distracted the man from the pain in his broken nose.

"The chair," he uttered.

Asher looked back at the chair the undertaker had previously occupied before standing to greet his potential customer. Leaving the man to support himself against the door, the ranger picked up the chair, aware of all the hiding places the piece of furniture offered. Sure enough, one of the legs was hollow and stuffed with a small cork. Inside were three lengths of knotted red string. He discarded the chair and ran his fingers over all three messages.

Asher would have laughed were his situation not so dire. All three messages had originated from Demry and had likely been sent to a handful of undertakers in Nightfall's employ. Specifically, it was a message for the court, informing them that they could find Asher in Lirian.

"Pragmatic indeed," the ranger muttered to himself, recalling Demry's own words.

Since the undertaker possessed all three messages, the Arakesh who had set a trap in the ruins must have received Demry's words somewhere else in the realm. That meant it was only a matter of time until the other two assassins came to Lirian and sought him out.

Leaving the undertaker to his bloody nose, Asher exited the office and took the three pieces of string with him, giving no thought to dropping them in the first muddy puddle he came across. He paused upon noticing the horse tethered to the post outside and spared the undertaker's front door a glance. Stealing a horse was punishable by death in most kingdoms, Felgarn included, but he already felt like a dead man walking and he cared little for Nightfall's lacky.

Mounting the horse, he guided it to the east, where they had previously cut through to the city. From there, he retraced their earlier tracks all the way to the pointed rock and turned the horse to the south. By then, the dark of night held sway over the heavens, with a cold moon and a palette of stars looking down on the ranger and his stolen mount.

For a little over two miles, he rode in silence, the only sound his horse's hooves crunching through fallen leaves and sinking into the mud. Arriving at the elven ruins, his chin was raised and his gaze set high. Made from stone, all that remained of the ancient architecture was a scattered number of arches and the hollow skeleton of a building, its function lost to time. Further to the south-west was a small building, though very little of it stood tall from the ground. It was impossible to say what had befallen the elves here, in the quiet of the woods.

The ranger dismounted and looped the reins around a broken pillar. It was tempting to give in to the belief that he would die and, therefore, it would have made sense to free the animal. There was, however, no part of his training that told him he was anything other than an apex predator. Survival was essential, whatever the cost. It was the same ideology that had prevented him from taking his own life.

Looking to the ground, he was impressed to find no tracks besides his own. That didn't mean he was alone. Instinctively, he reached for the blindfold on his belt then realised it was no longer in his possession. Forced to use his very human senses, Asher climbed up the remnants of a fallen wall and stepped onto the first floor of stone. It was a place for ghosts. The wind was funnelled through the decrepit shell, lending the ruin an eerie sound to its shadowy appearance.

"You got Demry's message then," he called out, attempting to coax his foe into the light of the moon. "It's a shame you don't have her courage. She challenged me to my face. And she fought well... to the very end," he added purposefully.

Light footsteps crossed the stone, turning the ranger to his left. There was naught but shadow to greet him. Moving into that darkness, Asher drew the short-sword from over his shoulder. He hugged the walls where he could, careful to keep his back covered if possible.

Footsteps padded over the ruins to his right, turning him back the way he had come. The ranger moved through a shattered archway and entered another chamber that had been exposed to the elements on two sides. Even the ceiling had a jagged hole in it that revealed something of the second floor, the building's highest level.

"This isn't much of a trap," he observed. "Rendal set a better one. He caught up with me just outside of Hogstead. He's still there now," he imparted menacingly. "Perhaps your successors will do better. Or perhaps I'll just kill them too."

"It's easy to kill a man." The sombre voice reverberated from every corner of the ruins. "Men have been killing each other since the dawning of the First Age," the voice continued, bringing back familiar words from The Night Codex. "It is said, however, that living with it can be difficult, a weight upon one's conscience." There was a pause before the voice returned with a mocking tone. "So say the weak," it announced. "Will you be able to live with yourself after killing us, Asher? With the number of bodies at your feet I imagine you to be on the road to madness by now. If only the Father had known how weak you truly were."

There weren't many words in any language capable of getting under Asher's skin, but the mention of Nasta Nal-Aket would forever be a weak spot in his armour. "Why don't you come out of the shadows and I'll show you how weak I really am?" he seethed, knuckles white around the hilt of his short-sword.

"And step into the light, as you have?" The voice that replied was not that of the first.

Asher was turning on the spot twice as fast now. This really was a trap, a trap of *two*. It was unknown for two Arakesh, each set to their independent task, to work together. Their pride, if not their joy, was in the hunt and the kill that they personally executed. It was at this point that Asher drew his broadsword, opting to wield both blades at once.

"The light," the second voice continued, "is no place for those unborn of the world and given to shadow and dust. We are blades in the dark."

"Maybe you should try it for a spell," Asher suggested, stalling for time. "The world might surprise you. Mrs Fairden's sweet meat pies will change your life." Everywhere he looked there was nothing but empty rooms and encroaching vines.

"The reality of man is a fabrication," the first voice returned with. "It is a lie you have chosen to embrace so you don't have to live with the horrors of the world."

"Death is real," Asher replied, punctuating the cold night air with his hot breath. "An absolute that has woven its thread through humanity since the dawning. Hold to this, for you are Death incarnate. You're not the only one who's read that depressing book. Though having it quoted to me is somehow worse," he muttered to himself. "Does Death have a name this night?"

There was a pause from his elusive enemies before the first voice declared, "I am Melekish. We've never formally met."

Asher turned his head to the right. "And you?" he called.

"Uthork," came the response.

The ranger knew that deeper voice had been familiar. He had met Uthork a handful of times and even sparred with him once. A man of The Ice Vales, he had been born of hardy stock. Asher also recalled the assassin displaying a significant level of immunity where pain was concerned.

"Well," Asher drawled as he ran out of wall to guard his back, "are you going to show yourselves or was the plan to bore me to death with ancient quotes?"

Uthork, the brasher of the pair, was the first to finally respond to Asher's taunts. Still, his initial attack came from the shadows in the top corner of the room and took the ranger by surprise. The Arakesh's first blow was a heavy downward stroke that met Asher's broadsword and sent the ranger rolling back across the stone.

Uthork was waiting for him when he jumped back to his feet.

They met in a clash of steel, each wielding a blade in both hands. Uthork was half a head taller than Asher and the length of his arms matched his impressive height, giving the assassin the advantage of reach. The ranger tried to bring his broadsword into the fight, his greatest tool if reach was to really matter, but combining it with his short-sword was proving ineffective and, at times, downright clumsy. The two blades weren't a good fit when used in conjunction. This became all the more obvious when Uthork batted the longer blade aside and sent it spinning over the edge of the ruin.

Reduced to a single blade while his opponent maintained his hold on two, Asher's odds of survival were beginning to shrink. Then Melekish made himself known. The second assassin swung down from the hole in the ceiling and caught Asher in the chest with both feet. The ranger flew from his feet and tumbled and slid down the slanted wall he had previously climbed up. By the time he had stopped falling over his own limbs, he was strewn awkwardly in the mud at the base of the ruins.

"Embrace the pain," he uttered to himself before a coughing fit robbed him of breath.

"So you do remember something of our teachings," Melekish observed from the first floor, his hearing impeccable with that red blindfold over his eyes.

Asher groaned and picked himself up, his back to the assassins. "Why don't you come down here and I'll show you some new things I've learned?"

A broad smile stretched Melekish's narrow face before he leapt and skipped down the crumbled wall, his every movement appearing effortless. He crossed the gap between them with one final jump, his blades held high over his head. It was a feint. At the last possible moment, he brought his left leg forward, intending to plant a boot in Asher's back. Melekish, it seemed, was hoping to draw out the battle for the sake of his own fun.

Unfortunately for the Arakesh, there was naught but air waiting for his boot. His back still to Melekish, Asher had pivoted in time with the incoming boot and was now able to roughly grab the assassin by his leathers mid-air, slamming him into the ground thereafter. It was then that Melekish's senses interpreted the truth behind Asher's supernatural instincts: the ranger's eyes were caked with mud, blinding him to the light of the moon.

Surprised as he was, Melekish was still able to react as Asher came down on him with his short-sword. The assassin batted the blade aside and twisted his hip to throw a kick across the ranger's face. It staggered Asher enough that Melekish was able to flip onto his feet and brandish both of his short-swords.

Tasting his enemy's steel on the air, Asher spat a mouthful of blood on the ground and assumed a fighting stance, his knees bent and weapon raised to his cheek. He wasn't going to rush Melekish but, instead, make the assassin come to him so that he might learn more about his foe. The slim Arakesh, however, was patient and held back. No. He wasn't holding back. He was waiting his turn.

Uthork leapt over a crouching Melekish and charged into Asher in the manner of a berserker. It was immediately apparent that Uthork had come to rely on his strength too much over the years and believed he could simply overpower Asher. He very nearly did. The blows impacting the ranger's blade reverberated down through the steel and into the bones of his arm. It was jarring and painful and almost forced Asher's fingers open, jeopardising his hold on the hilt.

Opting for speed over strength, Asher moved his feet, changed his stance, and evaded the next attack rather than parry it. Keeping his movements fluid, the ranger darted one way then the next, the tip of his blade scoring lines across Uthork's leathers. The scent of blood found his nose and he knew the short-sword had succeeded in cutting the Arakesh's skin, though it was far from a mortal wound.

"We're not sparring anymore!" Uthork growled, spinning around to bring both of his blades down on Asher. "Out here, it isn't about who spills first blood." The brute from The Ice Vales displayed a wicked grin. "It only matters who spills the last."

Asher pushed back against Uthork's blades, both pressing into his short-sword. The ranger proceeded to thrust a boot up into the larger man's chest, but Uthork blocked it with a foot and caught Asher in the gut with a kick of his own. It wasn't powerful enough to take the ranger from his feet but, detecting one of Melekish's blades sweeping in from behind, Asher used the momentum Uthork had lent him and threw himself down, under the coming short-sword.

Even before rolling back and onto his feet again, Asher's senses informed him of Uthork's flying kick. There was nothing he could do about it. The large boot impacted his shoulder and sent him back into a stone arch. One after the other, the Arakesh came at him. Asher ducked and weaved between their attacks, leaving the trained killers to strike the stone behind him. The ranger lashed out with counters, deliberately forcing the two assassins closer together. They were never trained to fight in tandem, or any groups for that matter. Inevitably, the pair clashed in their efforts to deliver the killing blow and left themselves exposed.

Again, Asher's steel tasted blood.

Melekish reeled away from the sting of the blade, but Uthork pressed on, unfazed by the new wound. He hammered the pommel of his short-sword into Asher's cheek before throwing a sharp elbow across his jaw, dropping the ranger to his hands and knees. There was no chance to recover as his ribs were swiftly lifted by Melekish's boot. There was more blood oozing from cuts on his face and dripping from his lips.

Uthork chuckled to himself. "That was easy."

Asher heard the assassin twist the blade in his hand, shifting the weapon into a downward position.

"Wait," Melekish bade, noting Uthork's preparations to drive his short-sword into Asher's back. "I want to savour this. He's supposed to be the best of us."

"There's always someone better," Uthork remarked, his hand squeezing the leather strapping around his hilt.

"There's always some*one*," Asher emphasised, leaning his weight into the stone arch. "Only one of you can claim the kill."

Melekish lowered the tip of a short-sword and touched Asher's cheek with the cold steel. "Don't even try it. You can't get in our heads."

"You've been beaten, Asher," Uthork added, scraping the mud from the ranger's eyes so that he might see his executioners. "The court sentences you to death."

The larger of the assassins returned his weapons to his back and heaved the ranger from the ground. Melekish moved in quickly and disarmed Asher, tossing his hourglass blade into the dirt.

"You could have had a swift death," Melekish hissed in his ear. "But too many of our kin have fallen to your blade. It is to be a traitor's death for you. A *slow* death."

Uthork launched his boulder of a fist into Asher's gut, doubling him over and making him more malleable. The ranger's mind was at war with itself. His instincts and training demanded that he find some way to fight back, to overcome Uthork's superior strength and Melekish's swiftness. But there was also the crushing guilt that reminded him a slow death was exactly what he deserved. Were the Murells present for this moment, they would only encourage the Arakesh to deliver more pain before the end.

As he was dragged back towards the main ruins, Thomas Murell was standing on the edge of the hewn stone, watching him, a witness to his end. Asher turned his head to maintain eye contact with the boy as he was forced up the sloping wall and onto the first floor. There, Uthork slugged him across the face and plunged another fist into his gut. Down on his knees, racked with internal pain, he could do nothing to prevent Melekish shoving a boot into his side, almost sending him over the edge. After that, he was hardly aware of the assassins and the tasks they set themselves to.

Instead, he lay motionless on the cold stone and held a silent conversation with the boy he had murdered. For all the apologies he laid at Thomas's feet, the boy remained unnaturally still, his observation not to be disturbed by the trivialities of the living. He was only there to watch.

The next Asher knew, he was being picked up from the floor and his hands were bound behind his back. He noticed the rope Uthork had slung over a jutting strip of stone overhead. There was a noose in the assassin's hand. Then there was a noose going over the ranger's head. He felt the knot press against the nape of his neck.

"The drop won't break your neck," Uthor told him menacingly. "You'll just suffocate under the weight of your own body."

Melekish came up on his other side. "You will either be broken down and built back up into something worthy of the name Arakesh," he began, quoting The Night Codex once more, "or you will be broken down and the pieces discarded. Your fate remains the latter, so say the court of assassins. Do you have any last words for the archives?"

Asher returned his eyes to Thomas Murell but the boy was gone, his image having left without a trace. Had he not come to witness the end of his killer? It occurred to Asher as being obvious, but he reminded himself the boy wasn't real; simply a ghost conjured by his mind, a manifestation of his guilt and shame. It also reminded him that he should have been dead long before, by his own hands. Yet here he was, still living and breathing, a man on fire with a singular reason to survive: to atone. He didn't know how many lives it would take to even out his scales against the deaths he had caused, but he knew he would save as many as he could now. Only then would Thomas Murell's death mean something other than tragedy. And Asher would shoulder the sickening burden of his actions for the rest of his days.

"You know nothing of my fate," he uttered to Melekish.

The slim assassin broadened his toothy grin. "I know it ends with a short drop and a sudden stop."

Uthork planted a heavy hand in the ranger's back and pushed him off the edge of the first floor. The stop was painful and far more jarring than the impacts Uthork's blades had inflicted on his bones. His legs straightened and his toes pointed to the ground, where they were so desperately trying to reach, but he remained a foot away from the dark mud. His whole body fidgeted left and right, his gurgling breath filling the night air.

Death was coming for him. It stalked through the forest like a malevolent Wraith, hungry to collect the soul that continued to escape its clutches.

Soon a new darkness would overcome him, a pitch black that even the night could never achieve. Where he would be taken to after that he did not know. He only knew that death would not be kind to him.

There was a burning in his lungs and his face took on all the heat from his body, swelling against the noose. Before he died, the ranger was sure he would experience every one of his veins explode under his skin. Behind his back, his hands repeatedly clenched into fists, but were unable to free him from the binding.

As death closed in on the ranger, robbing the fringes of his vision, both Arakesh leapt from the first floor and landed in front of him. They had not come down to watch his final moments, however, for neither turned to regard him. Instead, they faced the forest beyond and drew their swords. Asher told himself that he knew why they had done that, but his starving mind failed to connect all the dots. The answer came in the form of an arrow, and a well-placed one at that.

After cutting through the taut rope, the arrow went on to embed itself in the ruins. By then, of course, Asher had fallen the remaining foot and landed awkwardly on the ground, his lungs gulping in air. Lying on his side, he had a skewed vision of three Graycoats charging into the clearing on their horses. Behind them, with a hollering cry on his lips, was Geron Thorbear.

"Give them this," Asher had said, handing over his red blindfold.

"You want me to give this to the Graycoats?" Geron had asked incredulously. *"I thought you wanted to avoid them."*

"Go to their chapter house." Asher had instructed. *"Tell them everything you know about me. There's a good chance they will even know my name,"* he had added after recalling the young Graycoat who had heard Everic call out his name in Wood Vale. *"Make them believe you, Geron. Then take them to the ruins."*

"And what are you hoping that lot are going to do?"

"I'm going to spring the trap," Asher had explained. *"The Graycoats are going to get me out of it."*

Groggily, Asher watched the three Graycoats ride through the clearing, swinging their swords as they did. The Arakesh weaved effortlessly between the double-edged steel, but avoiding all of Geron was a much harder task. The burly ranger launched himself from his saddle and came down on Melekish. Uthork was quick to come to his brother's aid, but Geron was already swinging his claymore round in one hand, keeping the assassin at bay until he found his feet again.

As Melekish rose, all three of the Graycoats descended. Leaving their mounts to wander the ruins, they came at the slender Arakesh with the best training the realm could buy. Melekish did well to parry the first two and even draw a cut across one of their faces, but the third Graycoat waded in with a two-handed swing that chopped down into the assassin's thigh. He was instantly dropped to one knee, forcing his defences high. More blood was added to the volume pumping out of his leg when his hand was cut off at the wrist. His cry of agony and surprise was taken from him when the wounded knight drove his sword through Melekish's chest.

They left him dead in the mud and turned on Uthork, who was proving the better fighter against Geron. The ranger was being turned around and toyed with, a preamble to the killing blow. One of the Graycoats strode in and shoved Geron aside, taking his place in the battle. As did the other two. Three against one, the knights of the realm closed in from different angles.

Uthork was ready for them.

The Arakesh advanced aggressively and twisted the blade of the first swordsman aside, exposing the man's midriff. The knight took the assassin's short-sword through the heart in a flash of steel and blood. Uthork discarded the body and spun on his foes with a sweeping attack, filling the ruins with the ringing of swords.

Geron moved away from the fight and skidded to Asher's side. "I've got you," he reassured. The big man retrieved a knife from his belt and began sawing through the rope that bound the ranger's wrists together.

For a brief time, Asher was on his front, his face pressed to the ground where darkness enveloped his vision. His senses were momentarily flooded with information, but there was something about Geron that gave him pause, a taste on his tongue that was all too familiar. The bindings cut, the ranger was returned to enough light to extinguish the Nightseye elixir. He looked at Geron, his thoughts his own for now.

"We need to help them," he said with a pained croak in his throat. The words brought about a coughing fit and he spat some more blood on the ground before removing the noose from around his neck.

Geron regarded the intense battle. "This looks like Graycoat business to me, fella."

Asher pushed through his aches and pains and rose to his full height. Between him and the fighting trio stood his broadsword, the blade plunged into the ground. With every stride he took towards his weapon, the ranger visualised what he was going to do when he met Uthork in combat. He had a good idea now of the assassin's favoured fighting style, aggressive as it was. The combined efforts of the Graycoats would make him desperate, eager to drop bodies and start evening the odds. There was also a good chance he would see Asher as his greatest threat and move to attack him at the first opportunity.

Five steps and the broadsword was back in Asher's hand. Beside him, Geron had drawn his claymore again, though Asher had no intention of letting the fight go on. Six more steps and he had made himself an immediate threat to Uthork, whose superior senses had already detected this. The Arakesh swung his blades wildly to push the Graycoats back, giving him the space to turn and face Asher.

Three moves. That's all there was between now and victory, between now and Uthork's death.

It began by acknowledging the length of his broadsword, an advantage in reach that Asher intended to utilise. And, as predicted, Uthork's initial attack was from high to low, a strike that would benefit from his strength. Asher side-stepped, dipped his body, and moved through the gap created by Uthork's extended arm. More importantly, the ranger was simultaneously swinging his sword, maintaining a one-handed grip to keep his balance.

The steel sliced neatly through Uthork's waist. Though it was not a mortal blow, the first move had been completed.

The Arakesh was staggered by the wound and partially turned around. By then, of course, Asher was already on the move, pivoting on one foot and now with a two-handed grip. Down came his broadsword, chopping through Uthork's leg and completing the second move. The assassin fell to one knee and lashed out, but his short-sword wasn't nearly long enough to strike at Asher, who was able to keep his distance.

Though he couldn't see it, Uthork's senses would have detected the cold and bloody steel cutting through the air at speed. He raised his second short-sword to parry the incoming blade, but his recent wounds had slowed him down just enough that his defence was an inch behind Asher's third and final move. The ranger's broadsword slashed across the Arakesh's neck and sprayed blood across the ruins, staining the ancient stone.

Uthork dropped face down in the mud, never to raise his sword in the name of Nightfall again.

CHAPTER 32

I AM RANGER

Arkilisk - A distant cousin of the Basilisk, though, thankfully, much smaller and easier to trap. Having said that, the bite of an Arkilisk has a much faster acting venom and is capable of killing a man in mere minutes rather than the hours Basilisk venom requires.

You will find these most deadly of creatures in forests, their preferred habitat due to their bark-like hide that allows them to blend in with the trees.

Now, in all honesty, it is going to be rare that a contract comes up to hunt an Arkilisk down. They don't actively hunt humans and they never stray from their woodland domain. As a ranger, however, it is likely that you will share that same domain at some point or another and it's best to know your neighbours when they could kill you with a single bite.

Speaking of their bite, don't even think about an antidote. Even if one existed, you couldn't ingest it before their venom paralysed you, a symptom that begins in the hands of all places. Your only hope is to kill it fast or, better yet, from a distance. Just bear in mind that Arkilisks have six legs and move with significant speed.

The best advice I have for you is this: leave them well alone. If you don't pose a threat to either the Arkilisk or its prey, then it will leave you alone.

*A Chronicle of Monsters: A Ranger's Bestiary, 12th Edition,
Page 361.*

Korkali of the Oseki Tribe, Ranger.

Asher stepped back from the pool of blood spreading through the dirt and instantly became aware of the surviving Graycoats. Without moving too quickly, he carefully raised his green hood to conceal his face in deep shadow. His heart was twice its resting speed, flooding his veins with the thrill of the fight and the ecstasy of the kill. He had once welcomed the feeling, though it had always come after the switch had allowed his conscious mind to return from the quiet depths. Now that he lived every moment of it, choosing his every action with clarity, the ranger hated himself for revelling in death.

The edge of a sword came to rest on his shoulders. It was too soon. His instincts were still very much in control and his muscles responded accordingly. Twisting his body round, he flicked his broadsword in a swift arc and knocked the Graycoat's weapon free before he then snatched it from his grip.

In the blink of an eye, the ranger was now resting that same sword on its owner's shoulder.

The other Graycoat advanced and raised his sword to point directly at Asher's chest. "Drop it," he commanded.

Asher required another moment to collect himself and take a calming breath. When the ranger had stopped envisioning the ways in which he would kill both knights, he removed the tip of the blade from its threatening position and plunged it into the ground. Wanting to make his peaceful intentions even clearer, he returned his broadsword to its scabbard and stepped back with his hands slightly raised.

"You are the one called Asher?" the sword-wielding Graycoat enquired.

Asher nodded once, his head tilted just enough to keep one eye on the knights.

"Then this is yours," the Graycoat continued, tossing a red strip of cloth towards the ranger.

Asher caught the blindfold and returned it to his belt with another nod, this one a sign of appreciation.

"You're one of them," the other Graycoat accused, retrieving his blade from the dirt. "You're the Arakesh who killed our brothers and sisters in Wood Vale."

The ranger refrained from resting his hand on the hilt of his broadsword. "I am," he admitted.

"Your companion told us you walked away from Nightfall," the first Graycoat said, his sword still pointed at Asher's chest. "That explains your betrayal of these two wretches, but why would you exile yourself?"

"My reasons are my own," was all Asher replied.

"Who cares, Didrik?" the second knight spat, his own blade coming up now. "With them or not, he's a killer like the rest of them. How many innocents have died by your hands?"

"Two more if you don't lower your swords," Asher replied as a matter of fact, his tone laced with menace.

The Graycoats hesitated and exchanged glances. "You're coming with us," Didrik ordered. "You have knowledge of Nightfall. Lord Marshal Horvarth will want to question you himself."

"Your Lord Marshal can sit on his sword for all I care," Asher told them. "I'm not going anywhere with you."

"The hells you're not," the second, and far more aggressive Graycoat, retorted. "Another of our brothers has died because of you," he said, flicking the point of his sword at their fallen comrade. "You're going to tell us everything we want to know and then you're going to pay for your crimes against the realm."

Asher regarded the dead Graycoat and decided he wasn't going to let this particular death stain his hands. "He died doing his duty, which is exactly what they're going to say about you two if you don't step aside."

"Asher," Geron said with caution, but the ranger ignored him - he knew how to deal with Graycoats.

"We're not afraid of you," Didrik declared with creditable confidence.

"Look at what we did to your friend," the second knight hissed. "Killing Arakesh is what we do."

"You killed him three against one," Asher pointed out. "And you can bet the big man's going to fight for me," he added, nodding his head in Geron's direction.

"We'll take our chances," the angry Graycoat stated, his stance changing just enough to inform Asher that he was considering attacking.

"You needn't," the ranger remarked firmly, opening his palm to the knights. "I didn't arrange for you to come here so I could add a few more Graycoats to my conscience. I suspected a trap and knew you were the only ones in Lirian capable of facing an Arakesh. Had I known there would be two of them I wouldn't have sent Geron at all. As it is, you now stand the victors with two dead assassins at your feet. When was the last time anyone from West Fellion either defeated or retrieved the body of an Arakesh? How many assassins of Nightfall have you ever been able to study? Now you have their gear, their weapons. It's not much but you might find a few more secrets on them the Lord Marshal would find interesting. You can either take this win and the pat on the head, or you can join them in the dirt."

"You think highly of yourself," Didrik commented, his voice lacking some of his earlier confidence.

"I might not be able to take you both," Asher considered, "but I can guarantee one of you will never see West Fellion again." The ranger gripped his broadsword in its scabbard. "Make your choice."

Again, the Graycoats exchanged glances and held a silent conversation. At last, they lowered their swords and stepped back from the ranger, though they maintained the tension in their muscles, each ready to spring should Asher be deceiving them.

"As far as anyone is concerned," Didrik said, "you fled and we killed the Arakesh."

"Fine by me," Asher replied, moving to retrieve his short-sword.

The second Graycoat raised his chin after him. "We know your name now... *Asher*. And we will never stop hunting you."

With Geron in tow, Asher accepted the threat and replaced the hourglass blade over his shoulder. He considered taking one of Uthork's short-swords, but fighting with both blades was a style he wished to leave behind. Just holding the two short-swords would awaken unwanted memories stored in his muscles.

Giving no response to the knights, the ranger simply mounted his stolen horse. The big man ascended Hector, absent his usual cart, and brought the horse in beside Asher.

"What now?" he asked, looking back at the Graycoats nervously.

"Now you tell me the truth," Asher asserted. "*Everything*, Geron."

The big man winced as if the words had pained him. "Asher..." His tone was tired and tinged with apprehension. "After what we've just been through... Why don't we rest the night at least and talk about this at a more civilised hour? You nearly died back there."

"Rolan knew those people were going to die in Dunwich," Asher pressed, doing his best to fight his own fatigue. "I want the truth."

"There's nothing to tell," Geron insisted.

"Fine," the ranger said, kicking his heels into the side of his horse. "I'll get the answers myself."

"Asher!"

Geron's call did nothing to stop the ranger from taking off into the forest. He backtracked the two miles to the pointed rock and turned for the city, finally emerging from between the trees at speed, despite the limited lunar light. To his credit, Geron was only seconds behind him, but it was those precious seconds that saw Asher reach The Ranch unhindered.

Without bringing his stolen horse to a complete halt, the ranger was already climbing down one side. He slapped the mount on the rear and sent it galloping off into the quiet streets of Lirian. Geron's bulk prevented him from performing the same swift manoeuvre with Hector and he also needed the time to secure the reins to a nearby post. All the while, however, he was hollering Asher's name to no avail.

The Ranch's green door nearly flew from its hinges the way Asher stormed in. The main foyer was dark and Bail's anvil was silent beyond the supply room. Moving swiftly, the ranger was halfway down the stairs before Geron entered The Ranch.

Curiously, Dunkan was occupying one of the armchairs in front of the fire. Asher would have questioned the older ranger as to why he hadn't left for Dunwich yet, but he knew the answers he sought would only come from one. Leaving Dunkan to the warmth, Asher strode down the only corridor in the basement and made for Rolan Vask's office.

He didn't knock.

The door burst open, giving Rolan a good view of the imposing figure that stood between him and freedom. His calm demeanour instantly put Asher off balance. In fact, the older man looked almost bored, as if he had been waiting.

"I don't know what's kept you," Rolan remarked, taking in Asher's ragged appearance, "but I expected you some time ago."

The ranger entered the office and scanned every inch for traps, though Vask was clearly the only one to occupy the room, seated on the other side of his ornate desk.

"So you think you know the truth," Rolan continued, relaxing back in his seat. "Dunkan informed me of your questions. You must be wondering about the events in Dunwich."

"Asher," Geron pleaded, coming up behind him. "Leave it be. We'll talk about this on the road. Why don't we get some rest and tomorrow we'll strike out for—"

"You didn't clean your sword properly," Asher interjected, dumbfounding the big man.

"What?" Geron asked, making a cursory inspection of his claymore.

"By the ruins," Asher elaborated, "when you came to my aid. I could taste the blood you missed on your sword."

"What's he talking about, Geron?" Rolan asked.

"It wasn't the blood of an animal," Asher said, ignoring Vask for the moment. "It was *human*."

Geron's broad face lost its confusion and set like stone. "You don't know what you're talking about."

"*You* killed those people in Dunwich," Asher told him, confident it was the truth. "And you ordered him to," he said, turning to Rolan. "*That's* how you knew there would be two dead bodies in Dunwich. What was the plan, Rolan? Let fear take a hold of the town and then send Dunkan in with the suggestion of a monster and a contract? Is that how this has worked since the beginning? You choose a location, kill some people to make it look like a monster attack, and then arrive to take their coin and slay the beast?"

Rolan's relaxed demeanour turned sour and he leaned into his desk. "You had so much promise, Asher. An assassin of all things," he said, raising his arms. "But I can hear the self-righteousness in your voice. I didn't realise you were in a position to judge."

"This is no better than the life I abandoned," the ranger stated flatly. "You're all killers, you just murder people for a different reason."

Rolan slammed his fist into the desk. "And what would you know of our reasons? I know where you've come from," he said darkly, with a glance at Geron.

The betrayal stung in a way Asher had never known before. It was the kind of anguish that only came with trust and the ranger could see now that trust was exactly what had developed between him and Geron, a fact that had passed him by. Never again, he vowed.

"Has an Arakesh ever starved to death in Nightfall?" Rolan went on venomously. "Has an Arakesh ever known true desperation?

There is a line that exists between the living and the dead, Asher. 'Tis a lonely place where desperate men learn to do whatever they must to survive. It's there that you see what really matters to the realm, to the kingdoms. Out there, people only care about themselves - there is no help. At least in here, we can build something of our own, something that will always welcome us and provide harbour in the storm."

Asher stepped towards the desk and looked down on Vask. "From murderer to murderer, killing is killing, no matter how you dress it up. We both know there's no excuse that won't haunt us to the end of our days."

"Speak for yourself," Rolan replied, not backing off an inch. "I sleep like the dead."

The ranger wanted to reach over the desk and tear the smile off his face, but he heard more footsteps behind him. Besides Geron, Dunkan, Bail, and Kalantha now occupied the back of the room.

"Speaking of the dead..." Rolan drawled.

The signal given, all four rangers rushed Asher before he could turn and draw his broadsword. Geron reached him first, his bulk more than enough to barrel Asher over the desk. Rolan was waiting for him and wrapped a strong arm around the ranger's neck, pinning him down. Geron's hammer-like fist, closely followed by Bail's sharp elbow, came down on Asher's midriff.

Amidst the chaos, Asher heard the distinct sound of a dagger being freed of its sheath. He glimpsed the steel in the firelight as Kalantha came at him from the right, her weapon raised high. The ranger lashed out with a kick and caught Kalantha in the gut before she could land the deadly blow. Dunkan, however, was quick to step in and take her place, his thick arms coiling around Asher's ankle to prevent him from kicking again.

Now it was Rolan's turn to strike a blow. The boss leaned over Asher and dropped an elbow into his chest, though it proved a mistake on his part. Asher reached up and pulled on the back of his neck, forcing the boss's face into the ranger's knee, which left Rolan stunned before that same boot ploughed into Bail and launched him across the room.

Yet freedom was still beyond Asher's grasp, taken from him when Geron gripped him roughly by the leathers and heaved him from the desk. He was subsequently slammed into one wall after another, his body used to break various shelves and ornaments. The big man eventually tossed him out of the office and into the corridor, where another wall awaited him.

The pain tried to keep Asher down, luring him to sleep, but he embraced the punishment and pulled himself up the wall. Out of the corner of his eye, he saw a meaty fist coming for his face and managed to swing his head back before the impact. Geron cracked the wall but it didn't slow him down for a moment. His other hand whipped up and shoved Asher's head into the wall, a knock that doubled the ranger's vision. The next thing he knew, he was flying through the air and crashing through Hanaghan's door.

Splintered wood scattered across the floor and months of dust filled the air, assaulting the ranger's lungs. A hacking cough plagued his rise but he still heard the incoming footsteps, confident and aggressive. Dunkan had rushed in before Geron and was now in the process of throwing a punch that had gone out wide, like a swinging mace on a chain. Asher held his breath for the moment and raised one arm to block the heavy attack, though the force of it was still strong enough to knock him off balance.

Crashing into the end of Hanaghan's long table, vials of intriguing elixirs and potions smashed their contents in every direction, one of which, a vibrant orange, began to burn through the wood. The smoke it produced stung Asher's eyes and he pushed off from the table, meeting Dunkan's four subsequent strikes with four well-placed defences, his limbs moving with naught but instinct. The ranger whipped his palm up into the man's throat and sent him staggering back, giving Asher the distance to land a solid fist in his enemy's face.

Rolan strode into the room behind Kalantha and Geron, barking commands to knock Asher into the next world. The ranger shook his head and raised his shoulders as his fists came up, ready for the fight. The fight, however, came from behind. Hanaghan pounced onto his back with a shrill cry, his chain pulled taut. The weight of the small man pulled Asher back over the table where the two wrestled across even more of the alchemist's equipment.

One particular item, a small chest, was knocked over and its contents spilled across the table. Asher had only a moment before Hanaghan renewed his attack but, in that moment, he saw the empty glass vials that had been stored inside the chest. He had seen a vial of that exact size and pointed shape before, discarded on the beach outside Velia.

Before he could connect the rest of the dots, Hanaghan was swiping at him with his jagged nails. Asher shielded himself with one of his vambraces, the hard leather taking the raking nails in place of his skin. All the while, his free hand was running over the table in search of something to use as a weapon. A glass flask of some description, its previous use known only to the alchemist, was the first intact item he found. It was a strong piece of glass, but not as strong as Hanaghan's skull. The container shattered as it was slammed into the side of his masked face. The small man went down like a stone, not an ounce of consciousness remaining to even try and soften his landing.

Pushing off from the table once again, Asher was confronted by all six foot five of Geron Thorbear. The backhand he sent Asher's way was slow and obvious, but the ranger's previous head injury - also Geron's doing - was dulling his ability to react. Before he knew it, he was bouncing off another wall with a numb jaw. Kalantha darted in to the fray and launched her leg into his gut, doubling him over and lining his face up with Rolan's fist. Both blows hurt like hell but they weren't enough to take him from his feet. The same could not be said of Geron's next hammering attack, a closed fist to Asher's back.

On the floor and at their mercy now, the ranger had nothing left to give. The darkness that followed was inevitable.

The sound of crunching penetrated Asher's oblivion, worming its way into his consciousness. Soon, his eyes were attempting to open and a warm light filled his vision. It wasn't the first time he had woken up to find his wrists bound in rope and his freedom robbed from him. This time, he was on his knees with his arms stretched either side of him, tied to torch holders fixed into the walls. Judging by the lack of windows, he decided he was still in The Ranch's basement, though he had never seen this particular supply room.

Raising his head, he discovered the source of the crunching that had roused him. Seated on a stool, Geron Thorbear was slicing through an apple with a knife and devouring the pieces whole.

"You weren't supposed to find out so soon," the big man muttered between bites. "I was going to ease you in."

"You were going to ease me in to killing innocent people?" Asher quipped, though every word sent a jolt of pain through his jaw. "That's a far cry from your original pitch."

"It's not as simple as that..." Geron trailed off, perhaps seeing the simplicity in it after all.

"You killed those people in Dunwich," Asher stated miserably.

Geron nodded silently, his eyes fixed on the remainder of his apple.

"They weren't your first," the ranger pressed.

Now Geron shook his head. "And they won't be the last," he confessed quietly.

"Why?" Asher demanded.

Geron finally met his eyes. "Are *you* really asking me that? You're a *survivor*, Asher. You're just like me, like all of us. You dig your nails in and you *cling* to life. It doesn't matter how bad it gets or how desperate your situation becomes, you never give up. You have to keep your feet moving. You have to keep that breath in your lungs. And, at the end of the day, you'd do whatever you had to if it meant staying alive."

"How does killing innocent people in Dunwich keep you alive?"

Geron sighed. "Are you not getting it?" he asked with an edge of frustration. "The world out there never wanted us to begin with, Asher. It doesn't tolerate those of us who are willing to do whatever's necessary to survive. It wants us to bend and break like everyone else. That way the powerful stay powerful and the weak do their bidding. And because of this intolerance, they put us in cages. When we get out," the big man pulled back his sleeve to reveal the manacled tattoo of an ex-convict around his wrist, "they treat us like monsters. When, in fact, we're just more desperate than ever. Only now we won't just kill to survive - we'll do it *together*."

Asher let his head hang for a moment. "Was any of this ever real? The Ranch? The rangers?"

Geron took a breath and lost some of his intensity. "Aye, of course it was - *I* didn't write that bloody bestiary. The rangers have been around for centuries."

"Something tells me they weren't always prisoners with a grudge to bear," Asher commented.

"True enough," Geron conceded. "Though Rolan's the real deal," he added, flicking his head towards the door. "He's been hunting monsters since he was just a lad. He's the one that brought us all together. You see, the rangers hit hard times, and by hard times I mean they all died on the job. Vask was the only one left. Of course, no one wanted to join him - who would want to meet a gruesome end hunting monsters?"

"That's when he met you," Asher concluded.

Geron nodded with half a grin on his face. "That's when he met me," he echoed. "He saw my potential, just like I saw yours."

"You mean he saw you kill someone," Asher remarked.

"Not *someone*," Geron corrected. "I was in a caravan, a prisoner transport, when we were attacked by a Rakenbak." The big man's gaze grew distant as he looked into his past. "That thing peeled the bars off my wagon like they weren't even there. It had real hunger in its eyes and it terrified the others. Not me though. I knew that look. I knew those eyes. It was desperate, trying to survive. Rolan had been tracking it for days and caught up with the beast as it began eating its way through those in my wagon. Most of the guards pissed themselves and ran. There was no running for me - I was chained and bound for that hungry maw. It made *me* desperate. You know what it's like when that happens. You dig in and you find a way to survive. I managed to wrap the chains around its throat. Choked it to death. You won't find that technique in the book."

"And just like that," Asher said mockingly, "you were a ranger, a protector of the people."

"Not exactly," Geron replied, ignoring the jibe. "The guards that stayed tried to thank me for saving their lives by putting more chains on me. Rolan cut them all down. You see, by then he was also getting pretty desperate. He was getting older, slower. Tracking monsters took longer and slaying them was never guaranteed. He took me in and together we came up with a new model for the rangers. It just so happened that I knew some folk who would make excellent additions to our little enterprise." The big man eyed him with disappointment. "*You* were supposed to be the first in a new breed of ranger. No tattoos on *your* wrists."

"You didn't recruit me because I haven't done time in some dungeon," Asher told him. "You just saw another killer, someone who could stage an attack and make it look convincing. Another Mendal."

"It works, Asher," Geron said with some exasperation. "And we don't always kill people. Sure, the cities and some of the bigger towns need convincing that our skills are required and worth the coin, but we still find work organically. That Giant you felled up north - that had nothing to do with us. That was a genuine contract."

"And the Scudders," Asher continued. "How *genuine* was that? I chased someone through those tunnels and all I found was an empty vial of Darkest Night. I saw those same vials in Hanaghan's chamber. I'm assuming he made it for the Mendal brothers. That way they could navigate the catacombs with the Scudders they brought in."

Geron's face pinched into something akin to embarrassment. "Those fools had the easiest job and they still managed to mess it up." He tutted under his breath. "They couldn't tell an adolescent female from a male if it had a sign nailed to its hide."

"That's what happens when you recruit murderers instead of training real rangers," Asher chastised.

"Fair point," Geron conceded. "But you haven't grasped the bigger picture yet. This is all temporary - the killings. Once we're established in all six kingdoms and the high borns see our value, Rolan's going to get us the same deal the Graycoats get."

Asher coughed out a laugh. "You think the kingdoms are going to fund the rangers? There's ambition and then there's madness. Vask has you all wrapped up in the latter. To warrant that kind of funding, you're going to be murdering people every day of the week in every corner of the realm. Is that really worth the price of your *survival?*"

Geron was shaking his head. "This is why I was easing you in - it takes time to see the big picture." He leaned forward on his stool. "We're done surviving, scraping by. It's time to *thrive*. We're going to live like the high borns that judged us wretched enough to die in chains." His features softened then. "I wanted you to be a part of that. You've been a prisoner of Nightfall all your life. This would have set you free. It would have put you in charge of your own destiny. You could have known the real luxury that life has to offer."

"No one will ever again order me to kill another person," Asher answered before he sighed into his chest. "Still, I have to thank you."

Geron shifted on his stool. "For what?"

"A valuable lesson I shouldn't have doubted," the ranger explained. "I wasn't built to trust, but you broke that in me." Asher laughed to himself again, half-hearted as it was. "The first person I meet out in the world... If only Nasta could see me now," he uttered.

"I wouldn't worry about it, fella," Geron told him. "Soon, the troubles of the living will be a thing of the past."

Asher looked up at him. "If I'm bound for death why am I wasting my breath on you?"

"Still eager to meet the dead are we?" Geron remarked. "They're just deciding on the best way to dispose of your body. But don't worry," he added with sincerity, "when it comes time, I'll make sure the deed itself is quick and clean."

"What a friend you are," Asher replied sarcastically.

"I thought this is what you wanted," Geron snapped. "When we met you wanted death more than anything. And I've seen you sleeping remember. I know you're haunted by all that lies behind you. I had hoped a second chance would help to set things right from your past. But since you've spat all over that," he said with notable dismay. "Rest is finally coming."

"You did say the life expectancy of a ranger was short," Asher commented casually. "I just thought the monster that killed me would have more fangs." There was just enough venom in his tone to get under Geron's skin.

"If you truly wanted this life you should have kept your mouth shut and got on with it!" he bellowed, rising from his stool. "You had a chance to atone - I damned well gave it to you!" The big man paced up and down the cramped room. "You could have just walked away if you didn't agree with what we were doing. Got lost in the world and found your own way. You didn't have to make this a fight. It makes no sense!" he shouted, his frustration spilling over. "You're a killer, Asher! Compared to you and your assassin friends we're knights of the damned realm! How can *you* judge *us*?"

The question got stuck in Asher's mind, forcing him to really face it. He quickly came to wonder if he had been viewing his whole life from the wrong perspective. Since the switch in his conditioning had been broken, he had taken the view that he himself was broken, no longer the man he had always been. What if the opposite was true? he pondered. What if he had always been a good man and Nightfall had broken him? Perhaps it was wishful thinking to believe that there had always been goodness inside of him, yet here he was, his conditioning shattered by a deed so evil that the good man inside of him had finally come up for air. Now he saw right and wrong, good and evil, painful as those distinctions could be.

It led him to one simple answer. "Because I'm a *ranger*."

Geron frowned. "That ship has sailed, I'm afraid. The next time I walk through that door, it'll be to put you out of your misery." With that, the big man made to depart.

Left to himself, Asher immediately began to test the limits of his restraints, wondering just how well the torch holders were fixed to the wooden panels that layered the stone walls.

CHAPTER 33

DEATH INCARNATE

Darkling - The addition of this monster is something of a special case, but the rangers' council has agreed it warrants inclusion. The first thing you need to know when dealing with Darklings is this: they're already dead. These abominations are the creations of dark mages and the foulest of magic. From our archives, it appears I am the only ranger to have ever encountered Darklings and I pray to the gods that this will forever remain the truth.

I came across these dark mages in Snowfell. Their insidious cult, whose name I was never able to learn, was in the process of digging up the dead from their graves and breathing new life into them. Only, it was not the life they had known. No, these people were brought back as monsters, fiends who know only their master's command.

They're fast, ferociously violent, and they feel no pain, no fear, and they never tire. Under their master's spell, they hunt in packs and consume the flesh of any poor soul they come across.

Darklings do not return to death idly, and they killed my ward in the time it took us to discover a viable method of destruction. You must take their head or set them alight with fire. Nothing else works. They can lose limbs and take enough damage to drop a Rakenbak, but they will never stop coming for you. So I will say it again. Take the head or set them alight. Better yet, use both methods.

As I said though, these are not naturally occurring monsters. They are products of magic, the machinations of mad men. Though I never got the opportunity to kill one of these dark mages, there is a possibility that their death would end the spell and the Darklings with it.

A Chronicle of Monsters: A Ranger's Bestiary, 12th Edition, Page 148.

Omas Ban-Harqen, Ranger.

Coated in sweat, Asher finally stopped pulling on the ropes that bound him to the walls. His wrists were bruised and he was sure both of his arms were close to dislocation. At one point, he had even braced his legs against the wall behind him and attempted to pull the ropes from a different angle. The fixings on the walls, however, would not budge.

Returned to his knees, the ranger began to wonder how Geron was going to kill him. Perhaps he would run him through with his claymore. No. That was not the swift death he had promised him. Decapitation was quick and the big man certainly possessed the strength to see it through. A poison concocted by Hanaghan would also do the job and leave no mess. Given the people he had picked a fight with, it was entirely possible they would feed him to some beast in the wilds.

After another hour, Asher gave up on the images of his death. Whatever it was to be, there was little he could do in his current state. And Geron hadn't been wrong - death *would* bring rest. Most would tell him that rest was the last thing awaiting him in the after-life, his actions binding his fate to the lowest hell. But Asher didn't believe in any of that. He had been born, had his chance at life, and now he would die. That's all there was for him.

That should have been enough, but something had awoken in him, brought back to life by the *ranger*. Now he felt compelled to stop Rolan and the others before they took more innocent lives. Their every action spoiled the meaning of what it was to be a true ranger. That thought led him to the Mendal brothers. They hadn't been in The Ranch upon his return, having already been sent back out into the world. Where were they going? Who would they kill to drive up their prices?

A heavy thud sounded from the ceiling, drawing Asher's attention to the wooden beams and the raining dust. All thought of the Mendal brothers flittered away as an uneasy feeling settled over the ranger. That single thud soon turned into a ruckus above. The sound of shattering glass and snapping wood was interspersed with angry cries and colliding swords. This was quickly followed by the sound of rushing feet. Then there was more yelling and the apparent fight moved through The Ranch.

Cocking his head to one side, Asher heard someone tumbling down the stairs and into the basement. The cries became more distinct now as the rangers charged each other will killing someone. Bail, or possibly Dunkan, yelled something unintelligible before more swords came together in a violent dance. The wall to Asher's right was shaken by an impact and a handful of supplies fell from their shelf.

Rolan's voice cut through it all, the man swearing to all the gods that he was going to kill his opponent. Then came another thud; a body hitting the floor. Eventually, the fight spread into the corridor outside the supply room and a series of impacts struck the wall and door before another body hit the floor. By now, Asher had renewed his efforts to rip the torch holders from the walls, his pain be damned.

All the while, he had no choice but to listen to his approaching executioner fell ranger after ranger. Curiously though, Asher was sure he heard more than one of them rise from the floor and jump back into the fight. Indeed, the close-quarter battle appeared to be going on a while longer than he would have expected it to. Were the intruder an Arakesh, no ranger should ever rise once put on their back - efficiency was the corner-stone of Nightfall's methods. Yet, it seemed this particular assassin was merely maiming his foes, prolonging the fight.

Wasting no more time questioning it, Asher doubled his efforts and concentrated on one of his ropes. He had only to free a single arm and he could untie the other knot with his hand. There seemed some progress when the top two fixings began to budge, tilting the sconce by half an inch. Behind the supply room, one of the rangers finally met their death, evident by the gargling sound as they choked on their own blood. Whoever it was, they fell into the wall before dropping to the floor. A moment later, blood oozed under the door and entered the room.

The fight continued down the corridor and round towards Hanaghan's chamber. Rolan was still alive if his cursing words were still to be heard. There was another with him, pressing the intruder into the alchemist's lab. The sound of Hanaghan's chain resounded throughout the basement, though the fight had grown distant enough that Asher could no longer perceive individual movements.

Again, he heaved and groaned as he pulled on the rope. Feeling his arm coming dangerously close to losing its place in its socket, he was forced to stop and catch his breath.

"Come on," he rasped. "You've got out of worse."

Injured as he was, however, his muscles and fortitude faltered under the task. The fixture refused to relent any more than it already had. This was to be his place of death. He wasn't afraid to die, nor was he afraid of the manner in which he died, but he couldn't help but return to thoughts of the Mendal brothers, free to continue their wretched work. He was the only person who knew of their operation, the only one who could stop them. And so, it seemed, he was afraid of dying after all, afraid of dying before completing one last deed that would save lives.

And there it was, that unyielding requirement to survive.

The ranger dug deep and let loose a feral roar as he threw himself to the right and pulled as hard as he could on the rope tied around his left wrist. Another of the anchors began to lose its hold on the wall. A little more and he was certain the fixture would come free.

The door swung open.

Asher halted his efforts and stared at Dunkan. The older ranger remained standing in the doorway for another second before dropping to his knees and then his face. His body had been ravaged by steel, the cuts both shallow and deep marring his dark skin from head to toe. There was so much blood pouring out of him that it was impossible to say which wound was responsible for his death.

In his place stepped another. Entering the gloom of the supply room, this figure was draped in a large leather poncho, its edges frayed and dripping with blood. A hood made from the same material covered their head but the intruder wore a black mask that concealed every inch of their face, including their eyes. In one hand they gripped a razored sickle and in the other a hammer, both of which were plastered with red gore.

"Who in the hells are you supposed to be?" Asher demanded, though the intruder could have told him he was Death incarnate and the ranger would have believed him.

Motionless, the figure continued to stand over Dunkan's dead body. He could have been looking at Asher were his eyes capable of seeing through the black material that covered his face. With no indication as to why, the intruder dropped both the sickle and the hammer at his feet. By the time the ranger returned his gaze from the fallen weapons, the figure had retrieved something small from within the poncho. With a gloved hand, he flicked the cork off what appeared to be a slender vial and approached Asher with a limp in his step.

The ranger moved to lash out with his feet but the intruder was upon him. One hand pressed into Asher's head and pinned him against the wall, while the hand gripping the small vial came up under his nose. The fumes were potent and went to work almost immediately, robbing his senses of clarity. His muscles went limp and he was returned to his knees, his head hanging loosely around his chest. Holding on to any one thought became near impossible as his lips went numb and his sense of orientation span out of control.

Rough hands moved around his neck and over his body but never inflicted pain. When they finally stopped he could hear the intruder's breath in his ear. None of it made much sense to the ranger but, then again, he wasn't entirely sure what was up and what was down. The only thing he knew for sure was that the supply room was getting darker. Before he really had time to consider that, the light was gone altogether and Asher's mind with it.

When next he awoke, a deep sense of confusion battled with decades of training and conditioning. Multiple questions rose to the surface and demanded answers, but the ranger's last memory was one of danger. That was made all the more apparent when he laid eyes on Dunkan's body a few feet away.

A quick scan of the room informed him he was alone but, more surprisingly, he was no longer tied to the walls. His wrists burned with pain but it had been no effort of his that had freed him. Examining one of the ropes it was clear that it had been cut with something sharp. That led him to the razored sickle that had been left embedded in the doorframe.

Confident that he wasn't in immediate danger, Asher allowed some of his confusion to overcome his fight or flight instincts. His chief question involved the identity of the intruder. It had to have been an Arakesh but they looked nothing like an assassin of Nightfall, nor did they fight like one. Contradicting this was the fact that

Asher was still alive. No Arakesh would let him live - even Rendal had hunted him down and he wasn't on the court.

Determined to get answers, Asher crept towards the door and took the razored sickle as his own. The corridor behind was a scene taken right out of a nightmare. Blood had been splattered up both walls and across the ceiling and floor. In fact, the floor was more akin to a large puddle, the source of which appeared to be Bail. The smith's body lay on its side, propped up against the wall. Like Dunkan, he had taken far more strikes than was necessary to kill a man.

The intruder had enjoyed it. At least that was Asher's conclusion. If they were skilled enough to kill these men then they were skilled enough to kill them efficiently. Moving through the corridor, Asher followed a thick line of smeared blood to Vask's office but, reaching the corner, he was given a glimpse into Hanaghan's chamber. The sight gave him pause. The door was still broken from where Geron had thrown him through it earlier, but it was what lay beyond the entrance that had captured the ranger's attention.

Stepping inside the lab, he quickly came to stand over Kalantha's body. Her own sword was lodged in her gut and three daggers protruded from her back. Like the others, her death hadn't come swiftly. Kalantha, however, had not been the thing that drew Asher into the lab. On the other side of the chamber sat the Skalagat's skull, now stripped of its flesh and well cleaned.

Its pointed antlers branched high, there to hold up the small lifeless body of Hanaghan.

His blood had stopped running down the Skalagat bone now, leaving the antlers streaked with red. Asher moved close enough to touch the corpse and give in to some of his curiosity. Whatever hideous monster he had expected to find beneath that mask didn't exist, for there rested the head and face of an ordinary man. His white hair had been reduced to wisps and had grown in patches, but his complexion was merely that of an old man. What reasons he kept for concealing his face were his own and now they had died with him. It wasn't hard, however, to imagine that a great deal of shame lay at the heart of Hanaghan's reasoning.

Leaving the alchemist to his death perch, Asher scrutinised the rest of the chamber, making certain Geron wasn't lying dead under any debris. Perhaps his body was upstairs, the first to have faced the masked killer.

Keeping the sickle held out in front of him, the ranger made his way back to Rolan Vask's office and the trail of blood that ended at his door. He opened it and let the door slowly swing open. When no one tried to kill him he entered the office and discovered the oldest of the rangers slumped in his chair, his hands covering a bleeding gut wound. Beads of sweat adorned his pale face and flecks of blood stained his white beard.

He was still alive.

"What did you... bring down on us?" he managed through the agony that was clearly tearing through his gut.

Asher walked to the edge of the desk and looked from the sickle in his hand to the dying man before him. "I'm not sure," he admitted.

"I suppose," Rolan spluttered, "you think... we had this... coming."

"It's no more than you deserve," the ranger replied honestly.

Vask swallowed and slowly blinked. "If this... is what we deserved. Just think what's coming... for you."

It should already have come, Asher thought, still wondering why he was breathing at all.

"Geron should never... have brought you in," Rolan continued unsteadily. "You doomed us all."

Asher was only half listening to the man's ramblings now. His attention had shifted to the various parchments and scrolls that littered Rolan's office. Removing a particularly bloody map from the top of a pile, the ranger cast his eyes over a chart of sorts, written by Vask. It detailed where each of the rangers was in the realm as well as where they would be going next. Moving his finger down the list, a pattern quickly emerged. It seemed the Mendal brothers would visit a town or city first, having captured and transported the relevant monster, then one of the rangers would show up with just the right weapons for the job.

Looking further back, he could see that they had been assigned to Velia a week before Geron and himself had been tasked with investigating the deaths. Even further back, it appeared the brothers had been responsible for the Skalagat that Geron had been sent to slay.

Asher had to wonder how many of those travellers had been picked off the road by the Skalagat and how many had been murdered by Geron.

"Where is he?" Asher asked, cutting off whatever insult Rolan was concocting. "Where's Geron?" Vask gave something close to a shrug - what did dead men care about such things. "Where did you send the Mendal brothers?" he asked instead, unable to see the most recent entries on the chart, stained as it was.

Vask's eyes rolled up at Asher. "They're gone," he croaked.

The ranger moved around the desk and grabbed the man by his shirt. "Where did you send them?" he growled, recalling a conversation he had overheard. "They were keeping something outside the city. What monster did you have them capture, Rolan?" He shook the dying fool in his chair. "Where did you send them?"

"I sent them... to do their job. You can't stop... what I've started here. The rangers... will be glorious again." Tears began to streak down his face, following the lines furrowed into his skin. "It was my... responsibility. My duty."

Asher released him. "Your duty was to protect people from the monsters of the world, not become one yourself."

Leaving the man to his slow death, the ranger discarded the sickle and pored over more parchments, desperately searching for a clue that might lead him to the brothers. A small notebook in the top drawer looked promising, its pages curled from great use and the leather worn from handling. Inside were pages filled with more of Rolan's handwriting, reminders mostly, with instructions for himself as his memory grew soft with age. One such passage was a note to remind himself to visit Palios and search for suitable buildings that could house future rangers.

"That's mine," Rolan protested wearily. "Be gone... assassin. Leave me to my end."

Asher ignored the man and skipped to the most recent addition. It was a note to remind Hanaghan that he needed to source the ingredients for Selvin paste and give it to Kalantha.

"Selvin paste," the ranger muttered to himself.

Where had he seen reference to that before? Then he remembered. Looking at the books lining one of Rolan's shelves, he removed A Chronicle of Monsters: A Ranger's Bestiary and laid it out on the desk. He rapidly flicked through the pages with a partial memory of where to look inside.

There it was, right under the word *Basilisk*.

"Selvin paste," he said again, louder this time so Vask could hear him. "It's the only known balm that can slow down Basilisk venom. Why would Kalantha need that?" he enquired, before the despicable truth hit him. "She was to aid the victims, wasn't she? Slow down their inevitable deaths - draw it out to let the grief and the fear spread. They'd pay anything to be rid of the beast then, wouldn't they? Was that your plan?" he asked with disgust. "Is that what you've been doing all these years? Sitting behind your expensive desk and coming up with different ways to kill innocent people, to make them suffer."

Rolan gave no response, nor would he ever respond again. He was dead, eyes glazed over, and mouth ajar.

Asher sighed and leaned into the desk, his hands propping him up while his head hung low. The sun was coming up, its earliest rays beginning to penetrate the gloom through the narrow window set high into the wall. The Mendal brothers had a full day and night head start and he didn't even know what direction to take.

Out of the corner of his eye, the ranger caught sight of a familiar possession and, from the most unlikely place, hope was restored.

Moving with purpose now, he looked over the various items that had been left on top of the cupboard. They were all his, including the red blindfold that had been placed on his bundled green cloak. Resting against the wall was his broadsword, dagger, and hourglass blade, while on the other side of the cupboard lay his bow and quiver.

Before putting any of it on, he retrieved his blindfold and proceeded to cover his eyes. He needed an acute sense of touch if he was to glean their destination. Pushing through the almost sickening amount of blood and gore that bombarded his senses, the ranger returned to the chart and ran his finger over the stained area. His sensitive skin traced the remnants of the ink Rolan had used, following the curves and flicks that had been soaked in blood. First he checked the Mendal brothers and then Kalantha, making certain their locations matched up. Each contained eight letters with a break after the first four.

"Kelp Town," he said aloud.

The Mendal brothers were about to unleash a Basilisk on the people of Kelp Town. Asher's heart fell into his stomach. Every entry in the bestiary spoke of a truly ferocious fiend, its poison comparable to the reaching hand of Death.

Wasting no time, the ranger donned his cloak and strapped the various weapons to his body. Stepping over the dead, he made his way up to The Ranch's main floor, expecting to see Geron's corpse. The big man's fate, however, remained a mystery. There was no sign of him in the armourer's room and he hadn't been killed in the smith's yard.

Under a clouded pale sky, Asher walked across the street and entered the stable. Adding to the mystery, Hector was resting inside, absent his owner. The ranger checked the streets one more time. He had to be out there, somewhere. So too was the elusive intruder who had butchered the rangers and freed him.

Time against him, Asher saddled the horse and claimed Hector as his own, if for nothing more than the benefit of Kelp Town.

He only hoped he wouldn't be too late.

CHAPTER 34

A SERPENT FROM THE DEEP

Praitora *- Also known as the Fisherman's Bane. Praitora are most definitely the creatures that slithered out of the ocean's nightmares. If you've ever spent any time by the sea you probably have an idea about what an octopus is. For the sake of this passage I will assume you have. They are similar in appearance to the more harmless octopus, but they are considerably larger and have no qualms about encroaching on the shore. They hunt in the shallows and often claim nearby caves - the damper the better - as temporary dens while hunting on land.*

Some of the larger ones have even been known to capsize small fishing boats. Now don't even bother hunting these or even the smaller ones if they remain in the water; that's their territory. If one has come ashore, hunt it down or use bait to lure it from the sea if you must (see below for list of appropriate baits).

A Chronicle of Monsters: A Ranger's Bestiary, 12th Edition, Page 88.

Logan Hackett, Ranger.

. . .

With the wind behind him, Asher rode out of Lirian with all the haste Hector could give him. Taking The Selk Road, they were bound for The Ice Vales, an unforgiving land that promised winter's cold whatever the season.

Hector gave everything he had, galloping for two miles before slowing to a trot. By mid-morning they had passed through The Evermoore's western region and begun a new journey across the freezing wolds. It would be another day, however, before the most southern edge of The Vengoran Mountains came into view. From there, they had only to take the road north until it brought them to Kelp Town.

It seemed such a simple journey when laid out in the ranger's mind, yet no traveller had ever crossed The Ice Vales and considered it simple. The first night was blisteringly cold and the wind threatened to extinguish the fire at the heart of his camp. Then there were the shadows. Asher felt them moving about him as if he was constantly being watched. More than once he was convinced a dark figure had passed his camp and melted back into the night.

Having picked up meagre supplies on his way out of The Ranch, he was forced to ration his food and drink. And so he sat in the dark with naught but his pain for company. He could still feel every blow the rangers had punished him with. Especially Geron's. The big man knew how to use his strength to his advantage.

Then there was the blow of the truth. For just a moment, he had seen some kind of future for himself, a future where those around him had his back instead of always plotting to put a knife in it. The world had disappointed him again, revealing a new breed of killers just as eager to recruit him as Nasta had been. The lonely road was to be his path. He saw that now. Alone, he could never be betrayed. Alone, he could never be hurt.

After another sleep filled with nightmares from his past, Asher awoke to a rising sun. Time to go. Deciding to eat and drink on the road, he mounted Hector and drove the horse on, towards the mountains. He paid no heed to those sharing the road, his focus sharpening with every mile they covered. He so easily imagined a fully-grown Basilisk turning Kelp Town into its own hunting ground, picking off the animals and then the children.

Pushing on for another day, they finally reached the base of the mountains and the T-junction in the road. To his left, the road led south, to Grey Stone, while the path to his right weaved north, to Kelp Town. The ranger hadn't even stopped at the junction, directing Hector to cut across the corner and ride north. By the next nightfall, after continuing under the light of the moon for some miles, they were camped again, halted by the cold and fatigue. It was infuriating, yet neither he nor Hector were capable of pushing themselves any more than they already had.

It didn't help, however, with the images conjured by his imagination. Every passing minute in which he simply sat by the fire brought new and terrible thoughts about the potential victims. He had referred to the bestiary multiple times while camped, reading and rereading the passage about Basilisks. Amaya Hawkyns, the ranger who had chronicled the beast, named their kind as serpents of the deep world, suggesting they had originally come from the abyss beneath the surface world. Besides this ominous birth place, every detail about the Basilisks informed Asher that they were not to be faced alone.

The ranger had closed the book at that point. He would face the threat and either make the world a safer place or die trying. He was satisfied with either outcome.

By late morning the next day, Kelp Town appeared as a smudge on the northern horizon, sticking out from the base of the mountains. It was only then that he looked back over his shoulder and realised what he must have passed on the road. He wasn't certain of the exact distance, but the black gem couldn't be far from his current position. He didn't recall seeing the bowed trees that formed a natural arch into the wood, though, in truth, his focus had been miles ahead, where he was soon to face the Mendal brothers and their captured monster.

For the first time in weeks he felt the call of the gem. He so easily imagined the touch of it between his fingers. Not only that, but he recalled the feeling of invincibility it had always granted him, even if it couldn't save him from immediate death. It had always been bolstering to know that he could push himself through the worst of the worst and rise whole again.

The survivor in him wanted to backtrack and reclaim the ring, thereby ensuring life after Kelp Town. There wasn't time to retrieve it now. And he still wasn't sure he deserved such a powerful relic. A lifetime of pain was to be his punishment and even that didn't feel harsh enough at times. Before any more thoughts of reuniting with the ring could take root, Asher spurred Hector on, content to die if that was required to stop Rolan Vask's dark dream.

As the morning began to slide into the afternoon, Hector trotted under the wooden arch that served as Kelp Town's main entrance. Restless in his saddle, Asher already had one hand on his broadsword, his emotions stirred with both apprehension and relief. He had expected to come across some ghastly scene or a desperate situation in which the townspeople were running scared. Neither was the case.

All around him, Kelp Town went about its usual day. The streets were relatively busy, business was conducted per the norm, and children dashed between it all, throwing snowballs at each other. This was not a town that had suffered the wrath of a territorial Basilisk.

Doubt began to creep in. Had he got it wrong? Had the Mendals gone elsewhere? Was there a Basilisk plaguing another town even as he rode through these streets? He couldn't believe that to be the case. The letters concealed by Rolan's blood had read Kelp Town. His heightened senses were rarely wrong and he *had* learnt to read and write in the darkness of Nightfall.

So where were they?

He looked down every street and scrutinised every alley searching for the brothers' cart. It would have to be big and reinforced to house the plethora of monsters they routinely captured and transported. The ranger saw no such cart.

Bringing Hector to a stop in the middle of the main road, Asher climbed down and slowly turned on the spot. His fingers rubbed the red material of his blindfold, tempting him to use it in broad daylight. Refraining for now, he scanned every building, looking for the most likely place someone like Royce Mendal would rest his head. There were several taverns and a couple of inns situated in the heart of the town, all vying for dominance.

A frustrated growl rumbled out of the ranger's throat. He was going to have to check them all; what other choice did he have? They could unleash the Basilisk any minute. Or, perhaps, they already had and were simply resting while they waited for it to attack. Of course, the brothers had no idea what had transpired in Lirian, so they would likely be expecting Kalantha to show up any day now.

Hitching Hector to a post outside The King's Arms, Asher proceeded to enter the tavern and begin his investigation. He looked in every booth, hoping to catch a glimpse of a green cloak identical to his own. With no luck, he questioned the man behind the bar, giving him the brothers' descriptions and even offering coin in exchange for information.

It wasn't long, however, before he was back on the road and striding into Dandy's Inn. Using the same handful of words he gleaned that no one matching their description had stopped by the inn. On to The Hunter's Retreat, a potentially obvious watering hole for the Mendals given its name. Nothing. The ranger's concern was only growing as he crossed the road again and entered The Knight's Gauntlet, a tavern that appeared to be in the middle of a local brawl. Asher navigated the tussle, wanting nothing to do with it, and walked up to the barmaid on the other side of the counter. Her attention, unfortunately, drifted back to the two men swapping pathetic punches.

Asher sighed. "I haven't got time for this." Then he turned around and planted a knotted fist in the face of the closest man. "You win," he said gruffly, eyeing the other man. "Go back to your drink."

Seeing the animal that lived behind the ranger's eyes, the brawler did exactly that. Asher had already forgotten the man unconscious on the floor when he returned to the barmaid, her attention entirely his now. He gave her the Mendals' description and even added a detail or two about their personalities in case that jogged her memory.

"I saw the lads you're looking for," she replied.

Struggling to contain his anticipation, Asher demanded to know when and where exactly.

"They were sitting over there," she said, her chin pointing at the furthest booth. "Seemed to think they owned the place. And me," she added with exasperation.

"They're staying here?" the ranger pressed, his eyes looking up to the ceiling.

"No room," the barmaid told him. "I overheard them talking about The Crown's Inn. It's just round the corner."

Before she had finished with her directions, Asher was stepping over the unconscious man and marching back to the main road. With a glance he checked to make sure Hector was alright before rounding the corner.

A sign for The Crown's Inn extended out into the street above the door, drawing Asher to the black and white building on his left. Keeping a hand on his broadsword, the ranger stepped inside and rooted his feet in the middle of the room. From this position, he took in every patron seated in the bar area as well as the staff weaving between the tables.

"Can I help you, sir?" the bartender enquired.

"I'm looking for two men," Asher informed him, stepping closer to the bar. "They would look like me," he said, gesturing to his cloak and weapons. "I was told they might be staying here."

The bartender adopted an awkward expression, his shoulders rising. "I can't be telling strangers about paying customers now."

Whether he realised it or not, the bartender had just revealed that the Mendal brothers were, in fact, staying in this establishment. As the last syllable was forming in his mouth, Asher was turning to the stairs on the other side of the room. Accompanied by protests from the bartender, the ranger took the stairs two at a time and followed them round to the first floor. A short corridor awaited him with four doors either side. They were up here somewhere.

He had kicked in the door on his right by the time the bartender caught up with him. A new, and threatening, protest was on its way out of the man's mouth when Asher abandoned the empty room and drew his short-sword from over one shoulder. Be it the determined expression on the ranger's face or the naked steel in his hand, the bartender held on to his words and retreated back down the stairs.

Asher kicked in another door and discovered a half-naked couple pulling up the sheets of their bed to hide themselves. Moving on, he forced open the third door and found naught but a stripped bed and dusty cupboards. Approaching the fourth door, the ranger was given reason to pause. Like every human, his eyes instinctively spotted threats, and nature's most threatening colour was red. Standing outside the door, he could see flecks of red on the brass handle and the slightest smear on the dark wood of the door frame. Blood.

As he braced to kick the door in, he decided, instead, to try the bloody handle. His suspicions were correct: it wasn't locked. The door creaked as it slowly swung open. The ranger stepped inside to find a room with two single beds, each pressed against opposing walls. In one of those beds lay Davin Mendal. His throat had been slashed while he slept, leaving his corpse with a startled expression. His blood had poured out and soaked the bed before dripping onto the floor and spreading across the boards.

Sharing the floor space with Davin's blood was his brother, Royce Mendal. Face down and white as chalk, it looked to Asher as if Royce had risen to avenge his brother's death and suffered a similar fate for his troubles. Judging by the pool of blood beneath him, the ranger had been exsanguinated after someone had sliced through three of his major arteries. The dagger he still held in one hand was clean, suggesting he failed to wound his skilled opponent.

The grim scene triggered more questions in the ranger. Who, besides himself, had cause to murder the Mendals? The obvious answer was Geron, but this wasn't Geron's style - too surgical.

Considering the manner of their deaths, it had all the markings of an assassin to Asher, for the killer had to have picked the lock and crept in without waking either man. Then, they killed Davin with one clean cut and went on to use a very proficient method to ensure Royce's quick death. If it was the same figure who had brutally killed the rangers, they appeared to have changed their style, opting for stealth and speed. This hadn't been done for the enjoyment of it. This had been done for a specific reason, a goal that needed achieving.

As more questions rose to the surface, the sound of a laden cart, its large wheels finding every depression in the road, found Asher's ears. He moved to the window that overlooked the street and watched as a cumbersome cart, painted deep red and pulled by a pair of horses, emerged from an alleyway and made for the main road. Asher braced his hands against the windowsill as he got sight of the one holding the reins: a figure clad in black, the hood of their poncho covering their face. By the time the cart had turned onto the main road the horses were picking up speed, taking it towards the mountains behind the town.

In its wake were three watchmen, oblivious to the cart housing a Basilisk, as they strode towards The Crown's Inn. The bartender was leading them, waving his hands dramatically in their faces and pointing to the inn's first floor. At the same moment they passed over the threshold, Asher climbed out of the window and ascended to the roof. Though it was obvious to him, a trained killer, that the Mendals had been murdered hours ago, the town's authorities would happily pin their deaths on him.

That thought led the ranger to another, more ominous conclusion. The killer hadn't just murdered the brothers and stolen the Basilisk, they had murdered them and waited for him to arrive. Leaping to the adjacent rooftop, he realised the truth of the matter: he was being baited.

He could see the red cart now, moving past Hector and making for the trail that led to the mountain overlooking the town. He jumped the gap between two more buildings and rapidly descended to the alley floor. He broke away at a sprint and mounted his horse, turning the steed towards the mountains. Setting Hector to a gallop, he gave chase, quickly leaving the town behind.

The cart itself was already above him, weaving up the mountain left and right. Asher didn't give Hector a moment to rest, urging the horse to catch up with their prey. He couldn't allow the killer to open those doors and unleash the monster.

One of the cart's back wheels skidded over the edge of the trail and sent snow and pebbles down the side, littering the ground in front of Hector. The horse, notoriously afraid of its own shadow, tried to halt on the path and rear up. Asher had to work twice as hard to get the mount back on track and up to speed again. The pause, however, had given the cart valuable time to get off the winding trail and disappear from sight and sound.

After finally reaching a plateau, Asher examined the ground and followed the wheel tracks. At a trot, Hector crossed the flat area and brought them to a large cave entrance crowned with daunting stalactites of ice. The tracks cut through the snow and vanished inside the gloom. The ranger climbed down from his saddle and guided Hector to one of the three pine trees that stood tall beside the cave.

"Try and stick around this time," he muttered, tying the reins to one of the low branches.

Turning to the cave entrance, the ranger drew his broadsword and entered the shadows. The back of the cart soon came into view and, to his dismay, the thick bolts of iron had been shifted out of place and the doors had been opened.

He was immediately struck by the musty stench of its interior, and a part of him felt sorry for the creature that had been imprisoned in there for days. That same creature, however, was now somewhere inside the cave with him and it had to be hungry. The Basilisk wasn't the only predator lurking in the shadows though, for the killer had to be somewhere in the vicinity.

Up came the broadsword, both of his hands locked around the grip with white knuckles. In the same way he had faced the Giant, he now faced a Basilisk wholly unprepared. He hadn't taken the time to concoct any of the known poisons that slowed the monster down. He hadn't even taken measures to protect himself from those venomous fangs - the bestiary advising donning an entire suit of armour when facing the nightmarish serpent. And, for all the lessons Nightfall had imparted to him, none of them involved battling a Basilisk.

Putting his shortcomings aside, the ranger embraced the only part of him that really made sense anymore: he was a warrior. Be it man or monster, he would face them with grit and steel, fighting to his last breath.

Something moved at the back of the cave, catching a pale ray of daylight. From right to left, he witnessed a patchwork of scales glide across the rock face before the cart blocked his view. He moved to the other side, angling his blade to point ahead of him. There was no Basilisk to greet him, only shadow. Keeping his footwork slow and precise, he advanced towards the front of the cart. A grisly sight awaited him there. Both horses were dead, one with multiple puncture wounds across its neck and head, while the other looked to have been enveloped and crushed to death.

An ear-piercing *hiss* passed over his head and Asher shifted his stance to bring the tip of his blade up. There came no attack, though two of the murderous icicles fell away from their perch and shattered on top of the cart. The impact was loud, momentarily deafening the ranger. He turned on the spot to check his surroundings and saw a pointed tail disappear around the cart.

Deciding that he was done being toyed with, Asher reached for the blindfold tucked into his belt. The Nightseye elixir wouldn't make him stronger or faster, but it would grant him a level of awareness even the Basilisk didn't possess.

He hated the touch of it against his skin now. How many people had died each time he had tied that knot? Loathe it though he did, the ranger only succeeded in touching it between his finger and thumb.

The Basilisk had chosen its moment well.

The ranger dived to one side and rolled under the cart. Had he not caught sight of the beast in the corner of his eye, it would have snapped its jaws shut around his head. It attempted to pursue him under the cart but, past its reptilian head, the monster's body wouldn't fit. The cart bucked for a moment, straining in protest, before the Basilisk backed out and crawled over the top. By then, Asher had returned to his feet and grasped his broadsword in both hands.

Curled over the lip of the cart roof, the serpent was bathed in the afternoon light that pierced the cave, there to be seen in all its hideous glory. The head was an amalgamation of lizard and snake, with a jaw of small needle-tipped fangs and a pair of larger arching fangs that folded down from the roof of its mouth, each dripping with venom. A forked tongue darted from within to taste the air as its golden eyes, cut with a line of black, fixed on its prey below. Two of its six legs, each finished with serrated claws, dug into the side of the cart and helped to brace the creature in place. Beyond its striped body of blue and black scales was a swishing tail that ended with a flat bony spike. Every part of the Basilisk had evolved to kill.

"Everything bleeds," he whispered, repeating Nasta's words to himself. "Everything dies."

Satisfied with its chosen prey, the Basilisk lunged down at the ranger, its maw flexing unnaturally wide. Asher dashed to one side while being sure to delay the flick of his sword. As the monster was upon him, it met only the edge of his steel as it sliced through the inside of its mouth. The shock and pain prevented the creature from landing on its feet and its head crashed into the cave floor before its snaking body folded over itself in a heap of scaled muscle.

First blood was his, though he knew better than to believe that spelled ultimate victory. Bringing his broadsword up again, his knees braced low, he prepared for the next attack, and there was a next attack. The Basilisk's head emerged from the coiled body with narrowed eyes and a hissing jaw. Again, the ranger was able to side-step and evade the initial lunge, only, this time, the monster began to wrap around him. Not wishing to meet the same fate as the horse, Asher swung low and sliced through one of its six legs.

The shot of pain sent a spasm through its body and the thick midsection knocked the ranger back. His saving grace was the unfurling of the snaking body at the same time. Though the gap was narrow, Asher jumped through it and rolled across the ground to put some space between them. The Basilisk's remaining five legs, however, quickly compensated and brought its gnashing jaws about, pushing the ranger back towards the side of the cart.

Never one to stay on the defensive, Asher brought his sword to bear and swung left and right. Two of his blows landed true and struck the beast across its pointed face, yet it did not yield. By the time his back was pressed against the cart, the Basilisk had moved on to using its front claws. Rearing up, those front legs came for Asher and raked across the wood, missing the crouching ranger by mere inches.

There was no running away from it though, not when its wicked tail curled around and pierced the cart, blocking his path. Down came the broadsword, only the swing hadn't been powerful enough to sever the tail but merely wound it instead. Reacting to the injury, the tail whipped low and wide and took Asher from his feet. The knock to his head wasn't significant, but it hurt like hell and tried to rob him of his senses. Drawing on those reserves Nightfall had instilled in him so long ago, he maintained his awareness and saw a three-pronged claw speeding to swipe at his face.

Rolling to one side, the cave floor took the brunt of the damage in his place. The same could not be said of the second swipe. Asher roared with agony as the claws tore three ragged lines down his back, shredding his cloak and leathers in the process. A third strike was coming and he could either roll onto his back and face it or crawl away and simply hope he made it. The latter, however, wasn't part of Nightfall's training. Survival was all that mattered.

And so the ranger took the searing pain in his back and rolled over to see that third strike coming down on him. Gritting his teeth through the suffering that tore through his muscles, Asher raised his broadsword and held it horizontally with one of his hands against the flat of the steel. The Basilisk's claw met the weapon and pushed his elbows to the ground, but it was just enough of a defence to prevent any one of the claws from doing more than scratch his leathers.

Its claws, unfortunately, were not the monster's only form of attack. Bearing over him now, its jaws opened and hot saliva oozed between its fangs. One snap and it would crush his skull. Asher had no intention of dying with his head inside the mouth of a Basilisk. The ranger swiped his blade as far as he could to one side and twisted it as he did. The steel bit into the creature's claw before it could land another successful swipe. Asher then used what precious moments he had and lifted his weapon to point the tip up. The monster blindly retaliated and brought its claw down onto the sword, its cry of pain filling the cave.

With the sword lodged, Asher was flung high and cast aside in the violent reaction. He bounced off the cart and landed beside one of the dead horses, his broadsword miraculously still in his hand. Reduced to five of its six legs - and with only four capable of bearing any weight - the Basilisk limped towards the ranger with fury in its beautiful eyes.

Asher found his feet if not his breath and faced the monster with sagging shoulders. His back felt as if it was on fire and the impact against the cart had injured his ribs on the left side.

Still, his foe was bleeding.

Going on the attack, the ranger darted forward and swung his blade in both hands. The Basilisk was swift and brought its head back just enough to avoid a killing blow. It failed, however, to completely evade the sword and the edge cut through one of the two large fangs. The creature instantly recoiled, aware, perhaps, that it had just lost one of its primary weapons.

Asher doubled his efforts and advanced on his enemy. One swing after another sent the Basilisk retreating with red gashes marring its scaled hide. Every swing was crippling agony to the ranger and it took every ounce of his focus to keep up the attack. Deciding that he needed to finish it sooner rather than later, lest he push through his reserves and collapse from fatigue, Asher began to visualise the exact method he would use to slay the beast.

It was risky. But he saw the Basilisk's death in his mind so clearly.

Pivoting back a step from the monster, the ranger spun around and launched his broadsword high, seeing it spinning towards the icy spears above. He was running away from the Basilisk before those frozen spikes had even started falling - they were just a delaying tactic, after all. Three or four of them dropped on the monster as well as the ground between them and, somewhere beyond the beast a broadsword could be heard clattering to the ground.

Irked but not seriously wounded by the frozen daggers, the Basilisk did its best to bound towards its defiant prey. Asher had already retrieved the hourglass blade from over his shoulder and was now leaping into the side of the cart. The hard surface gave him something to push off and gain more height. Here lay the moment of greatest risk. If his timing was off by even half a second, or he had simply misunderstood the creature, he was dead.

Mid-air, hurtling back the way he had come, Asher now faced the Basilisk. Its jaws were opening, preparing to ensnare him in the middle of his leap. The timing wasn't perfect and, making matters worse, he had failed to take the monster's momentum into account. His short-sword stabbed down and forced the top jaw into the bottom, pinning them shut, rather than plunging down into the brain, a little further up. This still saved his life, but it did not stop the Basilisk's head from slamming into his chest and throwing him back into the cart.

Together, man and serpent tumbled to the cave floor. Infuriated and panicked by its new and painful predicament, the Basilisk writhed, knocking Asher about. The constant battering, however, worked to keep him conscious.

Clinging to his desperate plan, and with little air in his lungs, the ranger retrieved the last significant blade he possessed. With the curved dagger in hand, he seized his moment and jumped onto the monster's head. Ever precise in his attacks, Asher drove the dagger down between the serpent's eyes. When its skull offered some resistance, he opened his palm and hammered the pommel until the steel was buried in its brain.

That final strike dropped the Basilisk to the ground, dead.

Covered in sweat and blood, Asher slid off the side of the beast and slumped to the ground. Exhausted didn't feel an adequate description of the fatigue that crippled his body. If he closed his eyes, he knew he would sleep for a day at least. This was not a good place to slumber.

Battling the pain in his back and several other places, the ranger stood as tall as he dared and retrieved his hourglass blade and broadsword, both in need of a good clean. The broadsword, in particular, had never felt so heavy in his hand. Returning it to his scabbard sent jolts of agony up and down his back. He was also sure now that one of his ribs was broken.

Halfway out of the cave, his warrior's intuition gave him pause. Something wasn't right. He wasn't alone. The ranger turned around but it was too late, his senses too dulled. The hooded figure, masked and clad in black, was right in front of him. Mimicking the lunge of the Basilisk, the killer whipped out a single hand and struck him with something that pierced the soft hollow in the middle of his left shoulder. Staggering back two steps, it took Asher a moment to realise the thing protruding from his body was not steel nor any conventional weapon. It was the broken Basilisk fang.

Yanking it free, he glanced back at the cave to see the figure standing idly. With no further threat, Asher focused on the tip of the fang and the blood that soaked it. His blood. Even extreme exhaustion couldn't rob him of the obvious conclusion: he had Basilisk venom coursing through his veins.

He was a dead man.

CHAPTER 35

FULL CIRCLE

Drayga - If Scudders and Mud Worms weren't enough to steer you clear of swamps, let the Drayga be the warning you need. These pale beasts move on two legs as we do and even stand with the height of an average man, but they are feral to the bone.

Their sloped heads are more fangs than anything else but if you look into their black eyes you will see the sickness that lives there. Drayga are one of few monsters who hunt prey for no more than sport. Hungry or not, these creatures will rise from the swamps of Illian and tear you to shreds.

They do not, however, cope well out of water. Their ghostly pale hides dry up fast, a fact that causes them pain by all reports. If you can lure them onto dry land, away from their precious swamps, you will stand a better chance of whittling their numbers down. And they will have the numbers. Drayga move in family pods and always attack with every member, no matter how old or young they are.

Not to fear. If you are a competent swordsman these monsters will fall to your blade as easily as any man.

A Chronicle of Monsters: A Ranger's Bestiary, 12th Edition, Page 49.

Arthur Penvin, The Dancing Sword, Ranger.

A tumultuous storm raged inside of Asher. In the very real presence of impending death, his instincts began to take over. The need to survive overwhelmed any sense of guilt or belief that he deserved to die. It was there that logic and desperation battled for dominance, an immovable object colliding with an unstoppable force.

There was no cure for Basilisk venom. He knew this.

But he couldn't die. It wasn't an option his conditioning would ever entertain.

Dropping the broken fang, the ranger backed out of the cave and the dark figure slowly followed him. Any questions he would demand of the killer retreated in light of his current situation. Instead, his mind raced to come up with a solution that would save him. It was made all the harder by the searing pain that shot through his shoulder and the sudden nausea.

His gut spasmed, wrenching him over to spill the contents of his stomach across the snow. Upon lifting his head again, the ranger discovered a degree of dizziness now plagued him. Letting loose a feral groan, he turned and staggered back to Hector. He had no idea what he was doing but only knew he needed to be somewhere else. By the time he had freed the horse's reins, the figure who had doomed him was nowhere to be seen.

He didn't care.

The stranger was the least of his worries now. Climbing onto his saddle sent more pain through his shoulder and he nearly fell to the ground. Resting forwards, against Hector's chestnut neck, hopelessness crept into his thoughts. Logic was winning.

The dire situation took him back to his youth in Nightfall. He recalled a test in which he had been pitted against his entire cohort, all of whom had been armed with slender wooden clubs. He had failed to defeat them and was left at their mercy, a concept none of them understood. The beating he had received was severe and, at the time, felt like it would never end. Of course, it was known that none ever passed the test, for the test was not really one of skill or strength. The test was all about focusing while under duress. In that terrible place, Asher had to learn how to take his mind elsewhere and retain his conscious thoughts.

As the pain spread into his arm and across his chest now, he closed his eyes and retreated to that island where no one could hurt him, a place where only his mind could exist, free of the body's torments. It was there that logic served him instead of going to war with his survival instincts. The bestiary's words were lifted from their pages and returned to him. There was no cure. The venom could kill a fully grown man in hours, the rare exceptions being two known cases where the victims lasted a day. There were pastes and ointments that could ease the suffering and even slow the spread of the venom, but he had none.

If he survived this, he promised himself he would be a better ranger and prepare in advance. Since the bestiary had naught but bad news where Basilisk victims were concerned, it wasn't looking like he was going to get the opportunity.

There was one line from the bestiary, however, that offered a glimpse of hope. Amaya Hawkyns, who had died before finishing her introduction to the beasts, had written: *There is no cure for their venom save for a touch of magic perhaps.*

A touch of magic...

The thought tried to wander away from him as the venom made his mind suffer in ways a physical beating never had. A touch of magic, he repeated to himself. He was no mage and he knew of no spells, but he knew *magic*. All his life, he had been accompanied by it, even if he couldn't explain why. As the ranger conjured images of the black gem he heard that familiar, if mysterious, voice cry out from his most distant past.

"Run, Asher!" the woman hissed.

The ranger opened his bloodshot eyes and set his gaze afar, past Kelp Town below and to the south. The journey could be measured in hours but, somewhere along that route, the gem lay in secret beneath a rock, waiting for him to return. It was salvation. With the ring on his finger, he could will the magic therein to heal him.

He possessed no more thoughts beyond that revelation. Instead, he simply set Hector to the task of weaving down the mountain. Upon reaching the back of the town, he had sense enough to steer the horse around the edge and cut across some of the surrounding land until they were on The Selk Road. The question of how long he had before death finally claimed him rolled over and over in his mind. Did he have enough hours left to reach the gem? The survivor in him didn't even consider it a question, but the dark veins worming under his skin formed the root of his doubt.

The sound of foreign hooves on the road informed him that travellers were passing him by, but the ranger couldn't bring himself to open his eyes for any more than a few seconds at a time. He let them all go without consideration, be they threatening or not. With every second the venom ravaged his body his focus was only able to sharpen to a single point, putting the black gem alone in his vision.

As the sun waned in the sky, thick clouds moved in from over The Vengoran Mountains and sprinkled the world with snow. Whenever he opened his eyes he only did so to inspect the area to his right, where the base of the mountains were adorned with woods. He knew what he was looking for, but the urge to let go and pass out was pressing on him. Sleep would bring senseless oblivion, and he would slip into death without notice. The lashing whip of the Basilisk's venom encouraged him all the more to give up. Everything hurt now. His throat was beginning to close up, restricting his breath.

Then he saw it, the arching trees that welcomed any into the wood beyond. With what little strength remained in his hands, he directed Hector towards them. In his bid to sit up straight however, he was awash with intense nausea and a wave of dizziness. It was enough to send his head to one side and his entire body soon followed, taking him to the ground. Hector neighed and stamped his front hooves, but the horse was powerless to do any more.

The shock of falling to the ground gave the ranger a jolt of life he was in dire need of, though the pain caused by the impact was quickly superseded by the venom. Unable to get up for the time being, Asher crawled through the snow and the mud, challenged by a fallen log and a handful of rocks, as if they were as gargantuan as the mountains. It threatened to drain him of what precious energy he had left, and so close to the end of his journey.

The scree, produced by some ancient landslide, was within sight, on the other side of the snowy clearing. Pushing himself up to his hands and knees, a strong taste of iron bathed his tongue and he spat blood into the snow. There were no longer hours remaining on his life. He had minutes. Perhaps less.

Imagining Nasta Nal-Aket by his side, spurring him on to survive, Asher dug deep and continued forwards. His hands were practically numb by the time he was pulling himself up and over the protrusion of pale rocks. Halfway up, a coughing fit racked his chest and twinged his broken rib, folding the ranger into a ball of pain. But he was there. Wiping the snow from the small rocks, he discovered the flecks of dried blood he had accidentally left so many weeks ago.

Weakly, he removed the small stone he had wedged between two others. There it was, so small a thing yet it held the key to his future. He picked it up and rolled onto his back. His freezing hand could barely feel the metal ring that housed the gem. The ranger had only to slide it over one finger and the reunion would free him from Death's clutches.

In the next moment, however, both thought and air were taken from him as an arrow took him in almost the exact same place the Basilisk fang had pierced his shoulder. Despite the violent attack, Asher was assaulted by shock more than pain, for there was little that could compete with the fire that raged under his skin.

Crossing the small clearing limped the masked figure with a bow in hand. He thrust the bow in the air and the limbs collapsed in on themselves, just as Asher's did. The figure then cast the weapon aside and ascended the scree. Asher's fingers handled the ring clumsily, failing repeatedly to put it on. Just as it began to tip over one particular finger, a heavy boot pressed down on his wrist and prevented the tendons from working. The pressure was enough to splay his hand and reveal the gem.

A deep sigh escaped the killer and clouded the air at the rim of his faceless mask. "I told you I was going to get out of that hell," his voice rasped. "I told you I would use that ring to heal myself." The figure leaned down. "And I told you I would kill you."

With that, he pushed back his hood and removed the black mask. The eyes that looked down on the ranger were blue, a shade lighter than his own, though one of them appeared so damaged there was a good chance it no longer worked. Where there had once been thick blond hair was now a ravaged scalp, though the scars that marred it blended in to those that criss-crossed his face. He inhaled the cold air through half a nose and only one lip. Both of his ears had been almost shaved down to the skull and his slender neck revealed yet more wounds that continued down to his body.

Asher took a breath. "Everic," he croaked.

The younger Arakesh stood up straight, careful to keep Asher's wrist locked beneath his boot. "I had hoped for more surprise in your voice, but I can see that the venom has taken you to the very precipice of death. I quite like you there. I would show something of my elation," he added, gesturing to his face, "but I have very few expressions left to command." Everic crouched down again and scrutinised Asher. "You're looking a little tortured yourself. Basilisk venom," he mused. Asher groaned as the assassin yanked the arrow out of his shoulder and inspected the blood on the iron-tipped head. "Nasty stuff."

"Everic," the ranger began before the assassin cut him off.

"Save your breath, Asher," he bade with a light chuckle. "I didn't come all this way just so you could die with my name on your lips, though I confess I have dreamt of little else. And what a gamble this was," he went on in his moment of triumph. "I was greatly concerned to discover you no longer possessed the gem in Lirian. I feared I would be stuck like this to the end of my days. I had hoped that releasing you in such a state would lead me to it, but you seemed to care little about your wounds. When I heard you talking to the old man about *Mendals* and *Basilisks* - and with such passion - I knew you were no longer the Arakesh our brothers and sisters talk so much about.

"Kelp Town, you whispered," he continued, enjoying himself. "You made it so easy. Does your past disgust you so much that you would forsake the advantages Nightfall has given you? Had you relied on the elixir running through your veins you would have found those fools much faster, though you arrived so late it wouldn't have really mattered. It all unravelled so eloquently. A Basilisk of all things," he said, shaking his head in disbelief. "I needed you to court Death and there is no better way to do so than with Basilisk venom pumping through you.

"Of course, I had no idea where you had hidden the gem and therein lay the gamble. I was either going to watch you suffer a slow and excruciating death or you were going to reveal my salvation." Everic threw up his hands. "And here we are! Imagine my joy." The Arakesh surveyed their environment. "What significance this place holds for you I cannot say, but know that I will never forget it, this, the place of my rebirth."

"Everic," Asher tried again, his end creeping up on him.

"Shh," the assassin replied, holding up his hand. "I want you to see this, just as I promised. Only when I am whole again will I permit your death. And know this, traitor: from here I will make for Dunwich and kill Esabelle Murell." Everic's scars stretched into a beaming smile, revealing a mouth absent many of its teeth. "All this will have been for nothing."

Asher's lips parted again. He wanted to tell the northman that he was as good as dead the moment he read Demry's knotted message, leading him to Lirian. The effort to do so, however, escaped him. The younger Arakesh would see for himself soon enough.

Everic's blue eyes hung over the ring in Asher's palm. "To think, everyone believed you were the real thing, a child of Death itself and found by the father no less. But it was this all along," he concluded with awe. "With this I will be unstoppable. I will be the greatest Arakesh to have ever lived." The northman laughed to himself, contorting his scars. "Listen to me. Talk, talk, talk. I really should be getting on... I've a little girl to visit."

Even had he the power to, Asher would have offered no protest - he knew what was coming. Everic reached down and took the ring for himself, just as Menvin had in Skystead. Mimicking the dead mage, the northman's hand spasmed and seized around the gem. From there, every muscle in his arm tensed with painful pressure and rippled through his body until his legs buckled and what few teeth he had bit into his tongue.

Asher watched the assassin collapse onto the rocks and tumble down to the snow. Lying on his back, Everic's entire body convulsed as the magic in the gem rejected him. Blood spouted from the cuts in his mouth and his fingertips dug into the palms of his hands.

The event came to an end as suddenly as it began, leaving him very still in the snow.

The ranger rolled onto his front and crawled over the rocks, coughing up blood of his own along the way. Dragging himself through the snow, he slowly came up on Everic's side. The north-man's fingers were stiff, but he managed to prise them open and retrieve the ring. Feeling only seconds left of his life, the ranger wasted no time putting the ring on a finger and closing his fist. He imagined himself healing from his numerous wounds and the venom running like no more than water in his veins.

The relief wasn't instantaneous. He remained on his front and continued to picture his wounds healing up. It was all accompanied by some degree of pain, though it only lasted as long the wounds required to seal shut. With the effects of the venom dissipating,

Asher was able to inhale deep breaths again and his vision returned to its previous sharpness.

His full strength almost recovered, Asher began to pick himself up. His body no longer matched the damage his leathers and cloak had taken, ragged and torn as they were. He straightened his back, something the Basilisk's claws had prevented him from doing. It felt good. Everything felt good. It was exactly the feeling he had wanted to deny himself as penance. In fact, this had been the place he had intended to die. It didn't make him feel any better, however, to know that someone else had died here in his place.

Looking down at Everic, he could see the vestiges of life in the northman's eyes. "I'm sorry," Asher uttered, surprised for a moment by the power in his voice. "I should have killed you in Wood Vale. That would have been mercy." The ranger took a breath, elated to feel the air pass so easily through his lungs. "Mercy," he repeated wistfully. "That's probably a new concept to you. It was for *me*. I would say they made monsters of us, but I've recently faced a few and come to the conclusion that we are much worse. Monsters are just animals. They're ruled by eons of nature's guiding hand. They can be nothing else.

"But an Arakesh... We're *people*. We don't need to kill or maim. But we do. And we enjoy it. Nightfall twists us into demons and we believe there's no way back. That might be true. I don't know what I am anymore. But I know what I'm *not*." Asher crouched down. "I'm sorry you will never know another way. If there truly is anything beyond the veil of death, I hope it treats you better than life ever did."

Without warning, Asher removed the dagger from Everic's belt and pushed it down through his heart. The northman's eyes bulged momentarily before they took the last image of the ranger into the afterlife.

And, with his death, so ended the court of assassins. It did nothing to improve Asher's mood.

CHAPTER 36

LOOSE ENDS

__Trakian__ - There's nothing in this world more appetising to a Trakian than a dead body, and a human one at that. These fiends haunt graveyards up and down the six realms, disturbing the departed and leaving a ghastly mess in their stead. They might have no interest in the living, but that won't stop them from defending their feeding ground. Best to hunt them by day since they're nocturnal by nature. You can find their warren around the graveyard in question; they won't stray far from it, not even to sleep. Smoke them out and chop down anything that emerges from the den.

__A Chronicle of Monsters: A Ranger's Bestiary, 12th Edition, Page 281.__

__Varlan Bard, Ranger.__

Astride Hector, the ranger left Everic to his snowy grave and began the journey back to Lirian, his sense of purpose drawn to loose ends. Accompanied by his thoughts alone, his mind drifted to violent places. He couldn't help but wonder how many people he had killed since walking away from Nightfall. The number was staggeringly high, especially considering his actions in Skystead. And though he hadn't killed Rolan Vask and the other rangers, he certainly felt some responsibility there.

Having spent most of the journey reliving the various fights and brutal encounters, Asher came to one conclusion: he didn't really care. This conclusion bothered him, believing that so much death by his hands should weigh on his new conscience. But it didn't. They had all been deserving of their fate and all had entered their criminal life aware of the risks.

Asher couldn't decide whether this made him wicked or not. Whether it did or not, he knew the answer wasn't going to come to him there on the road. He had barely begun this new life and it had already surpassed his hopes in ways he couldn't have imagined. In time, should he live to accumulate such a thing, he would learn more about himself and what kind of a man he was.

For now, being a ranger would suffice. The title came with a sense of identity and a skill set he already possessed, making him ideal for the part. He certainly wasn't equipped to do much else. Of course, he had no intention of following the path set out by Rolan and Geron. Though he was returning to The Ranch, it wasn't to establish the kind of enterprise they had envisioned. He didn't want a base. Being still made him an easy target. No. He needed to be on the move, roaming from place to place in search of work.

Asher also didn't intend to murder innocent people to drive up his prices. He would forge his own path as a ranger, taking the profession back to its honest roots. This was a path paved with hope, hope that it would give him a chance to atone, hope that he would save more lives than he had taken, and, perhaps, hope that he would uncover the truth of his past and the woman who gave him the black gem.

As he passed between the trees of The Evermoore's interior, and into the streets of Lirian, Asher looked down at the ring on his finger. Questions had surrounded the gem for as long as he could remember, the original piece being as long as a finger before he had carved a small element off. In Nightfall, there had never been any time to seek the answers. Free to choose his own destinations now, there was nothing to stop him from investigating.

Who had he been before Nasta found him?

Why did he bear markings of the Outlanders?

How did he come to possess such a powerful relic?

These questions were important to him. But even as he voiced them in his mind, a new question arose in him and it burned for an immediate answer.

Did any of it matter?

Where he had come from. Who he had been. The kind of life he could have had if Nasta hadn't found him. What did any of that matter now? His past was a spiralling nightmare of death, blood, and misery. There was nothing good to be found in such a place. And what use was it to dwell on a life that could have been? All he had was the path ahead of him. There was little choice but to walk it and embrace the future.

This felt right to the ranger, though he knew those questions that had been with him since he was a child would only fade slowly. They had burned in him for too long to just be forgotten. If not forgotten, they could be put aside in favour of the future.

Riding through Lirian now, Asher was aware of the gruelling task that awaited him. In the dead of night, he was to load up Geron's cart with the dead rangers and bury them all somewhere beyond the city. He could already feel his muscles protesting.

First, however, he paid a familiar undertaker a visit. He had knotted this particular message on the road, using a strip of red cloth taken from Everic's blindfold. The ranger ordered the rather terrified undertaker to have the string passed on to the relevant couriers, a safeguarded system that would ensure his words got back to hell.

After keeping his head down in Sable's Tavern all day, Asher left under the cover of darkness and made for The Ranch. As he rounded the corner onto Ruskin Street, the ranger caught sight of a figure standing sentinel on the porch. Without hesitation, he steered Hector in the opposite direction and located a different stable that would take coin in exchange for housing the horse. Free to move on foot, he backtracked to The Ranch and surveyed the porch from the shadows of an alley.

The man guarding the green door didn't require more than a glancing scrutiny to be identified as a Graycoat. It seemed there had been a change of heart where Asher was concerned. With Geron's information they now knew where to find him and had sought him out, likely on the Lord Marshal's orders. Only they wouldn't have found *him* when they raided The Ranch.

The bodies must have taken them by surprise. The corpses had probably been seen to by now as well, leaving The Ranch to its blood-stained walls. They had to have pinned the murders on him, an easy conclusion for any Graycoat given their opinion of Arakesh. Besides guarding the scene of the crime, a job any watchman could perform, the Graycoats must be hedging their bets just in case he returned.

Asher pressed his back to the alley wall and tore his gaze from the knight. He had returned to smuggle the bodies out of the city and bury them all in the woods. That option had been taken from him and The Ranch itself had now become a place of great interest to an order of warriors who wished him dead. He wouldn't be able to return for a while, not until they realised he wasn't coming back. And they would. The Graycoats were spread too thinly to guard one location for more than a handful of months, if that.

Unfortunately, he needed to get inside one last time.

Taking a long-winded route to the back of The Ranch, Asher scaled a house and followed its roof to the edge, where it overlooked Bail's courtyard of weapons. Climbing down and into the courtyard, he made for the back door that brought him to the armourer's room, his destination. Piece by piece, he replaced his leathers, boots, and cloak from the cupboard that housed the newest equipment.

Satisfied with his attire, the ranger moved cautiously across the main foyer and crept down the stairs. Every step was stained with dark blood from when the Graycoats had extracted the corpses. It was nothing, however, compared to the mess in the basement. Healed and well rested, he saw the macabre scene with clarity now. Everic had slaughtered them all and with such glee at that. Asher thought nothing of the Graycoats and their options, but it sickened him to think that anyone could look at this and believe he was responsible.

Entering Rolan's office, the chair absent his body, Asher began to rifle through the man's previous belongings. It took some time, but he found what he was looking for: a list of every ranger they had ever recruited. Vask had a small file on them all individually, detailing their past and where they had come from. Most had a separate list for the crimes they had committed as well as towns and cities they should avoid. Asher fingered the tops of the parchments in search of Geron's information. Nothing. There wasn't a single scroll with his name on.

There was, however, another name among the others, right at the bottom of the pile. The ranger knew that name.

Asher pressed his finger into the parchment. "I'm coming for you," he vowed.

CHAPTER 37

FREE TO RUN

Lumber Dug - I don't know who named these monsters but lumbering will come to mind if you ever cross one. Hulking beasts of stone they are! At least most of their body is. If you dare face one from the front, and contend with the enormous horn protruding from its face, you could take a swipe at their soft underbelly. I wouldn't advise it though. What they lack in speed they more than make up for by being able to crush every bone in your body with one meaty fist.

You are better off poisoning their food (a dead deer will do nicely) or using fire depending on the environment.

A Chronicle of Monsters: A Ranger's Bestiary, 12th Edition, Page 87.

Sedwig The Trapper, Ranger.

Deep within the heart of Nightfall, where complete darkness enveloped The Cradle, Nasta Nal-Aket remained as still as the stone that surrounded him. Before the master assassin were two combatants in the throes of battle, their steel blades cutting and slicing through the air in a desperate bid to taste blood.

The Father observed with all of his senses, as did the rest of the cohort who formed a large circle around them. At eighteen years of age, they were nearing the time of their trials, beginning with the pit. Of the sixteen, at least half were destined for the bowels of some monstrous fiend. That fact weighed on him more with every cohort.

Thankful that his thoughts were his own, Nasta stepped forward, his movement enough to halt the duel. "You're both listening for the sound of the steel," he remarked. "Why? Because it is loud and obvious? You should be ready to respond before your opponent's blade has had a chance to move." With swift action, the Father raised one hand and rested his knuckles on one of the combatants' shoulders. "Did you feel that?" he asked. "You must feel as much as you listen. Feel the air move between us. Everything exerts pressure on the world around us. Understand this and you will know where your opponent's attack is going with only the slightest twitch."

Nasta had more to say on the matter but he heard the messenger's light feet running beyond The Cradle's doors. The Father held out his hand a moment before they entered and weaved between the cohort to reach him. The familiar touch of knotted string graced his palm and he closed his fingers around it. The cohort remained perfectly still, awaiting their master's command to do anything other than breathe.

As Nasta read the message, he felt numerous figures emerge on the surrounding balcony. Some of the masters were among them, though Master Krain entered The Cradle through the main doors. Four Arakesh arrived with him, their formation suggesting they were some kind of protective detail.

"Father," Krain began. "Is the message related to the court?"

Nasta felt the ripple wash through those gathered. The court of assassins had been the cause of great intrigue since the chosen few had been sent out into the world. The anticipation had grown with the news of every death. Everyone in The Cradle knew the message could only be one of two things. Since those on the court were required to routinely send a knotted message back to Nightfall, detailing their progress, this particular piece of string was either Everic checking in and potentially reporting Asher's death or it was something else entirely and equally intriguing.

After inhaling Everic's scent on the message, Nasta ran his fingers over the sequence of knots. He could hear Asher's voice in his mind.

"You sent four. I killed five. The court is dead. Send more and I will litter the realm with Arakesh. Let this be done."

Nasta pondered the five kills and quickly came to the conclusion that the fifth, and non-court member, was Rendal. He had failed to respond to the last two messages sent to Dunwich and neither had he returned.

"The court of assassins has failed," he announced. "As tradition dictates, Asher is no longer to be hunted."

Master Krain started forward. "He is free?" he questioned incredulously.

Nasta took a breath before replying. "Free is, perhaps, too broad a word for Asher's continued existence. Though we will not hunt him down, he is to be killed on sight. He will spend the rest of his days looking over his shoulder." *Alone,* the Father added sombrely in his mind.

"Is this your decree, Father?" Krain demanded.

"I speak of our ways," Nasta told him, "and our ways speak through me."

Krain's features creased into a sneer. "You weak old fool."

Ever composed, the assassins inside The Cradle didn't stir in the face of the provoking declaration, though Nasta felt several dozen muscles tense. Only Alidyr remained as he was, his relaxed demeanour suggesting a degree of boredom.

"You have a problem, Master Krain," the Father stated.

"My problem is you," he spat. "You have done nothing to advance this order. You are content to groom your chosen successor and naught else. A successor, as it stands, who has betrayed us all. His existence threatens Nightfall. This should have nothing to do with traditions. Asher should be eliminated at all costs. But I see your favouritism towards him has clouded your judgement. I will not let that stand."

"Hmm," was Nasta's flat response. "It appears you misheard me, Master Krain. I wasn't asking a question." The Father squared his stance and clasped his fingers behind his back. "Kill him," he said so all could hear his voice, "and the title of master will be yours."

Krain's expression contorted into confusion. "I have declared my challenge," he replied, his arms coming up. "Your commands mean nothing until our contest is resolved."

Nasta tilted his head. "You insulted me, Master Krain. I heard no such challenge."

As the distinct difference sank in, Krain's expression of confusion shifted with the dire revelation. "I challenge for the rite of—" He managed six words before the first attack came his way. Ironically, it was one of the Arakesh who had accompanied him into The Cradle.

Within seconds, every assassin, whether they had completed the trials or not, had descended on Krain. He had been an exquisite Arakesh in his youth, but the master was no match against such numbers. He had lost enough blood to ensure his death by the time Nasta was walking out into the hallway. By the time Krain's dying sounds faded from his sharp senses, the Father was already moving past the incident. It wasn't the first challenge to come his way and it wouldn't be the last. Though he had always hoped Asher would be the last.

His robes gliding about him, his bare feet padding against the stone, Nasta Nal-Aket made his way to the illuminated sleeping quarters. Unobserved, he slipped into the chamber that had belonged to Asher since he was no more than a boy. Locking the door behind him, he sat on the edge of the bed and let his senses absorb everything about him. It wouldn't be long before there was no trace left of Asher. No scent, no impression.

Then they would both be alone in the world.

He gripped the message tightly, the knots tied by Asher's own hands. "Live a better life than the one I showed you, my boy," he uttered, wishing he was still capable of shedding a tear. "Live well..."

CHAPTER 38
FINISHING IT

***Lewsha** - Of all the monsters you might face during your career, I guarantee you will never come across one so beautiful as a Lewsha. Beware these creatures, for they will appear to you as one thing when, in fact, they are something else entirely.*

The glands in their neck produce a toxin of some kind. It disturbs the air around them like the heat of The Arid Lands. Once you have inhaled this poisonous air, you will see only what you want to see: a beautiful maiden, a lover, even an old relative. With this they will lure you in, revealing their true and hideous nature when it's too late.

If Lewsha are your prey, you must ingest a potion of Hackweed and Lindis Grass. It will rob you of taste and smell but once it is in your gut it will counteract the Lewshas' toxins. Just try not to lose your nerve when you see their true form.

A Chronicle of Monsters: A Ranger's Bestiary, 12th Edition, Page 458.

Arnor Grimbold, Ranger.

. . .

The world turned and spring was left behind, the way paved for summer to wash over the realm. Then, as it would, the season blurred from recognition when autumn heralded winter's approach. Now, on the first day of those cold snows, a ranger walked into a bar.

The Mason's Lounge was crowded, though not overly so, allowing Asher to easily weave his way to the stools that lined the bar. Three men huddled around the end, deep in conversation with drinks in hand. Of the stools, only one was occupied and the figure's broad frame spilled over the edge, his green cloak touching the floor. His head of dark shaggy hair hung over the counter, his tangled beard concealing half of his tankard.

The snow was already beginning to melt from his cloak by the time Asher placed himself on the stool beside Geron. The bartender noted his arrival and made a question with his expression. "Velian mint tea, if you've got it," he answered. A flash of surprise raised the man's eyebrows before he got on with the order.

"I would say you're a hard man to find," Asher continued, his eyes wandering over the bottles beyond the bar, "but you're really not."

Geron lifted his head just enough to lay a single bloodshot eye on the ranger. "Then what took you so long?"

Asher knew exactly what had delayed this overdue reunion, but he kept that to himself for the moment. "Did you suspect the Arakesh were coming for me?" he asked the big man. "Before you fled that is."

Geron sighed and returned his attention to his tankard. "Fled?" He echoed in disbelief. "Forgive me if I couldn't bring myself to kill you."

Asher nodded along, sure that he wasn't hearing the whole truth. "But you were content to leave me there to die by the hands of others."

Geron glanced at him. "They're all dead I take it."

"Yes," Asher replied flatly. "The court of assassins murdered them all to get to me. The Mendals are dead too."

The big man chewed over that for a moment. "By your hand?"

"I was going to, but I was beaten to it."

"Those pesky assassins, eh," was all Geron conjured in reply.

"I did kill the Basilisk though," the ranger added as a matter of fact.

"Basilisk? You're racking them up, aren't you?"

Asher ignored the comment. "So you just ran then."

"I'll admit, I imagined your demons coming for us all. But that's not why I left. It's *not*," he insisted. "I've killed a lot of people in my time. Most deserved it too if you ask me. Maybe I saw something of you in me," he explained, presenting the ranger with a reprehensible comparison. "I just didn't want to kill you. Not like that anyway. You deserve to die fighting on your feet." The big man laughed to himself and waved his own words away. "I'm a survivor, Asher. You know what that's like. You just keep moving."

"If that's true then why are you still sitting here?"

The big man's coarse fingers drummed the bar. "I suppose you already know how you're going to kill me."

Asher took a breath and accepted his Velian tea from the bartender. "That's the thing about being me," he disclosed. "I know how I'm going to kill everyone." Indeed, he hadn't passed a single person since entering The Mason's Lounge without visualising the most proficient way to drop them.

"Right here?" Geron went on casually, as if his life wasn't in jeopardy. "Isn't this a little public for an assassin?"

"I'm not an assassin anymore," the ranger informed. "I do things a little differently now."

"Good for you," came the big man's easy response. "Different or not though, you're in for a bad day if you think you're putting me down."

"I've had bad days before," Asher quipped, before tasting his hot drink. "That is good tea," he commented.

Geron straightened his back, displaying his impressive size. "So what then? We draw swords right here, right now? They're not going to let me back in after I spread your insides across the walls."

"How did you get out of Lirian?" Asher asked, the only piece of the puzzle he had been missing.

Geron required a moment's thought as the conversation was taken in a different direction. "Paid my way onto a merchant caravan," he said with a shrug. "I thought blending in would help."

"Coming here so frequently was a mistake," Asher told him. "You came here twice in the summer and again in the autumn."

Geron frowned and raised his head a little more. "You saw me then?" He licked his lips, his eyes shifting to take in the room. "Why *did* it take you so long?" he asked again, this time with some suspicion in his voice.

"Hector's fine by the way," Asher went on as if Geron had never spoken. "A bit skittish for ranger's work, but he's a good horse. I think he's a little happier not having you in the saddle."

Seeing no threat but the man sipping Velian tea beside him, Geron relaxed a notch. "You're welcome to him. Perhaps you can think of him as some recompense for... well, everything."

"He's a good horse," Asher repeated, "but he's not that good."

The big man shifted on his stool. "This doesn't have to end in violence, you know. Everything else aside, we worked well together. Hells, I would even have called us friends. There's no reason why we can't make something of our future, something real, better even." Becoming somewhat excitable now, Geron turned fully on his stool to face Asher. "If the others are... *gone*, that leaves The Ranch in our names. I think a fresh start would be best for both of us. We could even turn it into a tavern! What do you think?"

Asher enjoyed another mouthful of tea before putting the cup down. "I think The Ranch is in *my* name. And I think you've had more fresh starts than you deserve."

His olive branch discarded, Geron's demeanour hardened. "What are you talking about?" he demanded.

"Of all the names on the charter," Asher explained, "mine is the only one that doesn't belong to the dead. That makes it mine. Not that I want it," he added.

"I think you've taken too many knocks to the head, little man," Geron replied with a smirk. "My name is on that list and, when we're done here, it will be the only name that matters—"

"Your name is on the list," Asher accepted, "though I believe we're talking about two different lists. Geron Thorbear *is* named on the charter and entitled to his share of The Ranch. But Geron Thorbear died just under a decade ago, in his home in Longdale, beside his pregnant wife, Lavinia."

The ranger let his words hang between them, filling the air with tension.

"Your tale was convincing," Asher continued. "It seems you knew Geron as well as he knew you... *Kradamir.*"

The big man stopped shifting uncomfortably and became as motionless as a snake before it strikes. "I haven't had that name spoken back to me in a long time," he said. "How did you learn the truth?"

"Rolan kept files on all of us."

Kradamir rolled his eyes. "I told him early on, after a particular night of heavy drinking. My fault, I suppose. You know as well as I the pitfalls of trusting others. So what now, little man? I'm assuming that self-righteous conscience you've developed can't bear the sight of me."

"Did you know his wife was pregnant?" Asher asked.

"Aye," Kradamir responded without missing a beat.

"When you said she wasn't granted a quick death, that's because..."

"Because I took most of the day," Kradamir finished, nodding his head with a despicable ounce of pride behind his smile. "Geron Thorbear took everything from me," he said darkly, leaning forward on his stool. *"Everything.* All that I had built, a lifetime of blood and sweat. He took it all and cast it into ruin. I had nothing. I was no better than an animal because of him."

"Animals don't enslave other animals," Asher pointed out.

Kradamir waved the remark away. "An assassin of your magnitude cannot judge. How many deaths are on your hands?"

"I granted every victim a swift death," Asher replied. "Most didn't even know it was their end until it was too late. I never snatched people from their homes and bartered them like cattle. How many are still tormented in chains because of your empire?"

"You're splitting hairs," Kradamir insisted. "I told you: we're both cut from the same cloth." He tapped the side of his head. "You're just broken."

"I know why you took his name," Asher announced, paying no heed to the comments. "Geron Thorbear was a good man. You knew this when you wrapped your hands around his throat and murdered him. You also knew he wasn't a hunted man, unlike Kradamir Damakas. What was it you said about the lords of The Arid Lands? *They're the worst humanity has to offer, and they never forget.*"

Kradamir lost some of his composure and began to stir on his stool. "What have you done, Asher?" He glanced over the heads of those seated at their tables as a bead of sweat worked its way down his temple.

"You made a lot of enemies in The Arid Lands," Asher stated. "It seems you were too good at being a slaver. Of the five lords who want you dead, I sought out the worst, the one with the most wretched of reputations and the biggest grudge to bear."

Kradamir's face lost some of its colour. "Kali Ras-Sabeem," he muttered.

"The very same," Asher confirmed. "It wasn't easy securing an audience with him, but your name opened a lot of doors. Apparently you killed one of his daughters."

"It was just business," Kradamir hissed. "He had a dozen daughters and twice as many wives. He should have just stayed out of my way."

"No, Kradamir," Asher replied, rising from his stool. "It's you who should have stayed out of my way." The ranger retrieved a handsome purse of coins from his belt and planted it on the counter, catching the bartender's eye as he did.

"What's this?" Kradamir asked.

"My reward," Asher replied, pushing it across to a rather confused bartender. "But I have no need of a slaver's blood money." Turning to the man behind the bar, he said, "That's for the damages. And the tea."

"What damages?" the bartender enquired with some apprehension.

"What have you done, Asher?" Kradamir asked again, watching the ranger make his way to the middle of the room. "What have you done?"

Asher turned around to face Kradamir. "You didn't kill me in The Ranch, but you did leave my fate to others. Now I'm doing the same." He tilted his head slightly to one side. "Did you hear all that?"

"We did," came the response.

The three tables surrounding the ranger came alive as their occupants stood up, numbering fifteen men in total. They pulled back their hoods or lowered their scarves to reveal their sun-kissed skin. Every one of them was a mercenary from The Arid Lands, and a pricey one at that. There was little, however, that Lord Kali Ras-Sabeem could not afford, and he had spared no expense in retrieving his old enemy.

Adjusting their clothing, the mercenaries exposed a multitude of blades, chains, and even a couple of maces. Asher had been told they specialised in *acquisition*, and Lord Kali wanted his prize alive. Leaving them to their job, Asher showed Kradamir his back and made for the door.

"Asher," the slaver called after him, his voice wavering.

One of the mercenaries moved to stand directly in front of the big man. "Kradamir Damakas. Our master is very much looking forward to seeing you again."

Those were the last words Asher heard before he stepped outside and crossed the street to retrieve Hector. He saw to a few sundries, supplies and the like, that were strapped to his saddle. All the while, a small war sounded to have broken out inside The Mason's Lounge. Furniture was broken, tankards thrown, and glass shattered, all the more so when one of the mercenaries came hurtling through the front window.

Asher had expected nothing less. He ascended to his saddle and took Hector's reins in hand. After another minute of listening to various men shouting and cursing in one of the southern languages, the doors burst open and Kradamir was dragged out by his arms while his toes cut through the snow in his wake. The slaver possessed just enough of his senses to peer up at the ranger through swollen eyes.

Then he was gone, thrown into the back of a carriage that emerged from an alleyway. Four jumped in after him and secured the big man with chains by the sound of it. The man that had been tossed through the window was collected and heaved in as well. The rest scattered like rats, disappearing into the shadows of the city.

Then the flick of reins sent the carriage down the street, where it turned a sharp corner and missed the group of watchmen approaching from the other direction. Asher watched them rush into The Mason's Lounge, too late to do anything.

"I think we've overstayed our welcome in Grey Stone," the ranger said, directing Hector towards the city's only entrance.

Crossing the icy ground, beyond Grey Stone's mountainous walls, they arrived at the crossroad. The choice was his, as all choices were now.

"Come on, Hector," he bade, steering the horse south, to Snowfell. "Let's hunt some monsters."

PHILIP C. QUAINTRELL

Hear more from Philip C. Quaintrell including book releases and exclusive content:

 PHILIPCQUAINTRELL.COM

 FACEBOOK.COM/PHILIPCQUAINTRELL

 @PHILIPCQUAINTRELL.AUTHOR

 @PCQUAINTRELL

ABOUT THE AUTHOR

Philip C. Quaintrell is the author of the epic fantasy series, The Echoes Saga, as well as the Terran Cycle sci-fi series. He was born in Cheshire in 1989 and started his career as an emergency nurse.

Having always been a fan of fantasy and sci-fi fiction, Philip started to find himself feeling frustrated as he read books, wanting to delve into the writing himself to tweak characters and storylines. He decided to write his first novel as a hobby to escape from nursing and found himself swept away into the world he'd created. Even now, he talks about how the characters tell him what they're going to do next, rather than the other way around.

With his first book written, and a good few rejected agency submissions under his belt, he decided to throw himself in at the deep end and self-publish. 2 months and £60 worth of sales in, he took his wife out to dinner to celebrate an achievement ticked off his bucket list - blissfully unaware this was just the beginning.

Fast forward 12 months and he was self-publishing book 1 of his fantasy series (The Echoes Saga; written purely as a means to combat his sci-fi writers' block). With no discernible marketing except the 'Amazon algorithm', the book was in the amazon bestsellers list in at least 4 countries within a month. The Echoes Saga has now surpassed 700k copies sold worldwide, has an option agreement for a potential TV-series in the pipeline and Amazon now puts Philip's sales figures in the top 1.8% of self-published authors worldwide.

Philip lives in Cheshire, England with his wife and two children. He still finds time between naps and wiping snot off his clothes to remain a movie aficionado and comic book connoisseur, and is hoping this is still just the beginning.

AUTHOR NOTES

If this is your first time reading a book set in the world of Verda, then welcome! For those of you who have devoured The Echoes Saga, welcome back!

For me personally, going from the saga to the archives has been like a soft exit after a series that consumed my life for 6 years. Rather than moving onto something with new characters, I get to stay in a familiar place for a while.

That said, this Asher is not the Asher I left in The Echoes Saga. Diving into the mind of a younger man, I had to rediscover exactly who he was, since he's a lot more defined with numerous years behind him in the saga. What I found was a very broken individual.

My biggest hesitation to write this book came from Asher's own words way back in Rise of the Ranger when he tells Nathaniel what he did that made him choose exile from Nightfall. As a father, it was incredibly difficult to write, with that particular scene taking me an entire day to get down. I considered not having it in at all and starting his story after he had become a ranger, but it also felt very important to see him as an Arakesh and to live through that horrendous moment with him, to feel the conditioning in him actually break.

I agonised over it though. How could anyone want to follow his story after this? I asked over and over. But, like always, it was the only story I had to tell and Asher's story was always going to be messy and hard to read in parts. It also explains so much about why the older version of him is so tortured by his past.

Given this part of his story, writing the first 12 chapters felt like I was wearing blinkers or viewing the world through a cone. Asher's mind was one of pure focus leading up to his meeting with Geron. It all felt very black and white to me in the beginning, his mind turbulent and his motivations dark. It was this contrast that led me to change the excerpts from the Night Codex to the Ranger's Bestiary.

Speaking of rangers, I couldn't write a book called The Ranger Archives and not have some good old-fashioned monster hunting. I hope you enjoyed these parts as much as I did. Leading on from this book, the remaining two in the trilogy are going to focus more on this since Asher survived the court of assassins and will start each book as a ranger. And, as you have seen from the excerpts, there's plenty of monsters to hunt in Verda.

One specific monster part I enjoyed was the slaying of the Giant. For those of you with long memories, you might recall that Asher kills a Giant in Relic of the Gods by driving his sword through its eye. This seemed like a book of beginnings for Asher and seeing him stumble and learn different ways to succeed at being a ranger felt like a good place to keep the narrative.

It was tempting to write him like Echoes Asher, whose experience is second to none and he's prepared for every eventuality. This Asher, however, had to be new to the ranger life and and be allowed to make mistakes along the way. Of course, with stumbling comes a good helping of physical punishment and you know how much I like to punish Asher. That ability to push through and always get back up is one of his main characteristics and, perhaps, his biggest draw for me.

With his punishment in mind, it felt good to have a character arc including the gem. Getting rid of it and then coming back to it, while entangled with his guilt and shame, was another step in Asher's journey. It also meant I got to have some fun with him since he couldn't heal so easily. For those of you who are reading this and haven't read The Echoes Saga, I don't want to string you along - there will be no definitive answers in this trilogy where the black gem is concerned. The mystery surrounding its origin etc is covered in the saga, beginning with Rise of the Ranger. For the archives, the ring is simply a feature of Asher much in the same way his sword or blindfold is.

For those of you who have read the saga, I wonder how many of you caught the little details I lifted directly from history mentioned in the saga. For instance, chapter 1 of this book, set in Wood Vale, Asher is kills a Hight Priest and seven Graycoats, as witnessed by Nathaniel Galfrey, the young knight. In Rise of the Ranger, Nathaniel tells Elaith that he first saw Asher in Wood Vale after he murdered a High Priest and seven Graycoats! I was very excited to actually get that scene in a book...

Another little nugget I enjoyed putting in was the brief conversation between Asher and Geron when they're discussing the big man's claymore. If you were to read Rise of the Ranger, you will find that Geron's response in this book is exactly the same as Asher's response to Nathaniel regarding the naming of a swords. It made me laugh...

There are little nuggets like these throughout that strengthen that connective tissue between the archives and the saga. I plan on doing this for all my books in Verda so they all feel part of the same universe.

Obviously, there's a good helping of violence throughout (to be expected since he transitions from one violent career to another). So I quite enjoyed the ending with both Everic and Geron. It felt like Asher had learnt more about how to conduct himself and how to win before entering a fight, or simply how to win without a fight.

If you know about my writing style already, you know I use an organic method rather than a planned one. I find my subconscious is better at writing the story than I am, and so the mirroring of fates for the mage Menvin and the assassin Everic was most satisfying. I had envisioned some big fight between them at some point, but Everic's motivations were very clear from the early on. It was tempting to orchestrate a fight between them, but the reality of the situation made more sense.

So I move on now to Blood and Coin. I'm looking forward to getting stuck in as the book's POV will be shared between Asher and one other character. I will write it as quickly as my fingers can type, but my daughter (my second child) was born this year so I have been enjoying life as a daddy of late. Still, I will write and write until my fingers bleed and the next Verda story is yours.

If you enjoyed this book I please ask that you take a minute or two and leave a review on Amazon for me - they all help immensely with getting the word out. Thank you! If you want to keep up with future releases and exciting announcements, check out my social media pages and feel free to email me.

Until the next time...

APPENDICES

<u>Kingdoms of Illian:</u>

1. ***Alborn*** (eastern region) - Ruled by King Rengar of house Marek. Capital city: *Velia*. Other Towns and Cities: Palios, Galosha, and Barossh.

2. ***The Arid Lands*** (southern region) - Ruled by Emperor Faros. Capital city: *Karath*. Other Towns and Cities: Ameeraska, Calmardra and Tregaran.

3. ***The Ice Vales*** (western region) - Ruled by King Gregorn of house Orvish. Capital city: *Grey Stone*. Other Towns and Cities: Bleak, Kelp Town and Snowfell.

4. ***Orith*** (northern region) - Ruled by King Merkaris of house Tion. Capital city: *Namdhor*. Other Towns and Cities: Skystead, Dunwich, Darkwell and Longdale.

5. ***Felgarn*** (central region) - Ruled by King Uthain of house Harg. Capital city: *Lirian*. Other Towns and Cities: Vangarth, Wood Vale and Whistle Town.

6. ***Dragorn*** (island nation off The Shining Coast to the east) - Ruled by the four crime families; the Trigorns, Fenrigs, Yarls, and the Danathors.

~

Significant Wars: Chronologically:

The Great War - Fought during the First Age, around 5,000 years ago. The only recorded time in history that elves and dwarves have united. They fought against the orcs with the help of the Dragorn, the first elvish dragon riders. This war ended the First age.

The Dark War - Fought during the Second Age, around 1,000 years ago. Considered the elvish civil war. Valanis, the dark elf, tried to take over Illian in the name of the gods. This war ended the Second Age.

The Dragon War - Fought in the beginning of the Third Age, only a few years after The Dark War. The surviving elves left Illian for Ayda's shores, fleeing any more violence. Having emerged from The Wild Moores, the humans, under King Gal Tion's rule, went to war with the dragons over their treasure. This saw the exile of the surviving dragons and the beginning of human dominance over Illian.

~

The Gods:
Atilan - King of the Gods

Paldora - Goddess of the Stars

Krayt - God of War

Naius - God of Magic

Ymir - God of the Harvest

Zephia - Goddess of Music

Sebela - Goddess of Marriage

Ibilis - God of Shadows

Athar - God of Agriculture

Mydowna - Goddess of Night and Day

Farg - God of Blacksmiths

Balgora - Goddess of the Afterlife

Atarae - Goddess of Destiny

Oemis - God of the Sea

Fimira - Goddess of Wisdom

Ikaldir - God of the Hunt

Nyx - Goddess of Life and Death

Nalmiron - God of Thunder

Lethia - Goddess of fortune

Vidilis - God of Dreams

A Chronicle of Monsters: A Ranger's Bestiary 12th Edition:

Skalagat - *A mistake of nature to be sure. These monsters are often referred to as forest knights or knights of the wood. They are not so noble as knights, however.*

Their black hides produce a sticky substance that binds whatever they can find to their bodies. Most commonly, they are found to be using bark from the trees, lending their exterior a look something akin to a suit of armour - hence the reference to knights.

It should be noted that Skalagats will use anything they can find, not just parts of the forest. They have been seen to wear the skulls of their victims like masks or even utilise the claws of other animals.

If you can get close enough to bring your sword to bear, they are vulnerable between these makeshift plates of armour. Getting close can be difficult though. Fully grown Skalagats can reach twenty feet in height, a fact that allows them to blend in with the trees.

Margotta Elysabef, Ranger.

Spider *- If you can squash it with your boot, it's not the breed of Spider I'm writing about.*
There are parts of the world where Spiders grow and grow until they could stand side by side with a horse (see A Charter of Monsters, Page 22, for known locations).
If possible, bring a mage into the contract; they're worth their weight in coins when it comes to Spiders. You see, Spiders hate the light, despise it. Now don't be thinking you can just take a torch into a nest - you're going to need a weapon in both hands. A mage can bring light to the hunt and it could mean the difference between life and death.
Your next advantage will be to keep moving. If you remain in one spot, which will be tempting when faced by waves of the fiends, you will be over-whelmed. See below for extensive list of strengths and weaknesses.

The knight with no name, Ranger.

Lech *- To the common folk, these monsters are known as Mudslugs. It's an apt description, though Lech are closer in size to a large dog.*
Typically found in bogs and marshes due to their preference for wet envi-ronments. If you can't see through the water and it's past your knees, take a care. The bite on these beasts is almost as painful as it is strong. Once they've got you in their maw, you're going to need fire to make their fangs retract.
Thankfully, they're easy to kill. They have no outer shell or any natural protection beside their ability to blend in with their surroundings.
They don't taste too bad either.

Dane, son of Heslin, Ranger.

Stravakin *- So wicked and foul a creature could only have been born of nightmares I tell you. Bone eaters our ancestors called them and rightly so. The first one I came across had left a bear carcass in its wake. Can you imagine finding a dead bear with all but its bones? A more unnatural thing I never saw.*

The bite on these beasts is next to none, their jaws capable of reducing bones to splinters. And, as large as their pointed maw might be, don't bother attacking it - those jaws will blunt your blade. Fire is your best bet. Set your trap and make certain you've plenty of oil about it. Don't hang about to watch it burn, mind you. Something in its gut gives off poisonous fumes when put to fire. Those fumes, however, are the perfect lure for the mate, and Stravakin always have a mate they're paired with until death.

Welek Tysarion, Ranger.

Basilisk *- These are likely to be among my last words, certainly my last written words. I have recently returned to Lirian after taking a contract in Longdale.*

It's a miracle of the gods that I made it back. I slew the Basilisk plaguing the outer villages, but not before it sank its fangs into my arm. There is no cure for their venom save for a touch of magic perhaps. A simple ranger, I possess no such talents.

I was able to make a small amount of Selvin paste (see Nature's Secrets, A Ranger's Companion, Page 88) with local resources. This helped with the pain and slowed down the deadly venom.

Now for what might help you. I found that luring the Basilisk was made all the easier using a blend of Gorsk oil and sheep fat. If you can also get your hands on a vial of Weet Green, add this to the bait. It will make the monster gag until it spills the contents of its stomach. This will be your moment to—

Amaya Hawkyns, Ranger.

Scudder *- Just because you've killed yourself a Lech or two, don't be* *thinking you can tackle a Scudder. These beasts are faster and far more aggressive than Mudslugs.*

And when I say fast, I don't just mean in the water - they're equally fast out of it. And when I say they, I do mean they. *These buggers do naught but eat and breed, increasing the size of their nest as they go.*

Thankfully, they're prey to a number of other monsters who help to keep their numbers down, but should they encroach on civilisation, they need rooting out as soon as possible.

There's always a female at the heart of the nest and she's the one you want if you're to put a stop to the nightmare. She's no fiercer than the males, though she is somewhat larger.

Now, there's nothing special required to kill the wretches. You just need something sharp and a strong swing behind it. (Read on for known sources of natural bait).

Handor Grain, Ranger.

Werewolf - *'Tis a curse, simply put. How this began is up for much debate, though talking about it makes little difference. Werewolves are real and they are among us.*

Contracts concerning these beasts should be left to the most experienced of our kind. I don't just say that because these beasts are seven feet tall with claws as long as your fingers. I urge the young among our ranks to leave these contracts because a wise ranger knows you don't hunt the wolf. You hunt the poor soul who received the cursed bite. They're stronger than the average person but they're weaker in their human form. Still, it's going to feel like killing a person. A deed like that will weigh on a good man.

Oh, and don't stock up on silver, it's a myth most likely started by a werewolf. You can kill it the same way you kill anything - with a good swing of steel.

Arnathor (the old hunter), Ranger.

Dragons - *The addition of this creature is a point of contention among my fellow rangers and for more than one reason at that.*
Firstly, no one has seen a dragon since the time of the elves, a thousand years ago. Some say they're extinct, others say they migrated to lands unknown. The truth is beyond this humble ranger.
Secondly, what legends there are speak of intelligent creatures of innate wisdom. Of course, we're still talking about an animal that has the power to level cities and torch entire forests.
Should you meet one, as unlikely as that is, pray to the gods that your death is swift and worthy of history's note.

** I would also add that more than one report has come from The Shining Coast in years of late. Rumour has it the mages of Korkanath have one under their spell, a pet of some sort perhaps.*

Fenrid Arlvark, Ranger.

Golem - *The first thing to know about these brutes is that they aren't natural. Golem aren't born, they're made out of pieces of the dead. Make no mistake, this is dark magic, necromancy work, crude as it may be.*
The most important thing to keep in mind is that they cannot be killed. Burn them, break them, cut them into bits - nothing stops them except a command from their maker.
That leads me to my next point, so be sure to read it twice. You're looking for people, not the Golem itself. Be it a mage, wizard, witch - whatever you want to call them. They're the key. You either trap the monster in something it can never get out of (good luck with that) or you convince the wretch who brought it into the world to stop it.
But be warned; a Golem will protect its master, and most Golems can rip a man in half with their bare hands. Trust me, I've seen it.

Hamish Lancet, Ranger.

Troll - *There exist variants of this creature, both big and enormous (read* *on for the breakdown of all types). They are brutes all and of limited intellect at that.*

Solitary beasts, they are rarely found in any numbers, though, be aware, their breeding season runs through winter. These areas can be found by following the sounds of recurring landslides.

Weak spots for most variants include the face, in particular their large eyes, and their softer midriff. I would advise using a surprise attack and with a spear, utilising the distance of such a weapon. If possible, coat the tip in Oylish poison (see A Ranger's Guide to Alchemy, Page 97) so that you might slow the Troll down first.

Gallad Corsair, Ranger.

Mer-folk - *The darkest depths of The Adean are said to be home to numerous creatures of intelligence, some even equal to our own (though that's entirely debatable), but it is those who dwell closer to our shores that move my quill this day. They be real monsters.*

Depending on when you are reading this, you may or may not know of Haven Run, a fishing village on The Shining Coast, just north of Velia. The creatures of the sea came in the night, slithering across the beach like snakes. All but myself were dragged from their homes into those murky waters, reducing the village itself to a lifeless husk.

I found no weakness in them other than with the swing of my sword, a skill the fishermen did not possess. Should a contract be posted concerning these monsters, share the coin with your fellow rangers - your only hope is in numbers.

Olav One-Eye, Ranger.

Vorska - *These monsters have gone by many names over the centuries. Your great grandparents likely called them Vampeer or Vampire. Before that, they were Gorgers and Blood Fiends. Whatever you wish to call them, know this: they are the real hunters. They have been preying on humanity since the dawn of time.*

Should you cross them in the light of day, you will see their true appearance and what a monstrosity they are, their nightmarish features forged in the pits of the lowest hell. But, by night, they will appear as the most beautiful person you could imagine. They will charm their victims into seclusion before their beastly tongue drains them of blood.
Silver, my friends. They abhor its touch. Use this to reveal them, then take their head with a good piece of steel.

Dobrin Vansorg, Ranger.

Sandstalkers *- Don't run. Never Run. Sandstalkers are among the most confident predators the world of monsters has to offer. Standing your ground will put them off balance and lend you an edge in the fight.*
If faced by one on its own - and this is unlikely - seek out the monster's weak spots, the softer flesh between the joints; their chitinous exterior can blunt the best of steel. That said, it is more likely you will encounter a nest. In this instance, run. Run until the heat of The Arid Lands beats you into the sand. A nest of Sandstalkers is not to be taken lightly, nor ever alone.

Jorven Dorn, Ranger.

Gobbers *- Gangly creatures of muscle and claw. What they lack in intelligence I have found they make up for in ferocity, a feature that is amplified all the more by their pack-like behaviour.*
They have speed on their side and you won't see them coming until they have you ambushed. Their scales are tough but not impenetrable - nothing a good axe can't deal with.

Kel Kregor, Ranger.

Wraith *- This foul creature is not of this world, but that of the Shadow Realm, a nightmarish place that only the most experienced mages can access (see Monsters of the Deep World).*
Half in this world, half in another, most folk call them ghosts but, as we all

know, there's no such thing. Though, fighting these beasts can sometimes feel like fighting smoke.

Killing the mage who conjured the Wraith won't change a thing; once it's here it's here to stay. Studying Wraiths is near impossible due to their hyper-violent nature, so we have no idea what they crave. We only know that their victims are drained of vitality and life: a painful process from all reports.

While magic is the best weapon against a Wraith, they can be killed with traditional means, including an unusual weakness to salt. For reasons unknown, salt disrupts their ethereal nature and reveals more flesh and blood. Good hunting.

Gudvig, son of Gendervig, Ranger.

Giant - *Not to be confused with Trolls. Their heights might cross over, especially where the Mawclaw Giant and Mountain Troll are concerned, but the Giants are, as their name suggests, the largest of Illian's monsters. Their level of intelligence varies across the subspecies. Through all my travels and all the contracts I've taken, it is my strong belief that the Ice Giants of West Vengora are the smartest and, therefore, the deadliest. Regardless of the subspecies, however, all Giants appear to suffer from bad hearing. Either that or they can't hear us tiny folk. Keep this in mind when springing your trap or ambush.*

Bragen Durth, Ranger.

Rakenbak - *If you haven't come across one of these beasts there's no mistaking them when you do. Imagine, if you can, a hedgehog and a bear brought together by monstrous forces and you have an idea what a Rakenbak looks like.*

They're fiercely territorial and their boundary grows as they do. This becomes a problem when the mother drops a litter close to a town or city, though you'll mostly find them in a woodland environment.

Now, once you've engaged a Rakenbak there's no walking away - or running away for that matter. At a flat-out run, they're faster than any man and they can climb anything you can. So don't attack the fiend until you know exactly how you're going to kill it. Read on for a list of suitable poisons and baits.

Weylan Ganes, Ranger.

Yarxal *- So fair a voice has never been heard, for it is like honey to the ears. How many travellers have fallen prey to this lure I cannot say, but I have discovered Yarxal nests decorated with more human bones than I could count.*

They are proficient predators that kill with admirable swiftness. This is a blessing in disguise I feel, as the beasts don't waste any part of their prey, whether it be devouring the flesh they strip from bone or using those same bones to secure their nests. These monsters prefer to hunt alone, only gathering in significant numbers for breeding purposes (don't even try hunting a Yarxal during this time).

Upright on three legs, they also possess three slender arms, their third limb protruding from their chest. Their grotesque heads will spread like the petals of flower, revealing a combination of suckers and fangs. It is also from where their unusually hypnotic voice comes from. The survivors I have encountered described the voice they heard as a lullaby, though they were all convinced it belonged to a beautiful woman.

Now, their skin breaks as easily as ours do, but I have found they suffer greatly when exposed to a particularly high pitch. I would recommend capturing a Banshee first (see page 400) and transporting it to the Yarxal nest. It's a lot of work, but a disorientated Yarxal is an easy kill.

Gelethaine the Grey Knight, Ranger.

Banshee *- Keep your head on a swivel with these noisy buggers. They've well-earned their name and they'll use their wretched screech to disorientate you - make you look one way while they attack from the other, and always from above.*

They live in swarms of up to twenty and prefer high vantages (see A Charter of Monsters, Page 107, for known locations). If you ever come across these pale predators, you'll understand why they're so well-suited to high vantages. You see, they possess a thin membrane that connects their limbs and hooked claws to the main body. Once they leap from their perch, their limbs spread out and this membrane allows them to glide without a sound.

Once they've got their hooks in your back their razored beaks will take chunks out of your head, so don't go blundering into a swarm. Locate them, then smoke them out (add Harlergrayde to the smoke and they'll get drowsy - see A Ranger's Guide to Alchemy, Page 214). Once they start dropping, get to work.

Yurik (The Beast of Bleak), Ranger.

Arkilisk *- A distant cousin of the Basilisk, though, thankfully, much smaller and easier to trap. Having said that, the bite of an Arkilisk has a much faster acting venom and is capable of killing a man in mere minutes rather than the hours Basilisk venom requires.*

You will find these most deadly of creatures in forests, their preferred habitat due to their bark-like hide that allows them to blend in with the trees.

Now, in all honesty, it is going to be rare that a contract comes up to hunt an Arkilisk down. They don't actively hunt humans and they never stray from their woodland domain. As a ranger, however, it is likely that you will share that same domain at some point or another and it's best to know your neighbours when they could kill you with a single bite.

Speaking of their bite, don't even think about an antidote. Even if one existed, you couldn't ingest it before their venom paralysed you, a symptom that begins in the hands of all places. Your only hope is to kill it fast or, better yet, from a distance. Just bear in mind that Arkilisks have six legs and move with significant speed.

The best advice I have for you is this: leave them well alone. If you don't pose a threat to either the Arkilisk or its prey, then it will leave you alone.

Korkali of the Oseki Tribe, Ranger.

Darkling - *The addition of this monster is something of a special case, but the rangers' council has agreed it warrants inclusion. The first thing you need to know when dealing with Darklings is this: they're already dead. These abominations are the creations of dark mages and the foulest of magic. From our archives, it appears I am the only ranger to have ever encountered Darklings and I pray to the gods that this will forever remain the truth.*

I came across these dark mages in Snowfell. Their insidious cult, whose name I was never able to learn, was in the process of digging up the dead from their graves and breathing new life into them. Only, it was not the life they had known. No, these people were brought back as monsters, fiends who know only their master's command.

They're fast, ferociously violent, and they feel no pain, no fear, and they never tire. Under their master's spell, they hunt in packs and consume the flesh of any poor soul they come across.

Darklings do not return to death idly, and they killed my ward in the time it took us to discover a viable method of destruction. You must take their head or set them alight with fire. Nothing else works. They can lose limbs and take enough damage to drop a Rakenbak, but they will never stop coming for you. So I will say it again. Take the head or set them alight. Better yet, use both methods.

As I said though, these are not naturally occurring monsters. They are products of magic, the machinations of mad men. Though I never got the opportunity to kill one of these dark mages, there is a possibility that their death would end the spell and the Darklings with it.

Omas Ban-Harqen, Ranger.

Praitora - *Also known as the Fisherman's Bane. Praitora are most defi-nitely the creatures that slithered out of the ocean's nightmares. If you've ever spent any time by the sea you probably have an idea about what an octopus is. For the sake of this passage I will assume you have. They are* *similar in appearance to the more harmless octopus, but they are consider-ably larger and have no qualms about encroaching on the shore. They hunt in the shallows and often claim nearby caves - the damper the better - as temporary dens while hunting on land.*

Some of the larger ones have even been known to capsize small fishing boats. Now don't even bother hunting these or even the smaller ones if they remain in the water; that's their territory. If one has come ashore, hunt it down or use bait to lure it from the sea if you must (see below for list of appropriate baits).

Logan Hackett, Ranger.

Drayga *- If Scudders and Mud Worms weren't enough to steer you clear of swamps, let the Drayga be the warning you need. These pale beasts move on two legs as we do and even stand with the height of an average man, but they are feral to the bone.*

Their sloped heads are more fangs than anything else but if you look into their black eyes you will see the sickness that lives there. Drayga are one of few monsters who hunt prey for no more than sport. Hungry or not, these creatures will rise from the swamps of Illian and tear you to shreds.

They do not, however, cope well out of water. Their ghostly pale hides dry up fast, a fact that causes them pain by all reports. If you can lure them onto dry land, away from their precious swamps, you will stand a better chance of whittling their numbers down. And they will have the numbers. Drayga move in family pods and always attack with every member, no matter how old or young they are.

Not to fear. If you are a competent swordsman these monsters will fall to your blade as easily as any man.

Arthur Penvin, The Dancing Sword, Ranger.

Trakian *- There's nothing in this world more appetising to a Trakian than a dead body, and a human one at that. These fiends haunt grave-yards up and down the six realms, disturbing the departed and leaving a*

ghastly mess in their stead. They might have no interest in the living, but that won't stop them from defending their feeding ground. Best to hunt them by day since they're nocturnal by nature. You can find their warren around the graveyard in question; they won't stray far from it, not even to sleep. Smoke them out and chop down anything that emerges from the den.
   Varlan Bard, Ranger.

Lumber Dug - *I don't know who named these monsters but lumbering will come to mind if you ever cross one. Hulking beasts of stone they are! At least most of their body is. If you dare face one from the front, and contend with the enormous horn protruding from its face, you could take a swipe at their soft underbelly. I wouldn't advise it though. What they lack in speed they more than make up for by being able to crush every bone in your body with one meaty fist.*
You are better off poisoning their food (a dead deer will do nicely) or using fire depending on the environment.

Sedwig The Trapper, Ranger.

Lewsha - *Of all the monsters you might face during your career, I guarantee you will never come across one so beautiful as a Lewsha. Beware these creatures, for they will appear to you as one thing when, in fact, they are something else entirely.*
The glands in their neck produce a toxin of some kind. It disturbs the air around them like the heat of The Arid Lands. Once you have inhaled this poisonous air, you will see only what you want to see: a beautiful maiden, a lover, even an old relative. With this they will lure you in, revealing their true and hideous nature when it's too late.
If Lewsha are your prey, you must ingest a potion of Hackweed and Lindis Grass. It will rob you of taste and smell but once it is in your gut it will counteract the Lewshas' toxins. Just try not to lose your nerve when you see their true form.

Arnor Grimbold, Ranger.